There's a Problem with Dad

Carlos Alba

Ringwood Publishing

RINGWOOD

First published in Great Britain in 2021
by
Ringwood Publishing, Glasgow.
www.ringwoodpublishing.com
mail@ringwoodpublishing.com

ISBN 9781901514971

British Library Cataloguing-in-Publication Data
A catalogue record for this book is available from the British Library

Printed and bound in the UK
by
Lonsdale Direct Solution

Dedication

To Hilary

Prologue

Roz surveyed the glossy, anti-crime posters on the walls and the jaded faces behind the Perspex screens and remembered vividly the last time she had been in a police station – March 1995, a Saturday, when she should have been seated in the main stand at Murrayfield, feigning interest in Scotland v Ireland. Instead, she was stuck in an interview room at Corstorphine cop shop, trying to explain to a pair of young constables why she'd been caught at the foot of an investment broker's garden with her knicker elastic stretched around her high heels, pissing all over his seedling rhododendrons.

It was her boyfriend's fault (the first and last time she'd been out with a fucking rugby player), she told them. He'd filled her full of cheap Chardonnay, which she hated, in a dingy Rose Street pub and then marched off with a gang of his fat necked mates towards the stadium to watch the rugby, which she hated, leaving her trailing cross-legged behind. A mile-and-a-half without a fucking piss break; what was a girl to do, she'd pleaded, flirting with them as best she could in the circumstances, still confident at that age that she had the collateral to carry it off. And she did. They let her away with the lesser charge of urinating in a public place when she could have been done with the more serious breach of the peace.

She should have been grateful, they told her. An inoffensive, buff envelope dropped behind the door of her flat a fortnight later containing an indictment, allowing her to plead guilty by letter and to pay the £80 fine in monthly instalments of £10, which she did from her student loan. She breathed a sigh of relief, worried that a more serious charge might have put an end to a career in politics before it had even begun. Such naivety: that idea had long since been kicked into touch, to borrow a rugby metaphor. Today she'd plead not guilty, pointing out that the pub had breached her human rights by not having a women's toilet.

She caught her reflection in a mirrored window that she guessed separated the booking desk from the custody suites and was shocked at how drawn and hunted she looked in her drab, black overcoat that was now a size too big for her. In her twenties and thirties, she might have got away with a dash for the red-eye flight from London the morning after two bottles of wine and 30 fags, but not now. Everything seemed so uncomplicated then – a baggy jumper and a pen in her hair were all she needed to appear effortlessly cool and desirable. Now it took a morning's work to avoid her looking like she collected cats.

She had dropped everything following Melvyn's cryptic, late night phone call and then barely slept, knowing she had to be up by 4 a.m. Her mother had been dead less than three weeks following an ugly illness that culminated in a slow, spiteful end, and now this. If she believed in a god, she might have thought he was trying to punish her for all the human trash she'd put out with the empties over the years.

Melvyn walked over, unthinkingly offering a hand before realising he never shook hands with his sister, patting her gently on the shoulder. Roz was glad she didn't have a touchy-feely family; she feared that even a moderately forceful hug would see her disappear within his grasp, like sand draining from a bag.

'Where's Dad?' she asked.

'He's in an interview room with a couple of detectives.'

She waited for him to expand but there was no more.

'So, what are they doing?'

'I don't know.'

'Have they charged him with anything?'

Melvyn bristled.

'I said I don't know.'

'I only asked.'

'I don't know any more than you do. If I did, I'd have told you.'

Yards away a jaundiced woman with a protruding jawbone conferred loudly with a disinterested desk sergeant through the screen. She held up a hand that was wrapped in a blood encrusted bandage to the officer who was paying minimum wage attention to her garbled tale of casual abuse in the bootleg opiate market as he took a draft from his mug of tea. The woman could have been 30 or 50 with her flyblown, sunken eyes and blackened bombsite for a mouth. Roz had seen similar sights in rehab a dozen times before and she wasn't shocked. Despite the relentlessness of the woman's hard-luck story, she still managed to laugh, coarsely and uproariously, at frequent intervals, while the policeman's face remained deadpan.

Roz decided she could no longer resist the siren call of nicotine. If she were to survive the next day or so, or however long it would take to get this thing sorted, she would have to nourish her addiction, which would have the added benefit of helping to ration contact time with her non-smoking brother.

'I'm going out for a fag,' she announced.

Melvyn had arrived in a cab – he didn't want to bring his car in case someone recognised it in the car park – and he wore jeans and an old fleece he had found at the back of his wardrobe which, he figured, he must have last worn more than 20 years before. In the taxi he had noticed a badge pinned to its breast in support of a workers' sit in from the 1990s. He remembered the case well; it involved an American company that owned a clothing factory in Kirkcaldy where the machinists had all been sacked for refusing to accept new contracts. Egged on by their union, they refused to leave the building and the newspapers were full of stories about these feisty Scottish women determined to take on their rich Yankee bosses. Melvyn was a trainee at a no-win-no-fee law firm representing the machinists and it was one of the first cases he worked on.

It was his role to interview the women and keep them up to speed on how the case was going, a job none of the more senior lawyers would dirty their hands with. It was still one of the most difficult things he'd ever done. Perhaps it was because he was young and green, but there was more to it than that. He could hardly understand a thing the women said because of their thick Fife accents and he found it hard to communicate with them. His boss kept telling him to form a 'connection' with them but, no matter what he tried, it never seemed to work. In truth, he didn't really know what his boss meant.

In the end the company had to go to court to force the women out. It won, but six months later it closed the factory, claiming demand had plummeted because of all the bad publicity. The only winners were the City lawyers representing the company who were handsomely rewarded for gaining the court order. Melvyn was let go by his boss who claimed they should have won. The tabloid papers reported that in many cases the women were the only breadwinners in their homes because their husbands had been made redundant from a local coal mine. That was information Melvyn should have gleaned from the women as it could have been an important detail in swinging the case, his boss told him. He figured someone, probably Roz, must have pinned the badge on his fleece for a joke. He pulled it off and threw it out the window of the taxi.

Roz returned smelling of cigarette smoke and Chanel No5.

'Tell me again what happened,' she demanded. 'I'm still not entirely sure why we're here.'

He was not minded to tell his sister anything, even the little he did know. He had only just managed to quiet the raging voice inside his head urging him to throttle her. It was at her suggestion that he had invited their father to his company's ball in the first place. Left to his own devices he would never have placed him in such an unpredictable environment, less than a month after their mother's death. Roz knew full well what he was like. If only he had trusted his own judgment and resisted her righteous pleadings, none of this would have happened.

'I've told you all I know. A complaint has been made against him.'

Of course, he wouldn't throttle her. He wouldn't even tell her he wanted to throttle her. The worst he would do would be to breathe heavily as a sign of his exasperation. Externally he would be as calm as a statue while his stomach was a spin cycle of resentment.

'Do you know any more about what the woman is claiming?'

'The woman's 17,' he shot back.

'That's old enough to know what she was doing. I remember some of the things I got up to when I was 17.'

'Not everyone's like you.'

Suppressing murderous rage toward his sister was, of course, preferable to the guilt he felt for having brought everyone to this pass in the first place, not that he could ever reveal the truth. How could he possibly tell them they need not be here at all, if only he had had the guts to stand up to his father-in-law? It was true that, if George had been at home, safely away from other people, this incident – alleged incident – would never have happened. That much was certain, and it was something he would cling to as vindication, come what may. Was it his lack of judgement or understanding that had got the better of him and allowed the situation to spiral out of his control? He'd been outmanoeuvred by Robert, the wily old bastard, who had glided into his office with the sort of portentous flourish that told Melvyn he needed to have his wits about him.

'Something's come up, old man,' he declared in that annoying *I know something you don't* way which he revelled in. 'I think you ought to know that your father has caused something of an upset.'

Melvyn said nothing, while Robert set out his wares with the verve of a showman.

'Now, before I proceed, I should say there's no reason why this needs to go any further. No one wants a scandal, least of all the girl's parents, and we all agree it's in everyone's interests for it to be contained.'

So typical of Robert to spot an opportunity to profit from a 'scandal', Melvyn thought. It was meat and drink to the old man, to put himself at the heart of the matter and engineer it so that Melvyn would end up owing him for sorting it out. He'd been outmanoeuvred by him so many times in the past and he still couldn't work out how. He was so much quicker and smarter than Robert – he'd demonstrated that in business many times over and so, in situations like this, he should have been able to run rings around him. But it never quite worked out like that. Well, not this time, old man, he'd resolved. Not this fucking time.

'If the girl's complaint is genuine, she should go to the police,' Melvyn stated with a dry calmness.

Robert held Melvyn's gaze for a couple of moments, wearing a deniable smile.

'Now hold on, no one's mentioned the police,' he said coyly.

'Why not? What is it that her parents are afraid of?'

That was clever, he was pleased with that at the time; putting the old man on the back foot, making him answer the questions for a change.

'Don't be ridiculous, Melvyn. You know perfectly well that's not the issue.'

Of course, he didn't expect Robert to answer any questions, he was far too elusive for that.

'No, Robert, I don't know what the issue is. From my perspective, it is perfectly clear. If someone is making a complaint of this nature, then the normal thing is for them to go to the police. Wouldn't you say?'

Robert shook his head, projecting that image of apparent incomprehension he normally reserved for board meetings. Of course, Melvyn never expected the old man to actually go ahead. This sort of thing was always handled 'in-house', in an organisation like theirs. Robert was full of stories about how he had smoothed things over, calmed tensions, called on his impeccable connections to protect the reputation of the firm over the years. But not on this occasion. Once again Melvyn had been well and truly wrong footed.

A man and a woman emerged from the door next to the booking desk and made straight for Roz and Melvyn. The woman asked if they were relatives of Mr Lovelace, which made Roz think they had been watched from behind the mirrored window. Melvyn made a typically officious attempt to introduce himself, accompanied by one of his weighty handshakes. The man introduced them as Detective Sergeant something and Detective Sergeant something else – for a journalist, Roz was hopeless at registering names at the best of times, but her mind was suddenly numbed by the realisation that the situation was real.

He wore an attention-grabbing shiny grey suit whose impact was nevertheless compromised by his even more striking bottled winter tan and recently whitened teeth. The woman was dressed more casually and had the kind of androgynous look Roz guessed was still beneficial for a woman to succeed in this line of work.

The male detective sergeant said they had suspended questioning of Mr Lovelace for the time being but that

7

they would require him to return, later in the afternoon, accompanied by his lawyer. If he didn't have access to a solicitor, then one could be provided.

'Why does he need a lawyer?' Melvyn asked urgently.

'We think it would be in your father's best interests if he were to have a solicitor present,' the female detective said.

'Is that strictly necessary, Detective Sergeant? I'm sure we can clear this up now without having to take up any more of your time.'

Roz muffled a sigh and cast her eyes skyward.

'We think it would be in your father's best interests if he were to have a solicitor present,' the policewoman repeated, taking a step forward as though to reinforce the importance of what she was about to ask. 'Does your father suffer from any conditions that we should know about?'

Roz and Melvyn exchanged glances.

'What do you mean?' he asked.

'Does he suffer, or has be ever suffered, from any mental health issues?'

'No, he never has,' Melvyn stated emphatically. 'Is that a question that you ask of all your interviewees?'

'No, it's not, sir – it's just that if there are any circumstances relevant to your father's situation that we should know about before questioning him, then that is clearly something that should be volunteered sooner rather than later.'

They all stood in silence for a few moments.

'So, you're clear there's nothing we should know about?' the detective said.

Roz moved forward slightly as though she was about to say something, but her brother took hold of her arm and pulled her back.

'We're absolutely sure, Detective Sergeant, there's nothing we can tell you. As you can see, having met our father, he is as sane as you or me.'

The pair watched as the detectives disappeared back

through the door. They returned a couple of moments later with George, who was dressed in his standard uniform of blue blazer with pressed slacks and tan moccasins polished to a high shine. He greeted them with a grin that Roz feared the police might mistake for defiance, but they didn't know him the way she did. Smiling was simply his way of letting them know he would not let a minor setback like this defeat him. She walked forward and took hold of his arm.

'How are you, Dad? Are you ok?' she asked.

'Oh, nothing that six numbers on the lottery wouldn't put right,' he replied with a grin. When they were children it had been eight score draws on the football pools. When Roz was little it gave her a warm sense of reassurance, knowing that things were normal, but now it sounded ridiculously out of place. She had been desperate to see him but now they were together she didn't know how to behave or what to say. Despite his hail fellow bravado, there was no mistaking that he looked lost.

'How are you, Roz? You look terrible,' he said, suddenly displaying that he hadn't lost his uncanny ability to defy expectation.

'Thanks, Dad, kind and supportive of you to say so,' she snapped back.

She felt an immediate rush of anger combined with guilt that only her father could provoke. His comment was typically insensitive and hurtful and yet, of all the things he could be accused of, lack of support was not one of them. George may have had his faults, but as a father he was always dependable and loyal to a fault. There was not a ballet performance, sports day, parents' evening or gang show where he had not stood by dutifully, always at the front of the queue, always first to buy the tickets, always front row centre. He was the one who checked her homework, prepared her packed lunches, drove her to school discos, taught her to drive, helped her to fill out her university application forms,

9

while for the most part her mother lay in a darkened room with an ever-present bottle of sleeping pills.

Roz knew what a truculent and unpleasant teenager she had been and how her behaviour must have challenged both of her parents to the limits of their endurance. But she was also aware that whatever she did or whoever she became, George would be there to watch over her and to pick up the pieces when she fell apart. He'd never been the most demonstrative parent – she couldn't remember a hug or an expression of love – but he was always the one she could rely on; the one who appeared, rigid and mute, at her hospital bedside when, at seventeen, she had an abortion; who paid off her overdrafts and visited her in rehab for six weeks without missing a single day. Sometimes she felt irritated by his elaborate displays of practical devotedness because she felt that, for him, that was a less difficult alternative to a simple show of warmth or a few words of affection. But it was perhaps more than she should have expected, she thought, now that she was old enough to know how difficult and demanding parenthood could be. He had done his best and it was the best that he could do, and she loved him for it.

It occurred to her that neither of the officers had said anything about the complaint and she winced at the prospect of having to ask her father about it. He was a painfully private person, especially about anything to do with sex. It was one of several issues that were never discussed when she was growing up. Adolescence and puberty were periods of her life when parental responsibility was devolved entirely to her mother. If the subject of sex were ever raised while he was in the room, he giggled or said something smutty and childish. Displays of nudity or romantic love scenes on the telly created a tension and made him agitated, and invariably, he left the room. But she had never expected this of her father, not from a man in his seventies.

Chapter 1

Corstorphine, Edinburgh, three weeks earlier

John Lennon was born on October 9th, 1940 at Liverpool Maternity Hospital in the city's Oxford Street. From the age of five until he was 22, Lennon lived at Mendips, 251 Menlove Avenue, Woolton, a semi-rural suburb, in the care of Mary Smith née Stanley – an aunt whom he called Mimi – and her husband, George, to whom he was particularly close. The couple, who had no children of their own, assumed responsibility for Lennon's care because his mother, Julia, a young and flighty sexual libertine, was deemed incapable of looking after him. George Smith died on June 5th, 1955, aged 52, as a result of a liver haemorrhage which made Lennon, then 14, very sad. His mother, who lived separately but with whom he was unusually close, died suddenly on July 15th, 1958, aged 44, after being hit by a car driven by a drunk off-duty policeman named Eric Clague. Lennon was very sad at her death too. He later wrote a song in her memory entitled Mother, which included the lyric 'Mother, you had me/but I never had you', interpreted by some commentators as an expression of regret that he never had sexual intercourse with her before she passed away.

Another song written by Lennon in her memory, Julia, was included in The Beatles, their ninth official album, known informally but commonly as The White Album, released in 1968, and the band's most successful album of all time. The track was more in the genre of a traditional love song though it, too, was scrutinised for potential Freudian clues as to Lennon's unusually close relationship with his mother. The Beatles (The White Album) debuted at number one in the UK charts on December 1st of 1968, where it remained for seven weeks, until it was replaced by The Seekers' Best of

11

*the Seekers on January 25th, 1969, dropping to number two.
However, the following week it returned to the top spot where
it stayed for an eighth and final week. It spent a further four
weeks in the Top Ten, before dropping down the charts.*

**'I hope you're going to take some time off work,
George.'**

Donald Leman took a step to the side, hemming George
in as he returned from the bathroom. He had been trying to
finish the first chapter of his book, but without much success,
as he had been constantly interrupted by people knocking
on the door, asking if he was alright. Leman now had him
trapped between two groups of people, to the left and right,
with the Euclidean plane wallpaper immediately behind him.
Why he hoped George should take time off work, he had no
idea. George could not remember ever discussing his work
with him. He was sure Leman did not even know what he did
for a living, far less why he should be taking time away from
it. Maybe Leman was taking time off work and he wanted to
talk about that, so he was turning it around on George in the
hope it might kick-start a conversation. Leman was wearing
a fixed, inscrutable expression and it did not look as if it was
likely to change without further conversation, which George
was not in the mood for, so he just nodded and stared at the
floor.

**'I mean, there's no reason for you to rush back, is
there?'**

Leman, husband of Carole whom Susan had met at one
of her night classes. George could not understand why they
had become friends. They had nothing in common. Carole
wore flip-flops in winter and asked how you were doing
all the time. Doing what, George was not quite sure, but

he knew if he said 'fine' like everyone else did, she would leave him alone. Leman had a habit of jerking his head and blinking, like he had something annoying in his eye. George had once asked him if he could possibly stop doing it as it was intensely annoying, but he failed to respond – he just smiled, and the room went silent until Susan changed the subject. She later gave him a dressing down because, she said, Leman had Meige Syndrome, which made him twitch and he couldn't help it.

George glanced up briefly to see if Leman's expression had changed. It hadn't. He was sure he detected a half-smile but what with the constant twitching it was difficult to tell, so he looked down again. Leman was wearing a silk tie with flecks of orange and brown, like the pattern on one of the angling flies which George's father had kept in his tackle box below the stairs when he was a child. Orange over brown equalled Conehead Marabou Muddler, particularly good for salmon, he recalled.

'My brother died last year, and I went back to work far too early. Big mistake. Hit me like a tonne of bricks a few days later.'

George nodded vigorously, still looking down. There was a gap between two beams of the laminate flooring that he had noticed, coincidentally, on the same day Susan died. The flooring was laid in the summer and the beams had contracted as soon as the weather turned cold. He had warned the fitter at the time that he should use cork buffer strips below the skirting boards, to allow for seasonal expansion and contraction. He even printed a diagram from the Internet showing the quantities of contraction that could be expected with that type of wood, but Susan told him to 'leave the poor man alone' and the upshot was that there was now a gaping chasm in the floor.

13

'It barely gave me enough time to get over the shock, far less to grieve.'

Leman, row seven right, seat six in the crematorium, one of only seven out of seventeen men not wearing a black tie. Not wearing a black tie to a funeral was a sign of disrespect and there was no excuse for it. PAINTING!

Why hadn't he remembered Susan's painting when he had written her eulogy? That was a serious omission. He was sure people must have noticed. He recalled her other interests, but painting was such a big part of her life that those who had known her for a long time must have noticed his failure to mention it. He should have included it in the section immediately preceding travelling.

TRAVELLING: (Isle of Mull, October Week 1995, accompanied by George; Cornwall camping holiday, three weeks in July 1997, accompanied by George; Majorca, fortnight in August 1998, accompanied by George; Turkey twice, fortnight in July 1999 and 2000, both accompanied by George; France driving trip, three weeks in July 2000, accompanied by George; guided coach trip of Austria and Germany, July 2004, accompanied by George; Madrid city break, Easter 2009, alone; Rome city break, October 2010, alone; Cyprus, fortnight 'beach holiday', July 2011, alone; Portugal 'beach holiday', August 2012, alone; Kos villa rental July and August, 2013, alone; Almeria villa rental June-September, 2014, 2015, 2016, 2017, 2018, all alone).

He had omitted to mention the family holiday they took together, with Roz and Melvyn and their respective spouses and children, to visit Susan's family in Toronto in 2011, not only because it was the last time he holidayed with his wife, but also because it had been such an unmitigated disaster and he still felt too angry even to think about it, far less to speak

14

publicly about it. Despite him having spent several weeks organising (and paying) for everyone's trip; making special arrangements for both the children (Anthony was 11 years old at the time and Isla two) to be seated next to him on the flights from Edinburgh to Amsterdam and then Amsterdam to Toronto, so that he could entertain them throughout the entire ten-hour journey, he had received no gratitude or even an acknowledgement of his efforts, either from Susan or from Melvyn or Roz.

Before departing, he had sourced individual presents for all of Susan's relatives – including bottles of exceptionally expensive single malt whisky, which had been aged in sherry casks for 30 years – for her father and brothers. For her mother and sister, he had hand woven kilts made to measure by a specialist kiltmaker on the Royal Mile in an original tartan designed to mark Scotland's historic ties with France, in recognition of the family's Gallic heritage. Yet, when he attempted to explain to the assembled company, gathered at Susan's parents' home, the history of the Auld Alliance, which dated back to 1295, he'd barely reached the influence of Mary Queen of Scots – and her import of many French customs and aspects of French culture and language into the Scottish Court after returning from exile in France in 1561 – when he was told to 'shush' by Susan, who said she thought that 'everyone has heard enough'.

If that was not humiliating enough, Susan spent the rest of the holiday engrossed in conversation with her parents and siblings, while Roz and Melvyn did their own thing with their respective families, leaving George side-lined and ignored. When he tried to raise the issue of Susan's ostracism of him with Roz, she told him not to be ridiculous and that it was normal that her mother should want to spend time with her relatives whom she hadn't seen for several years. He felt doubly betrayed, that Roz failed to appreciate or to understand the strength of his anger and frustration. So much so that every evening, after dinner, he opted to go for a long walk, alone, in the neighbourhood – not that anyone ever asked to join him – where he cried quite uncontrollably such was the level of frustration he felt.

Reading was another of Susan's interests upon which he expounded at length in her eulogy.

READING: (Favourite genres) i) Crime, particularly but not exclusively Agatha Christie, PD James, Victor Hugo, Colin Dexter and, more recently, Ian Rankin and Henning Mankell; ii) Historical, particularly but not exclusively, Charles Dickens, Alexandre Dumas, CS Forester and, more recently Julian Barnes, Margaret Attwood and Phillipa Gregory.

Cooking: (birthday presents included variously but not exclusively Oyster Regency mixer/blender/food processor, 1979; Cordon Bleu classes at Stevenson College September–December, 1986; Kenwood food processor, 1992; visit to Rick Stein's cook school in Padstow, 1998; Keith Floyd box set, 2002; major topical cookery book for 25 consecutive Christmases, 1980–2005 until Susan said she wanted something else).

His final comment had raised an unexpected laugh, not unwelcome as humour was now regarded as an acceptable part of a funeral service, but it was confusing as none of his other scheduled jokes had drawn so much as a titter. He was particularly perplexed that none of those present had laughed at his comment about how Susan would probably have stayed away from the service on such a foul wet day had it been another person who had died, rather than her, because she hated the rain.

He could not help thinking that failing to mention her interest in painting had been a significant faux pas. It would have fitted perfectly into the section on the third stage of her life, after the children had left home, pre-retirement, which he had known from the start was going to be the toughest to research. He had enough material to fill her early years, what with her degree in Law and her gap year trip to Rhodesia where she taught the coloureds how to read, and then her albeit short-lived legal career.

Then there was the children and their upbringing, which had taken up more than half a page of notes. He'd noticed that, for the latter stages of her life, he found it more difficult to think about what she did or, more accurately, what he was aware of that she did. There had been a short stint of voluntary work with The Cyrenians, but he didn't feel qualified to explain what she did there or her reasons for leaving, largely because she never properly explained any of it to him.

Why hadn't he remembered the painting? She had taken night classes for almost ten years before ending them abruptly on June 27th, 2007. She had been so enthusiastic about it for such a long time and she must have invested thousands of pounds over the years in materials – including a particularly expensive easel, brushes of various gauges, provided by a specialist supplier in Surrey, and multiple boxes of pastel crayons, oil and watercolour paints that were routinely delivered to the house. But in truth she was not a good painter, an opinion George had imparted to her on the few occasions when she showed him examples of her work. There was particular disharmony, he recalled, after he opined that her charcoal sketch of a dog was not in the least realistic. She responded angrily, saying it was an abstract painting, and he asked if, by 'abstract', she meant that it looked like a horse. She did not speak to him for four days afterwards.

George precisely remembered the date of her final class because she had interrupted his viewing of the ten o'clock news on the BBC. It was Tony Blair's final appearance as

Prime Minister in the House of Commons. He had been unable to gauge precisely how she was feeling because, while she exhibited some signs of anger she was, at the same time, quite calm. She said she had given up painting because, she felt, he had 'consistently undermined her pursuit of it as a pasttime'. It was not simply that he had never encouraged her in the endeavour, but also that he actively demeaned her at any given opportunity; an accusation he refuted strongly, challenging her to name a single occasion when he'd done so.

She mentioned the incident with the painting of the dog, which he found confusing and frustrating, because he was simply stating an opinion. He told her his recollection was of a frank but reasonable exchange on the merits of the work. After that, there followed a largely angry volley of statements from Susan, none of which George recognised as accurate or fair, and the discussion ended with his observation that Susan's withdrawal from painting classes was characteristic of an historic shortage of stamina on her part when it came to the pursuit of her supposed interests. This exchange resulted in a five-day period of silence from Susan.

'He died of bone cancer, quite suddenly. He was diagnosed in September and by December he was gone. I was awfully close to him and I found it difficult coming to terms with the loss.'

George ignored Leman. He had caught sight of Roz on the other side of the room, pouring herself another drink – by his count her third since they arrived back from the crematorium. She had insisted on having a large one in the morning before the limousine arrived, to 'steady her nerves' she said, although she didn't appear particularly nervous to George. He asked what there was to be nervous about at a funeral, unless, of course, the coffin lid opened suddenly during the service and her mother sat upright. That was intended as a joke, but it simply served to make Roz more nervous than before.

He noticed how she poured vodka into the glass until it was almost half full, albeit on top of a couple of ice cubes, with just a splash of tonic water. As a result, what had been a new, litre-sized bottle – purchased by him only the day before, specifically for guests at the purvey – was now only a little over half full. He had worried for a long time about the damage Roz was doing to her health through her persistent heavy drinking. What was initially dismissed by Susan as youthful excess, had continued long after Roz graduated, and now it now appeared to be an irreversible part of her lifestyle. He had lost count of the number of times Roz had assured him she would cut down, or give up drinking completely, only for him to be disappointed by her continued drunkenness. Because she lived in another city, it was difficult to keep track of her alcohol consumption, and time and again her pledges of abstinence were forgotten as though she had never made them.

George found it difficult to comprehend why, if she knew about the destructive effects of alcohol abuse, she continued to drink so heavily. It had already jeopardised her marriage, her relationship with her daughter and now it was beginning to take its toll on her appearance, and yet she continued unabashed. Having given up on appealing to her to change her behaviour, he had since resorted to physical interventions, whenever possible. On one occasion he had gone as far as journeying to South London to collect her from a clinic to which she had been admitted to 'dry out' and he had driven her home to Edinburgh to nurse her back to health. She spent six weeks sleeping in her childhood bedroom, being cared for by him and Susan, before she felt well enough to return to her life in London.

He now had a duty, he realised, to reach the other side

of the room to seize the vodka bottle and hide it before Roz was able to drink anymore. He tried to edge around Leman without touching him, but members of the group standing closest to them were each holding paper plates of food from a buffet supplied by a catering firm hired by Melvyn, and George was concerned that if he nudged any of the people, they might drop them. Liz Frost waved an arm demonstratively and, in doing so, she dipped her elbow in Derek Derwent's Russian Salad and, George observed that, unless he intervened, she was about to rub it on the back of Simon Poynter's jacket. As he considered his options, it occurred to him that perhaps he would be ill- advised to interrupt her while she was mid-sentence. He was uncertain, at that moment, whether his priority should be to allow her to finish speaking or to prevent Poynter from getting Russian Salad smeared on his clothes.

It seemed likely Poynter would not want his jacket stained; it was a black and white pinstripe and, in George's best judgment, of a higher-than-average value – clearly an item to be worn on special occasions. The main ingredient of Russian Salad was mayonnaise, whose principal component was oil. Removal of oil from what appeared to be a pure wool suit would certainly require the services of a dry cleaner at some cost to him, yet, on the other hand, Liz Frost might well take exception to being interrupted, particularly by having her arm handled to prevent contact with Poynter's back. In the event, the decision was taken from George as before he could make a properly considered judgment, contact was made and a quantity of mayonnaise was transferred from Liz Frost's elbow to Poynter's jacket.

'I figured that if I threw myself into my work, then the pain would be easier to manage. But then the grief hit me suddenly and that, I suppose, is always the danger. You don't want that to happen.'

The gap in the laminate flooring appeared to have widened in the past week, George thought. He tried to ignore it and to concentrate instead on getting to the vodka bottle, but it kept drawing his glance. The fitter had used a brown, cellulose adhesive to bond the planks and now that they had separated, the gap resembled a thin, chewy membrane like a bad mussel after it had been steamed open. The sight of it made him feel queasy because he remembered when, as a sixteen-year-old, he had fitted violently after eating a mussel for the first and last time, in an Italian restaurant his parents had taken him to for his birthday. He recalled kneeling on the pavement outside the restaurant, vomiting into the gutter as drops of oily rainwater washed up from the wheels of passing cars splashed against the side of his head.

He knew he couldn't make eye contact with Leman and yet, when he looked at the floor, at the membrane, his head spun. He had to get away from it before he became nauseous. He pushed past Leman, who was mid-sentence, only to find himself tight up against Liz Frost, whose face reddened instantly, like he had caught her doing something she shouldn't. She was by far the fattest of Susan's friends and she was bursting out of a black dress like an overstuffed cushion. There was an abrupt halt to the conversation around her and George wondered if he had said something aloud that he shouldn't.

He could not recall his lips moving or hearing himself say anything but that was no guarantee he hadn't spoken. On a previous occasion when she and her husband, Calum, had paid a visit to Susan to drink coffee on a Saturday morning, George entered the room looking for a screwdriver. The television was switched on, with the sound turned to mute and Dawn French, the so-called comedienne, was being interviewed on some morning show. It occurred to George that Liz Frost looked fat enough that she could have eaten Dawn French but, instead of just thinking it, he said it aloud, which got him into all sorts of trouble with Susan after the Frosts left.

She smiled at him and he noticed several specks of orange breadcrumb from a Scotch Egg at the corners of her mouth, adhered to what seemed like over application of scarlet lipstick. He decided not to refer to that.

'How are you, George?' she asked, pressing her hand against his arm, which he quickly pulled free.

'Oh, nothing that six numbers on the lottery wouldn't put right,' he said.

'I thought you did marvellously well at the Church. It can't have been easy, standing up in front of all these people.'

'Ah well, you do what you have to, Liz. It doesn't do to wallow.'

Derek Derwent and Simon Poynter halted their laughter abruptly when they saw George was standing next to them.

'Hello, George,' they chorused.

He smiled appropriately.

'How are you?' Derwent asked.

'Bearing up, Derek, bearing up.'

'I hope you're not going to be in the house on your own tonight', Poynter said.

George was still analysing this sentence when Poynter continued.

'I mean, surely the children will be able to stay for a couple of nights until you get used to being ... well, until you get used to things.'

Poynter was the husband of another of Susan's friends and their children had gone to the same school as Roz and Melvyn. Rangy, with dark, penetrating eyes, he had been a consultant obstetrician before changing jobs to become a hospital administrator and now he spent most of his time abroad and talked a lot about the cost of operations. George had always thought Poynter would have made a good bus ticket inspector given his officious, concentration camp guard demeanour. He never responded whenever George mentioned that to him, which was quite often, because it was one of the few things that he could think of to say to him. Poynter would just stare at him for longer than was usual with a kind of half smile.

Some years ago, he found Susan and Poynter together in a broom cupboard at the home of Andrew and Jennifer Littlefield during a graduation party held for their daughter, Samantha. Susan appeared angry that George had disturbed them and so he apologised for his intrusion and left, closing the door behind him. On the way home in the car, she explained unprompted that they had been engaged in a private conversation about arranging a surprise 57th birthday present for Jennifer, and insisted they weren't having an affair. George apologised again for his intrusion and told Susan he had no reason to suppose they were having an affair. In fact, he told her that he regarded the very notion as preposterous, particularly with a man who looked like a Nazi bus inspector, which seemed to make her even angrier.

'No, it wouldn't be good for you to be alone for the next while. That wouldn't be good at all.'

George could no longer see the chasm in the hardwood floor because Liz Frost's weighty frame was in the way, but it continued to prey on his mind. He visualised the small pot of wood filler in the central section of his toolbox in the garden shed. It would only take a few seconds to retrieve it, and then the job would be done. It wouldn't be perfect, but it would mask the horror until he could source some replacement boards. He had spent a fortune and given up hours of his time planning exactly how the room should look, having walls knocked down, the ceiling raised partially, bookshelves fitted, and the floor was the only blot on an otherwise pristine canvas. No one had mentioned it, but he knew they would notice it. It was an offensive stain. He could smell its repulsive, fishy odour and it was growing stronger. He had to sort it, to breach the chasm, to obscure the offending stretch of ugly adhesive. He felt trapped within a crossfire of unwanted ephemera and he wished they would all shut up. He needed silence and space to think, to decide what his priority should be – reaching the bottle of vodka or fixing the gap in the floor.

Despite what Poynter said, he was not going to be alone, not for long anyway. Linda Walker would be moving in soon. Or he would be moving in with her, one or the other. He wondered if it was appropriate to mention it there and then. He did not believe there was any good reason why he shouldn't. He had spent months nursing Susan through a terminal illness, and he had nothing to reproach himself for if he decided now to get on with the rest of his life. But he could not be sure how people would react. For that reason, he hadn't yet told Roz or Melvyn. He thought Melvyn might understand, but Roz tended to overreact to such things. Where relationships and feelings were concerned, she was a stickler for doing the right thing. She had an ability, more than anyone else, to make him feel uncomfortable with her intrusive questioning, never seeming to listen to what he had to say. No matter how many times George repeated the same things, there was always another element to her argument, another cul-de-sac of tortured logic into which she could trap him.

Liz Frost moved away to refill her plate, offering George an escape route which was immediately blocked by Georgina, Susan's sister who had flown over from Canada for the funeral and whom, until that point, he had managed to avoid. She had spent most of the day crying – he was aware of her ostentatious sobbing throughout his eulogy – and, although she now appeared to have calmed down, her face was pink and inflamed. He ignored her, staring at the

24

floor while Derwent continued with his pronouncements on George's living arrangements.

'Until now you've had the funeral to focus on, and people around you to keep you going.'

The first thought that had entered George's mind when he held a compact mirror to Susan's face to ensure she was no longer breathing, was that now she was dead he would be obliged to live alone for the first time in his life and that his routine would be disturbed, just as Lennon's had been after he separated from Yoko, during what became known as his 'lost weekend'. That was a grotesque misnomer as they were actually apart for a period between 1973 and late 1974, the length of which was disputed but which was undeniably significantly longer than a weekend. It was also referred to in some quarters as an 'eighteen month lost weekend' which, as well as being an oxymoron, was also misleading because, by most reliable accounts, it was a period some way short of eighteen months.

Whatever the timescale, there was no doubt in George's mind that Lennon's was a troubled, even a tortured, mind during those dark days and would have been more so were it not for the ministrations and attention provided by May Pang, his secretary and interim lover. Alcohol misuse undoubtedly featured prominently, but George had always thought it incredibly unfair that a period of solitude and solemn soul-searching should be characterised in the public mind by an unfortunate incident involving Harry Nilsson in the Troubadour Club, in Los Angeles, when Lennon emerged from the public lavatory wearing what most American media accounts referred to as a 'menstruation towel'. It was an issue upon which George had written extensively in the letters' pages of the music press over the years and, more recently, on various online fan forums.

Despite evident prejudice against May Pang by some fans, her relationship with Lennon had had the blessing of Yoko who viewed her as a guardian rather than a rival. Like George, Lennon always had the presence of a woman in his life – his mother, his Aunt Mimi and Cynthia, his first wife – and it occurred to him that perhaps Linda would be his May Pang. He felt sure that Susan, were she looking down from a celestial peak (which he doubted because he was an atheist), would feel the same sense of benevolence toward their relationship as Yoko had done to that between Lennon and May Pang. There was no logical exception which she or anyone else could take, now that she was dead, to his 'moving on romantically', so to speak.

'Have you decided what you want to do with Susan's ashes yet?' Georgina asked.

George was reminded of a quote from a Jann Wenner interview in Rolling Stone magazine that referred to Lennon's relationship with Yoko, but which might easily have been applied to his relationship with May Pang or, for that matter, to George's impending relationship with Linda Walker. It seemed, at that moment, to be quite apposite to his circumstances – an elegant counterpoint to the mundane chattering around him by people who had no clear idea of his needs or desires, forcing him ever tighter into a corner and preventing him from sorting the gap in the flooring.

The voices grew louder and the troubling scent of shellfish more intense and George felt an impulse that, rather than listening to individuals lecturing him about what he should or shouldn't do or feel, he should instead demonstrate what was important for him to all the people assembled. His volume of collected Jann Wenner interviews sat on the bookshelf, directly behind Derwent's shoulder, tantalisingly close, but George did not need it to be able to recite Lennon's observations, verbatim – the words, like everything he had ever read by or about his hero, were etched indelibly in his mind.

He stepped forward and raised an arm aloft to facilitate his breaking through the knot of people in front of him. As he did so, he knocked Donald Derwent's glasses off, and then he began to speak. Recognising that his words were not being heard by most people, who continued with their conversations, he raised the level of his voice louder and louder still until the room fell silent.

'There is no reason on earth why I should be without her!' he shouted. 'There is nothing more important than our relationship, nothing. And we dig being together all the time.'

Several of those present – mostly the women – smiled warmly, and one or two voiced sympathetic sighs.

'And both of us could survive apart, but what for? I'm not going to sacrifice love, real love for any fuckin' whore or any friend, or any business, because in the end you're alone at night. Neither of us WANTS to be and you can't fill the bed with groupies, that doesn't work. I don't want to be a swinger. Like I said in the song, I've been through it all and nothing works better than to have someone you love hold you.'

After he had finished, the room remained silent for a few seconds until Roz approached him and took him by the arm.

'Those are lovely sentiments to express about Mum,' she said as she led him from the room toward the kitchen.

As she did so, he reached over to the drinks table and retrieved the bottle of vodka.

Chapter 2

Soho, Central London, the following day

It didn't take Roz long to find the place in Soho where Crossman had suggested they meet. It was the only address on the street with a bouncer stationed on the door. She couldn't understand why a cafe would need a bouncer, especially at eleven o'clock in the morning. Perhaps the owner feared a rush of trainer-wearing office workers tanked up on cheap supermarket caffeine. The place wasn't what she'd have expected of Crossman – it was modern and minimalist with a smattering of abstract art scribbled on the walls and a few items of low-slung furniture with any semblance of comfort designed out of them. She had him down as a gentlemen's club kind of guy, all dark wood and red leather with a real fire with an army of uniformed minions to bring him crystal tumblers of malt whisky and warm, pressed copies of the first editions.

The place was empty, so she took a seat in a corner. She was wearing high heels, an arse-hugging micro skirt which, she noticed, had caught the attention of the waiter as she entered, and a low-buttoned, white cotton shirt with a dab of glitter on her cleavage. She was not looking to win any prizes for subtlety. She'd been told by Becky, the comment editor, that Crossman liked his female writers to be 'visual'.

He was late. It was a tactic he employed to give him a natural feeling of superiority, Becky said. Roz considered leaving and walking around the block so she could arrive after him and, perhaps, put him off his stride a little but she didn't have the nerve. There would be a moment of awkwardness with the waiter, and what if she met Crossman on the way out? How would that look? It would be obvious to him what she was doing, and she could not risk fucking

28

him off.

Why had he even asked her to meet him anyway, she wondered for the umpteenth time since his secretary had rung her the previous afternoon to inquire, with her inscrutable, dentist receptionist's formality, if she were 'available', knowing damned fucking well that, whatever she was doing, she would make herself available. She had not heard that voice for months. The last time she met Crossman was to renew her contract, and that was at her behest. It had taken weeks to pin down a date that was suitable for him and, even then, he had changed it at the last minute because of a big, late-breaking story. Now, out of the blue, he wanted to meet her, and quickly. Her first instinct, naturally, was that it was bad news.

Briefly, she had considered the possibility that perhaps he might have wanted to offer his condolences for the death of her mother, but dismissed that just as quickly. It wasn't his style. If he were to make any kind of intrusion into her private life it would be in the form of a stiff, hand- written letter, on headed company notepaper, sent to her home. There was always the prospect, of course, that he wished to promote her, although that was not something upon which she allowed herself to dwell for long, to avoid a greater sense of disappointment when it failed to happen.

A burst of tinny electropop from her mobile ringtone made her jump. She had wanted to change it to something more sedate since she bought the thing six months ago, but she didn't know how. She thought it was Crossman's secretary cancelling but when she looked at the display, she saw it was Melvyn and she breathed a sigh of relief. A telephone conversation was just what she needed right now. It would provide her with a cover of activity should Crossman walk in, making her look busy and in-demand. It would also give her the opportunity to test the quality of her voice following the damage it had received at the funeral the day before.

Ruaridh had been asleep when she arrived home after midnight. She had had to kick him out of bed earlier because he had slept in again. He was already on a final warning from the Toby Man and, unless one of the other stall holders had ringed off his pitch, he was in danger of losing it. It was a stroke of luck that she had woken up herself as both had slept through the alarm. She had no idea how much she had drunk at the funeral, though she had a vague recollection of the air stewardess's glare of disapproval when she ordered another couple of vodka miniatures. There were three cigarettes left when she checked but she couldn't remember if that was the end of her second or third pack.

'Hi Melvyn,' she said groggily. 'Hi. Are you ok?'

'Yeah, I'm fine.'

She knew her brother was doing his best to show concern, but it made her feel intruded upon.

'I'm waiting for my boss.'

Melvyn did not answer.

'How did it go after I left?' Roz asked to break the silence.

'It was fine. We went back to check on Dad after we dropped you at the airport and he was busy writing in his little notebook. He's writing a book.'

'He told me.'

'Mary offered to make him dinner, but he'd eaten a lot of sandwiches at the funeral, so we left him to it.'

'Do you think he'll be alright?'

'Yes, he's fine,' Melvyn replied.

'Are you sure?'

'Yes, of course. Why do you ask?'

'Well, I'm concerned about what happened yesterday,' she said.

'What do you mean, his impromptu speech?'

'No, it wasn't just that. Derek Leman told me he'd been rude to him. Dad asked him why he wasn't wearing a black tie and said it was a mark of disrespect.'

30

'That's just Dad. We all know what he's like,' Melvyn insisted, trying to sound reassuring. 'I spoke to Derek and he was fine about it. He said he could only imagine what Dad was going through and that no offence was taken.'

Roz was concerned not to be drawn into another dead-end discussion about her father. She knew Crossman would be walking through the door any minute and the last thing she needed was a protracted filleting of George's behavioural tics. Her parents' marriage had not been the happiest, but she did not doubt he was sad at his wife's death and that there would be some bumps along the way as he mourned her passing. She noticed how dependent he'd become on her latterly. She had always cooked his meals, according to his exhaustive set of dietary requirements, shopped for his clothes and taken care of his domestic needs but recently she had become almost a proxy for him, answering for him in company, acting for him in dealings with officialdom, anticipating potential flashpoints with friends and neighbours and heading them off.

Emotionally, he was as resilient as ever because nothing seemed to touch him, but then he could respond quite absurdly to the slightest things. He took the death of his parents remarkably calmly, applying himself to the practical tasks of arranging their funerals, disposing of their belongings, administering their estates. The untimely death of his grandson, Melvyn's son, at a young age, made him grieve but in an unusual, almost trite, way, like he was taking his cue from an instruction manual. The devastation wrought by the event on the rest of the family served only to highlight to Roz how unmoved he was by the tragedy. The only time she had ever seen him cry was when she was a child, after John Lennon was shot.

'He must be feeling better, he asked Linda Walker out,' Melvyn said with a hint of a snigger.

Roz was flabbergasted.

'What do you mean, he asked her out?'

'He asked her out for dinner.'

'Christ, where did he do it?'

'Outside the church.'

'The church?'

'Yes. That's not right, is it? That's just not right. I mean, there's a time and a place,' Melvyn said, sounding unsure of himself.

Roz was used to her brother's unusual sense of understatement, but she was still shocked at the blithe way he had imparted the information.

'It's not just that he did it at the church, Melvyn. Linda Walker, for fuck's sake.'

'Yes, right enough, Linda Walker. It's not right.'

'How do you even know?' she asked.

'She told me.'

'And how was she?'

'Fine. Enjoying retirement, I think.'

Roz felt a rush of anger at her brother's obtuseness. Everyone was always 'fine' as far as he was concerned, no matter the circumstances. She could have just been run over by a bus and he'd say she was 'fine'.

'For fuck's sake Melvyn, I didn't mean how was she, how was she? I meant how was she about being asked out on a date by a man who's about to cremate his wife?'

'Eh, I don't know, it was difficult to tell.'

She also resented that he had chosen this precise moment to dump such an explosive piece of information on her, when she should be at her most composed.

'What do you mean it was difficult to tell? She must have been mortified. Could you not tell that she was mortified?'

'No, she seemed OK.'

'She couldn't have been OK, otherwise why would she tell you? Christ, you're useless in situations like this.'

Roz spotted Crossman entering the room.

'Look, I'll have to go. My boss has arrived.'

Crossman glided serenely across the floor, without seeming to move his legs. He wore a grey-flecked pure wool overcoat, with the collar turned up and the hem hovering a couple of feet above a pair of immaculately white tennis shoes. His height was not the first thing she would have mentioned if she was describing him, but Christ, was he tall, and he seemed to grow the closer he got. She stood to greet him and felt her legs weaken as he swept his heavy, greying fringe away from his eye and flashed a grin. Why was it that posh men had lustrously thick heads of hair, she wondered?

'Hello, Rosalind,' he said as he clasped her hand tightly and brushed her face with his expensively scented cheek.

She couldn't remember if his background was South African or Australian, it was one or the other, and his accent gave no clue, having been scrubbed clean of any external influence by the purifying effect of a top English public school and an Oxford college.

'I'm fine, Peter, how are you?'

Roz's accent was by no means broad, in fact it was often mistaken for a soft Irish lilt, but in Crossman's company she felt indecipherably inner city Scottish. As she sat down, she pulled her shirt sleeves back to reveal her forearms in an unconscious gesture of supplication to demonstrate that she hadn't spent the morning shooting up in a squalid council high rise. He smiled at her warmly and she felt immediately submissive. No one she had ever met had such an effect on her as Crossman. She didn't fancy him; she was sure of that and she had thought about it long and hard. He was too effortless and brimming with intellectual certainty, like he had never put a foot wrong in his entire life. Even when he was wrong, he was right. She liked to be challenged but not that much. She felt sex with him would be demanding and exhausting like being gangbanged by the entire winning team of University Challenge. She imagined approaching orgasm and being asked to recite Pi to 23 decimal places. Like most newspaper editors, Crossman expected to get his own way and she felt an irresistible compulsion to please him.

The waiter appeared and nodded familiarly at Crossman, clearly satisfied that the company he kept was legitimate after all. Roz would have killed for a sharpener to take the edge off her hangover, but she did not want to risk incurring Crossman's disapproval, so she ordered a black coffee instead. He asked for an orange juice because, he made a point of stressing, he was due on court in an hour. He played tennis every day and always won, except on the days when he played *The Sentinel* proprietor's son, when he always lost.

Roz endured an uncomfortable period of silence as he removed his coat, revealing a pristine set of whites. She wondered if she should initiate some small talk, perhaps inquiring after his wellbeing, but decided it would probably sound too familiar. She knew that, with Crossman, boundaries were important, and she was, by now, savvy enough to know which ones not to cross. She had seen plenty of examples of underlings being seduced by his easy manner and faux jokiness and then being swatted like flies when they strayed too far above their pay grade.

Suddenly she became conscious of her hands. Wherever she put them felt heavy and awkward like she had only just acquired them and didn't yet know what to do with them. She crossed her arms and immediately uncrossed them, aware that it made her look defensive. She placed one on each knee but feared drawing too much attention to the shortness of her skirt. Finally, she settled on laying them flat on the chair on either side of her, with her palms facing upward and the tips of her fingers tucked under her thighs.

Crossman leaned back with his legs crossed languidly.

'So, Rosalind, what's happening in the world?'

She had forgotten about his peculiar, nebulous line

34

of questioning, which everyone at the office warned the unsuspecting about in advance. As a national newspaper editor he was better placed than most to comment on what was happening in the world, so why was he asking her? Was he being ironic or was it a mischievous, inverted way of setting out their respective positions at the start? Perhaps he was asking what was happening in her world and, if so, did he mean her professional or her personal world? Or maybe she was being over analytical, and he had just said the first thing that had popped into his head, an unthinking bit of social banter to ease their passage into shop talk.

'Oh, this and that,' she said wanly.

She hated her lack of verbal spontaneity, she was much better with a keyboard, when she had time to think about how profound she was going to be. Think, think, she told herself. What is he interested in? She knew his son was due to sit his mock A Levels soon.

'I saw an interesting report by a parliamentary sub-committee the other day on the subject of grade inflation by the main exam bodies. We all know it's happening, but this seemed to suggest that there was new evidence of collusion with the Department for Education about keeping...'

The waiter arrived with the drinks and she stopped talking as he placed the tray on the table.

'I think it's definitely worth doing something on it in the run up to the exams.'

Crossman looked at his watch.

'I was sorry to hear about your father's death,' he said.

'My mother,' Roz replied embarrassedly as if it were she who had dropped a clanger.

'Yes, your mother, of course it was. I'm sorry. I knew it was your mother.'

And so you fucking well should, she thought, I've written about it often enough. Had it been anyone else, she would have thought such behaviour unforgivably crass. If you're an employer and a member of staff suffers a family bereavement, it's incumbent upon you at least to research which fucking relative has died. But with Crossman, she made allowances.

'No, it's fine, she'd been ill for a long time and we were expecting it.'

He nodded and took a miniscule sip of orange juice. She felt the crushing silence and an irresistible urge to fill the void.

'In fact, it's a relief more than anything else not to see her suffering any more. She'd lost the will to carry on long ago, but nature had to take its course.'

Yet more silence. This was another of Crossman's tactics – say nothing and let the helpless underling before you dig a coffin-sized hole for herself with a massive shovel fashioned from trite, witless drivel.

'It makes me angry thinking about the pro-life lot who believe that a person's existence cannot be cut short no matter what the circumstances.'

'So, how is the column going?' he asked suddenly, drilling straight to the heart of the matter.

In those few words Roz immediately realized the reason for their meeting. Momentarily, her body froze, and she touched the crosswire of her bra to ensure her shirt was unbuttoned just low enough to reveal a bit of cleavage. Her finger acted like a conductor, drawing Crossman's eyes to her tits and buying just enough time for her to think of a response.

His question held within it the evident truth that he believed her column was going badly. That would explain why he'd taken time out of his busy schedule to meet her. She calculated that if he'd set aside an hour, he wasn't minded to engage in any protracted ruminations about how her column might be improved. More likely he planned to get a quick firing in before tennis and, traffic allowing, to be back at his desk for afternoon conference. Christ, that was so fucking Crossman, she thought. Less than a minute ago he was commiserating the death of her mother, feigning sympathy, and now he was about to sack her.

'I think it's going really well,' she said, erecting a line of defence in what she feared may already be a fast-sinking sand bank.

'Really?' he asked, with a hint of a smile playing on his lips.

Perhaps he was toying with her, she thought. Was he using his authority, placing her in a state of fear, and then challenging her to flirt her way out of a dismissal? She was unsure quite which way to turn, fearing that the wrong decision could be fatal. Make the wrong judgment call and she would be out of work by lunchtime. What the fuck, she thought.

'Well, I don't get many complaints,' she said, touching her top lip with her tongue.

Crossman uncrossed his legs and stared at her for a couple of seconds though it seemed like much longer.

'I bet you don't, but what about your column?' he asked, beaming an erogenous grin. She leaned forward with slow deliberation over the low table that separated them, ostensibly to top up her coffee, hating herself for what she was doing. She wondered what her 25-year-old self would make of such behaviour. How would she explain to her sisters on the student association's equalities committee what she was doing, seducing a shit like Crossman just so that she could continue writing for his hateful, misanthropic rag? Perhaps she would tell them to fuck off and to drag their pansy white, woke arses into the real world and realise that her willingness to work for Crossman was nothing to do with money or expediency, but rather a sign of her professional and political maturity. People like him and his readers have always existed, and they always would until brave, class conscious women like her stop sniping from the self-satisfied comfort of the liberal broadsheet comment pages and sought to change the system from within. Only by working for the right-wing press and challenging its prejudices could she, or anyone else, begin to make a real difference.

Did she believe that? Did she really believe that? Yes, she did ... or at least she had when she staggered over to Crossman's table at the Press Awards, after too many return trips to the free bar, and clutching her Columnist of the Year gong, told him, in no uncertain terms, that what his pitiful rag lacked was her brand of muscular liberalism to shake its entitled, loafer and twinset-wearing, middle English readership out of its Mogadon-induced complacency. Or something to that effect. She couldn't remember her exact words, but she clearly recalled the sensation of her lips touching his ear and of her hand draped gently around his slim neck as she fought to have herself heard above the din of Roger Daltrey's live stage set arranged, Crossman had made a point of telling her, courtesy of his impeccable connections. He replied that exposing his readers to her 'Marxist feminist rantings' would make them 'shit in their chinos' and lead to violent insurrection in Rotary Clubs and WI chapters around the country.

She had woken the following morning in a fug of stale booze and crippling embarrassment, hoping that none of her colleagues had seen her or, God forbid, been told what she had said. But then, a few days later she picked up a call from Crossman's secretary asking if she was available to meet with him the following morning.

'Like I said, I don't get any complaints.'

His grin ebbed slightly.

'Perhaps that's the problem,' he said, grounding the mood of flirtatious levity.

'So, there's a problem?'

He shifted uncomfortably, clearly on softer ground when

being asked questions.

'We don't object to our columnists receiving complaints. In fact, we expect it. It shows they are doing their job properly. That they are testing the assumptions of readers, challenging a few shibboleths.'

She nodded soberly, keen to demonstrate that she knew what a shibboleth was.

'We don't expect to be flooded with letters of congratulations. The worst of all outcomes is to be ignored.'

Her body froze at the suggestion. She lifted her cup, concentrating heavily to ensure that her hand didn't shake, and drew it deliberately toward her bone-dry mouth. The coffee was tepid and bitter, and the taste made her shudder. She would have killed for vodka to steady herself.

'I get a lot of emails that you don't see,' she said, sounding more defensive than she would have liked. 'I had a big response from frontline staff following my piece about cuts to maternity budgets.'

'What issues have you covered in the past couple of months?' he asked pointedly.

It was a straightforward enough question, but her mind went blank. She tried to clear her thoughts and to concentrate but she couldn't even remember what she had written the previous week, never mind two months ago. Crossman reached into his coat pocket and retrieved a piece of paper which he unfolded slowly with his long surgeon's fingers. Not for him, the crude modernity of an iPad. Christ, things were more serious than she had imagined. He had done his homework.

'The health service, the schools' system, the criminal justice system, the health service, nursery provision, the environment, the health service, the higher education system, local government accountability, the health service...do I need to go on?'

The smile of a few minutes ago had been replaced

with a threatening deadpan. Some of the subjects she had covered started to come back to her. They seemed topical and relevant at the time and she certainly would not have characterised them in such summary terms, but she knew better than to question his judgement. Experience told her that when Crossman went to such lengths to make a point, he didn't generally do so to invite debate.

'You think I need to spread the net wider, cover a greater range of issues?'

He looked at his watch again and sighed.

'I didn't hire you to write academic theses on health service spending and the administration of local government. That's not what we're about.'

She nodded nervously, like a recalcitrant schoolgirl being given one last chance by a head teacher who was fast losing patience.

'Our readers don't really care about that.'

'Really?' she asked.

Crossman pursed his lips and his eyes closed over in a gesture of evident frustration.

'They pretend that they care about these things and, who knows, maybe they are of fleeting importance once every five years when our readers go to the ballot box.'

'To vote for the Tories?' she suggested, immediately regretting her plainly failed attempt at playfulness.

'They don't want to read about these worthy issues day in, day out. You're with us to bring a female sensibility to the great issues of concern to our readers. You do understand that, don't you?'

She nodded.

'Well, let's look at the range of issues you could have covered in the last two months.'

She thought he was going to produce another piece of paper but clearly, he didn't have to. He had a list stored in his head.

'Immigrants, rapists, transsexuals, benefits cheats, drug dealers, immigrant rapists, transsexual rapists, immigrant transsexuals, immigrant drug dealers, immigrant benefits cheats, immigrants getting sex changes on the NHS, rapists getting sex changes on the NHS, immigrant rapists getting sex changes on the NHS, transsexuals using women's changing rooms in swimming pools, transsexuals using women's toilets, immigrants claiming benefits, rapists claiming benefits, immigrant rapists claiming benefits...'

'Immigrants selling drugs to transgender benefits cheats in rape crisis centre toilets?' Roz suggested.

Crossman didn't respond.

'Do I need to go on?'

He looked at his watch for a third time and nodded ostentatiously at the waiter to bring the bill.

'No, you don't,' said Roz.

Chapter 3

Central Edinburgh, the same day

Lennon was raised in the Anglican faith, a tradition within the Christian religion linked, historically, to the Church of England, its beliefs, worship and structures. The word Anglican derives from 'ecclesia anglicana', a medieval Latin phrase dating back to the 13th Century, which translates as English Church. He attended Dovedale Primary School between 1952 and 1957 before moving up to Quarrybank High School after passing the Eleven Plus, an examination administered to some students in the United Kingdom in their final year of primary education and governing admission to various types of secondary school from 1944 until its abolition in 1976. As a child, Lennon was described, variously, as 'happy-go-lucky', 'good humoured', 'easy going', 'lively', and as a 'prankster' and a 'class clown'. Following the death of his Uncle George and his mother, he was described as 'violent', 'cruel', 'moody', 'bullying', 'disruptive', 'rebellious' and 'destructive'. Some writers and commentators have suggested that these situations are connected.

George had been thinking about writing a book about his hero for a long time but, when it came to putting the words down on paper, he barely knew where to start. He had a clear picture in his mind about how he wanted it to be but bringing the ideas together to make sentences and paragraphs was another matter entirely. He agonised about whether he should start with the day Lennon was born or whether he should go back further. Most of the biographies he had read started with his father, Alfred, and his mother, Julia Stanley, and made what he regarded as a series of fatuous points about how they came from different backgrounds and how ill-suited they were as a couple, as if that had some significance for the way their son wrote songs, he thought. Some books started even earlier, with his grandfather who was a musical act in the United States of America for a spell.

He knew from the outset he did not want that. He wanted his to be a proper record of the musician's life and career. Following extensive consideration, he decided it wouldn't address the question of whom, between he and McCartney, was the greatest songwriter in both their Beatles and post-Beatles careers, nor would it seek to set the record straight in that regard. It was to be in no respect a vendetta against John Cherry and his 2009 travesty *Better than Lennon* (Peppertree Press) as Susan had suggested. That chapter of his life, which had caused perhaps the biggest strain on their marriage, had ended and he had no wish to revisit it.

In his opinion, Susan had offered no support whatsoever to his campaign to have this 'exposition of McCartney's supposed superiority as a songwriter and musician' withdrawn from sale. His issue with it, as he reminded her consistently, was not to deny Mr Cherry his rightful freedom of speech – a point he made forcefully and with some erudition in his letter published in full by the Chapel Hill Herald, Mr Cherry's local newspaper in North Carolina (several other, so-called, quality publications refused to carry it). In fact, George suggested he would have been perfectly happy to see the book reissued with a specified number of factual corrections, under an amended title.

His main point, he made clear, was a matter of the Law. As it stood, *Better than Lennon* was potentially defamatory for the simple reason that it was a title presented as a statement of fact. If it had been phrased as a question, or clearly identified as an opinion, then there would be no reason to change the wording of the title, only the punctuation accompanying it. *Better Than Lennon?* or even '*Better Than Lennon*' would have been acceptable alternatives, for example.

Susan's contention that 'the man is dead, what does it matter?' was, unconsciously, making the point that the dead cannot be defamed, but she missed an important caveat under English Law: that a statement can be held to be criminally libellous against a dead person if it is intended to be, or has the effect of being, scandalous to that person's relatives or the guardians of his estate such that they might commit a public order offence. In that sense, it could be argued that Lennon's sons, Julian and Sean, or his widow, Yoko, may have been defamed in his absence by Better than Lennon if they were to be provoked into committing, for example, a violent assault on the author.

George's argument failed to prevail. The book remained on the shelves, largely unremarked upon (one mixed review on Amazon), and he received a letter from Mr Cherry's attorney warning that he faced legal action if he did not 'desist from any further 'harassment' of [his] client', a point which George had disputed in his lengthy response. That too was not an issue upon which he wished to dwell, although he bitterly contested Susan's characterisation of the episode as an 'obsession'.

George made no apology for seeking to prove his point. It would have been all too easy for him to sidestep the issue of who was the greatest, like many eminent contributors had done before him. George Martin, the Beatles' producer, for example, had written that comparing Lennon with McCartney was like comparing oil with vinegar, while the truth was that one did not work without the other; a statement which, in George's opinion, was palpable nonsense. Vinegar could easily be deployed without the addition of oil and vice versa, as he had demonstrated in a blind test with Susan, over three nights.

He planned to complete an entire chapter while he sat waiting for Mr de Nascimento to emerge from the Scottish

Government building at Ocean Terminal, in Leith, but Mr de Nascimento had now been inside for an hour and George had managed only five paragraphs. Given his self-imposed deadline, he began to wonder whether he should have taken the driving job on at all. On the face of it, the conditions were well suited to his needs. It wasn't the highest paid position in the world, but it allowed him lots of free time to get on with the book and there was no requirement to speak to people beyond anything that was purely functionary. He simply collected passengers – mostly businesspeople – from the airport, drove them to their destination, waited for them until they had finished and then drove them to their hotel or back to the airport.

One or two of them would want to talk, but it was simple stuff like how to get to such and such a place, or perhaps they wanted to know a little bit of the history of the city – nothing that was going to trip him up or put him on the spot. Many were non-native English speakers, which had its benefits as well as its disadvantages. If they asked him something difficult, when he wasn't altogether sure what they were getting at and he couldn't see their expression in the rear-view mirror, he could always hide behind the language barrier. But then, often they used unusual or unfamiliar phrases.

On one occasion an Indian gent asked him for the 'timing' of his return flight when, what he meant was the 'time'. When George told him, he didn't know how long the flight was, the gent became quite irritated, repeating the question several times as though George was a simpleton. On another occasion, he was driving an American businessman back to the airport with the car radio playing when the passenger said: 'Can you not have the radio on while I'm trying to concentrate?'

George was confused because it seemed to him quite self-evident that it was possible not to have the radio on.

45

He simply nodded in agreement and left the radio on which he often did as it broke the silence and made the passengers less inclined to engage him in conversation. He continued driving until the passenger yelled suddenly: 'Will you switch that fucking radio off, godammit?'

The worst passengers were those who asked personal questions and wanted to know about George's background. In many cases, he managed to end the questioning by offering a single word response or by changing the subject, but some were quite persistent. In those circumstances, George could get upset at their direct probing, which felt suffocating. On one occasion, he lost concentration and steered the car onto the hard shoulder, which led to the passenger complaining about him to his boss.

The worst occasion was when he made the mistake of telling a passenger that he was formerly a tax specialist because it turned out that the passenger was also a tax specialist and he wanted to know all about how a tax specialist had ended up being a chauffeur. George was forced to make up a whole story that did not involve grievance procedures, industrial tribunals, garden leave and all the other stuff he had spent years trying to forget about. George was no good at lying because he knew it wasn't real and anything that wasn't real confused him. He ended up contradicting himself and, invariably, the person or people to whom he was talking knew that he was lying.

This time he decided that lying was better than being drawn into a long explanation about how he had to protect his family from all the lies and personal vilification that was ranged against him for no reason other than that he was too good at his job for some of his former colleagues to handle. That was why they had it in for him and were prepared to go to extraordinary lengths to protect their own interests and, in so doing, to ruin his life. Despite it being a difficult episode, he took pride in the fact that he held firm and retained his dignity. He had gone through the entire process without flinching and without exposing Susan and the children to the worst insults they could level against him. But he would do anything to avoid talking about it.

Mr de Nascimento came striding from the main entrance of the building, so George had to drop his notebook and exit the car to make sure he was holding the rear passenger door open, just like he had been told to do by Mr Greening. Mr de Nascimento was short and greying, but George guessed he was probably not much older than 50. He was dressed in a pale blue suit that looked expensive and George noticed he wore high Cuban heels. The man smiled at him as he held the door open and he said 'thank you' as he slid onto the back seat, which made George feel good. Very few of them said 'thank you'.

When George got into the driver's seat Mr de Nascimento was already reading some papers and he appeared to be preoccupied, which meant George could concentrate on driving and didn't feel compelled to fill the silence with words. He checked the schedule again before pulling away, to make sure he had the sequence right in his head. He had to take the passenger from the Scottish Government building to the offices of *GrantAitkenMacIntyre* in Morrison Street, where Mr de Nascimento would attend another meeting, at 14:00 hours, and then he had to drive him back to the airport, for 17:15 hours, where he would catch his return flight to London.

George already knew the detail of the schedule, but he always liked to go over it again as it made him feel more secure. After dropping Mr de Nascimento at the airport, he'd allocated himself a generous 50 minutes, allowing for rush hour traffic, to make it back into the city and to be at Newington by 18:15, in time to be outside Linda's house by 18:30. Because she wasn't expecting him, he anticipated that, even if she was planning to go out – and on a Tuesday

47

evening the chances were unlikely – she'd still be at home at that time; unless, of course, she was intending to visit the theatre, but he checked the schedules and it didn't appear that there were any shows or plays or concerts currently being performed which suited her tastes, or those tastes that he was aware of.

As he drove onto Leith Walk, the car became snared in traffic, just as Mr de Nascimento packed away his documents. George thought about switching on the radio, but Mr Greening had warned him that, following the previous incident, he should have the radio on only if the passenger requested it. After a few moments he could bear the quiet no longer.

'I see you're a dancer,' he said.

'I'm sorry?' Mr de Nascimento replied.

'I see you're a dancer,' George repeated.

Through the rear-view mirror he could see Mr de Nascimento's thick black eyebrows bunch together, which he recognised as a frown. That meant he was confused.

'Your shoes. I see from your shoes that you dance.'

His frown became even more pronounced.

'You see my shoes and you think I dance?' Mr Nascimento asked in heavily accented English.

George watched him shake his head and the silence continued.

'You live in an interesting city,' Mr de Nascimento said after a few moments.

George thought so too, so he did not feel obliged to say anything in response.

'I have had a look around since I have been here and there are many beautiful buildings.'

George stared straight ahead, without commenting on what he recognised to be a self-evident truth.

'I know many people who have been to London but not so often in Edinburgh. I will tell them, the next time you are in the UK, you go to Edinburgh.'

The traffic lights changed to green and George put his foot down hard on the accelerator.

The car pulled away sharply, but it managed only about 50 yards until he had to stop again at the next set.

'You have always lived in Edinburgh?' Mr de Nascimento asked.

'No,' George replied.

He decided to block out Mr de Nascimento's presence to allow him to concentrate on what he was going to say to Linda later. He had exchanged a few words with her just before Susan's funeral, but they were interrupted by all the mourners milling around and the timing wasn't ideal as it coincided with the coffin being carried into the church. Linda had not turned up for the reception, which disappointed George, but it hadn't surprised him as she and Susan were not on speaking terms when she died. The brief conversation he had with her at the church was the first time he had heard her voice for several years, but they had always had a connection, of that he was sure.

The car pulled up alongside the *GrantAitkenMacIntyre* building, but all the parking spaces were filled so George had to double park, which he didn't like doing because it made him tense. The traffic was busy; there was virtually no space between the cars queuing on the road and the traffic lights were changing rapidly, which meant there was little movement. The noises of engines revving and horns blaring meant he almost lost his balance as he made his way around the car to open the rear, passenger-side door. Mr de Nascimento said something as he emerged, but George could not make it out and he had to ask him to repeat it.

'MY PLANS HAVE CHANGED,' he shouted. 'I WILL BE STAYING IN EDINBURGH FOR ONE MORE NIGHT AND I WILL NEED YOU TO DRIVE ME SOMEWHERE THIS EVENING.'

George did not like sudden changes of arrangements. When he thought of the endless permutations and potential outcomes of a single alteration to a plan, over which he had no control, he felt dizzy. Staring down and concentrating hard at the tips of his shoes helped. If he could see his feet fixed in a particular position, he felt safer. He closed the car door after Mr de Nascimento left and he gripped the handle. His eyes were closed to block out the presence of the people around him. He sensed a commotion; a queue of traffic was backed up behind his car, waiting for him to move it and the drivers were becoming impatient, hooting their horns and shouting. A man approached and stood immediately beside him. There was a sickening smell of stale tobacco from his clothes and George could tell he was fat because he felt the soft yielding of his belly against the sharpness of his elbow.

'Urr you gonnae stand there aw day like' the man asked.

Like what, George wondered, but he had lived in Edinburgh long enough to know not to ask. He forced himself to release his grip on the door handle and he edged slowly around the car, until he reached the driver's side and he slumped on the seat. The noise and fleeting movement of different shapes and colours continued to attack his senses and he fumbled with the key, managing at the second or third attempt to force it into the ignition. He eased his foot onto the accelerator and the car pulled away.

He concentrated as hard as he could on driving but his legs were shaking and he was unable to properly control his feet on the pedals, making the car lurch forward. He had to shove the gear stick into neutral to stop it from crashing into the car in front. He felt the coldness of his sweat-covered shirt constricting his chest and back, drawing attention to the heaviness of his breathing.

The traffic lights turned to green and the cars in front of him pulled away, creating a free run. He engaged the car in gear and used his free hand to hold his accelerator leg steady long enough for the car to build speed. He didn't know where he was going or even in what direction, but he knew he needed to be out of there.

Chapter 4

Central Edinburgh, an hour later

Before Lennon's musical ability was recognised, he displayed a talent for drawing and writing. Some people believe that all abilities within these spheres, whether cognitive or aesthetic, derive from a single innate source known as creativity. Those who are talented, or creative, across a range of disciplines, are known as polymaths. One such polymath was Leonardo da Vinci who was a talented scientist, mathematician, engineer, inventor, anatomist, painter, sculptor, architect, botanist, musician and writer. Furthermore, some people contend that creativity is linked to madness. For example, Edgar Allan Poe said: 'Men have called me mad; but the question is not yet settled, whether madness is or is not the loftiest intelligence – whether much that is glorious – whether all that is profound – does not spring from disease of thought – from moods of mind exalted at the expense of the general intellect.' Lennon's drawings frequently featured pictures of cripples and spastics and, while performing on stage with the Beatles, he often pretended to be mentally handicapped. In Lennon: The Definitive Biography (Harper, 1993), author Ray Coleman said he developed an obsession with cripples, spastics, human deformities and people on crutches, and that he had a fascination with warts. In his debut book, In His Own Write (Simon & Schuster, 1964), Lennon invented a character called Partly Dave who, when confronted with a negro bus conductor, heard a voice in his head saying, 'would you like your daughter to marry one?' prompting him to leap 'off the bus like a burning spastic'. This is also an example of racism, according to some observers.

George stopped writing and remained still for a few

moments. With the windows closed, the inside of the car felt peaceful and secure. His breathing had returned to normal. He was parked on a double yellow line at the far end of a cul-de-sac, hemmed in on either side by tall, dirty tenement buildings in a part of the city centre that was home only to a few shuttered wine shops and a decrepit 'hotel' for the homeless. He sat motionless for around 30 minutes until a stern-faced traffic warden approached, swinging an arm from behind his back to consult his watch which, George guessed, was his cue to leave. He tossed his notepad aside and started the engine.

When he returned to Morrison Street, Mr de Nascimento was standing on the pavement outside the GrantAitkenMacIntyre building. He was in the company of another suited man who was considerably taller than him and was holding an umbrella under which they both huddled as protection against the rain. Mr de Nascimento raised an arm as George approached and hurried towards the car, holding a folder over his head. George moved to exit the car to hold the rear passenger side door open for him and he shuffled onto the back seat.

Watching Mr de Nascimento through the rear-view mirror, George could see droplets of water trickling down his face and steam rising from the shoulders of his suit jacket which created an unpleasant smell, like a wet dog. The businessman removed his glasses which had steamed up and he wiped them with a royal blue, silk handkerchief that he retrieved from his breast pocket.

'You're wet because you're short,' he said.

Mr de Nascimento stopped what he was doing and stared at the back of George's head for a couple of seconds. His eyes narrowed, as he tried to focus without his glasses.

'I'm sorry?' he said.

'The other fellow was holding the umbrella too high above your head. You'd be dry if you weren't so short.'

53

The businessman's eyes narrowed further.

'I don't understand what you say.'

George found the confusion funny, like in a comedy sketch show, and so he laughed.

'You're short, like a midget, that's why you wear high heels' he said, doing his best to be helpful.

Mr de Nascimento shook his head quizzically, reminding George of the sort of dumb foreigner character he remembered from the Benny Hill Show which was his favourite comedy programme of all time. That made him laugh even more.

'A midget ... a dwarf ... like in Snow White and the Seven Dwarfs. You know? Dopey, Grumpy, Sleepy...'

'Just drive,' Mr de Nascimento said, waving his hand dismissively.

George had yet to broach the subject of the changed plan and the prospect was preying on his mind. He considered telephoning Mr Greening and telling him directly about Mr de Nascimento's sudden and unreasonable alteration to the agreed schedule, but he knew in advance what his boss' response would be. He would repeat the same mantra about doing whatever the client wants. George remembered the instruction word for word: 'Whatever the client wants, you do. If the client wants driven around the city, you drive him around the city. If the client wants taken to the airport, you take him to the airport. If the client wants fired out of a cannon wearing his sister's dress, you do it.' The last bit was a joke. George had worked that out for himself.

'Where would you like me to take you, Mr de Nascimento?' he asked when the car was stopped at traffic lights.

'To hotel,' he replied sharply. 'Then we go to the Scottish Government where we collect two colleagues who take me to football match for which they have tickets.'

'To the Balmoral Hotel?' he asked.

The businessman's head turned sharply; his top lip was curled up slightly at the end and his eyes narrowed.

'Yes, to Balmoral. Same hotel as before.'

George had more questions he needed answered but he decided to wait until the lights had changed. He knew he would have to concentrate on driving as the streets were busy with people and he never knew when someone might step off the pavement unexpectedly. He managed to negotiate another two sets of lights before stopping again at the junction of Princes Street and Charlotte Square.

'What shall I do after I've dropped you at the hotel?' he asked.

Mr de Nascimento breathed heavily through his nose.

'I tell you. Wait.'

'Wait for what?'

'For me to have shower and change into new clothes.'

'How long will that take?'

'Not long.'

'How long?'

Mr de Nascimento paused, and he breathed heavily again.

'I don't know how long, maybe 50 minutes, maybe one hour. Why is this of your concern?'

His voice sounded harsher and higher pitched than before. George guessed he was angry about something, so he resolved to stop talking which, from experience, he found often helped to change the other person's behaviour, to make it more equable. He glanced at the green digital clock on the dashboard and saw that it was now 16:12 hours. He calculated that if they arrived back at the hotel by 16:30 and it took Mr de Nascimento 50 minutes to shower and change, they would be ready to depart for the Scottish Government building at 17:20. Assuming heavy rush hour traffic, it would take a further 20 minutes to drive there by which time it would be 17:40 hours.

Mr de Nascimento had not mentioned which football ground he wanted taken to, but George knew that whichever it was, it would never leave him enough time to be in

Newington and outside Linda's townhouse by 18:30 hours. After another couple of blocks, he realised his forehead was damp with sweat. He needed further clarity on the altered schedule.

'Which football ground do you want taken to?' he asked.

'I don't know,' his passenger replied tersely.

'You don't know?'

'No, I don't know.'

George felt this answer was irrational, which increased his sense of irritation and he felt a stabbing sensation in his chest. His skin tingled like he had been given a mild electric shock.

'How can you not know where you're going?' he asked.

'I tell you I don't know. My colleagues, they have tickets, they tell us which place to go.'

'Is it Tynecastle?' he pressed.

'I tell you I don't know.'

'Easter Road?'

'I don't know.'

'Hibernian or Heart of Midlothian?'

Mr de Nascimento exploded with anger.

'Hey mister, you ask too many questions. I said I don't know. You stop asking me. How many times I have to tell you I don't know.'

George could see flecks of Mr de Nascimento's spit land on the shiny leather seat beside him and calculated it was time for him to stop talking.

Chapter 5

Edinburgh New Town, a fortnight later

'What is this?' Robert stood waving an opened copy of the Law Society Journal, his face flushed with anger. Melvyn had noticed, in recent weeks, a slight tremor in the old man's hands as well as a hint of uncertainty in his voice, but he knew better than to mistake those signs of age for frailty.

'Eh, it looks like a copy of the Journal?' Melvyn said calmly.

In the past he might have attempted to appease the old man, but he now realised that what Robert wanted was to be allowed to point out Melvyn's perceived shortcomings in the running of the firm, and thereby demonstrate his enduring grip.

'Yes, I know it's a copy of the Journal, Melvyn, but what I want to know is why we appear to be in it.'

Melvyn took hold of the offending item. He had not yet seen the latest edition of the magazine, nor the full-page advertisement for *TMBL Law* that he had placed in it the week before. He had purposely avoided mentioning the marketing campaign of which the advert was a small part because he knew, from long and painful experience, what his reaction would be

'Because I thought we could do with raising our profile following the rebrand?'

'Our profile?'

'Yes, our profile.'

'And why, pray, should our profile need to be raised?'

Melvyn looked again at the ad, bearing the firm's bold new logo that he had retained a digital creative agency to design six months previously. There were many quality standards against which the old man measured the firm's successes, but marketing outcomes and brand identity were not among them. For reasons Melvyn did not claim to understand, he considered commercial advertising vulgar and his anger was aroused not only because Melvyn had embarked on such an endeavour, but crucially, that he had done so without his approval. However, Melvyn knew better than to point this out to the old man who was, after all, the company's chairman and, more importantly, his father-in-law.

'Jesus God, Melvyn, it was bad enough that you invited that mob of brilliantined spivs in to tell us how to do our job and charge us a bloody fortune into the bargain. Now we're getting the begging bowl out for customers, and as if that wasn't humiliating enough...'

'This strategy was agreed by the board,' he ventured, attempting to remove any personal element from their exchange and to put it onto a purely business footing with which he felt more comfortable.

Breathless with anger, the old man took a moment to compose himself.

'Well, the board in its wisdom is not always correct and it's my job as the chairman to point out to the managing partner when I think he has made a poor strategic decision'

Melvyn arrived at his desk at 6.30 a.m. every day in the full knowledge that he was there only by virtue of an historic act of spite on the part of his father-in-law. He had acquired his position as managing partner of the firm, not because of his qualifications, experience or talent, but simply because he wasn't either of Robert's two nieces. Robert and his late brother, Albert, had launched *Templeton's* in 1958, each investing £200 in establishing a criminal law practice in a room above a pub on the Lawnmarket, a stone's throw from the Sheriff Court. Five years later, they had saved enough money to move into a shop front in South Clerk Street and within a decade, their firm occupied three floors of a converted Georgian townhouse in the New Town's Abercromby Street.

By the mid-1970s, following the recruitment of Albert's two recently married daughters, Elspeth and Rhona, the firm relaunched as *Templeton McGregor Ballantyne*.

In the early days, their respective wives were employed as administrative assistants in the Lawnmarket and South Clerk Street premises. The brothers' estrangement was rooted in a perceived slander by Bert's wife, Ingrid, on the alleged inability of Robert's wife, Agnes, to properly bind a legal brief. Further, equally grievous, slights are alleged to have been levelled to compound the initial injury, including charges that Agnes served non-branded caramel wafers to a visiting sheriff with his tea and misspelt the name of the wife of a Justice of the Peace on the firm's annual Christmas card list. Progressively, the brothers moved onto more substantive disagreements, culminating in Bert's effective withdrawal from the day-to-day running of the practice and a silent stalemate between the brothers.

Following Bert's death, his daughters resolved to perpetuate their father's side of the wordless vendetta. Their mutual distrust and dislike of one another permitted Rab to elect himself as senior managing partner and, in return, they accepted salaried positions. When the old man was finally persuaded that, at the grand old age of 76, he should think about stepping down, largely as a result of a sustained campaign of harrying by Mary, ownership and management of *Templeton McGregor Ballantyne* was a labyrinth of historical, operational caveats and make-do-and-mend compromise. The refusal of the founding partners to communicate directly had, by necessity, created a strangulated network of executive sensitivities and fragmentary command and communication channels, a situation exacerbated rather than relieved by the arrival of the younger generation.

In selecting a successor to Robert as senior managing partner, the board had the choice of appointing Elspeth, then head of litigation; Rhona, head of criminal law; or Douglas Hunter, an otherwise perfectly able managing partner who, because he had been appointed by Robert, was viewed by Elspeth and Rhona as a hollow-headed stooge. In its wisdom, the board elected Melvyn who had not only failed to apply for the post, but had no experience of, interest in, or to his knowledge, flair for lawyering in general, far less running a busy legal practice.

What he did possess was a chequered background, having scraped a third-class honours degree in Law and then failed his Diploma of Legal Practice. Several inauspicious attempts at employment followed, culminating in him gaining a junior position with an ambulance-chasing firm of road accident, medical negligence and personal injury lawyers whose favoured premises were a series of pop-up stalls in shopping centres.

He was, however, deemed to be the ideal compromise candidate on account of him not being any of the other three genuine contenders. News of his successful appointment was broken to him by Mary in a manner which felt more like a rape than a seduction. Only after he was sitting at his desk behind a brass plaque inscribed with his new title did it occur to him that, as a board member and senior shareholder in the new practice of *Templeton McGregor Ballantyne Lovelace*, his wife was now effectively his boss. His father-in-law elected to remain in place as non-executive chairman which, from that point on, gave him carte blanche to stalk the corridors as self-appointed senior counsel in charge of such lofty matters as advertising veto.

'Now, are you remembering it's the Gala Ball at the weekend?' Robert asked, taking the conversation in a sudden change of direction.

'Yes, I'm remembering,' Melvyn replied, trying vainly to disguise the truth.

'Have you taken your kilt to the dry cleaner?'

'Eh ... no, I don't think so ... I think Mary may have done it,' he stammered, reproaching himself inwardly for not thinking faster on his feet.

Robert flapped his hands hard against his sides and sighed loudly.

'Christ on a bike, Melvyn, you need to be on top of this. We cannot have a repeat of last year's debacle. I will not countenance you turning up, yet again, in a tatty rental suit looking like the best man at a Larkhall wedding. The head of the firm always wears the Templeton tartan to the Gala Ball. It's a tradition and people expect it to be maintained.'

'I do know that, Robert – it wasn't my fault. The shop mislaid my kilt, and I had no option but to wear a dinner suit.'

'Well, make sure you take it to another dry cleaner this time. I will not apologise for you again. People notice these things and they talk, Melvyn. Don't think for one moment that they don't.'

'I know they talk, Robert, and I will go to another dry cleaner and I will get it back in time, so you have no cause for concern.'

Robert eyed him closely, clearly unconvinced.

'Now, if you don't mind, I'm extremely busy with other matters and I'd rather not be standing here complaining all the time. I know these things might seem unimportant to you, but they count. People pick up on details like that, you know.'

'I'm busy too, with the civil service sexual harassment tribunal case,' Melvyn said.

'Ah, we're handling that, are we?' he asked, clearly forgetting that the issue had been the subject of prolonged discussion at the most recent board meeting. 'Good oh, as you were then.'

The old man retreated through the doorway with an outstretched arm, his tailcoat sashaying in the narrowing gap behind him. Melvyn slumped back onto his swivel chair and he grimaced as he experienced a twinge of lower back pain. No matter how often Melvyn reminded himself that Robert had no real power over him, a truth routinely reinforced by Mary, he couldn't help but feel bested and humiliated by his father-in-law following such an exchange. He was certain, and the direction in which he'd led the company since taking control confirmed, that he was a far superior businessman to Robert. His knowledge, judgement and vision left the old man in the shade, and yet when it was just the two of them in a room, it became a battle – because Robert always made it a battle – of wits, character, personality or whatever you wanted to call it, he felt hopelessly ill-equipped, even to compete.

He surveyed the drab office, the appearance of which he had done nothing to improve since his arrival more than 20 years previously, and which Robert, who had occupied the same rickety chair before him, had done nothing to improve since entering it in 1964. Or was it 1966?

He would need to consult one of the leather-bound, limited edition copies of the firm's official history – which his father-in-law had commissioned a professional biographer to write, to mark its 50th anniversary – to be sure.

A dark-wood panelled crime of faux-baronial kitsch, the room had a sad, outmoded smell of bygone ideas and unrealised plans. The floor was a jigsaw puzzle of fitted oak parquet chevrons, tired and vague with age, which bore a tell-tale whitened footpath to a mock antique filing cabinet in the far corner in which Robert had kept his whisky, which he habitually dispensed in large glasses to clients, whom he entertained on a now worn, tan leather sofa.

Sitting in the office made Melvyn feel like a character from a Graham Greene novel, cast haplessly into an alien environment over which he had no control. The principal emotion he felt was frustration, not at the job itself – in fact, he rather enjoyed it and, against expectation, found that he was good at it – but at the dead hand of Robert's continued presence and influence. The reason he had done nothing to improve the appearance of the room was not through neglect or disinterest, but because it no longer served any useful purpose. It existed solely as a fig leaf to satisfy the old man's naïve and misguided conviction that the Abercromby Street practice bore any meaningful relation to the company as it was now constituted.

Melvyn had long since moved the firm's centre of decision making to a new headquarters that spanned several floors of a high-rise, glass-fronted tower at Haymarket Square, in the city's financial and commercial district, to which he would decant the moment Robert exited the building. In the old man's day, Templeton's may have been his idea of a steady and dependable fixture of the Edinburgh legal establishment but, under Melvyn's guidance, it had been transformed into *TMBL Law* – a full-service, international legal consultancy with branch offices across the UK and Europe,

The change of name alone had been enough to cause the old man near apoplexy and it was, like most other major decisions, forced through only on a vote of the board. More significant for Melvyn was that, in the old man's confused and outdated thinking, he failed to appreciate that the small number of criminal cases handled by the Abercromby Street office now accounted for a tiny fraction of the global business conducted under the *TMBL Law* banner.

What neither Robert nor his nieces anticipated was that, while Melvyn had limited abilities pleading cases and next to no people skills, he excelled quite magnificently at spotting patterns and that, in the modern business environment, was a highly bankable asset. It was while attending lowly Justice of the Peace Court hearings during ambulance chasing duties with his former employer that he spotted a trend in the pleas of mitigation offered by solicitors representing clients who had received citations for non-payment of parking fines. In some cases, the cumulative amounts owed by defaulters ran into thousands and even tens of thousands of pounds and some of the most egregious offenders were jailed for up to 60 days if they were unable to pay the fines or financial penalties handed down by the court.

What struck Melvyn was the sheer number of occasions solicitors claimed their clients had unsuccessfully appealed against parking fines. It seemed there were no, or vanishingly few, circumstances in which the imposition of such fines could be overturned. Most motorists simply paid them to avoid the negative consequences of not doing so and wasting time with an administrative appeals process that overwhelmingly favoured the plaintiff.

He also noticed that the system to collect fines had been established and was administered by the city council, which had an unambiguous financial interest in maximizing the revenues that it generated. Not only was there a presumption of guilt when a parking ticket was issued, but the burden of proof was on the motorist to prove his or her innocence and the only appeals process was to a non-independent agency controlled by the plaintiff. This was a blatant money-making scheme and a flagrant breach of natural justice.

Some cursory research by Melvyn established that, in the previous year, the council had issued 850,000 tickets, generating some £27 million in fines. After accounting for differences in demography, vehicle use and collection rates, he estimated that local authorities – or agencies acting on their behalf – across the UK had the potential to raise more than £1.1 billion in revenues, with a margin for error of plus or minus two per cent. On taking control of *Templeton McGregor Ballantyne Lovelace*, one of his first actions was to constitute a small team of solicitors for the purpose of pursuing a class action against the Edinburgh City Council. The lawyers had no difficulty in conscripting motorists recently issued with parking fines to agree to participate, on a no-win-no-fee basis. After the *Evening Chronicle* ran the story, the number of appellants joining the class action became hundreds and, by the time the case was heard for the first time at Edinburgh Sheriff Court, the firm was representing more than three thousand disgruntled drivers.

Despite losing at the initial hearing, Melvyn was determined to pursue the case further and he lodged an appeal. By the time the case was called at the Court of Session, Robert had taken an interest – not least because it had attracted the attention of his legal cronies – and it gave him an opportunity to dust down his wig and gown to tread the judicial boards. Melvyn was happy to give the old man his moment in the spotlight and he had to admit that, in front of the bewigged, three-judge panel and a room full of his peers, he had delivered a bravura performance.

Arguing that the city council had 'used its ordinance to put its thumbs on the scales of justice to extract millions of pounds from motorists through a subversion of the judicial system', the old man made an impassioned plea to his learned colleagues:

'From the outset of this flawed procedure, there is a presumption of guilt, contrary to centuries of precedence set by statute and case law, accompanied by threats of increased fines, impoundment and illegitimate court cases, should the respondent fail to fall in line. The appeals process, such as it is, is a kangaroo court in which the plaintiff becomes the judge. 'Milords,' he pronounced as he bestrode the courtroom floor, with his thumbs tucked into the sides of his waistcoat, 'This is as clear an example I can think of for natural justice being denied, in principle and practice, not to a single individual or a small group but to an entire class of citizens, and I urge you to take the right, and indeed, the inevitable path, in favour of our many thousands of clients.'

The immediate windfall for the firm as a result of winning

65

the case represented its biggest ever pay day by a multiple factor. Melvyn could not remember how much revenue the High Court victory generated but, to him, that was not important. Nor was the fact that, by the time the widely used procedure for collecting parking fines and administering appeals across the United Kingdom was scrapped and replaced with a fairer system, Templeton McGregor Ballantyne Lovelace was representing more than 50,000 motorists in class actions against 103 local authorities. More significant was that he had established a business model for the company that would take it in an entirely new direction. From then on, neither the focus of its work nor the level of its ambition would be dictated by past practices or indeed by the city limits. The only constraint on its growth would be the horizons of his own imagination.

Before he set off for Haymarket Square, he resolved to call Mary to make sure she took his kilt to the dry cleaner, lest he risk the calamity of the previous year which had warranted an hour-long inquest at the subsequent board meeting. The annual fundraising Gala Ball was held in the clubhouse at the Grange Golf Club – home to the Royal Company of Lothian Golfers – and was the final piece of the firm's business over which Robert continued to exert total control. As a result, Melvyn's anxiety levels increased exponentially as the date grew nearer.

All its current and former staff still living were invited, along with clients, past and present, fellow advocates, solicitor advocates, advocate deputes, sheriffs, judges and local dignitaries. Every year Robert invited the Lord Advocate and the Solicitor General and every year they sent their apologies with barely serviceable excuses. Few of the current staff would bother to turn up if Melvyn did not institute a three-line whip, enforced with threats and promises and, even then, most of the tickets were bought by former clients and colleagues of Robert for whom he had done favours over the years.

As chairman, the old man had bestowed upon himself the sole responsibility for choosing which local charity would benefit from the funds raised and, as a matter of principle, the beneficiary was always a cause associated with the care or protection of children.

Melvyn sat lifelessly, collecting his thoughts, waiting until he could be sure Robert had left the building and he heard the haughty drone of his claret Daimler depart the car park. The silence was broken by the ringtone of his mobile phone, which made him jump. It was Roz and he considered ignoring her call again, as he had done twice already, the previous evening and again earlier in the morning. On the fourth ring, having reasoned that clearly she had something important to say and that by failing to answer he was delaying the inevitable, he pressed the green pick-up button.

'Hi Roz, I got your messages, and I was going to call but I've been up to my eyes in it,' he said with breathless haste, trying his best to sound harassed.

'It's OK, I just wondered if you'd heard from Dad.'

She sounded concerned.

'I haven't spoken to him since the funeral. I'm really up against it. This civil service class action is proving much more complicated than any of us thought. More women have come forward claiming to have been sexually assaulted. There's going to be a media shitstorm.'

'It's just that he's lost another job and I'm quite concerned about him. He's been round pestering Linda Walker again and this time she sounded really pissed off.'

Melvyn closed his eyes and let out a slow, frustrated breath. He experienced a sudden flash of anger. He knew his sister was not to blame for his father's infuriating behaviour, but she always seemed to be the one to give the bad news and it felt like she revelled in the role of messenger.

'What happened with the job? I thought he was enjoying

67

it. He told me at the funeral that he was enjoying it.'

'He left a client in the lurch. He was supposed to be taking some financial bigwig to a football match and he just dumped him at his hotel and drove off.'

'Oh, Christ.'

'I couldn't get a sensible explanation from him. As usual, none of it was his fault. It was only when I phoned the chauffeuring company and spoke to his boss that I got the full story. I tried pleading his case, but they were having none of it. They didn't say as much, but I got the impression there had been other incidents and this was the last straw.'

Melvyn wanted to tell Roz they should cut their father loose and let him get on with his life and them with theirs. He had always been a difficult character so why, at this stage in his life, should his family be expected to continue making allowances for him? If he could not hold down a job, that was his lookout. Why should he even have a job? Most people of his age had retired, so why couldn't he do the same?

Of course, he knew that Roz's reply would be that he had always been active, he needed something to occupy his time, he wasn't the sort of person who could relax or potter around, that he needed a project. Melvyn had heard the same arguments and platitudes about his father for years and he was sick of them. This was an opportunity for him to speak up – this was his moment – and as usual, he bottled it.

'So, what happened with Linda Walker?' he asked.

'He turned up on her doorstep while she was having some girlfriends round for dinner. She tried to tell him, subtly, that it was not a good time, but he did not take the hint. He hung around until, eventually, she had to set an extra place for him and, of course, he didn't eat anything because none of it was suitable, then he spent the whole night boring everyone shitless about John Lennon.'

'Oh, Christ.'

'He stayed until the bitter end and even when all Linda's

friends had gone home, he seemed in no hurry to leave. She got the distinct impression he was angling for an invite to stay the night.'

'Oh, Christ.'

'She only managed to get rid of him by threatening to call one of us.'

'Was she angry?' he asked.

'She said she wasn't. I think she was more concerned than angry. I told her I was worried about him being on his own and she felt Mum's death may have affected him more than he's letting on.'

'Did she say as much?'

'She agreed that he's not the sort of person who would cope well with a sudden change of routine.'

'What's this leading to Roz?'

'It's not leading to anything,' she protested.

'He's not moving in with us. We have been through this before and I have told you it is out of the question. Mary will not have it. Nor will I for that matter.'

'I'm not suggesting that he moves in with you.'

'Why do these things always land on my doorstep? Just because I live closest to him does not mean I should have more responsibility. I didn't force you to move to London.'

Melvyn was just ten years old when he realised that he found it difficult and frustrating being in his father's company for long. George arrived home from work and announced, with some fanfare, that they were going to be 'a proper father and son' and, to mark the occasion, he had bought an Airfix model of HMS Vanguard for them to build together. He had heard a work colleague boasting in the staff canteen about what a great relationship he had with his son and he was determined that he would have the same.

He set about the task in the same, methodical manner he applied to all his 'special projects', by reading up on the subject at the local library until he'd exhausted every possible source, from Darwin and Freud to Spock and anything in between with 'father' and 'son' in the title. Melvyn recalled the look of deep embarrassment on his father's face as he attempted to explain to him the facts of life. The few details he was still able to retrieve from his childhood memory included dealing efficiently with sperm leakage following masturbation and proper foreskin hygiene. They were logged in bullet point format in a notepad, under the heading 'FOL Discussion', alongside other activities including cycling, fishing, wrestling and camping. Neither George, nor as it turned out Melvyn, had remotest interest nor proficiency in any such activities and the father and son bonding project was promptly shelved within a few days.

'Calm down, Melvyn, the last thing I want to do is to create tension between you and Mary.'

'Well, what are you suggesting?'

'All I'm saying is that you should keep an eye on him. Involve him more in your life. Go round to the house and have a cup of tea with him, take him out for a pint or for lunch and talk to him.'

'Talk to him?' Melvyn scoffed. 'Have you tried talking to him recently? Are we discussing the same person?'

'Look, I know it's difficult and I promise I'll take my share of responsibility.'

'Why can't he come up to you?'

'I have asked him, but he won't do it. And besides, don't you think he has enough change to cope with, without taking him out of his comfort zone and transplanting him in a flat in a corner of South East London he knows nothing about?'

Melvyn sighed, battered by a tide of reason and fair-mindedness, and he knew he had no option but to comply.

'OK, I'll see what I can do,' he said resignedly.

Chapter 6

Corstorphine, Edinburgh, the following week

Lennon met Paul McCartney at a church fete on July 6, 1957 and invited him to join The Quarrymen, precursor to The Beatles, as a result of which they formed what was to become the most successful song writing partnership in musical history. McCartney introduced George Harrison to Lennon the following year and he joined as the lead guitarist, aged 14. Their first recording, in June 1958, was That'll be the Day by Buddy Holly, whose insect inspired backing group, The Crickets, gave band members the idea to rename themselves The Silver Beetles, a name that later evolved into The Beatles, a linguistic reference to the popular Mersey Beat movement of successful Liverpool-based musical acts. Lennon wrote his first composition, Hello Little Girl, when he was 18 years old. It would become a UK Top Ten hit for The Fourmost, nearly five years later in 1963. Along with Stuart Sutcliffe and drummer Pete Best they performed 'gigs' at venues in Liverpool as well as three residencies in Hamburg, Germany, in August 1960, April 1961, and a third in April 1962. The term 'sex and drugs and rock 'n' roll' might well have been coined for The Beatles in Hamburg which, as a port city, was a hotbed of vice and depravity. The quarter where they played, known as The Reeperbahn, was populated with bars and strip clubs where prostitutes, homosexuals and transvestites openly paraded. It is speculated that during their time there, each of the band's members had sex with up to 50 women a week and that they regularly took stimulants, including Preludin and amphetamines. Lennon's caustic wit was deployed with great alacrity during their performances there, when he would often greet the German audiences with Nazi salutes and cries of 'Heil Hitler' while holding the edge of a black comb under his nose, pretending it was the Fuhrer's moustache. Such amusing behaviour would not be tolerated today because of 'political correctness gone mad'.

George stopped writing because Melvyn had invited him to his company's annual ball later that evening and, having had nothing planned, he agreed to attend. Other than Melvyn, his wife, Mary, and his father-in-law, Rab, it was unlikely he would know anyone at the event. Mary had suggested George should arrive at their home beforehand, so that they could make their way to the ball together. The time of the event, she said, was '7pm for 7.30pm', a typical example of the sort of ambiguity that confused George. He knew it would have to start at either seven o'clock or half past seven and Melvyn had been unable to explain properly which it was. When he called Mary at her office at the university for clarification, she said that, officially, it would start at 7pm but that arriving any time up until 7.30pm would be fine which, George pointed out, meant they would be late. When pressed on the matter further, she said 'Oh, Christ' several times.

He decided that, rather than risk being late, he would time his arrival at their house for 18:15 hours which meant he would have 30 minutes to bathe, shave and defecate and to dress appropriately for the occasion, and a further 30 minutes to prepare and eat his evening meal. Melvyn had told him the dress code for the event was 'formal', which meant he would have to wear a black dinner suit, white shirt, black bow tie, black socks, and black brogues, all of which he had in his wardrobe.

Alternatively, Melvyn said, George could wear Highland dress, as he himself would be doing, which meant he would have to wear a tartan kilt and matching tie, a checked shirt, sporran, knee-length hose with flashes, sgian dubh and black ghillie brogues, which he decided against as he had never worn Highland dress and had none of the requisite items.

Melvyn said there would be a buffet meal at the event, but he was unable to provide a detailed list of what foods would be available. In such circumstances, George always made it a rule to eat beforehand, as the menu might be unsuitable to his requirements which, invariably, was the case. There were a lot of foods George was unable to eat, either because he didn't like the taste or, more frequently, because they had an alien texture which made him vomit or want to vomit.

Such foods included nuts, eggs, most fruits (apart from cooked tomatoes and uncooked apples), most vegetables (apart from raw baby carrots and celery sticks) especially garlic and onions, most foreign cheeses (but not cheddar or Edam), cream, yoghurt, some soups (with lumpy bits) raisins, currants or sultanas, jam with seeds, jelly, peanut butter, all cold meats (apart from Sainsbury's own boiled ham), crumbly breakfast cereals, all Chinese food, all Italian food and anything spicy.

Throughout his life, his food likes and dislikes had attracted comment. When he was a child, adults routinely called him 'fussy', 'difficult' and even 'spoilt', which made him feel frustrated because he didn't choose to dislike particular things and he often became fearful, even tearful, if someone tried to force him to eat something that he knew would make him sick. As an adult, he suffered from gluten intolerance, which was a blessing in disguise because then he could blame that for him refusing to eat things that he could reasonably claim didn't agree with him.

Melvyn had suggested George should take a taxi, which would allow him to drink alcohol at the ball, but he decided against that because, in his experience, taxis were invariably late and their drivers frequently chose routes that were neither familiar to him nor, in his opinion, the most time efficient. In many cases, they wanted to engage him in conversations whose subject matter was of no interest to him, such as driving restrictions in the city centre and the reproduction rates of brown immigrants.

George preferred to drive himself and, generally, it didn't stop him from drinking as he found that alcohol did not negatively affect his reaction speeds to any significant degree, as was claimed by many police spokespeople, road safety professionals and other members of the Nanny State. He had regularly drunk and driven over a period of more than 50 years and, in all that time, he had been involved in only one minor incident, in August 1991, when he misjudged the angle of a bend in a road and his car careered down an embankment and landed on its side in a ditch. The incident was principally caused by a lack of street lighting, rather than by the influence of alcohol upon his judgment, in George's opinion, and he escaped relatively unhurt, with only some minor cuts and bruises. He judged that the statistical probability of him being involved in another road incident caused by drink-driving to be negligible, so he continued the practice to this day. Generally, he avoided mentioning it to others who tended to take an unnecessarily censorious view, particularly Mary, who became agitated and challenging if she suspected him of doing so.

He left home at 17:15 hours, taking with him his tube of saccharine sweeteners and a breath freshener, a sample of toilet paper, whose firmness and texture he knew he could trust should he be caught short, and his notebook with which he could retreat to a quiet corner to pen an additional page or two, should he encounter a situation with which he was unfamiliar or felt challenged. He arrived at Melvyn's and Mary's house at 18:00; he had planned to get there at 18:15, some 30 minutes earlier than Mary had suggested because he didn't trust her margins for error, but the traffic on the bypass was quieter than he'd predicted, with the result that he was in situ a good 45 minutes ahead of schedule, which gave him a warm, satisfied feeling.

He parked on the street and walked through the main gateway, along the winding, stone- chipped path that led to Aite Beannaichte, the Robert Adam-designed sandstone villa where Melvyn and Mary lived. There was a strong wind, and it was cold, even for the time of year, and he regretted his earlier decision not to wear an overcoat. The final bend of the path was dominated by a large, overhanging horse chestnut tree that had shed most of its leaves and they crackled noisily underfoot as he walked over them in his brogues.

The front of the house was dominated by four large, sash bay windows that were illuminated from the inside and, in the fading light of the retreating day, they looked warm and inviting. The main entrance was framed by a stone portico, supported on either side by a pair of Doric columns and, within it, a Regency-style, lead stained-glass doorway. The hallway featured a marble floor in deep red, with flourishes of blue and gold, and it was dominated by a neoclassical staircase.

Upon discovering the provenance of the house, shortly after Melvyn and Mary had moved in some eight years previously, George had taken a good deal of interest in its history and he even unearthed its original plans at the National Library of Scotland. Over several months he undertook exhaustive research to identify the style and sources of all the materials used to fashion the property's main features, including its ceilings and intricate cornicing work, flooring, balustrades and main fireplaces.

He discovered details of previous occupants in documents stored at the National Archive of Scotland and the General Registry of Scotland and by consulting local parish records. He found that among its residents was a former Solicitor General of Scotland, a successful slave merchant and a Baillie in the Royal Burgh of Linlithgow. He wrote, edited, professionally bound and published a fully sourced and illustrated volume on the history of the building, including chapters on Adam himself and the local parish.

Sadly, the reaction to his endeavours was not what he had hoped for. Mary objected to his frequent visits to the house to inspect various items and, most vociferously, to his requests to have fireplace facades removed temporarily, to locate the trademark of the master craftsmen responsible. She had also taken exception to him approaching a neighbouring family, one of whose forebears, George discovered from parish records, had been guilty of 'a heinous felony severe enough to merit Transportation'.

He rang the doorbell and waited for Melvyn or Mary to answer. When, after around 30 seconds, neither appeared, he became agitated, but he resisted the temptation to ring again, as he feared another tart rebuke from Mary, as had happened on a previous occasion. Another 20 or so seconds elapsed before he saw her elegant outline glide down the stairway. She answered the door without smiling and offered her right cheek for him to kiss. Her hair was soft, shiny and red and shaped in a helmet bob. People said she looked like Jane Asher, but she reminded him of Amber, 21, from Basildon – a model he'd seen in a pornographic publication several years earlier but who remained fresh in his memory right down to what clothes she wore (before she took them off) and what poses she struck. He often wondered what had happened to Amber, 21, from Basildon, because he had never seen her again, no matter how hard he looked in subsequent issues of that and other top-shelf magazines.

'Your father's early again, Melvyn!' Mary shouted as she retreated into the hallway.

He found Mary's attitude toward him unreasonably and bafflingly hostile. He could have a perfectly pleasant time in her company, albeit that she was quite often short and unspecific, and then, days later, Melvyn would reveal she had accused him of doing something terrible, though in his mind quite trivial, to offend or upset her.

The most excitable he remembered seeing her was immediately after the death of Anthony, their son. George had paid a visit to Aite Beannaichte on an unrelated errand concerning the recent release, by the Royal Mint, of a collection of 28 distinctive 50p pieces, each bearing the motif of an Olympic sport on the reverse side, to commemorate the 2012 Games in London. Some 14 million of the coins had been distributed into the economy and, immediately, he had set about preparing a collection, with a view to future sale or transfer. However, quickly he realised that not all the sports featured in equal numbers, as a result of which, some coins were rarer than others.

He had no great problem acquiring those bearing sports distributed in the highest numbers such as athletics, canoeing, table tennis and triathlon, but he found it difficult to locate those distributed with least frequency, notably modern pentathlon, tennis, wheelchair rugby, wrestling and football. He sought assistance from Melvyn, asking him to tell the staff in each of the *TMBL Law* branches to regularly check their change in case they should come across some of the more prized versions. He would, of course, reimburse them with other, non-collectible 50p pieces, he made clear.

Despite numerous reminders from him by telephone and email, Melvyn had failed to follow-up on his request until suddenly, on the morning of May 12th – a Saturday – he called to say that three of the five elusive coins had been located – tennis, at the Aberdeen office, wrestling in Manchester and football in Bristol. Between that phone call and George's arrival at the house, news of Anthony's death had been delivered by a policeman, whom he passed on the driveway, via the British Consul in Santa Cruz. It transpired the boy had sustained a fatal skull fracture after falling from the fourth storey of an apartment block in Tenerife, while drunk, landing head-first on a concrete concourse during a holiday with four of his school chums.

Melvyn met George at the door and told him what had happened, then led him into the lounge where Mary was perched on the edge of a chaise longue, located along a wall near the bay window, at the far end of the room. She looked distant and distracted and Melvyn suggested she move onto a more central settee, near the fireplace, where she would be more comfortable, but she ignored him and continued to stare straight ahead. She didn't seem to be crying but her face was red and wet, and she made occasional groaning noises over which she appeared to have no control.

Melvyn paced back and forth, anxiously. Several times he appeared to be on the verge of saying something but then he didn't. George stood between them, in the middle of the room, without knowing what to do or how to behave. He had been in the company of people who had suffered bereavement in the past, notably when his own mother and father died, in both cases when they were quite elderly and after long illnesses. He knew from experience that, in such circumstances, respectful silence and the appearance of solemnity were the order of the day. But this situation was of a different magnitude principally, he thought, because of the suddenness of Anthony's death and his relative youth, and due to the recent nature of the news which, he was able to observe, created a high level of tension in the room. The telephone rang suddenly in the hallway, making Mary jump with fright. Melvyn left the room to answer it, leaving George alone with his daughter-in-law, which seemed only to intensify the silence.

She continued to sit upright, her body suffering periodic minor convulsions and her face remained damp from the ongoing production of noiseless tears. Mary continued to stare straight ahead. George stood upright, with his arms held vertically straight down each side, clutching in his right hand his tweed cap, which he had removed at the door, as a gesture of respect. Though he had never served in the forces, he felt his demeanour displayed an appropriate level of martial stoicism. Melvyn returned from the hallway, following his telephone call, and resumed his stance in front of the Adam-designed fireplace.

'That was the Foreign Office,' he said quietly, his voice weak and faltering. 'They're sending someone over to discuss arrangements for...', he didn't manage to finish the sentence, losing his footing and landing awkwardly on the settee. Mary offered no response, and the silence resumed. George decided that his presence was serving no useful purpose and that he should leave.

'I'll go then,' he said, addressing Melvyn. 'You'll have a lot to get on with and I'll just be in the way.'

Melvyn looked at the floor and nodded slowly. George stood for another minute in the silent room.

'I'll make a move then,' he said.

Melvyn managed to raise himself from the settee and walked toward his father with his right arm outstretched to offer a handshake. They had never been a 'touchy feely' family – George didn't encourage unnecessary physical contact with either of his children – but, on this occasion, he felt it was appropriate that he should reciprocate. As he raised his arm, he felt that perhaps a handshake was too formal a gesture, given the circumstances, and so he moved his hand past Melvyn's with the intention of patting him on the upper arm as a means of comforting him. Anticipating this, Melvyn raised his arm and their knuckles clashed.

There was a momentary awkwardness as both sought to apologise for the mix up, but their voices were low and mumbled, and their words came out as groans. Following a moment of further mutual indecision, both then simultaneously sought to take the initiative by raising both their hands and placing them on the other's shoulder, which gave the impression of them being locked in a wrestling clinch. Embarrassed, both retreated with uncommon haste, each voicing a low, inarticulate apology, before George decided the entire enterprise was ill-fated, brushing past Melvyn and heading for the doorway.

'It's OK, you don't need to see me out,' he said with his head down.

He made it into the hallway before it occurred to him that he had forgotten the original purpose of his visit. Gingerly, he pushed open the door to the lounge and took a tentative step back into the room.

'Melvyn, could you look out those 50p pieces for me, please?'

Mary looked up like she had heard a gunshot and the life seemed suddenly to return to her eyes, her gaze boring into his face with a piercing intensity.

'GET HIM OUT OF HERE!' she screamed.

Melvyn looked stunned and remained motionless.

'GET HIM OUT OF HERE,' she repeated.

George stood alone in the hallway, unsure of what to do, for around ten minutes until Melvyn appeared at the top of the stairway. He looked uncomfortable in full Highland regalia which appeared to overwhelm his thin frame. That and his prematurely grey, balding pate were at odds with the traditional image of a bulky, ginger haired Scot that George associated with such attire. His son appeared flustered and irritated, simultaneously pulling at his shirt collar while scratching at his right inner thigh under his kilt.

George said nothing. Melvyn walked past him into the lounge, leaving the door open which, George guessed, was a cue for him to follow. He moved across the room to a vintage bar cart located beneath a row of antique bookshelves upon which sat a crystal decanter of whisky and several cut-glass tumblers. By the time George entered the room, he had poured himself a large measure and was swigging it from the tumbler. George would have liked a glass himself – Melvyn kept a range of superior aged malts which he could not afford to buy – but he wasn't offered one. The pair waited in silence until Mary arrived, wearing a black overcoat and clutching a black, patent pocketbook that matched her shoes. She stood in front of the wall mirror and applied a coat of lipstick.

The golf club was located on the outskirts of the city, a 30 minute drive away along the bypass, and the three of them spent the journey in silence. George had visited it on only one previous occasion many years before, after Melvyn had begun playing golf there with his father- in-law, who was a member. After doing some cursory research, he learned the building was designed by Robert Adam's father, William, in the early eighteenth century and that the estate had previously hosted King James VI for a hunting expedition. Both facts he found fascinating, but Melvyn was uninterested and appeared more concerned with reducing his handicap, which became something of an obsession, to the point where Rab refused to play with him.

When they arrived, Melvyn and Mary exited the car ahead of George and walked briskly toward the entrance of the grandiose building where they were met by a group of men, all dressed identically to Melvyn in formal Highland dress. By the time George reached the doorway, they had already gone inside and had disappeared into the gathered crowd. The lighting in the foyer was a dim yellow and a thrum of amiable chatter melded with the aroma of expensive perfumes and high notes of alcohol. The scene was one of warm conviviality with which George was warily familiar and the combined assault on his senses caught him off guard.

This was his first social outing since Susan's death and he had not anticipated how exposed he would feel. He inched forward into what he identified as the main function room which was swarming with people, none of whom he recognised. He tried to imagine what he'd have done if he had his wife to provide support and cover. What was so comforting about her presence was that he didn't need to do anything. She acted as both a shield and a diversion. After standing in the same spot for several minutes he decided that perhaps he should try to start a conversation with the one person in the room, other than Melvyn and Mary, that he knew.

He edged past several tables, all identically covered in white damask tablecloths and silver service cutlery and adorned with ice buckets of champagne, glossy programmes, miniatures of malt whisky and assorted favours for the ladies, until he reached Rab, who was standing with a group with three men all of whom appeared to be about his age, which made George feel slightly more comfortable. They appeared to be engaged in a conversation about some aspect of the law but George couldn't understand a lot of the terms. He stood silently on the edge of the group for several minutes but, when Rab failed to acknowledge his presence, he decided to move further forward until he was among them. As he elbowed his way between two of the members, they smiled and nodded at him, but Rab continued to ignore him.

When one of the group finished what he had to say, there was a momentary break in the conversation as none of the other members of the group seemed minded to continue it, so George took this as his cue to say his piece.

'Rab, were you aware that this building was designed by the father of the architect responsible for designing Melvyn and Mary's house?'

The three other gentlemen turned their attention to Rab, who was taking a sip of whisky.

'Yes, you have told me,' he said drily.

There was a further pause in the conversation before one of the other members opted to speak.

'Aren't you going to introduce us, Rab?'

Rab appeared flustered as he turned to face George for

the first time.

'Of course, do excuse me. This is George, Mary's father-in-law.'

The three shook George by the hand and introduced themselves before Rab turned his back on him and resumed their discussion.

George thought that perhaps he should buy a drink from the bar; he found that drinking alcohol had the effect of making him feel calmer and, despite the queue for the bar being exceptionally long, he took his place at the end of it. He pulled his wallet from the inside pocket of his suit and withdrew a £50 note. He had budgeted to spend a maximum of £35 on alcohol during the evening leaving him £15 to pay for a taxi should Melvyn decide to overrule his plan to drive home from Aite Beannaichte. The queue was irregular and unstable, and he had difficulty discerning where it began and ended.

Directly to his right were several young women, he guessed in their late teens or early twenties, who were in high spirits, swapping humorous observations, laughing and, on several occasions, shrieking loudly. They were heavily made up and dressed minimally in bright colours, displaying a large amount of flesh both above and below the waist. They were scented with strong, unsubtle perfumes whose smell conjured thoughts of sexual intercourse in George's mind. One of the girls staggered slightly and fell against him and the top half of her left breast brushed against his hand. Her flesh was warm and yielding and he experienced a sensation of arousal.

'Oops, sorry,' she said, giggling.

'That's alright, no harm done,' George said.

She was tiny, compared with him, but her raised footwear gave her added height and her hair was a rich, chestnut colour, cut short and fashioned with hair products to give it a spiky style as if she wanted it to look unkempt which seemed, to him, a strange ambition. She wore a short chessboard-patterned skirt, revealing bare legs to the upper part of her thighs, and a black, low- cut sleeveless top made from material thin enough to reveal a scarlet, lace bra.

She had the sort of looks that he would have found desirable in a woman when he was younger, and he admired her clear sense of fun and extroversion. Susan would never have worn such revealing clothing, despite his frequent entreaties for her to dress more suitably for her age. For many years, he had been convinced he was married to the wrong woman as Susan had not shared his interests and, more recently, he had come to think that perhaps he had been born into the wrong era. Sexual liberty seemed to him to be far less prevalent when he was growing up than it was for younger generations for whom everything – dress, music, television, alcohol – seemed purposed to facilitate enjoyment.

The queue moved at a slow pace and eventually, when he arrived at the bar, he was confronted by a barman who was dressed smartly in a black tuxedo and bow tie. He ordered a blended Scotch whisky which was served with ice, in a crystal glass placed on a cushioned paper coaster adorned with the golf club's crest. He always admired the little touches of luxury at Melvyn's dos, and he wished that he had worked in circles where such opulence was afforded. He proffered his £50 note, but the barman failed to take it and instead, he mouthed something which George couldn't make out. He thrust the banknote again at the barman but, again he refused to take it.

'It's a free bar, sir,' a male voice said, immediately to his left.

The barman moved onto another customer, which made George feel anxious because he had not yet taken his money, nor given him any change. He perched a shoe on the footrail to give him greater reach across the bar, and again he thrust the note in the barman's direction with his outstretched hand.

'Excuse me, I haven't paid yet,' he said.

He felt someone grab hold of his elbow and he was pulled back.

'It's a free bar,' a young man said.

George turned around and stared at his face in the hope that it might provide some clue as to what his words meant. Taken together they made no sense. What was a free bar, he wondered? Was this bar free? If so, why should the cost of the bar be relevant to this situation? Why should he have any interest in the bar given that it was his first and, quite possibly, last visit to it?

'It's a free bar, mate,' a female voice to his right repeated.

He turned around and looked in her direction and was met by a chorus of smiling young female faces. He felt his face redden and he wanted to cup his hands over his ears to block the noise, but he resisted the temptation. Susan had admonished him for doing so in the past, saying it made him look simple-minded. His mind blanked over and all he could think was how he was going to extricate himself from the situation.

The young girl in the chequered skirt stepped forward and took hold of his hand. She put her arm around his shoulder and led him to the side of the bar. Gently, she unfurled his fingers, removed the damp banknote from his palm, folded it in quarters and slotted it into the breast pocket of his suit.

'It's alright, you don't have to pay, she said, smiling. 'All of the drinks have been paid for in advance by the company.'

She returned to her friends and he breathed deeply and with a sense of relief that someone had taken the time to explain the situation to him in straightforward terms and without the use of complicating idioms. She looked over at George and smiled again and he smiled back.

Chapter 7

Roz woke with a shock, from the warmth of a comforting, half-remembered dream into the cold reality of an unheated flat. On another morning she might have experienced a gentler drift, when the blissful absurdity of sleep fused with a moment of creeping clarity ahead of the realisation that she was back in the real world. Today there was no such hiatus; instead, the joy of quiet, dismembered thought was swept away instantly as her brain resumed its obsessional stories of the night before.

For the past week, she had slept until she couldn't sleep anymore; when there was nothing left to dream about, she sat alone for an hour or two, with only the background chatter of Radio Four as a distraction until she was tired enough to fall asleep again. She summoned the strength to raise her head from the cold pillow and looked at the clock. It was almost eight o'clock and, through a gap in the curtains, she saw traces of night continued to hover. Her mind ached and she felt an irresistible urge to pull the duvet over her head and shut herself away from the world, but she had an appointment she couldn't miss and she knew she'd have to force herself out of bed.

She swung her legs over the edge, sat upright and shivered. As the sole of her left foot made contact with the cool floorboard, she let out a whimper and summoned the will to bring the other foot down. She stood up and walked to the single-paned, sash window that was coated with a layer of frost and she fashioned a hole with the tip of her finger, peering out onto the frosted pavement. She hadn't expected London mornings to be as cold as they were in Scotland.

She bought the flat five years ago at a knockdown price,

cheap even for this unlovely chunk of the Capital. It required 'moderate upgrading', according to the selling agent but, with the prospect of Crossrail and ongoing gentrification of the area, she was assured it was a cushty little nest egg for which well-heeled twinkies would soon be biting her hand off. To date, she hadn't got around to upgrading anything and Crossrail had been delayed, yet again. Without double glazing, central heating or even carpets, she convinced herself it was a 'work in progress' but now she was coming to the realisation this was just how she lived.

She pulled her dressing gown around her shoulders and made her way through to the kitchen-living room where the previous night's embers had long-since expired in the tiny open grate, leaving a pathetic mound of calcified rock. She fumbled with a box of matches to light a ring on the gas hob to warm her numbed hands. They began to thaw and she summoned the resolve to make a cup of tea, filling a pan of water and waiting for it to boil, hunched over the stove for warmth. She looked at her mobile phone, which showed she'd missed another call from Melvyn. She dialled 1571.

'Hi, it's me. Give me a ring, there's a problem with Dad.'

Surely not another problem, she thought despairingly. She had spent an entire morning earlier in the week trying, and failing, to get to the bottom of exactly why George had been fired from his latest job. These things always fell to her because Melvyn simply offloaded responsibility onto her for clearing up the latest mess their father had got himself into. She made a mental note to call her brother later in the day. In the meantime, she had enough to contend with keeping her own life on the straight and narrow and, increasingly Ruaridh's mind focused on just getting by.

She thought she remembered his clumsy manoeuvrings in the freezing darkness earlier in the morning, but it might have been a dream. She wondered if he'd overslept again. He would have had to go to the lock-up to load up with stock, before heading to the market, because he hadn't done it the night before, so she hoped he'd left himself enough time. He'd been late to secure his pitch twice the previous week and the rent collector had warned him that he'd lose it if he did it again. It was a decent spot near the entrance to the market, so there was no shortage of stallholders waiting to step-in and grab it given the chance. He only managed to retain it the previous week because the bloke on the neighbouring stall, who sold fruit and veg, had parked his van on it until Ruaridh arrived. Roz decided not to think about it any longer, otherwise she would start to catastrophise – a despicable non-word she'd heard on a CBT podcast.

...the world is a benign and predictable place...there is no conspiracy to defeat me...most of the things that can go wrong in my life will not go wrong...

After summoning the resolve to get dressed, she wrapped herself in an old parka, which was the warmest item of clothing she owned, and braced herself to face the day. She walked to the end of the street, past the yellow-brick Gurdwara and a small row of shops where the boys in Mr Uncle's Fried Chicken Shack were getting ready for the lunchtime trade from the local school. It was barely opening time at the Who'd a Thought It? but she could see through the unwashed, mock-Tudor windows that several of the bar stools were already occupied. Its charmless dinginess was a deciding factor in her decision to buy the flat – that and the fact that it was far enough away from the nearest train station to discourage even the most determined of her colleagues north of the river from launching an expeditionary force to seek out her quaint little pied-à-terre in 'the East End'.

Her first few visits to the pub were promising enough; she'd taken up residence in the most secluded corner of the lounge bar, equipped with a conversation-blocking paperback and a tacit understanding with the barman to keep the large vodkas and tonic flowing in her direction. A growl had been enough to repel any approaches from the few barflies still compos mentis enough to register her presence. The arrangement worked for a few weeks until a self-loathing social worker, who routinely took-out his professional frustrations on the spirits gantry, recognised her picture by-line from his tattered copy of *The Sentinel* and from then on, the writing was on the wall. It wasn't her newfound celebrity that troubled her so much as the prospect of news leaking out about how she chose to spend her leisure time. After that she began to spread her patronage wider, to other bars in the area and, while most could claim a more salubrious ambiance and a more discerning clientele, none could offer the same level of detached indifference to the heroic volumes of alcohol she chose to consume as the Who'd a Thought It?

She didn't have to wait long for a bus and, as the doors swung open, she felt a relieving blast of warm air. It was midmorning and only a handful of passengers were aboard; she knew a few of them by sight but, this being London, none of them returned her smile. The only one to acknowledge her with a cursory nod was a peanut-headed youth she'd seen before, perched on the backbench and whom, she suspected, wouldn't have needed much encouragement.

Until now, she hadn't mentioned Ruaridh to Dr Cheng. She figured that she hadn't known him long enough for him to have any impact on what she did or how she felt. She also didn't want to discuss him, only for her to then reveal a few weeks later that he was out of the picture and to self-analyse why they had broken-up, what it said about her attitude to relationships and whether she was truly capable of being anything other than a monumental psycho fuck-up. For the first time since they'd been together she found herself wondering what she was doing with Ruaridh.

Even acknowledging such thoughts convinced her that their relationship, if you could even call it that, was in its final throes. That, of course, was before the bombshell.

Funny how finding a little blue line on a piece of plastic, with your knickers stretched across your knees in a McDonald's toilet, could have such a cataclysmic impact on your life and prompt such a profound, internal dialogue about who you are and where you are headed. She could have hoped for a more salubrious setting in which to consider questions of such high, existential import, but then those are often the cards you are dealt. It had quite put her off her double cheeseburger with fries.

She was still unsure about how or if she would approach the subject with Dr Cheng. Until then their discussions had mainly been about her family. By their discussions, of course, she meant her discussions. Dr Cheng never said anything other than to offer the occasional prompt, such as 'What makes you say that?' or 'Why do you think you did that?'. Sometimes Roz felt like screaming, 'No, why do you think I did it? You tell me. You're the fucking psychiatrist!' She still felt patronised even having to attend the sessions, angry that a few throwaway comments to her GP about 'feeling a bit down' had spiralled so quickly. She wasn't the sort of person who needed a psychiatrist, she told herself. People who need psychiatrists are the poor souls in psychiatric care units who dribble their food or businessmen found striding across Westminster Bridge in their underwear during rush hour.

But it turned out not to be what she expected. Rather than the heavies being summoned to strongarm her into the lobotomy suite on her second visit, she found herself wondering if Dr Cheng might just be a little bit more pro-active in her approach. A bit more digging into her psyche to discover what made her tick wouldn't go amiss, she thought. In fact, she found her astonishingly incurious about anything to do with Roz's life or childhood experiences or attitudes to sex or any other things she associated with psychiatric inquiry. But then, as the Dr Chen told her, it wasn't her job to tell Roz what problems she had and what might have cause them; it was for Roz to talk about what she thought might be at the root of her problems and, through self-realisation, to come to a better understanding of them and herself.

So, how would she explain Ruaridh and why she had decided he'd become another problem in her life? Was he even a problem, or might he just be the solution? When they first met, she'd found his carefree attitude to life and money surprisingly appealing because it contrasted so profoundly with that of George, who over-managed his life and those around him to an infuriating degree. She let him move in with her because he didn't care about how much things cost, or about being on time, or about following instructions to the letter. He didn't get up at the same time every morning and follow an identical ritual; he didn't have rigid structures to his behaviour and he didn't criticise those who didn't do the same. She had found someone who wasn't prone to acts of often cruel insensitivity; who didn't freeze, change the subject, or leave the room when challenged; who didn't react in extreme, disproportionate ways to the smallest provocation; who didn't have irrational dislikes and fears and obsessional interests; who wasn't solitary and withdrawn; who didn't find it difficult to engage in conversation; who wasn't predictable to the point of distraction. Ruaridh may not have done any of those things, but that wasn't the same as finding someone she really liked, far less loved. She liked to think that her threshold of acceptability in a partner should be more than anyone who was not like her father.

As the bus pulled away, she recalled a conversation she'd had with her mother, years before, about why she and George married. The main things that attracted her to him, she said, were his dependability and ambition. He had

91

his future mapped out before him from a young age, Susan said. When he was still at school he had already decided that he would graduate with a first-class honours degree in accountancy from the University of Edinburgh and that he'd begin his career with one of the big auditing firms, advancing to manager, director and then partner level. He would have children at the best public schools, drive expensive cars and live in the sort of highbrow, wax-sealed townhouses that featured in the Sunday supplements. He would sit on boards, join prestigious clubs and societies and rub shoulders with the great and the good in the best balcony seats at the Usher Hall – all perks that someone of his education, bearing and ambition should reasonably expect.

Of course, none of it happened and the reasons why had become the subject of a lifelong inquest. It wasn't that he lacked the intellect, drive or talent – he failed to fulfil his potential and ambitions because he had all of them in too great abundance. His failure to impress, the pass-overs for promotion, the difficulties in making friends and cultivating colleagues were all part of the same mendacious prejudice, the same inevitable plot to do him down and deny what was rightfully his, engendered by the bilious, conspiratorial envy of others.

From the moment her parents met at a Beatles concert in April 1964 at the ABC cinema, in Edinburgh, George had pursued Susan with a determination that Roz found deeply romantic. Susan was in Scotland on holiday from her native Canada and she had gone to the concert on a whim, to see why such a fuss was being made in all the British papers about this new pop group from Liverpool. He was already a fanatical follower of the group, with an encyclopaedic knowledge of its members, their careers, songs, and musical abilities. He described his love of the band and its music with a passion she found charming, if a little intense. He was particularly taken with John Lennon, she remembered, and she thought such hero worship was odd for a man of his age.

A couple of weeks later she returned to Toronto and, despite living thousands of miles away, George showered her with attention, sending her effusive, sentimental love letters – sometimes several in one day. She said he made her feel like she was the most loved woman in the world and that he was determined to know everything about her life, her background, friends and family, her likes and dislikes. He delighted in the fact that she was from another country and he made energetic efforts to find out as much as he could about her culture, learning Quebecois French in a matter of months and bombarding her with obscure facts about the province, some of which she didn't know, despite having lived there all her life.

Six months later, he suggested they spend Christmas together at her parents' house. She was cool on the idea at the start, but she relented under his persistence. It seemed that once he had set his mind on something, he was determined it should happen, which she also found attractive. He arrived in a taxi from the airport laden with gifts for each member of her family, which he had chosen based on brief bits of information she mentioned about them in her letters to him.

He wasn't the most attractive man she had ever met; he had dirty, fair hair, and his nose was too sharp – someway short of her tall, dark and handsome ideal – but she fell in love with him because of his enthusiasm and chivalry. Certainly, Susan's parents had no concerns about this polite, well-doing Scot who had travelled thousands of miles to show his devotion to their daughter, a welcome departure from the scruffy Beatniks who sniffed around her at school.

Looking back, warnings of issues that would later surface in their marriage were already there. He was extremely fussy about what he ate and drank, restricting himself only to what was familiar. He bought a travel guide to Toronto and insisted on sticking faithfully to its recommendations, despite assurances from Susan that, as a native of the city, she knew more interesting and offbeat places to visit. He didn't like surprises, she noticed, even small ones like a late change to a dinner plan or an impromptu decision to hail a taxi. And he was fastidious about time keeping, becoming quite irritable if there was even an outside chance of being late.

She recalled that, during his visit, they planned to spend the day together visiting several tourist attractions he had identified in his guide, and then to have an early dinner in a downtown restaurant that the guide had identified as being English influenced, which he found appealing. While they were viewing St Michael's Cathedral, Susan's father and both her brothers arrived unannounced, in the company of two male friends, and said they had managed to get hold of an extra ticket for the evening's big ice hockey match, which they thought George would enjoy. All were extremely excited about the match, as was Susan who was keen on the sport, but George seemed unimpressed, reluctant to change his plans and he was only persuaded to attend the match after Susan pointed out, quite forcefully, that the tickets were very expensive and hard to come by and that to refuse might appear rude to his hosts.

When the six men returned later in the evening, all but George were still high with excitement about the match which their team, the Toronto Maple Leafs, had won by six goals to five, which was particularly impressive, coming off the back of a zero to seven defeat to the Boston Bruins the previous night. George, however, remained silent, and when Susan asked him about the experience his only comment was that the crowd had been too noisy and that he wasn't fond of team sports. Susan's father later told her that George had spent most of the match standing alone, away from the rink where the action was, and that he barely spoke a word to any of the other members of the party, all of whom commented

94

how shy they found him.

At the time Susan attributed such behaviour to him being nervous about being in a foreign country. She even found it quite gallant of him that he was prepared to take the lead in organising their time together, to save her the trouble, even though he was in a country of which he had little experience. In hindsight, however, she felt she should have been more questioning of his behaviour and challenged his unwillingness to be accommodating and flexible.

As usual, Roz arrived at the health centre with time to spare. On one of her early visits, she had been a few minutes late and she was sure she saw Dr Cheng writing something about it in her little notebook. She wondered if everything she did was being watched and judged, as though being late or excusing herself to go to the bathroom said something meaningful about her mind. She had resolved not to give her any more ammunition though she wondered if the psychiatrist possibly may have just written the date. Whatever it was, it made her more punctual.

The building was low-slung and functional, set in a rough part of the borough in the shadow of a series of tower blocks. It was located next-door to a bookmaker's shop and, among the rabble of smokers crowded on the pavement outside, it was difficult to distinguish which were patients and which punters.

Roz edged past them, stubbing what she knew would be her last fag for more than an hour under the sole of her boot as she entered. Despite being seven minutes early, the receptionist told her she could go straight to her appointment. She entered same the small, featureless room where all of her sessions were held and found Dr Cheng seated on one of two orange, plastic, bucket chairs laid out so that they would face one another. She already had her notebook open at a blank page on her lap but she didn't write anything. Roz was still taking her parka off when the psychiatrist launched her opening pitch.

'So, what do you want to talk about this time?' she asked with a weak smile.

Fucking hell, Roz thought, no 'How are you? How have you been? How was your mother's funeral? So, you haven't topped yourself yet?' For a columnist, virtually anything would be better than 'What do you want to talk about this time?' She felt like she'd been put on the spot, as though she should mix things up a little, deliver something topical and punchy that wasn't the same old material from their last session. Christ, this was worse than a meeting with Crossman, she thought, but at least it had the effect of making up her mind for her.

'Actually, I want to talk about this guy,' she said.

Dr Cheng didn't acknowledge what she'd said. She wrote something in her notebook patently lengthier than the few words she'd spoken, and she wondered what additional detail she might be recording. What could she possibly extrapolate from the single revelation that Roz wanted to talk about a guy? The thin scratch of pen and paper was the only sound in the room adding to a slight tension. Roz knew this was her cue to continue; the psychiatrist had done her bit by asking what she wanted to talk about, now it was her turn to fill the void for an hour. But she didn't know where to start. Dr Cheng stopped writing and placed her pen in the groove between the pages. Now there was total silence. She waited for a few moments longer before she looked up and smiled.

'And what guy would that be?' she asked.

Roz felt herself blush like a teenager. She'd never introduced Ruaridh to anyone and she hadn't thought about how she might describe him.

'Oh ... just this guy I know,' she said stumbling over her the words in her head.

Dr Cheng paused, with her hand hovering over the

notebook as though she was going to pick-up the pen, but then she laid her palm flat on the page. Roz noticed how long her fingers were, and how they seemed slightly out of proportion with the rest of her body which was so petite and compact. She figured they must be around the same age, but she looked younger. Dr Cheng smiled again. It was a warm, sympathetic smile and it occurred to Roz that, in different circumstances, they might be friends.

'How do you know him?' she asked with a hint more firmness in her tone.

'Eh, I met him in a pub.'

Roz found she couldn't hold the psychiatrist's gaze and she looked past her, through the window, which faced the grey exterior of another building.

'We live together,' she added.

She chanced a glance at Dr Chen's face and saw that her smile had broadened.

'So, he's your partner, then?'

Roz smiled back.

'Yes, I suppose he is,' she said as her voice broke into a short, self-deprecating laugh.

The psychiatrist didn't ask any more questions, but Roz felt a dam had broken and she found herself talking freely about Ruaridh in a way she had been unable or unwilling to do before. What had attracted her to him, she asked herself, apparently out of nowhere. On first impressions, she thought, it was probably because he was nothing like her father. The reality of her articulation of such an idea in the company of another person made her cringe, but she pushed on regardless to further observations. He was a regular in one of the more civilised bars where she drank, which was close to his carpentry workshop, and their 'relationship' was informal from the start. Roz liked this because it gave her a feeling of control and kept expectations to a minimum. If he became too demanding, she felt it would be easy to end it because, at the end of the day, he was just a guy she was sleeping with rather than a proper boyfriend.

Conversationally, they never seemed to progress beyond the humdrum. Initially she told herself she liked the fact that he was practical rather than intellectual and that she'd had her fill of self-important, chattering class dipsticks who thought they knew the solution to world hunger but couldn't change a tap washer. She found it quite sexy that he could do things with his hands around the house, that he knew where the stopcock was and that when a gas engineer came round to fix her 25-year-old boiler, Ruaridh saw through the jargon and flim-flam and saved her the cost of installing an entirely new system when all it needed was a new pilot light sensor. When he admitted he didn't like reading books, she felt a shock. In fact, thinking about it later, it was less of an admission than a statement relevant to another point he was making and yet, despite his lack of sophistication, he could be articulate and even poetic. Unlike any of the other men Roz had been with, she found that when he told her how he was feeling (which he did often, always unsolicited, sometimes tearfully) she knew instinctively that he was being truthful and authentic. She had warned him at the start that, under no circumstances, was he to tell her that he loved her, and true to his word, he never did. But she could tell in ways other than words that he did.

She found him physically attractive which, when she took him home to bed, seemed to be the only thing that mattered. He had a boyish, uncomplicated face and he appeared incapable of deceit. On the rare occasions that he attempted to dissemble, usually about how little work he'd done, he couldn't survive even the gentlest interrogation.

'So, what is it about Ruaridh that you want to talk about?' Dr Chen asked, without looking up from her notebook.

Roz had been doing her best to discuss him without actually getting to the bombshell, as she felt that might be a more effective way of learning how she felt about him, rather than starting the revelation that he'd knocked her up and then trying to talk herself into staying with him. For the first time, she recognised the insight and craft behind Dr Chen's seemingly random prompts. She knew she had no choice.

'I'm pregnant,' she said.

The psychiatrist continued writing.

'And how do you feel about that?' she asked.

Roz knew she didn't have an answer to the question which was the real reason why she'd delaying the arrival of this moment for as long as possible. She understood the impact it would have on her life, that she would have to deal with her drinking and that it would force her to make-up her mind about how she honestly felt about her relationship with Ruaridh. But all of that was irrelevant chaff compared with the real issue of how she felt about being pregnant and the truth was that, for now at least, she didn't feel anything. She realised she couldn't stay silent so she opted to ignore the question and to continue talking about Ruaridh in the hope that through that, she might arrive, tangentially, at some greater revelation.

Although technically he could be described as a carpenter, he wasn't a very committed one, she thought. His business was based in a local lock-up garage and on a single process of turning blocks of cheap wooden offcuts that he sourced somewhere or other on a lathe. After fashioning a basic wooden circle, with a rim, he polished and varnished it and inlaid with one of a series of ceramic tiles, featuring uninspiring pastoral scenes that were delivered in boxes by a supplier somewhere in the Midlands. It was a simple, functional process that produced a range of unimpressive household items including coasters, cheeseboards, fruit bowls and teapot stands. He could do it standing on his head, which might just have taken some of the boredom out of it.

She knew he was better than that, that he had a talent he wasn't using, because she'd seen examples of his more artistic and creative work that lay unfinished and abandoned at the back of the workshop. Pieces of furniture with intricate carvings that he copied from books borrowed from the library and never returned. The pieces showed artistry and creativity but also inventiveness. Because he had never been trained properly, he had to make everything up on the hoof and, when he got to a technical process he hadn't learned, or that he couldn't find a way to improvise, he gave up.

Roz had tried to convince him to learn new techniques, to attend night-classes, even to read the words in the books rather than just trying to copy the designs. He smiled and assured her he would while his face betrayed unmistakably that he wouldn't, that he didn't know how and that, even if he learned, what would be the point as no-one would buy them. So, what could she do? If her own life wasn't so chaotic, perhaps she'd have a leg to stand on but she was hardly a role model of personal and professional get-up-and-go. Besides, if he turned into the next Thomas Chippendale, where would that leave her? Why would he want to stay shacked up with a half-drunk old hack with her best years behind her?

She knew that the sight of herself in the bathroom mirror the morning after yet another self-destructive orgy was an inescapable and irreversible record. The patina of addiction sat in her hair and on her skin, shining through whatever modern miracles of skin rejuvenation and truth-defying cosmetics she applied. It was there in her expression and her movements like a humiliating, corporeal footprint of bad behaviour and deeds that couldn't be undone. She feared being seen at her worst but now she wondered what, if anything, her worst represented. Was any night worse than any other? She tried to think of one that was longer, lonelier, more excessive, more forgettable, but she couldn't. The truth was that her worst was now commonplace.

'So, perhaps you and Ruaridh can help each other,' Dr Chen suggested.

It was the first time Roz had heard her say anything that wasn't a question.

'You could help him to become a better carpenter and he could help you to be a better person.'

Roz felt a sudden rush of optimism.

'So, do you think I should have the baby?' she asked.

Dr Chen smiled.

'I can't answer that question for you. Only you and Ruaridh can decide. What do you think?'

As she left the health centre, Roz remembered the message from Melvyn so she called his mobile.

'Did you get my message?' he asked hurriedly.

'You said there was a problem with Dad.'

There were always problems with dad.

'He's been arrested by the police on suspicion of sexually assaulting a 17-year-old girl.'

Chapter 8

Police Scotland, Fettes Avenue, Edinburgh, the following morning

While at art school Lennon met Cynthia Powell, his future first wife with whom he would sire a son, called Julian. He later split-up with Cynthia, following a six-year marriage, because she had become a tiresome burden to him and his career and, in his opinion, because she failed to live up to her early promise as a suitable spouse. The couple divorced a short time later, allowing Lennon to marry his second wife, Yoko Ono, a Japanese, avant-garde artist with whom he was more suited and enjoyed a healthy and fulfilling sex life.

It has been recorded in several biographies that Lennon was somehow 'cruel' to Cynthia and that he did not treat her with an appropriate level of respect or so-called 'tenderness'. Examples cited included leaving her stranded on a station platform in a scrum of Beatles' fans and Press, when he and the rest of the band departed London for Bognor, Wales to indulge in Transcendental Meditation sessions with the Maharishi; having sex openly with the wife of a mutual friend and then writing about it in the song Norwegian Wood, which he penned for the Rubber Soul album in 1965; and moving Yoko into the marital home at Weybridge, Surrey, before telling Cynthia that their marriage was over.

While, arguably, such incidents might have been handled better from a 'PR' point of view it is, in my opinion, misguided and deeply unfair to suggest that somehow all the blame for the failure of their marriage should be laid at the door of Lennon. From my observations, from the start, Cynthia should have been more attentive to her husband's life, career, interests and goals. It is all very well for her to complain later, as she did in her hatchet job autobiography

'A Twist of Lennon' that she became overwhelmed by the force of attention heaped on her and her family but, in my view, she was aware from the start of her husband's career as a musician and she should, therefore, have been prepared for all eventualities.

While no one can say for sure what passed between Lennon and Cynthia – except for the people themselves – I can fully understand how frustrated he might have felt from my own marital experiences. It is, in my opinion, totally wrong for a woman, at the start of a relationship, to mislead her future spouse into believing that she has an interest in something and then to pay no attention whatsoever to that thing after they are married and, through commission or omission, for her to effectively undermine him by failing to accompany him to concerts and specialist or themed trips; to take little or no interest in the release of Beatles and Lennon singles, albums and publications; on one infamously memorable occasion, actually to complain when he plays 'too much' Lennon music, describing one particular album as 'a collection of dirges'; and to show a criminal level of disrespect by failing to properly mark the man's tragic, brutal and untimely death or to make any sort of personal sacrifice as a gesture to the grieving process.

'I'm afraid you'll have to put the notebook down, sir,' said a female voice.

The person standing in the doorway wasn't wearing a police uniform, so George didn't know who it was or if they had the authority to tell him what to do. The room was small, cold and windowless and there was a strong smell of stale cigarette smoke and disinfectant. The only furniture was a pale wooden office desk defaced with graffiti, and three upright chairs, one of which he sat on while the remaining two, facing him, remained unoccupied. An old Sanyo radio cassette player sat on the desk, the like of which he hadn't seen since the early 1990s, along with three unopened Pioneer cassette tapes with their foil still unbroken.

Writing was the only diversion that stopped George from feeling cramped and sick so he carried on, or at least he tried to, but he couldn't concentrate because the person continued to stand over him, repeating that he would have to put the notebook down, only this time their voice was louder than before. The person had the voice of a woman but the appearance of a man. They were young, around the same age as Roz, he guessed, but they might have been older. Their face was yellow and puffy, like a teddy bear's but without the fur and they had corn-coloured hair that was spiky and rigid. They wore a baggy, sleeveless shirt with a messy pattern in navy blue and orange, of the kind a darts player might wear, with its tails hanging over an ample stomach and a pair of lived-in, black slacks that reached only as far as their shins. On their feet was a pair of cushion-soled, red leather boots that reached up to their calves.

Immediately, George ruled out the possibility that the person was a lawyer, by their appearance alone. More likely they were a member of the constabulary's civilian staff, he thought, or perhaps an 'appropriate adult' – a role he'd read about in various sources of literature although, from their deportment, he couldn't imagine for what they might be appropriate.

'Mr Lovelace, my name is Detective Sergeant Lanigan,' they said.

That didn't help to solve the mystery. George scoured their face for signs that might provide some explanation as to why they were telling him this information, but there was none.

Their expression appeared neutral although he knew from previous experience that might not be the case. Reading peoples' faces was a skill he lacked and one he'd endeavoured to learn over the years, with mixed success.

He'd been able to rely on Susan in the past, particularly in social situations or when dealing with officialdom. It was particularly frustrating watching a play or a film as often there were developments he missed because he didn't feel they had been explained properly. He often had to ask Susan how a particular character knew such and such about so and so and she'd say, 'because she read it on the person's face'. This made no sense to him whatsoever.

'So, you are a police officer?' George said.

'Yes, that's right, Mr Lovelace, I'm a police officer.'

'Oh, I see, because I wasn't sure.'

'So, once again, could I ask you to please put down your notebook?'

Detective Sergeant Lanigan smiled a bit. They pulled one of the chairs from under the desk and sat down, causing it to screech along the wooden floor which made George's head hurt.

'Are you a man or a woman?' he asked.

They looked at him and the smile disappeared, but then it came back.

'I'm a woman, although I agree it's not obvious.'

'No, it's not,' he said.

'But that's ok, I don't mind.'

'Nor do I. It's just a bit confusing.'

She picked up one of the cassettes, removed the cellophane wrapper and loaded it into the recorder.

'Why are you still using cassette tapes?' he asked. 'You'd get much better sound quality with a digital MP3 recorder.'

She laughed a bit.

'Don't you have a digital MP3 recorder?' he asked.

'You're joking,' she said.

'I'm not,' he replied.

'We're hardly at the cutting edge of technology in the force. We still toast bread on an open fire.'

'Really?'

A man entered and closed the door behind him. He wore a shiny grey suit, a starched white shirt with cuffs secured by silver-plated cufflinks and a lilac tie with a chunky Windsor knot. His black, slip-on shoes were fashionably pointed and polished. He didn't say anything but took his place on the other seat and stared at George. His face was bronzed and creased at the corners and he had a stern, focused expression that made George feel uncomfortable, so he lowered his eyes and fixed his gaze on the desk, reading bits of graffiti, most of which were obscene.

Pigs fuck arses
Fucking queer cop bastards
Lanegan's got a fucking big cock

He heard the buttons of the tape recorder being pressed down and the spools squeak as they started to turn. The man spoke first.

'In the room are Detective Sergeant Ronnie Mackay, Detective Sergeant Jane Lanigan and Mr George Lovelace. Mr Lovelace has agreed to be interviewed and he has waived his right for a solicitor to be present during questioning. For the tape, would you please confirm that your full name is Mr George Eric Lovelace of 32 Deanbridge Avenue?'

George hesitated.

'Would you please answer the question?'

'Why do I need to confirm my name for the tape?' he asked.

The detectives exchanged a brief glance.

'We need you to confirm who you are for the record.'

'You said for the tape.'

'It's a figure of speech. I meant for the record,' he replied.

'Oh.'

The pair looked at one another again, this time for longer.

'So, can you confirm, for the record, that your full name

is Mr George Eric Lovelace and that you live at number 32 Deanbridge Avenue?'

It took Detective Sergeant Mackay longer than would be normal to speak, in George's opinion, because he seemed to enunciate slowly like he was stating a series of unrelated words rather than asking a meaningful question.

'No,' George said.

The policeman maintained a fixed gaze, directly on his eyes and his mouth seemed to tighten.

'You won't confirm, for the record, that your full name is Mr George Eric Lovelace and that you live at number 32 Deanbridge Avenue?' he asked.

'No.'

'Why not?'

'Because it's not true,' George said.

'What's not true?'

'That statement is not true.'

'What, all of it or part of it?'

'Part of it.'

'Which part?'

'The name part.'

'That's not your name?'

'No, that's not my full name.'

Detective Sergeant Mackay took a deep breath and exhaled slowly.

'What is your full name then?'

'Mr George Lovelace.'

'Then why are you listed on the electoral register as Mr George Eric Lovelace?'

'Because of an anomaly.'

There was another period of silence.

'Would you care to explain?' he asked.

'No,' George replied.

The policeman moved his seat backward a few inches, causing the legs to screech again, and he shuffled his body slightly.

'Are you refusing to explain?' he demanded, his voice higher than before.

'No, I'm not refusing but you asked me if I'd care to explain and I wouldn't care to explain.'

George became suddenly aware of the silence in the room when no one was speaking and he felt the closeness of the walls, like they were almost touching him. He imagined for a second or two that he was struggling for breath although he knew, logically, that couldn't be the case. He was confused about the question and the intensity with which the policeman continued to stare at him.

'Interview suspended 11.33 a.m.,' Detective Sergeant Mackay announced suddenly, looking at his watch.

He switched off the tape and he and Detective Sergeant Lanigan stood up and left the room. George watched them talking through the glass panel in the door, although he couldn't hear what they were saying because the room was soundproofed. He felt a release of pressure and he slumped against the back of the chair. Feeling more relaxed, he applied his mind again to the question Detective Sergeant Mackay had asked, evaluating any other possible interpretations. After a few moments, they returned and sat down.

'Were you saying that you wanted me to explain the anomaly in my records?' George asked.

Detective Sergeant Lanigan smiled, while Detective Sergeant Mackay's face remained expressionless. Neither responded to his question.

'Because, if that is the case, then I will explain, although I reserve my original position that I wouldn't care to explain.'

Both frowned and they looked at one another again and then back at him.

'You will see that my officially recorded name is George Lovelace. However, after my parents had registered my birth, they decided I should have a middle name, Eric, after my maternal great-grandfather, and so I assumed the name George Eric Lovelace and that is the name I have maintained in common usage throughout my life.'

Neither of the detectives offered any reaction, verbal or facial, so he took that as a cue to continue.

'So, you will see that, when you asked me to confirm my full name, while it is true to say that in common usage my full, assumed name is George Eric Lovelace, for official purposes, that is to say, for the purposes of that which is recorded on my birth certificate, my full name is simply George Lovelace.'

Detective Sergeant Mackay's mouth opened, as if to speak, but then he closed it again.

'We think you need a lawyer,' said Detective Sergeant Lanigan.

'Have I committed a crime?'

The pair exchanged another fleeting glance.

'Why do you ask that?' she asked.

George hesitated for a moment to gather his thoughts. He had a response in mind but, when he thought about it in more detail, he realised he didn't have enough evidence to support it. It would be, he decided, more reasonable to present it as an impression rather than a statement of fact.

'In my experience people who require the services of a solicitor during police questioning have something to hide and are, therefore, more likely to be guilty.'

'In your experience?' Detective Sergeant Lanigan asked.

'Yes, in my experience,' he replied.

'And what experience would that be?'

'I refer not to personal experience, but to experience gleaned through reading about criminal cases in journals and other publications. Notably, that of Mark David Chapman, John Lennon's assailant, whose questioning by police I would be happy to discuss with you. I have read the transcripts of the interviews at length and I regard myself as something of an authority on the subject.'

They regarded George again without responding.

'So, would you like a lawyer?' Detective Sergeant Lanigan asked.

'If you think I should have a lawyer then I am bound to accept your superior judgment,' he replied.

'Does that mean you're guilty?' Detective Sergeant Mackay interjected.

He hadn't spoken for a while and his voice sounded short and croaky.

'I don't know. Perhaps I am guilty, but I won't know until you tell me what I'm being charged with.'

They led him from the interview room into a corridor that was flooded with sunlight from a large gable-end window. At the far end was a door next to a window through which he could see into the main reception area and as the three of them approached it, he spotted Roz trying to retrieve a drink from a coffee machine. He was immediately struck by how awful she looked. He had hoped that her tired appearance at Susan's funeral was down to how much she'd had to drink, but she looked just as bad today. He worried about her health with an intensity incomparable with any other feeling he experienced. When he compared how she looked now with his memories of her as a little girl, dressed in flowery cotton frocks and with her hair tied in ponytails, he felt overcome with a terrible sadness. He remembered crying on only three occasions in his adult life – on holiday in Toronto, after he heard the news that John Lennon had been shot and when Roz was born. He would never forget the moment, as he cradled her in his arms and she looked up at him through her tiny blue eyes that were blurred and unfocused, as they struggled to adjust to the hospital lights. His shape was her first experience of a new and uncertain world and the discord of her helplessness with the overwhelming sense of responsibility he felt toward her gave him a sudden burst of joyous energy. He'd created this perfect little being that was his to mould and protect and nurture. In that moment he knew that nothing would ever be as important as his duty to this beautiful burden and that his life would never be the same. Nor would he want it to be. His qualities would be hers, her successes, his.

Remarkable as it now seemed, he never considered that he would also feel responsible for her disappointments and setbacks and yes, her failures, which he should have foreseen would come as inevitably and naturally as a new day. He'd been blinded by the delusion there would be no downsides to parenthood beyond the physical and the mundane. The smells and the noise never bothered him, nor the sleepless nights, childhood illnesses or the frequent changes in routine. He embraced the progressions, with both Roz and Melvyn, from crib to pushchair to school to braces, as stages to be navigated and challenges to be overcome.

But as they got older, graduating imperceptibly from childhood to adolescence to adulthood, those challenges became opaque and indefinable; no longer practical, but emotional and harder to predict. He'd seen his children as extensions of himself, but now his example was no longer enough. They developed opinions and attitudes he didn't understand, traits he neither recognised nor approved of and his unconditional love for them became contaminated by their sedition which gave him an emasculating feeling of losing control. More devastating was the retrospective impact their growth had on his legacy as Susan began to identify roots of their behaviour in things he'd said or done, tones he'd set, episodes in which he'd played a leading role. As if that wasn't confusing and unpredictable enough, there were the absences – words that hadn't been said, emotions that had gone unexpressed, touches withheld. He refused to accept that Roz drank because he wasn't affectionate enough or that Melvyn deliberately cut himself with a razor blade

111

when he was 14 because of something George had failed to say. All of that created further conflict, lengthening the already unbreachable rift between him and his children.

Roz spotted him and hurried over, but she didn't return his smile which he took to be a bad sign. His mind filled with anger at Melvyn's flagrant disregard for his instructions – he'd warned him specifically not to attend the police station and not to tell Roz he'd been summoned for questioning. He thought their presence premature and, in any case, it wasn't their business. He was glad of the continued presence of the two officers as he knew it would delay the inevitable questioning to which he'd be subjected by his children.

Roz asked him how he was bearing up.

'Oh, nothing six numbers on the lottery wouldn't fix,' he said brightly.

It was a response that had served him well over the years, suggesting he was possessed of spontaneous wit whilst also seeming to draw a satisfactory line in the sand when small talk threatened. In most cases people nodded and smiled and they didn't make any further conversational demands on him.

Detective Sergeant Lanigan told Roz and Melvyn that their father would be obliged to return to the police station later in the day, accompanied by a lawyer. If he couldn't obtain the services of a lawyer at such short notice, then one would be provided, she said. Melvyn briefly thought about suggesting one of *TMBL*'s criminal lawyers, but he didn't want to involve the firm if he could possibly avoid it, handing further ammunition to Robert, so he suggested George should avail himself of a publicly appointed solicitor, a proposal he accepted.

They agreed to reconvene at the police station more than two hours hence, which suited George as he calculated it would allow him to repair to a local library he'd spotted across the street, to complete the chapter he'd been working on in the interview room. When he mentioned this to Melvyn and Roz, they refused, insisting he should accompany them to a nearby café to inform them of what had been discussed with the detectives.

This made George angrier as, not only had Melvyn contradicted his earlier instructions, but Roz was now complicit in seeking to appropriate his plans, disrupting his writing timetable. He had built some reasonable slippage into the timescale for his book, but such disruptions could not be tolerated and had the potential to place the entire project in jeopardy. Reluctantly, he agreed to join them but the whole enterprise made him uneasy. He calculated that, allowing for some limited conversation, he might yet be able to negotiate an early departure to spend some time in the library.

The menu in the Café Amalfi was typically confusing to George containing, as it did, several different names for bread rolls and varieties of coffee and all seemingly in Italian. It made him slightly envious that other people seemed able to look at an unfamiliar menu in a café or restaurant and order something without having to think too hard about it. Susan often ordered things she'd never tried before which George regarded as reckless. When she started going on holiday on her own, she returned with tales of how she'd eaten from foreign language menus without even knowing what she'd ordered. She said such uncertainty made her feel alive and excited. The thought made him feel physically sick.

A young waitress stood over him with a pencil point poised on a notepad. He asked her for a cup of plain tea, which she agreed to provide but, despite descriptions of the food being included on the menu, he couldn't visualise how any of them would appear on the plate. Roz suggested that he should order what she explained was a roll and ham. He asked the waitress if it was boiled ham from Sainsbury's; she said she didn't think so, but she'd go away and check. She returned a few moments later and said the ham was from

Parma, in Italy so he said he'd just leave it. Despite being hungry, he'd sooner have nothing to eat at all.

As the waitress left to service their orders, a hush descended over the table, with eyes fixed firmly on George. He felt he couldn't let the moment pass without commenting on Melvyn's behaviour.

'It's not that I'm not pleased to see you both, but your presence here is in direct contradiction to my wishes. I expressly told Melvyn I didn't think it was necessary or desirable that you should take time out of your busy lives to pander to what is nothing more than a distraction, that -'

'Dad, tell us what happened,' Roz said.

He continued: '- that, in time, will be resolved to the satisfaction of all parties and will be shown to have been predicated upon nothing more than -'

'The police station, Dad, tell us what happened in the police station,' she pressed.

Of course, he understood they would expect him to divulge details of his inquisition, but history had made him wary. When asked to recount his experience of meetings or events, he always seemed to focus on the wrong things as far as other people were concerned. Gauging what might be of interest to them was never easy and this often led to displays of intolerance and ill temper.

'Well, what do you want to know?' he asked.

Melvyn stared at the floor as Roz leaned across the table and took both of George's hands in hers and she placed her face a few inches from his. When he tried to pull away, she tightened her grip.

'Tell us what happened,' she said firmly.

Roz's face was pretty rather than beautiful, George had always thought. Her nose took up slightly too much of her face and her lips were a bit thin, but he commended her for making the most of her looks in the sense that she spent a lot of time and energy making herself attractive to the opposite sex and, as a result, she'd been quite successful with men.

'Nothing happened,' he said.

'Of course something happened, otherwise why would we be here and why would they ask you to have a lawyer present when they question you again?'

He leaned back in his seat to put some space between his face and Roz's, while she maintained a tight grip of his hands.

'It's just a misunderstanding, that's all,' he said. 'Some person appears to have gained a misleading impression of something and that's what we need to clear up. But I'm sure it can be cleared up to the satisfaction of all parties.'

'And this person, this girl...?'

'Yes, she is a female person,' he said.

'What is the something that you think she has gained a misleading impression of, Dad?'

He winced at Roz's ending of a sentence with a preposition – a transgression he regarded as offensive given the amount of time and effort that he spent instilling in his children a proper appreciation of grammar. But he knew that to raise such an issue then would not be politic.

'Well, that's exactly what we need to get to the bottom of with the police,' he said.

Roz loosened her grip slightly and maintained her smile.

'What do you think it is that she gained a misleading impression of, Dad?'

He thought for a moment.

'I'm afraid it would be improper for me to speculate,' he concluded.

When she was younger, Roz imagined that her father's laconism was a sign of some deeper insight and that, in his verbal economy, he was somehow scaling heights of understanding she wasn't old or wise enough to appreciate. His silences and questioning glances from the back of the room at her parents' soirees seemed, to her child's imagination, to offer more substance and sagacity than the louder proclamations of those around him who talked plenty but didn't say much. She was more admiring of him than the bloviating bores who dominated the conversations at these get-togethers, but it was mixed with feelings of pity and frustration that he always seemed to be listening rather than contributing, hugging the periphery, busying himself with small chores, keeping himself to himself.

Eternally loyal, she waited patiently throughout her childhood and adolescence for the moment when he would come forward with the big reveal, when he would stop being a passenger and take hold of the wheel. Having watched and listened, analysed and calculated, she anticipated that, finally, he would emerge from the shadows with a devastating synthesis of some greater, Herculean search for truth. But it never happened. She glowed with pride when Linda Walker said at one such event that George Lovelace didn't say much, but when he spoke everyone listened because it was sure to be something worth listening to. As she grew older and her thoughts matured, Roz continued to wait and hope.

She let go of his hands and slumped back, sighing with exasperation.

'Christ, we're your family, your son and daughter. You're not giving evidence to a parliamentary inquiry,' she said loudly.

'Calm down, Roz,' Melvyn said, glancing across the café at the handful of customers who appeared to have taken an interest.

The waitress reappeared and set out cups of frothy coffee for Roz and Melvyn, along with George's tea which was served in a tall, glass beaker on a saucer with the teabag still inside and a half slice of lemon at the side, along with two sachets of sugar. This was not what he'd expected. Where was the milk? In his experience of drinking hot beverages in public, milk was provided as a matter of course. He wondered if, perhaps, the serving of lemon was a cultural peculiarity of this café owner's regional or ethnic background. Not having been to Amalfi, he was unable to say for sure. Or perhaps it was a modern fad, which until now had passed him by.

He retrieved his tube of sweeteners from his trouser pocket, and then returned it, resolving not to complain, but simply to leave the tea untouched in the hope it wouldn't be noticed. Even if the waitress agreed to provide milk, he couldn't countenance drinking tea from a glass beaker and certainly not in the vicinity of a slice of lemon.

'Melvyn, there must be more that you can tell me about what happened,' Roz said after the waitress had gone.

Melvyn sighed.

'All I know is that the girl is the granddaughter of one of one of our clients who was at the ball with some of her friends and they were drinking and dancing and having a good time. Then at some stage, I think toward the end of the evening, the girl appears to have been on the dancefloor with Dad and something happened.'

'On the dancefloor?' Roz asked.

'Yes, I believe so.'

'Dad, do you remember dancing with her?'

George stared at the slice of lemon, wondering if he should say something about it. He could call the waitress over and ask her to remove it, but that would simply draw attention to him at a time when he was already receiving more attention than he was comfortable with.

'The girl appears to have been upset enough to tell her parents about it when she got home,' Melvyn continued. 'They reported it to Douglas, who reported it to the board. Robert finds the whole thing unbearable and, if it had been the daughter of one of his friends, he might have tried to deal with the whole matter in-house. When he found out the girl's father was one of our new "nouveau riche" clients that I recruited, he thought nothing of throwing us to the

117

wolves, no matter the damage it might do to the firm and its reputation.'

He stopped talking for a few seconds while he took a sip of coffee.

'What a shit,' Roz interjected. 'Rab really is the fucking limit, isn't he? He knows Dad, for Christ's sake. Can't he see that's not the sort of thing Dad would do? Can't he see that, for fuck sake?'

Melvyn felt his complexion darken as he struggled to withhold the truth from the others; if he had stood up properly to Robert, then the police might not have become involved.

'At that stage, having spoken to Dad who denied doing anything wrong, I had no option but to suggest to him that he should go to the police himself, voluntarily, to demonstrate that he was willing to cooperate with any inquiry they might wish to launch. That, as I told you on the phone last night, is all I know.'

Roz shuffled her chair around the table, so that she was sitting at 90 degrees to her father and she placed an arm gently around his shoulder, making him bristle.

'Do you remember dancing with the girl, Dad?' she asked patiently.

He placed his hand on the table to push the saucer with the slice of lemon away.

'Did you have any contact with the girl after leaving the dance floor? Try to think, Dad, it's important.'

'You're wasting your time,' Melvyn said. 'You're never going to get anything out of him.'

'Don't talk about him like he's not here, it's not his fault. Had you had a drink, Dad? Is that the problem ... can't you remember what happened?'

The number of questions and their frequency created in George's head an image of a crowded room where lots of people were asking different questions, all demanding answers at the same time and he didn't know whom to address first. He couldn't focus on any single thing, so he squeezed his eyes shut and tried to block the sounds around him. After a few moments he stood up and walked slowly across the café, between tables – he was vaguely aware of Roz's raised voice, but he resolved to ignore it. He made his way out the door, across the pavement and onto the road, where he continued without stopping to check for traffic, determined to reach the calm of the public library.

The next memory he had was of being inside the library where two female members of staff were seated behind a desk that had a sign saying Reception. The only other occupant was a wiry man, seated reading a newspaper, who didn't look up. George slumped into a chair and breathed deeply, feeling at peace for the first time that day. He was glad to be away from Melvyn and Roz and Detective Sergeants MacKay and Lanigan and the girl from the *TMBL Law* annual charity ball and Rab and Mary and Mr de Nascimento and Linda Walker and Donald Derwent and Simon Poynter and Derek Leman and Liz Frost and, if truth be told, from Susan as well. He pulled his notebook from his pocket and turned the pages until he found his place and, only then, did he feel properly settled. He had important matters to take care of and for those he needed peace and time and to be alone with only the memory of John Lennon for company.

Chapter 9

Crouch End, North London, three days later

Roz stepped off the bus onto the Broadway two stops early to string out the journey, like a student binge watching a Netflix series to delay the painful moment of opening a book. She liked to walk the final mile or so, both to acclimatise to the middle-class surroundings and to squeeze in a concentrated nicotine hit ahead of the next two or three hours of enforced abstention. The thought that visiting her daughter felt like a penance made her want to cry.

She'd arrived in London the previous evening after she and Melvyn agreed she was serving no useful purpose in Edinburgh. She said she'd return if there were any further developments in George's case but, in the meantime, she had her own hollow existence to get on with. She lit a second smoke. The walk was a good three fags' worth, smoked in quick succession, but enough to hold down each acrid, salty breath for as long as possible and to cherish the sensation of the soothing nicotine molecules crawling into her bloodstream.

Ahead of a previous visit she'd tried to squeeze in a fourth, but even she couldn't walk that slowly and smoke that quickly, and such a heavy concentration of nicotine in a short space of time had left her feeling queasy and unsteady on her feet. No, three smokes were the minimum and, as it turned out, the maximum she required before going under Martin's angle- poised table lamp for the Third Degree.

The walk took her past a row of shops that included an off-license, but she knew a quick sharpener was out of the question. To arrive with the smell of alcohol on her breath would be the death-knell for any further contact with Isla. She was, as Martin continued to remind her each time less hilariously, drinking in the last chance saloon as far as access to their daughter was concerned. Besides, she knew she shouldn't drink in her condition. She hadn't touched a drop for three nights which was the longest period of abstention she could remember. She knew she shouldn't be smoking either but that was too much of an ask in the same week. It was silly, really, as she'd already decided she probably wouldn't go ahead with the pregnancy, but it had kept her off the sauce for 72 hours, so perhaps it was no bad thing. But when she thought about not having a drink for nine months that's when she realised she couldn't go through with it.

Despite the sense of dread she felt start to build from Wednesday onwards ahead of each alternate Saturday with Isla, she couldn't live without these absurdly scripted encounters. They were nothing more than duty visits and she couldn't say with any honesty she enjoyed them while she was there. How could she, with the tyranny of the wall clock and Martin's censorious presence rendering any contact with her daughter as sterile as a prison visit? But it was the only link she had left to a life as she thought it should be lived; to a relationship where the love offered to her felt pure and untainted by fear, hurt or shame. No matter what she'd done in the past, her daughter's feelings for her remained the same and, while she knew that as Isla grew older she couldn't take that love for granted, it mattered to her now more than anything else.

Despite the way Martin and Deborah made her feel about the visits, making them was the most important, regular thing she had to aim for. Even writing her column, which used to make her believe she was still relevant and listened-to, now filled her with anxiety and doubt as she wondered if her writing had lost its punch, if anyone still took her seriously. At least she knew her daughter would love her and that she looked up to her, if only by virtue of her age. Although, with her approaching her 12th birthday and being party to the kind of conversations Martin undoubtedly shared with Deborah about her, she wondered how long that would last. Despite everything, Roz remained determined to improve on the low benchmark of parenting set by her own mother and father who, separately, had their own virtues and qualities but who, combined, had become a joint enterprise of destructiveness and dysfunction.

She arrived at the turn into a nondescript suburban street of redbrick terraced houses, each differentiated only by the colour of its door and an occasional, expired pot plant squatting forlornly on the yard or so of ground that separated them from the pavement. The estate agency blurb that Roz had downloaded from the Internet described number 21 as a 'distinctive, four- bedroom period property' – 'distinctive' being the kind of ubiquitous filler that could describe anything from a Home Counties manor in its own grounds to a dose of vaginal thrush, and whatever period to which it referred hardly seemed like it had been a golden era of architectural accomplishment.

Deborah had pointed out on more than one occasion that the road was included on an internet list of the least expensive in Crouch End – a trope of inverted snobbery she employed without a flicker of self-awareness, observed Roz, who had checked with the land registry and discovered they'd bought it for £950,000 – hardly a pauper's hovel – shortly before Martin threatened histrionically to 'go legal' unless she stopped her 'campaign of online stalking'.

The road represented a station of bourgeois advancement from which she felt entirely excluded. She and Martin split-up before they had moved out of rented rooms in Balham and that's where she remained until she bought the Plumstead flat. In the meantime, her then soon-to-be ex-husband and his shiny new partner were scaling the dizzying heights of the London property ladder. It was only partly a matter of resource – she could have scraped together the deposit for one of these identically mundane shoeboxes which existed, virtually brick-for-brick, in any number of unfashionable, provincial English towns where they were worth less than a tenth of the price – but progress was afflicted by a form of paralysis; a conviction that the elements of a normal, middle class, professional life should be denied to her because she wasn't worthy.

Martin answered the door looking like a model from a Boden catalogue with a slim fitting cashmere crewneck pullover and a pair of expensive looking jeans – a far cry from the sweatpants and Sloppy Joe look she remembered from their marriage. He had lost the stomach he used to carry around and his face was thinner and healthier looking.

'Going somewhere?' she asked.

'No, just doing some stuff around the house.'

He let her in and closed the door.

'Isla's at a friend's party. She should have been back by now, but the girl's mother phoned to say they'd been caught in traffic on the way back from the cinema. She shouldn't be long.'

Roz considered making a fuss but thought better of it. The house was quiet with only the indistinct chatter of a Radio Four matinee emanating from downstairs.

'Where's Deborah?' she asked, doing her best to sound nonchalant.

'She's staying with her parents for the weekend.'

Roz felt a surge of glee at the prospect of potential trouble in paradise.

'They live in Eastbourne. She doesn't see them often,' he explained.

She already knew where Deborah's parents lived, and she wondered if the apparently innocent explanation was for real. Whatever the truth, she was glad she wasn't around.

'Coffee?'

He led the way down the narrow flight of stairs to the

123

basement kitchen which, at that time of the day, was partly masked in shadow. The only light came from a small, grilled window at the near end, through which you could see the feet of people walking along the pavement. The room had been countryfied by Deborah with chunky, rustic furniture and expensive looking ceramic tiles featuring hand-painted farm animals. The coup de theatre was a large, burgundy oil-fired Rayburn for which they'd had to specially reinforce the floor to accommodate its weight. She thought the entire scene pathetically contrived. On the wall nearest the fridge was a cork message board with letters from Isla's school and memos written in Deborah's handwriting that made Roz feel sick.

'How's Ruaridh?' Martin asked.

She felt a stab of hateful resentment every time he asked after Ruaridh, which he'd taken to doing routinely ever since Isla had told him and Deborah all about 'Mummy's new boyfriend'. Martin's first mention of him was accompanied by a torrent of sickening smugness about how 'genuinely happy' they all were for her, and how delighted he was personally 'that she was making a new life for herself'. As she picked at a plate of wholemeal farfalle with organic broccoli pesto and homegrown sage that Deborah had knocked up shortly before heading out to her book group, she felt like stabbing him in the throat with her fork. She could imagine the condescending conversations the pair of them would have about her hairy, illiterate joiner after Isla had gone to bed.

'He's fine,' she said brightly. 'How's work?'

'Fine, you?' he responded as he filled the kettle.

'Oh, you know, just the same.'

Roz was trying to forget about work and she hated Martin for bringing it up. She'd dropped by the office earlier in the week to gauge the mood on a day she knew Crossman wouldn't be around. It was mid-morning and there were only a couple of people on the desk – the comment editor had been invited to a corporate jolly at Glyndebourne and his deputy, Chris, was on the phone to someone, a guest pundit by the sound of the laboured instructions he was delivering. He looked up at Roz and smiled and then made a dialling gesture with his finger next top his temple to suggest the person with whom he was dealing wasn't the brightest. Roz took his joshing as a good sign but then she wondered why, if the person were such a bore, Chris hadn't drawn the conversation to a halt so that he could chat to Roz who was, after all, supposed to be their star columnist and an infrequent visitor to the office.

The only other person around was Joy, the comment desk secretary. Roz sidled up to her desk and shoved a large pile of printouts and yellowing back issues to one side to allow her to perch a buttock on its edge. Joy was tapping frenziedly at a keyboard.

'So, what's going on?' she asked.

'Same boring shit, different day,' Joy said without looking up.

Joy had started at the paper on work experience about a hundred years ago and had clearly loved it so much she never left. Either that or she was completely unemployable anywhere else. She began by performing all the tasks no one else would touch, including proofreading, chasing-up copy, running from desk to desk with page printouts, dealing with petty complaints from prima donna writers about semicolons that had been moved without their permission, making the tea, ordering taxis, being sworn at, lying to wives and husbands, and pretending not to notice the frequent acts of casual misogyny and fumbling sexual opportunism that had passed for acceptable behaviour until #MeToo delivered a thermonuclear ballistic bromide suppository up the arse of every man who had ever stepped foot inside a newspaper office and who, overnight, became models of gender equality.

Over the years Joy had built a little empire around herself and now, with the shoe on the other foot and knowing where the bodies of all the former sex pests were buried, she was one of the most powerful people in the building and one whom the writers and editors went out of their way to cultivate. Among her duties was processing the writers' expenses claims and rejecting the more outlandish ones that, over the years, had notoriously included a four-figure casino tab, an 80inch plasma television, a Kawasaki Z1000 motorbike, a pedigree greyhound and a Russian- made rocket launcher. She had, memorably, refused to wire cash to a particularly obnoxious foreign correspondent to fund his flight from a warzone because he had felt her up while she was pissed at an office Christmas party.

She also dealt with readers' letters to the editor, which made her one of the few reliable indicators of who, among the writing staff, was most popular with the readership. Not only did she have first-hand knowledge of what stories and columns were provoking the greatest interest, she was also responsible for separating the wheat from the chaff, selecting those letters which should be recommended to Crossman for publication and those which should be consigned to the spike. Crucially, she was the first line of defence against any legal complaints or references to the Independent Press Standards Organisation. If something you had written was going to land you in the shit, Joy knew about it first. Through her privileged position, she was also a fount of any petty detail worth knowing regarding the personal and financial circumstances of every member of staff.

'Any gossip?' Roz asked.

'Nah.'

There was a short silence, which Roz thought might be a signal for her to leave, but then Joy stopped typing.

'Actually, there was a funny thing that happened last week,' she said, smiling conspiratorially. 'Crossman was late in on Wednesday and he was spotted by Maurice in circulation using the commercial department's car park, which is unusual because he normally parks his car with all of the other top floor cock jockeys in the executive bays. Anyway, who should be seen emerging from the passenger side door of his fuck off big Beemer, but Isabel?'

Joy waited for a reaction which wasn't forthcoming.

'Don't know her,' Roz said.

Joy sighed. 'She's the new deputy news editor, came from The Independent. Pretty little thing with tits like a dead heat in a Zeppelin race.'

'Right,' Roz said, trying to sound fascinated.

'So, Crossman bursts in with a flourish and strides across the editorial floor to his office with his usual nonchalance. A couple of minutes later, Isabel slopes in silently and shuffles over to her desk, wearing the same clothes as the day before, without any make-up, with her hair all over the place and smelling like a wet fish shop at Friday closing. You'd have thought after pumping her and then dragging her straight into the office without so much as a change of knickers that Crossman would have let her use his executive shower room, but no such luck for the hapless Izzie.'

Roz tried to look engaged, hoping Joy would bring the story to a sharp conclusion so that she could quiz her about what Crossman had thought about her most recent column.

'Nigel was on days off, so Isabel had to go through the news list in conference and everyone thought she'd be given an easy ride by the Editor.'

'As opposed to the coarse-grade sandpapering he'd no doubt given her arse the night before,' Roz chipped in with a snigger, suddenly warming to the theme.

'Not a bit of it. Crossman went through her like a bayonet through a ripe watermelon. Told her the list was 'pathetically thin gruel' and asked her what the fuck she'd been doing all morning. Apparently, you could have fried eggs on her face.'

'Poor cow,' Roz said, reflectively.

'Poor cow nothing. If she can't take the flak, she's got no business calling herself a fucking journalist. You don't need to be Woodward and Bernstein to work out Crossman's a grade A shit. The only person dimmer than Isabel is his hollow headed missus holed up in Chipping Norton labouring under the delusion that her husband's some sort of workaholic monk.'

'Yeah. Stupid cow,' she said.

Joy resumed her frenzied typing. Roz watched the hypnotic, rapid movement of her hands across the keyboard. Like all self-taught typists, including Roz herself, she only used four fingers but repeated practice over the years had given her the speed of the fastest touch typist.

'So, anything making waves at the moment?' she asked breezily.

'What, you mean apart from Crossman's overactive penis?'

'No, I mean content – stories, columns, features. Are any writers grabbing the readers' attention?'

Joy looked up and smiled knowingly.

'You mean have any readers written in to say what a brilliant columnist you are?'

Roz blushed.

'No, I just wondered if there were any issues that -'

'I know what you wondered,' Joy said sharply, cutting her dead. 'The answer's no.'

'What, none?

'None that I can remember.'

'What about the other columnists? Have any readers responded to their pieces?'

Joy thought for a moment.

'No, don't tell me. I don't want to know,' Roz said.

'Wait a minute, there was one letter about something you wrote, last week I think it was, from some guy who took issue with a claim you'd made that it's the middle classes who always have the messiest divorces.'

'Oh, right ... and what did he say?' Roz asked hopefully.

'He said he'd Googled you and you should know.'

Martin busied himself with a coffee machine that used small cartridges to make real coffee and a hand-held, electric whisk to froth the milk. Roz had seen them for sale during one of her window shopping trips to the Conran shop and knew they cost a bomb. She tried to think of a topic of conversation that was non-contentious and yet which wasn't so bland that it would dry up after a couple of sentences, but nothing came to mind. It depressed her to think she should feel so ill-at-ease in the company of a man she'd shared her life with for almost ten years.

'I read your column about divorce,' he said.

'Oh, right,' she replied warily.

'I thought it was good.'

For a moment she almost considered urging him to write a letter to Crossman, but then she knew he was lying. When they were married it was taken as read that what she wrote was good. The only time he ever mentioned her work was when he had an issue with it.

'Well, people do get divorced, you know, Martin. We got divorced. It's an important issue for a lot of people,' she said, a mite too defensively.

'I know it is. That's why I said I thought it was a good column.'

'Yes, but I know what you meant.'

He placed a mug of frothy coffee on the table in front of her and smiled.

They had met at university while they were both studying journalism. At the time she was the more political of the two, having been vice-president of the student union and active in her local Labour Party branch. Martin, was more focused on his career, with ambitions to work on the nationals. They both started out on local papers in North London and Roz realised quickly that her interest in politics was more to do with the late-night drinking that was equally prevalent in journalism while Martin became disillusioned with the routineness of news reporting and took a job as a researcher with a small, independent television production company. He now worked as a senior executive for the BBC with responsibility for political programming. It was there he met Deborah who was a senior producer in the Westminster media centre at Millbank.

'We can't all cover budgets and cabinet reshuffles, you know.'

'I was just trying to make conversation,' he replied in a tone that appeared caught between contrition and frustration.

They sat on opposite sides of a long oak dining table, distressed to look older than it was, without talking. A woman walked past the window and the clean crack of her heels on the pavement seemed to intensify the silence. Martin cupped his hands around his mug and sat back, pursing his lips.

'What are children reading these days?' Roz asked.

'Sorry?'

'What's Isla reading? What books?'

He looked blankly.

'I don't know, the usual, you know?'

'No, I don't know, that's why I'm asking you. Crossman wants me to write a column about how children are all watching internet porn instead of reading Swallows and Amazons and it's robbing them of their childhood. He thinks I'm an expert on all that shite for the sole reason that I've given birth.'

'Why don't you ask Isla?'

'What?'

'She's best placed to tell you what she's reading.'

'Thanks, Martin.

'What do you mean, 'thanks Martin'? All I said was "why don't you ask your daughter to tell you what books she's reading".'

'Forget it.'

He stood up and walked distractedly to the sink where he picked up a tea towel and pretended to dry dishes that had been sitting on the draining board. Roz wondered why the same level of anger she'd felt towards him during their break-up endured without let up. At least if it had changed in character, that would be something, but it was the same, insufferable melancholy tinged with resentment at how he'd never been clear about how close they were to splitting up. If he'd been more explicit about how her behaviour was affecting their relationship, perhaps she could have tried to change. Surely it couldn't have been entirely down to her drinking. She wasn't as bad then and he always seemed so supportive of her, albeit half-hearted, attempts to cut down.

She felt there was a fundamental misunderstanding at the heart of their marriage and that she'd been deceived. Compared with her parents' marriage she thought they were blissfully happy, and while her parents remained together until the bitter end, hers had fallen apart and still she couldn't work out why. She'd listened to a woman in rehab talk about how it had taken her three years to get to the point following the break-up of her marriage where she was ready to move on, as though that was an eternity. It was now six years since Martin had walked out on her and there appeared to be no let-up in the bitterness and paralysis she felt. She tried to talk to him about it before they divorced, but his response was always the same – his feelings had changed, and he wanted to move on. She couldn't understand why his feelings should play such an important role; they were married, they had a daughter together and he even admitted that he still fancied her. That, of course, was before she knew about Deborah.

Her position on things remained essentially the same,

while his had moved so far that it was difficult to believe he was the same person. From the books and CDs on his shelves to the things he talked about and the friends he mixed with, everything about him seemed more current and relevant. Talking to him now, she was embarrassed about things they'd done together or issues that seemed important when they were married. Being in his company felt like looking at an old photograph of herself in clothes that were once fashionable, but which now seemed embarrassingly dated. It was like the world had moved on without her.

It didn't help that she and Martin were thrown together regularly on these occasions. She had argued against him always being present but quickly realised there was no point. She'd agreed to his suggestion that they should sort out their domestic arrangements between themselves, without bringing in lawyers, which essentially meant accepting his terms, because she knew that if they involved the courts, the conditions imposed would have been harsher. How could they have been anything else after what she'd done?

'There's something I need to discuss with you before Isla gets home,' she said. 'I wasn't going to mention it, but I don't want her to hear about it from anyone else.'

'Oh, yes,' he said.

'There's a problem with Dad.'

'I'm listening.'

'Some girl has made a complaint against him and he's been charged with indecent assault.'

Martin threw the tea towel into the sink and walked slowly across the kitchen.

'You don't seem surprised.'

'Are you?' he asked.

'Fucking hell, Martin, he might be a bit eccentric, but...'

'But he's been charged?'

She sighed.

'Yeah, he was dancing with a girl at one of Melvyn's

dickie bow bunfights and something happened. We don't know what.'

Martin said nothing, making Roz feel obliged to fill the gap.

'It's not like she's underage or anything. She's 17 and by all accounts her skirt was so far up her arse she was practically wearing it as a hat.'

'So, molesting her is all right then?'

'Who said anything about molesting?

His expression remained blank.

'You're the one who writes every other week about the sexual exploitation of young girls.'

'What's that got to do with anything?'

'That young girls are being sexualised too early.'

'They are.'

'That they're victims.'

'They are.'

'Except when they're assaulted by your father, then they're saucy little provocateurs who deserve what they get?'

'Oh, for fuck's sake, Martin, you're taking two issues out of context.'

'Am I?'

Silence resumed.

'Look, I'm sorry, I shouldn't have said that,' he said.

Roz was furious with him, but she knew that venting her anger would backfire and she'd be painted as the one in the wrong, again.

'Look, I won't mention it to Isla for the moment. Let's see what happens,' he said.

'Thanks.'

'In the meantime, if there's anything I can do to help, let me know.'

She nodded.

'You didn't answer when I said you didn't seem surprised.'

He looked at her in the same interrogative way he did

when he was quizzing her about how much she'd had to drink. She'd always liked his eyes, which were a comforting, earthy brown.

'I don't know if I'm surprised or not,' he said.

'Which means you're not.'

She felt tears welling in her eyes. Martin tore off a square of kitchen paper and handed it to her.

'Look, all I meant was that it doesn't surprise me entirely that your father has found himself in this situation. I don't mean I ever thought he'd be accused of something like this, but he did always seem to be on the brink of one disaster or another. Do I think he's capable of indecent assault? I'd hope nobody that I know is. Do I think his behaviour is, at times, peculiar? Yes, probably. And I can see why a seventeen-year-old girl might feel a bit creeped out by him.'

A burst of laughter broke through Roz's tears.

'He is a bit fucking odd, isn't he?'

'Mad as a Mad Frankie Fraser.'

They both laughed.

'I can only imagine what the poor girl must have thought when she saw Dad hoving into view clutching his collection of Olympic 50p pieces.'

It occurred to Roz that this was probably the first time since their divorce that she and Martin had laughed together. She knew they must have shared moments of humour, she remembered them both laughing, just not at the same time.

'So, how do you rate his chances?'

'Who knows? You know how he is – we can't even get him to talk about what happened. All he says is that he's 'not guilty as charged' whatever the fuck that means.'

'Can't you talk to his lawyer?'

'He told his solicitor he didn't want any details of the case discussed with anyone but himself. The only information we've had so far is from the charge sheet. Whenever we try to pin him down on anything specific, he says something facetious and then shuts up.'

'Sounds like George.'

Another silence descended but, after the interlude of levity that they'd shared, this one didn't seem so oppressive.

'Look, I know this is a difficult subject, but Christmas isn't far off and Isla will want to see her grandfather.'

In previous years Martin had allowed Isla to stay for a few days with Susan and George, usually between Christmas and New Year, to let them develop their relationship and to give her a break from her London routine.

'Do you think that, with all of this going on, it's appropriate that she should be alone in his company?' he asked.

The last of the afternoon sun was suddenly stolen from the room and it was plunged into a grey darkness. Roz hated the dark, which she always associated with the swish of the heavily lined curtains in her childhood bedroom being drawn, blocking out sound and light. Even in summertime, when the warm, peachy dusk simmered late into the night providing a canopy of light for children to play games in neighbouring gardens, she remembered the finality of their smooth, noiseless movement. But for one exceptional evening when the door was thrown open, long after she should have been asleep, releasing a momentary flash of brightness from the hallway, before it closed again just as quickly and returned the room to its state of obscurity.

It was a Saturday night, she recalled, when her parents were hosting one of their dos and the house was filled with the sound of chatter and the comforting aroma of adult sociability. The free expression of laughter was a rarity in her house and, for that reason, it was memorable to her.

Earlier in the day she'd helped her mother to decant crisps and nuts into china bowls, to skewer cubes of cheese and pickled onions onto cocktail sticks, to prepare sausages rolls and vol au vents for the oven, exotic comestibles unknown and untried because of her father's strictures about food. She'd been sent to bed shortly after the arrival of the first guests, but she was unable to sleep, buoyed by the excitement and the pleasing, sweet smell of alcohol and freshly lit cigars.

She tensed at the strange presence now in the room alongside her, sensing somehow instinctively that it was illicit. The sound of her father's voice was followed by that of another person, a woman, in a low whisper, urging him to speak more quietly. Hers was the only room in the house with a spare bed and her parents' bedroom had been turned into an impromptu cloakroom for the evening. She didn't recognise the other voice. Over the years she'd struggled to recall much of what she said, remembering only the tense discomfort of her whispered protestations.

'We'd better go down. We'll be missed.'

The muffled, humiliating sound of furtive movement, of flesh rubbing on flesh and stifled groans, appeared painful and yet, curiously fascinating, to her. She lay facing the wall with her back to her intruders, rigid with fear, afraid even to breathe and yet inside she felt a strangely familiar stirring that wasn't unpleasant.

'We've been away for long enough. What if someone comes to look for us?'

The movements became more frequent and rhythmic, the groans sharper.

Afraid, she prayed for the episode to end, dreading the prospect of discovery and punishment, disgusted at herself for bearing witness to a scene she didn't understand, far less for daring to admit that it was in any way pleasurable. She tensed her limbs until they ached, her skin burned and only when, suddenly, she gasped for air did she realise she'd been holding her breath.

The movements stopped abruptly, and the room was plunged into a pulsating silence. The cheerful chatter downstairs seemed like a dreamlike counterpoint. She closed her eyes tightly and held her position, not daring to move.

'Is there someone in the room?' the woman's whispered voice demanded.

Her father said nothing.

'Is there someone else here? Jesus Christ, this isn't one of the children's rooms, is it?'

There was an eruption of movement and the sound of clothing being hurriedly applied and straightened, followed by the lightning flash of the door being opened and closed. The other figure remained motionless and silent for a few minutes – long enough for Roz to think they might have fallen asleep. She longed to move but dared not take the chance. The pain of retaining such stillness became almost unbearable and she felt tears well in her eyes. She prayed for release from the torture, even if it meant discovery and confrontation but even then, she couldn't bring herself to move.

Eventually she heard the soft slide of movement and footsteps on the worn carpet, at first not knowing in which direction they were travelling, but then she became aware of the static warmth of a body standing immediately over her. She tensed, imperceptibly to her onlooker, but enough to intensify the pain she already felt, and she screwed her eyes tighter.

'Roz, are you awake?' her father whispered.

His voice sounded gentle and caring and she struggled to resist the instinctive urge to roll over and respond to his paternal concern, to smile warmly and to say, 'yes Daddy, I'm awake. I can't sleep, can I have a drink of water please and a kiss goodnight'. But she held her position and refused to yield.

'Roz, are you awake?' he repeated, this time more quietly, as though by virtue of asking he would make the answer negative.

A moment later he disappeared and Roz cried herself to sleep. The incident was never discussed by her, not even in rehab. She thought about recounting it on several occasions and she even rehearsed the details in her head, when she was alone, to anticipate how it might sound to a dispassionate observer, but she couldn't bring herself to mouth the words to another person.

Roz shivered as she watched the silhouette of Martin's frame disappear into the shadow where he switched on an overhead light. The darkness was gone and the silence of the kitchen was broken by the sound of the front door opening and the chatter of Isla and her friend's mum in the hallway. Martin continued to stare into her face, requiring an answer.

'What do you think then? Should we let Isla stay with her grandpa for a few days over Christmas?'

'No,' Roz replied. 'I don't think that would be a good idea at all.'

Chapter 9

Corstorphine, Edinburgh, three days later

Perhaps the greatest mystery in the life of John Lennon is the question of whether he was ever intimate with the Beatles' manager, Brian Epstein. Much speculation surrounds the pair's relationship and, while it was undoubtedly close, hard evidence as to whether it ever spilled over into the bedroom department remains tantalisingly out of reach. It was known to all the Beatles, and to many music industry insiders, that Epstein was homosexual; the term gay was not then widely used to denote the practice of sodomy. From an early age, Epstein exhibited signs of effeminacy and frivolousness which may have informed a keen eye of the potential dangers of a later slide into homosexuality.

Despite never professing to have carnal designs on Lennon, Epstein is said to have been poor at hiding his true feelings. He was, apparently, unable to look Lennon directly in the eye for fear of revealing his sodomistic designs. Lennon's behaviour, in contrast, was more difficult to understand. Publicly, he was a macho heterosexual who enjoyed a great deal of casual sex with female 'groupies' and latterly, he was a married man with a child. Yet in interviews in later life, he admitted to having had a 'relationship' with Epstein, albeit one that was never consummated and that he enjoyed 'playing it a bit faggy' (vernacular for homosexual behaviour). Yoko Ono said in a 1981 interview that she considered Lennon a 'closet fag', revealing that he liked her because she looked 'like a bloke in drag'.

Events came to a head in 1963 when Lennon accompanied Epstein on a holiday to Andalusia, Spain. Cynthia was pregnant with their son, Julian, and decided to stay at home; however, recognising that her husband needed a holiday,

she gave him her blessing to travel. A version of the 'truth'
propagated in several quarters suggests that, after having
spent months suppressing his homosexual feelings towards
Lennon, Epstein saw this as an opportunity to corner his
quarry and to 'have his way'. The pair are said to have
frequented clubs, bars, cafes, shops and bull fights and to
have talked openly about homosexuality. Lennon is said to
have asked a lot of questions, wanting to know about the
ins and outs of the homosexual act. However, he always
maintained that it never spilled over into outright buggery.

The phone rang and George stopped writing. Frankly, he
was glad to take a break from what, for him, was a troubling
subject. Homosexuality was not an issue that he could claim
to understand in any detail, despite having made some effort
to do so in the past after discovering that a work colleague
had a penchant for such proclivities. It was something that,
really, he only became aware of comparatively late in life
when, to his mind, the number of homosexuals multiplied
exponentially as society appeared more tolerant of their
existence. He'd heard it argued that his reasoning was
perverse and that, in fact, the number of homosexuals had
remained largely static over time but that, as public tolerance
of their activities increased, so-called 'gays' felt more at
liberty to make themselves known.

That may have been the case, he thought, but all he could
say from his own experience was that he was not aware of
many existing at all until he was close to what might be
referred to as middle age – certainly when he was married
with children. Of course, one heard of rumours that so-and-
so was 'that way inclined', such as Neville, Susan's hair
stylist, and the young man with bad skin and a high voice
who worked at the chip shop on Corstorphine Road. Both
were certainly effeminate, but you couldn't go accusing
every person who was the slightest bit slack wristed of being

a fairy. That sort of thing would certainly land you in hot water.

The realisation that there were many more homosexuals than he had hitherto supposed didn't trouble him particularly, as it appeared to do with many of his contemporaries, some of whom harboured what might be described as a violent dislike of the homosexual act and the mincing characteristics of many gays. In fact, he was ambivalent about the thought of having sex with men, or certainly as indifferent as he felt at the thought of having sex with Susan for long periods of their marriage, leading him to conjecture at one stage that, perhaps, he was bisexual.

Changing attitudes to what was 'acceptable' certainly caused him some difficulties and led to him being upbraided in social and professional circles for using language that, only a short time before, had passed unremarked-upon. It confused him, for example, that he should be rebuked for using the term 'shirt-lifter' which, to him, seemed to be an instructive illustration of an act preparatory to buggery, while talk of 'queers' and 'poofs' were, to him, significantly more pejorative terms and yet were deemed to be perfectly acceptable, often used by gays to describe themselves. On one occasion he heard an openly homosexual, so-called comedian, refer to himself on television as a Fellow of the Royal Society of Fudgepackers, which resulted in howls of appreciative laughter from the audience, but which left him unmoved.

The bell rang and he answered the door to an overweight young man dressed in a grey anorak, unfastened, with a white shirt and a brown, paisley pattern tie, secured loosely with a large knot. He introduced himself as Brian somebody from the Midlothian something or other which George didn't catch because of the wash of traffic noise. His hearing had long been a bone of contention, particularly with Susan. Despite being unable, for most of his life, to make out individual voices, particularly in crowds or against moderate background noise, he'd been told by no less than five separate clinicians there was nothing they could do to improve his hearing. Three of them had examined him during childhood and adolescence and they all assured his parents they were unable to prescribe any treatment because they could find nothing medically wrong with his hearing.

Susan refused to accept these early diagnoses and insisted his hearing should be tested on two further occasions, once shortly after they were married and again, several years later, when the issue became an increasing source of frustration to her. On both occasions, doctors came to the same conclusion. Susan refused to believe George, accusing him of distorting or misrepresenting what they said because he was too vain to wear a hearing aid, which was certainly not the case.

He waited for the traffic noise to abate and asked the boy to repeat himself.

'My name is Brian McGarvey from the Midlothian Advertiser,' he said.

George thought that, had he been the boy's superior, he'd have sent him home to change his clothes and wash his hair.

'Oh yes, and what can I do for you?'

'This is the home of George Lovelace?' he inquired.

George said nothing, assuming it to be a statement of fact.

'Is this the home of George Lovelace?'

George noticed a chip in one of the boy's upper incisor teeth.

'Are you looking for the home of George Lovelace?' he asked.

The boy's eyes were wide and rheumy and surrounded by red circles. They narrowed at his question.

'Yes,' he replied.

'Then why would you suppose that this is not the home of George Lovelace?' He grinned in a stupid way.

'And are you George Lovelace?' he asked.

'Yes, I am,' George replied.

The boy asked if he could come inside. George asked him why he wanted to do that, and he said because it was cold and they would be more comfortable indoors, which George thought a reasonable suggestion, so he invited him in. He led the boy into the living room which hadn't been tidied for a while – George had done no housework since Susan's funeral as he regarded it a distraction from the more pressing need to complete his book – and the accumulated clutter on the furniture meant there was nothing available to sit on.

The boy asked if he could move some piles of newspaper and magazine cuttings from the settee, but George told him he would rather that he didn't. He said he was free to move some items of crockery from the coffee table and to sit on it but warned him that a large pool of congealed gravy covering part of its surface – the result of an overheated steak and kidney pie – risked staining his trousers and so the boy said he'd stand.

He unfurled a ring-bound notebook until he arrived at a blank page and pulled a biro from the pocket of his anorak. He asked a question which George didn't register because his mind was focused on the notebook and pen. He asked the boy why he'd produced these items and he said he intended to interview him. George told him he didn't recall agreeing to be interviewed and the boy apologised for not being explicit, adding that he'd taken for granted, him being a journalist, George would have realised his intentions.

George wondered why a journalist should want to interview him. He thought perhaps word had spread about his collection of Olympic memorial 50p pieces, details of which he'd been active in disseminating through relevant online discussion forums in recent weeks after learning that Olympic organisers planned to issue a series of 100 Yen coins, featuring five new Olympic sports, to commemorate the Tokyo games. He didn't recall having discussed his collection with anyone in the Edinburgh and Midlothian areas but then, when one is corresponding with strangers on the internet, one is generally unaware of their location, he reasoned.

The boy asked if he could have a cup of coffee and George said no, he couldn't. He asked why not, and George said because he didn't have any coffee. The boy said tea would do. George said he didn't feel minded to make him a cup of tea but added that, if the boy was going to help him to publicise his collection of Olympic memorial 50p pieces, then perhaps he might oblige. The boy stared blankly at him for a moment and then smiled and said he took milk and three which, after a moment of reflection, George took to mean three teaspoons of sugar.

When he returned to the living room a few minutes later with the mug of tea, the boy was standing by a bookshelf in the far corner of the room holding a framed photograph of Melvyn surrounded by George, Susan and Roz, taken outside the Old College quad building in North Bridge, immediately after his graduation.

'Is this your son?' he asked.

George said it was and handed the boy the mug, which he took without thanks and placed on the bookshelf.

'Melvyn?' he said.

George didn't answer.

'Your son, that's his name, isn't it – Melvyn?'

George nodded.

'So just to be clear, you are the father of Melvyn Lovelace, the chief executive of *TMBL Law*, the legal firm?' the boy asked.

'Yes, that's right,' George replied.

'And who else is in the picture with him?' he asked.

'Ah, well, on his left is Roz, his elder sister. That's what we call her, but her name is Rosalind. She's a newspaper person, the same as you.'

'She's Rosalind Boucher, the columnist for *The Sentinel*?' he asked.

'That's right.'

The boy nodded enthusiastically.

'I'd rather you returned the photograph frame to the bookshelf,' George said.

The boy did so.

'So, she uses her married name,' he said after a slight pause.

'Yes, that's right.'

'My dad reads her stuff. He says she's very good.'

'Yes, she's very up on all the modern trends, by which I mean social trends, that is to say, lifestyles, living habits, parenting arrangements and the like. She wrote a rather interesting piece recently about these new social media networks on the internet and how they -'

'So, she is married then, I assume?' the boy asked, cutting off George in mid-sentence. 'I mean, if she uses her married name, then obviously she's married?'

'Not necessarily,' George replied, smiling.

He rather enjoyed such occasions when statements based upon flawed assumptions could be exposed as erroneous.

'You see, she's divorced,' he explained.

'Ah, divorced,' the boy echoed and wrote in his notebook.

It struck George as peculiar that the boy should be interested in Melvyn's academic record and Roz's marital status in preparation for a newspaper article about his collection of Olympic memorial 50p pieces, but he resisted the urge to voice his reservations. He glanced skywards with the end of his pen resting on his bottom set of teeth. George couldn't make out which had the less attractive appearance, the stressed, fragmented writing tool or his chipped incisor.

'Lovelace, that's quite an unusual surname.'

George felt a surge of adrenalin at the opportunity to expound upon one of his favourite subjects.

145

'Actually, it has an interesting history, its origins being in medieval Glamorganshire, before the Norman Conquest,' he explained. 'It's derived from the old English word 'laweles', which means 'lawless' and is ultimately -'

'So, there's just the two of them? Lovelace children, I mean?'

'As I was saying, the name derives from a nickname for a person who was an outlaw or, in some senses legally unconstrained. The Gaelic form of Lovelace is Laigheis, which is particularly interesting because -'

'So, you're the only George Lovelace? I mean, there are no other men in the family called George Eric?'

Irritated and frustrated at the boy's apparent disregard for the matter at hand, George offered to fetch his collection for him to review.

'What collection?' he asked.

'My collection of Olympic memorial 50p pieces,' George replied.

The boy thought for a moment.

'Alright,' he said.

George raced upstairs and retrieved the collection, which was stored in his bedroom, under the bed, in Susan's antique jewellery box. Antique furniture had been an interest of George's and he'd always been intrigued by this item which was rosewood veneered and inlaid with mother of pearl and pewter stringing. He guessed it was from the early Victorian era, circa 1840-50 and was in good condition. It retained its original brass lock, hinges and top catch and it was complete with a silk tassel. The interior of the box and the tray was velvet and slightly distressed.

He'd suggested to Susan, on more than one occasion during their marriage, that she should have it valued professionally, with a view to selling it. He believed it could fetch a sizeable sum, certainly running into the high hundreds of pounds, but she'd resisted, insisting it had belonged to

146

her great grandmother and possibly earlier, that it was an heirloom and that it had tremendous sentimental value to her. He pointed out that the term 'sentimental value' was an oxymoron as sentiment had no market value, but she told him he was an 'idiot who was trying to destroy her mind'. She told him that 'if he so much as looked at the jewellery box, she wouldn't be responsible for her actions'. While it had served a useful purpose since her death, as a receptacle for his collection of Olympic memorial 50p pieces, he fully intended to have it valued and, assuming an acceptable price could be obtained, sold, immediately after this business of the girl and the charge of indecent assault had been disposed of.

He checked to make sure the coins were in the proper order. He'd purchased a quantity of re-sealable polythene pouches for each, to avoid the coins becoming tarnished by oxidisation or with dirt deposits or other contaminants and then he'd organised them, according to sporting category – for example, track and field, equestrian, swimming and diving, shooting, cycling and team sports – and, within those headings, he had further sub-categorised them alphabetically.

He resolved that he would allow the boy to view the collection only under strictly controlled rules. He would hand them to him, one coin at a time, and he would not allow them to be removed from their resealable sheaths, to avoid a repeat of a previous misadventure when he, ill-advisedly, permitted an exhibition at Susan's insistence, to the Poynters and the Lemans. This resulted in the anarchic spectacle of the coins being plundered from their casings and handled indiscriminately, with heed neither to their condition nor their classification. Consequently, George was forced to evict the assembled guests from the house.

When he re-entered the living room carrying the collection, he found the boy regarding a seascape in oils overhanging the fireplace that had been painted by Susan during her artistic phase. George had never liked the piece, in fact it positively offended him, and he had determined to remove it from its place and to dispose of it immediately upon completion of his opus.

'This is really good,' the boy said.

'No, it's not,' George replied.

'Yes, it is. I studied art before I became a journalist, and this is a cut above anything I ever saw at college. There's a real originality about it.'

He'd heard it said, on several previous occasions, that Susan's work was 'original', but this meant little to him.

'And by originality, I can only assume you mean that it bears no meaningful resemblance to its professed subject matter, beyond featuring what can be described only in the most abstract terms as a vaguely boat-shaped object.' he said stridently.

The boy's face turned pink.

'And perhaps you'd care to explain to me how a vessel with a main sail of such absurd disproportion to its hull, might be expected to achieve buoyancy?'

'I only meant that, as a work of art, it shows some skill and imagination.'

George could barely contain his anger, not only that this slovenly interloper should seek entry to his house, avowing interest in his collection of Olympic memorial 50p pieces, and then to patently ignore it in favour of sundry issues that bore not even a tangential relation to the matter at hand, but that he should then adopt the side of an argument that had, for long, been a significant bone of contention between Susan and him.

'Oh, I see you only meant it as a work of art, did you? And doesn't it occur to you that for a work of art to achieve even moderate credibility, it must first be possessed of an element of realism?' he demanded.

The boy's head wobbled, George thought, like a nodding

dog he had once seen on the rear shelf of a moving car.

'Have you even been on a sailing boat?'

The boy's lips quivered silently, but George wasn't going to let him off the hook that easily.

'Have you ever been on such a vessel?'

'Eh, no,' he said falteringly.

'Then how can you presume to tell me what is and what isn't a valid piece of nautical art. I mean look at it – it's barely legible. It's a splurge of paint identifiable only as a boat in the context of its surroundings and even then, it's debatable that the objective observer would be able to make out what surrounds it is the sea.'

George was close enough to the boy to see small seeds of perspiration popping onto his forehead and around his nose. He backed away and sought to return to the subject of his collection of Olympic memorial 50p pieces. He swept aside a swathe of cuttings from the settee, fashioning a clearing and he invited the boy to occupy it, but he declined.

'No, you must sit,' George insisted. 'I haven't explained the story of how the collection was achieved, which is important because, you see, they were not circulated uniformly.'

'I'm afraid I have to go,' the boy insisted. 'I have another job in 20 minutes and then I've got to write this up in time for a seven o'clock print deadline.'

George wasn't listening.

'You see, some sports, like handball, were distributed in smaller volumes than others to give them a rarity value,' he explained. 'They are already being sold for higher than their face value on internet auction sites. Let me switch on my computer and I'll -'

'How do you get on with your children, Mr Lovelace?' the boy asked.

'The Royal Mint said that more than ten million of the coins had been taken out of circulation by members of the public, more than any other commemorative coin released since decimalisation.'

'How do you get on with your children?' he repeated.

'You see, many people believe these coins will have a collectors' value in the future. I read that in the Daily Mail, so it must be true.'

'How do you get on with your children?'

George stopped.

'Not very well,' he replied.

'Why not?'

He thought for a moment.

'I suppose because they think I'm somewhat odd.'

'Odd?'

'Yes, odd.'

The boy scribbled in his notebook. George couldn't make out what he'd written because it was in a strange, illegible script like hieroglyphics, which he took to be a form of shorthand.

'Why do you suppose they think that?'

He thought again.

'I don't know, you'd have to ask them. Perhaps I am.'

'Odd, in what way?'

'I don't know. A school friend of my daughter's once said she thought I was creepy.'

'What made her say that?'

'I don't know. My daughter agreed that I can be a bit creepy sometimes.'

'Did you do anything to her or her friend that might have made them think you were creepy?'

He thought for a period, longer than before. He didn't feel comfortable with the direction the boy's questioning was going. It didn't feel right. The questions had nothing to do with his collection of Olympic memorial 50p pieces and he didn't want to answer them.

'I think you should go now,' he said.

George walked to the front door and held it open.

'One final question, Mr Lovelace,' the boy said. 'Will you be pleading guilty or not guilty to sexual assault at Edinburgh Sheriff Court tomorrow?'

'I think you should go now,' George repeated.

Chapter 10

The Braids, South Edinburgh, the following morning

Mary finally relented following an argument with Melvyn that lasted for most of the morning. She agreed to collect George from his house and drive him to the Sheriff Court for his committal hearing, while Melvyn remained at home keeping a low profile and, she was sure, obsessing about the effect the unfolding events might have on his career. It was assumed, without question, that she should drop everything to pander to his weakness and neuroses, she shouted, in a show of frustration and unkindness she later regretted.

That she had been due to attend an important meeting of her senior management team to discuss the impact of the latest education cuts on her departmental budget was, apparently, of secondary importance to her requirement to accompany her husband's father to court. There was no recognition that her attendance there might possibly compromise her position at the university given that her father-in-law's alleged victim, a seventeen-year-old girl, was the same age as many of her students.

Nor was there any acknowledgement by Melvyn that looking after George shouldn't be her responsibility; she had more than enough on her plate, holding down a demanding job, managing the household and dealing with the challenges of her own parents' failing faculties which she did, she argued, with understanding and tolerance but with no help from Melvyn. Her concerns were expendable, it seemed, in the greater crusade to build his professional legend.

All this, despite George being his father and Melvyn having earlier agreed to accompany him to the court. Her husband had even told his sister there was no need for her to travel to Edinburgh for what would be a routine appearance, to confirm that he understood the charges against him and for him to enter a plea. Roz's support would be needed further down the line, if and when the case came to trial, and so she should conserve her energy until then, Melvyn counselled with an admirable display of sensitivity and concern that he appeared to reserve only for people who weren't his wife.

His display of altruism vanished instantly however, the moment he picked up the latest edition of the local paper at the breakfast table and proceeded to cough his coffee all over the splash headline.

DAD OF SEX CASE LAWYER ON INDECENCY CHARGE
KIDS THINK I'M AN ODDBALL, SAYS OAP

Melvyn's suspicions had been aroused the previous evening when George telephoned him to say he'd been visited by a reporter from the local paper and that a story about his collection of Olympic memorial 50p pieces would be appearing in the following day's edition. Melvyn tried to question him about how the reporter had found out about his collection of Olympic memorial 50p pieces, why he or his readers should have the remotest interest in them and how, precisely, their conversation had developed, but George had remained characteristically vague. The article provided some answers:

The father of a top city law firm boss representing
dozens of women who claim they were sexually
harassed at the Civil Service has been
charged with molesting a 17-year-old girl at a
glamorous company bash.
George Lovelace (76), father of *TMBL Law* boss, Melvyn
Lovelace, is accused of indecently assaulting the girl at the
black-tie ball, thrown by the firm
earlier this month.

Parents of the alleged victim, who cannot be named for
legal reasons, alerted police following the event at the posh
Grange Golf Club. The pensioner is expected to appear
at Edinburgh Sheriff Court today.
In an interview with the Advertiser, Lovelace, whose
daughter Rosalind Boucher is a high-profile columnist
for a national broadsheet paper,
said his kids thought he was
'odd' and 'creepy'.

Mary suggested that if a member of her family or even
a close friend were in the same situation, she would have
agreed to help immediately, in any way she could. Melvyn
refused to accept this which, if anything, she found more
upsetting than his unwillingness to help his father when
he needed him most. She might have felt slightly better
disposed towards her husband if he'd reacted to his father's
predicament in a more heroic manner than collapsing onto
his knees in the hallway and repeatedly headbutting the
floor while shouting 'FUCKING, FUCKING, FUCKING,
FUCKING, FUCKING, FUCKING, FUCKING, FUCKING
OLD CUNT OF A BASTARD' at the top of his voice.

She stood behind him, almost hypnotised by the rhythmic
motion of his forehead pounding the carpet in time to every
declaration of 'FUCKING', and she felt a combination
of revulsion and fascination, wondering if his actions had
the potential to do his brain any lasting damage. With an
uncharacteristic lack of charity, which she later regretted,
she found herself questioning whether her choice of such a
luxuriously thick pile Axminster had been a wise investment.
She tried to remember a time when she might have done
something to stop him, perhaps to take him in her arms and
whisper some calming words of reassurance. She felt no
such urge now. He stopped and lifted his face to the ceiling,
as though he were praying to a greater force.

'WHAT WILL THIS DO TO THE BUSINESS?' he pleaded.

Mary opted to treat the question as rhetorical.

'AFTER ALL I'VE DONE TO BUILD IT UP. HE'S DETERMINED TO FUCK UP MY LIFE. THIS IS WHAT ALL OF THIS IS ABOUT. HE WON'T BE CONTENT UNTIL HE'S TOTALLY FUCKED ME OVER.'

He began to sob and just as Mary thought his anger had given way to tearful self-pity, he stopped and started pounding his head on the carpet again.

'FUCKING, FUCKING, FUCKING, FUCKING, FUCKING, FUCKING, FUCKING, FUCKING, FUCKING, FUCKING, FUCKING, FUCKING, FUCKING, FUCKING, FUCKING, FUCKING...'

He offered no response when she suggested that perhaps his first instinct should have been to protect his father and to think about the effect events might be having on him, rather than on the reputation of the law firm. What did he think his father's reaction would be when, in his moment of greatest need, the person he should be able to rely on most, his own flesh and blood, was more concerned about how badly his company's share price would be affected? Melvyn stared at her blankly with, she thought, all the understanding of a ruminating heifer.

A series of subsequent incoming telephone calls changed things, initially for the worse. The first was from Roz, informing him that a journalist from the Press Association had called her, asking her to comment on the criminal charges against her father, reported in his local paper, and inquiring whether the family would be standing by him. The second was from an indignant Tom Parker, *TMBL Law*'s Director of Communications, demanding to know why he hadn't been briefed on the charges against his father and had only just learned about them from BBC Scotland's Business Editor who had called to ask if Melvyn would do an interview for their lunchtime bulletin.

Fortunately for Melvyn, Parker remained calm and professional, urging him to approve an immediate statement of reassurance to mitigate any potential impact such a damaging story might have on the company's share price. He also suggested that Melvyn should telephone the various youth and women's groups that *TMBL Law* sponsored to reassure them that his father had no role in the company, that he denied all charges against him and that he would 'vigorously contest' them. Melvyn's face grew pink at the prospect, and he declined, suggesting such a message would be better coming from Parker as he had no connection to the case. He did his best to make his reasoning sound objective and based on sound logic, but he came across to Mary as frightened and overwhelmed.

With these matters taken care of, Melvyn's mood appeared to lighten, and within minutes he was behaving as though nothing had happened. Mary tried to challenge him about his earlier reaction, but he responded as though they were discussing two different events. He failed to accept that his behaviour was in any way disproportionate or inappropriate and he insisted that, far from losing control, he had no reason at all for which to reproach himself.

'Since this whole thing started you haven't once asked me if I am alright or if I'm coping,' Mary complained.

'What's it got to do with you?' he demanded.

'What's it got to do with me?'

'It's not your problem. He's my father. The only way it might affect you or your father is if it damages the business.'

She felt exhausted and close to tears.

'I'm your wife, Melvyn. Doesn't it occur to you that if you or anyone close to you is in trouble, it affects me?'

'How?'

'Because of the way I feel.'

'How you feel? I don't understand, why should it make

you feel anything? It's my father who's in trouble, not yours.'

She turned her back on him and took her car key from her coat pocket as she made to leave. She had been in similar situations countless times before when Melvyn had behaved irrationally or thrown a tantrum and his attitude never failed to surprise and anger her. She knew that to continue to argue with him, to keep pressing him in the hope that asking the same questions in a slightly different way might provoke an alternative response was futile, but she couldn't help making one final appeal.

'Don't you ever think about how the things you say will affect me?'

He tipped his head forward and frowned.

'Can't you see that such behaviour might be cruel?'

'I'm not trying to be cruel,' he pleaded.

'But you are. Can't you see that, intentionally or not, your behaviour is upsetting?'

He continued to avoid eye contact, training his line of sight slightly below her chin. She wondered, not for the first time, if the slightly convex shape of his mouth was a poorly disguised grin.

'When was the last time you thought about what's good for me?'

He remained silent and his eyes darted. She continued.

'Does it ever cross your mind that it might be helpful to say something comforting – just a few words to make me feel reassured that you're with me and looking out for me?'

'You'll have to leave now, or you'll be late for Dad,' he said.

He tried to walk past her toward the lounge, but she blocked his path.

'Have you ever woken up and thought, "You know what, I'm not going to do what's best for me today, I'm going to put Mary's interests first"?'

He tried to manoeuvre around her, but she moved again

to cut off his route and stood firm.

'Do you ever think about my interests?'

A sudden glint of recognition appeared in his eyes.

'What about the golfing break I offered to take you on?' he asked plaintively.

'Not those kinds of interests, you stupid shit. I mean my wellbeing, my welfare.'

'I booked us an expensive golfing holiday on the Costa del Sol, and you refused to come.

I lost a lot of money on that holiday, but did I complain?'

'Stop, Melvyn, stop. Every time we have an argument, you bring up that bloody golf trip.

It's your answer to everything.'

Sometimes Mary felt like she was married to an actor playing a deliberately obtuse role for the benefit of an audience.

'You say I don't think about you or your interests but that's an example of something kind I tried to do for you, and you threw it back in my face.'

There was a flatness in his delivery that made his words seem inauthentic and lacking in emotion.

'If I try to show you kindness and it's rejected, then why should I bother again? Einstein said that the definition of madness is repeating the same actions time and again and expecting a different outcome.'

'Bollocks to Einstein, Melvyn. If Einstein ever tried having a conversation with you, he'd know what fucking madness was.'

Melvyn looked injured and she felt shamed again.

'Besides, that golf trip was ten years ago.'

When they first met, Mary had made the mistake of not entirely disabusing Melvyn of the impression that she liked golf. She encouraged him to take up the game because, she thought naively, it was something he and her father might do together, that throwing them together on a golf course might help to forge some kind of relationship between them. What she failed to predict was that within a few months Melvyn would have a lower handicap than Rab, who had by then been playing golf for close to 50 years, and that her husband's obsessiveness about the game would be too much, even for her father. Melvyn enjoyed playing golf, but as with everything else he took part in, only when he was alone. For him it was a solitary pursuit, to be performed repetitively to the point of distraction, for a limited time until his obsessiveness about it subsided and then it was forgotten about with equal haste and never referred to again.

As well as playing golf he had become a compulsive devotee of motorcycling, gliding, marathon running, rare whisky collecting and online chess – all of which involved only minimal and transactional contact with other people. While he hadn't played golf for many years now, Mary's role in his discovery and short-lived romance with the sport, had created its own legacy in the form of a stick with which he seemed determined to routinely beat her.

She moved closely toward him until they were only inches apart, to ensure his undivided attention but also because she knew that such proximity unnerved him. He tried to move backward, but she grabbed his arms tightly and used all her strength to hold him in place. She noticed how dry his skin was. Tiny flakes had dislodged from his forehead and settled in his eyebrows. It was one of the things that, in the past would have concerned her and she'd have told him to moisturise – not that he'd have paid any attention – but now it irritated her and made her feel slightly repulsed.

'I hate golf, Melvyn. I've always hated it. I hate everything about it,' she said bitterly. 'I hate its smug, well-fed, little Englishness and its odious, unrepentant misogyny. I hate its arbitrary, self-selecting etiquette, designed to weed out those who don't quite fit, and its byzantine, incomprehensible scoring system with its stupid little names like birdies and boogies.

'Bogeys,' Melvyn corrected.

'I hate its middlebrow, silver plate narcissism and its clownish, unselfconscious camp. I hate its top-of-the-range, drinker's nose, clubbability and its conceited, changing room locker key exclusivity.'

Melvyn stared uncomprehendingly.

'But most of all I hate the detestable cunts who play it – the pot-bellied, back-of-the-bike-shed, overgrown schoolboys who have nothing better to do with their time than bat a wee plastic ball along the grass with a stick.'

'It's played with clubs, not sticks,' he protested.

In all the time they were married, Mary couldn't recall experiencing a genuinely malevolent impulse toward Melvyn, but his lingering expression of bovine incredulousness made her want to reach down and punch him in the balls.

'Why did you never tell me that before?' he asked plaintively.

'I thought I had,' she sighed.

'No, I'm sure I'd have remembered.'

'Did you never take the hint?'

He frowned.

'I've never played golf, Melvyn. I've never expressed a desire to play golf. I've never been to a golf tournament or watched one on television. I've never read a report of a golf match in a newspaper or knowingly initiated a conversation about golf. The only time I've ever been near a golf course is at the annual *TMBL Law* charity ball which I'm required to attend out of some misguided obligation to you and my father. I may not have expressed my dislike of golf in explicit terms before but surely ... surely, you must have picked up on the signals?'

'I haven't,' he said with evident sincerity. 'Really, I didn't know.'

He looked trumped and, fleetingly, his expression was

indistinguishable from the one his father wore when it was clear he didn't quite understand something. That Melvyn was becoming more like his father the older he got was a reality Mary had long done her best to ignore. Physically, they were quite distinct as Melvyn had inherited his mother's slenderness and sharp features and he was also half a foot taller than his father. Yet there were increasingly noticeable similarities in their behaviour and even their language. They spoke with an economy that might be interpreted as bluntness or even arrogance by those who didn't know them, and they could both also appear quiet and reserved though, in reality, neither were. In addition to their mutual desire for solitude, they both had a sad vulnerability, though one whose attractiveness faded in the firing line of life's slings and arrows.

When Mary first met Melvyn, she thought his reluctance to express his feelings were symptoms of shyness. Like many men of his generation and social background, it didn't do to be too eloquent or to show your feelings, she told herself, and she believed she could help him to change. She imagined his emotions to be buried under several geological formations and all she had to do was to drill down deeply enough to release them. Now she realised she'd been wrong – he didn't experience emotion in the same way she did, or anyone else she knew for that matter.

His response to the death of their son had done most to change her attitude to him. Beforehand she'd been prepared to give him the benefit of the doubt, to accept that having lived with his parents for so long and having endured what she believed must have been a fairly repressed upbringing, and that freeing him from those effects would require time and patience. Now she was sure that, if such a reversal were possible, it would require someone with greater skill and more stamina than she possessed.

She recalled the unbearable moment she learned of

Anthony's passing, how she'd been dressing in their bedroom, after taking a shower, when the policeman called to deliver the news. She was drying her hair when the doorbell rang, so she was only aware of the officer's presence when she switched the hairdryer off, and she heard the distant, muffled voices on the level below. The exchange lasted only a few minutes and was conducted entirely at the front door – Melvyn hadn't thought to invite the policeman inside – and so, by the time she made her way downstairs to inquire about their caller, he'd already left.

'Did Anthony have travel insurance?' was the first thing Melvyn asked her as she appeared on the landing.

That was the last time she'd heard Melvyn mention their son by name. He never missed a day of work – even on the day they learned of Anthony's death, he sat in his study preparing a report on a planned expansion of the company – and he took a change of clothes with him to the funeral so that he could make his way directly to the office following the wake.

He refused to deliver a eulogy at the funeral, quite understandably many of her friends and colleagues said. He'd have found it too upsetting, given the sudden and devastating circumstances of their son's death, and what father could say with conviction that he'd have acted differently in the same position? Mary's bereavement counsellor said people deal with grief in different ways and perhaps Melvyn's way of coping was to remain active and to keep his mind focused on more mundane matters

'He's a man and they think differently from women,' she explained when Mary complained about his lack of emotion. 'They demonstrate their feelings in practical ways.'

Mary believed differently – she knew Melvyn hated speaking publicly because he found it too nerve-wracking, being at the centre of attention, and she couldn't blame him for that, but still she felt real and deep discomfort at the level of commitment to work he was able to maintain and how, if he suffered any grief at all, he didn't show it. She felt trapped by her own cynicism and readiness to see a coldness in her husband's behaviour that no one else seemed to notice, which she couldn't express for fear of appearing heartless. When she should have been mourning her son, her greatest treasure for whom she felt the strongest possible love, all she could think about was the fear she felt for her husband.

As the rush hour traffic inched slowly forward, Mary caught sight of her damp, mascara- blackened eyes in the rear-view mirror and, for a moment, she didn't recognise herself. She hated the way Melvyn made her look and feel about herself. She tried to recall what had gone through her mind when she agreed to marry him. While she could remember vividly the inside of the restaurant, right down to the pattern of the tablecloth, what she had thought when he popped the question was a blank. She felt suddenly old and sick with regret.

He proposed weeks after they met at the university, where he had worked briefly as a postgraduate research assistant before he landed his first job with a back street law firm. She'd seen him sitting alone at the same refectory table at lunchtimes, engrossed in papers. When their paths finally crossed it was in the waiting room of the occupational health clinic where they were both waiting to see the nurse. All the other patients studiously ignored one another in case, she presumed, the subject of why they were there came up, but Melvyn brazenly struck up a conversation with her about a persistent sweat rash. He was rangy and athletic and erratically clothed, she remembered, like he'd been dressed by committee. His appearance was something of a joke in Law Faculty where she heard a colleague comment that his glasses looked like they'd been given away free with another pair of glasses.

She found his gawky appearance sad and disarming. He

had a long, pleasant face, like a dependable pet – some of her friends described him as handsome in a dated, black-and-white film sort of way, like a young Fred McMurray or Humphrey Bogart – but what she found attractive was his diffidence that was the antithesis of the kind of predictable, showy attention that she got from other men. He was thoughtful and serious, not in an austere way, but rather as someone who demanded to be taken seriously. And he was certainly passionate, albeit about technical and esoteric things.

Their coming together, while not romantic, was warm and funny – at least they hadn't met in the pub, she told friends in what became a refrain that, she wondered later, was perhaps a subliminal liturgy of self-justification. Even his solitude hadn't put her off; that he had no friends, she interpreted as a sign that he wasn't a typical bloke, that he preferred his own company, he wasn't good in crowds and, besides, it meant they'd have more time for each other.

Suddenly, she was an inch away from the car in front. Her foot jammed on the brake but not quickly enough to prevent a bash. Despite travelling at only a few miles per hour, her body jerked forward, hard against the seatbelt and her head rocked violently back against the headrest. In the moment of impact, she was momentarily elsewhere followed by a flash of sudden clarity – she'd felt sorry for Melvyn and she didn't have the heart to say no.

She sat, rigid, with her hands clasped tightly to the steering wheel, her knuckles taut and red, as though stuck by an irresistible force. And she cried. Tears had become an almost daily routine of her life since Anthony's death but not on this scale. Cold droplets rolled down her chin, collecting on her breasts and soaking her blouse. Salty mucus caught in her throat and she struggled to breathe. The pressure inside her head reached a point of discomfort but there seemed no means of release and she thought she might convulse. She became suddenly panicked, caught in an impossible limbo. There was a rap on the window that caused her to inhale suddenly and deeply. She started breathing normally again, but her hands remained fixed to the steering wheel and the tears became torrential. There was another knock on the window, but she felt too humiliated to turn her head and she was certain she'd be incapable of coherent speech. The door opened and she was aware of a presence; she knew it was a man before he spoke because of his smell. He remained silent for a few awkward moments as she sobbed bitterly.

'Look, don't be so upset, love, it's only a small dent.'

She continued to cry hard and loud.

'There's barely any damage, hardly a scratch, I'd say.'

Still unable to decouple her hands, she moved the top half of her body forward slightly and rested her forehead on the steering wheel.

'Look, let's just forget it, shall we? There's no need to trouble our insurance companies over this.'

She opened her eyes and watched as her silvery tears dropped in quick succession onto the well at her feet.

'Are you sure you're alright, love?'

She summoned what seemed like an enormous reserve of strength to lift her head a couple of inches from the steering wheel and nodded gently.

She arrived at George's house to find him on the road, pacing obsessively. When he clocked her car, he glanced at his watch with the kind of studied irritability that always made Melvyn anxious when he was on the receiving end of it. His face was bright red. She was relieved at his anger because it meant he was unlikely to venture the kind of lingering, wet mouthed, full-on kiss that he seemed habitually to mistake for an affectionate greeting. She hoped he wouldn't notice she'd been crying.

'I've been trying to get you on your mobile for the last nine minutes,' he said.

Some hope that he'd notice anything about her, she thought.

'I couldn't answer, I was driving,' she said, making a point of not apologising.

'You've got hands free.'

'I didn't hear it. It must be switched off.'

He glanced at the illuminated screen of the phone, sitting in the hands-free cradle.

'It's not switched off.'

Mary couldn't decide if his persistence was intended to reinforce his displeasure at being kept waiting or a crude attempt at teasing an aggressive response from her. Whatever the motive, she noticed that his manner in such circumstances always remained formal and consistent. There were times when she wondered if she was in the wrong and that he might appear to a neutral observer as perfectly reasonable. At other times she was sure his behaviour was so obviously unsettling, even hostile, that it had to be prompted by feelings of ill will. A professional might call it passive aggressiveness, but she didn't believe George had the craft to employ such deceit. Despite the irritation and occasional menace of his behaviour, she didn't feel he was anything other than sincere. Whatever prompted this behaviour, she was sure he felt entirely justified.

She hoped they would spend the car journey in silence. There were days when George offered no conversation at all but, regrettably, this was not one of them.

'So, what's the talk in the staffroom this week?' he asked, word for word, the same question he asked whenever they were thrown together. When she was feeling generous, she might venture a response but not today.

'Oh, nothing much,' she said with barely suppressed impatience.

'I see the universities are demanding more funding from the Government. It's as if they're not already swimming in public cash. I mean, where do they think the money's going to come from, all these academics in their ivory towers? It's not like it grows on trees.'

Mary knew she shouldn't let herself to get drawn into an argument, but she was also certain he would offer no comeback if she challenged him.

'Well, actually, George, the decision not to allow Scottish universities to raise their own funds by imposing tuition fees was a political one made by the Government, so the money has to come from somewhere. You can't have it both ways.'

As expected, he didn't respond. She'd noticed long ago that George didn't follow the normal rules of conversation. For him, the process was non-reciprocal: he seemed unable or unwilling to process the responses of others but rather offered only a series of disparate comments – often comically obtuse non-sequiturs – as though he'd rehearsed them in advance.

They drove past the Botanic Gardens, whose prolific greenness Mary normally enjoyed at this time of the year. Strong winds had scorched the tall, mature Horse woods that overhung the road, stripping them of their leaves and giving the impression it was the depth of winter. It had rained earlier in the morning, leaving the road dark and slick, and a sudden movement of grey cloud cover made her feel sad and hopeless. They spent the rest of the journey in silence, which suited her although she couldn't relax because she wasn't sure he wouldn't venture some observation or other at any moment to which she'd feel obliged to respond.

She recalled the first time she met George, shortly after she and Melvyn had started going out together. She'd been invited to his parents' house on a Saturday for afternoon tea. Susan had been welcoming enough, she recalled, asking her about her career plans and her family background and encouraging her to have more tea and another piece of shortbread. But her overall impression was of a cold formality, as though the entire occasion was planned from a book and she sensed a mood of relief when she and Melvyn got up to leave. George barely uttered a word all afternoon. Susan explained he was in a bad mood because he'd been refused permission to make his usual Saturday afternoon visit to a flea market in Leith that he scoured routinely for items of Beatles memorabilia.

Mary apologised but he ignored her, scowling like a truculent adolescent. She noticed then that Susan made even the smallest decisions on his behalf, from which chair to sit on, to which biscuit he should eat, and she frequently upbraided him for minor acts of incompetence and breaches of etiquette. Occasionally Mary caught him staring at her and, when their eyes met, he averted his gaze and blushed. The experience embarrassed her, but she didn't remember feeling unnerved or threatened by his behaviour. She recognised at once his awkwardness in company, like Melvyn's, but she also detected something approaching confusion, as though what was going on around him was unusual or novel. She discovered a short time later that she was the first girlfriend Melvyn had brought home, so she thought that perhaps he'd been especially nervous.

She pulled a right onto Chambers Street and they came within sight of the grandiose court building, nestled behind large and imposing wrought iron gates. Mary's heart sank as she saw a gaggle of press photographers and TV cameramen huddled around the entrance. She sensed George tense and heard him mutter something under his breath. He remained fixed to his seat, hunched and rigid. Miraculously, she found a parking space diagonally across from the court on the other side of the street, but George refused to leave the car until the photographers and cameramen had left. Mary tried to explain to him that his situation would only be worse if he failed to appear in court, that he could be arrested and held in prison until his trial if the judge decided that he was a flight risk, but he wouldn't budge. Drops of perspiration had formed on his top lip and his hands trembled slightly.

She told him she would go into the court and try to find his solicitor. As she walked across the road, a pair of chastened men in black gowns hurried past her, their eyes trained on the ground, followed by a group of smoking, pram-faced girls with mordant scowls, evidently prepping one of their number for her appearance before a sheriff. She asked the clerk at the entrance to the court for the name of George's solicitor and she was pointed in the direction of an unshaved man standing in the lobby, with a pile of papers at his feet, who appeared to be reading hurriedly through a buff coloured file. He had tired eyes and a drinker's face and he wore a shabby, ill-fitting black gown. She introduced herself as George Lovelace's daughter-in-law, but he seemed none the wiser.

'Your client,' she prompted.

He hesitated and his eyes darted.

'He's been accused of sexual assault.'

'Ah yes, the sex case,' he said.

'He won't leave the car,' she announced.

'Why not?'

'I don't know. I think he was spooked by the sight of the photographers.'

'Well, if he doesn't appear in person, he can't enter a plea.'

'I know.'

'And a warrant will be issued for his arrest.'

'I know.'

'And he may be held in custody until the date of a new hearing is set.'

'I know.'

The solicitor appeared stumped, like he'd already passed on the sum of his knowledge and he had nothing left to give.

'Remind me of the details of the case,' he said.

Mary lost patience.

'You mean you don't know them?' she asked incredulously. 'You're representing him in less than an hour. Are you telling me that you haven't even looked at his file yet?'

'He's only entering a plea. It's not essential for me to know all of the details of the case at this stage,' he said fluently, as though it was a practiced speech.

'It might be helpful if you knew some of them.'

A note of indignation crept into his voice.

'I'm appearing on behalf of half a dozen different clients this morning, all on different charges, and another four this afternoon. I can't be expected to have expert knowledge of them all.'

Mary sighed heavily.

'Look, I just want to know what I should do.'

'Let me go and get his file,' the solicitor said.

He hurried away and returned sometime later carrying another buff folder containing a thick sheaf of papers. Mary wondered how such a quantity of documents could have been accumulated over seemingly so little procedure. The solicitor was breathless and appeared nervous and she couldn't help feeling sorry for him.

'I've had a quick look and what the case appears to hang on is whether your father-in-law had an erection at the time he was dancing with the plaintiff.'

George's erect penis was not an image upon which Mary wished to dwell longer than necessary, but she felt she needed some clarification.

'So that's what she ... the girl ... alleges, is it? That George had an erection while they were dancing?'

'Yes.'

'Does she allege that he took it out of his, err...'

'No, the wording of the allegation is that he infringed her dignity by pressing and rubbing his erect penis against her, without her consent, causing her fear and alarm.'

Hearing his alleged behaviour described in that detail made her feel sick and yet part of her was relieved it wasn't any worse.

'So, what does that mean? I mean, how serious is that? Is it serious?'

The solicitor thought for a moment.

'Well, he's been charged with indecent assault, so the procurator fiscal clearly believes it's a serious matter. Your father-in-law could argue that, because his penis was not exposed then, strictly speaking, contact did not take place although, in my view, that's unlikely to be accepted by the judge. Indecent assault can also mean touching another person's breasts and that is generally held to mean through clothing.'

'Right.'

'My guess is that the fiscal has gone for a charge of indecent assault, leaving the door open for your father-in-law to plead guilty to the lesser offence of sexual harassment.'

'But he says he's innocent, so why should he plead guilty?'

'Well, because he'd avoid the ordeal and the publicity of a trial, and a conviction for a charge of sexual harassment is unlikely to carry a custodial sentence. Most likely, he'd get away with a fine or community service.'

'So, will that be your advice to him, to cut his losses and plead guilty to sexual harassment?'

'I'm simply pointing out the risks involved. Convictions for indecent assault are more difficult to obtain, particularly in a case like this where, essentially, it's her word against his. In my experience, which I have to concede is not extensive in this area, a jury is more likely to believe an otherwise respectable, retired professional man who has raised a family over a scantily clad teenage girl who's had too much to drink and whose sexual history could and should become a matter

171

of public inquiry.'

She nodded, trying to maintain a neutral expression, to avoid betraying her feelings of revulsion.

'And, of course, the jury would have no prior knowledge of his previous conviction which would, however, become a significant factor if he were to be found guilty and convicted, in which case he would certainly be looking at a custodial sentence. As I've said, if he was to plead guilty to the lesser charge, he could avoid the prospect of prison altogether.'

Mary felt her mind freeze.

'Previous conviction? What previous conviction?'

The solicitor blinked nervously.

'You didn't know,' he said, as a statement of confirmation to himself rather than a question.

'No, I didn't know, a previous conviction for what?'

He rustled through the sheaf of paperwork until he came to the right page.

'He has a previous conviction for sexual harassment, from December 1980. He pleaded guilty and was sentenced to 150 hours of community service.'

'Sexual harassment?' she said disbelievingly. 'Against whom?'

The solicitor ran his finger hurriedly along the lines of the page, mouthing the words to himself.

'It doesn't say. The victim's identity was protected by an order of the court.'

'Does it reveal anything about her, her age or where she came from?'

The solicitor's face reddened.

'Actually, the victim was male.'

Mary felt her skin tingle like she'd received a shock. The first thought that entered her head was about her son. Rapidly changing images flickered in front of her eyes like photographs spilling in front of her of the times George had been alone with Anthony. Had he bathed him when he was a baby? Had he changed his nappy? Had they played squash together? Had they ever slept in the same bed? She hated herself for thinking such things, but she felt she had no control over them.

'I don't want to alarm you, Mrs Lovelace, but we need to get your father-in-law into the court,' the solicitor said. 'I understand he'll be feeling nervous about the press but that's something he'll have to overcome. There's nothing more likely to infuriate a sheriff than no-show. Show me to your car and I'm sure I'll be able to talk him around.'

She led him across the road to her car but when they got there, George was gone.

Chapter 11

Somewhere in Edinburgh, the following morning

By the early 1970s Lennon had become something of a political activist and a supporter of assorted leftist, anti-establishment movements, some of which had distinctly nefarious connotations. His early activities were restricted to voicing support for various mainstream political 'causes du jour', including the anti-Vietnam War movement, exemplified by his now famous 'Bed-in for Peace' at the Amsterdam Hilton Hotel while on honeymoon with his new wife Yoko Ono, and for the aims of the terrorist Irish Republican Army (IRA), following the Bloody Sunday massacre in Londonderry, Northern Ireland in November 1972 where 14 unarmed civil rights activists were shot dead by the British Army. He and Yoko also showed solidarity for workers at the Upper Clyde Shipbuilders (UCS), who were staging a work-in, in protest at planned shipyard closures and also for John Sinclair, an American poet and founder of the White Panther Party who was serving a ten-year jail sentence after being convicted of selling two marijuana reefers.

Lennon's political activism moved in more esoteric, some might say extreme, directions with support for several fringe organisations including the Black Panther Party and the International Marxist Group. In 1969 he and Yoko Ono supported the family of James Hanratty, hanged for murder in 1962, in its quest to prove his innocence. Lennon said those who condemned Hanratty were, 'the same people who are running guns to South Africa and killing blacks in the streets...The same bastards are in control, the same people are running everything, it's the whole bullshit bourgeois scene.' It was the voicing of such seditious sentiments that led to a dark period in Lennon's life and resulted in him being denied

American citizenship, spied on by security services on both sides of the Atlantic, including being followed, having his telephone bugged and his mail read under the direction of J Edgar Hoover, the paranoid and sexually perverted director of the Federal Bureau of Investigation (FBI) and ultimately to him being assassinated under the orders and cooperation of the Central Intelligence Agency (CIA) of the United States of America.

George couldn't concentrate properly because he'd left his notebook at home and he was writing in a new, inferior version that he bought at a supermarket in whose cafeteria he was now seated. At the back of his mind was the thought that he'd have to copy it all out again when – if – he eventually retrieved the original. Despite the inconvenience, not to say immense upset, caused by not having this item on his person, he couldn't risk returning home because he wasn't sure who might be staking it out, waiting for him to return.

When he left Mary outside the court building, he didn't have any clear idea about what he would do or where he would go. All he knew was that he would not be presenting himself to the authorities to play the stooge in whatever show trial they had planned for him in their kangaroo court. If the way he had been treated by the media was anything to go by, justice could go hang and that, he suspected, was the fate that awaited him, metaphorically, if he were to submit to the clutches of the criminal justice system.

He selected the supermarket after some deliberation as it was located in an area of the city that was strange to him, to limit the chances of him being spotted by a family member or an acquaintance. Seated directly behind him was a diminutive man, unshaven and with a somewhat dishevelled appearance who wore small, wire-rimmed spectacles and carried with him a powerful odour of stale urine, and whom George suspected, like him, had slept rough the previous night.

Although they were the only patrons in a somewhat large expanse of otherwise vacant tables, neither felt compelled to converse with the other, which suited his requirements.

On the table before him were three cups of cold tea, along with six milk portions in small plastic pots and six sachets of white sugar, all untouched. He felt obliged to continue purchasing cups of tea at regular intervals to justify his continued presence, as per the hospitality retail principle, but he couldn't drink them because he'd left his tube of sweeteners, along with his notebook, at home, and he couldn't drink tea that wasn't sweetened. He could have purchased another tube – he knew for a fact that the supermarket stocked his brand – but he made a point of not opening a new tube until the previous one was finished, allowing him to decant the contents of the most recently purchased into the original which he'd had for several years.

It was nine o'clock. He had been in the cafeteria since opening time three hours before when he last Googled himself on his smartphone to see if he'd become any more infamous since the last time he checked. His name, coupled with Edinburgh Sheriff Court, produced seven results, one more than the previous evening. The latest hit was an article in the local evening paper, reporting that a warrant had been issued for his arrest. He felt a firesome rage building inside of him so intense it was difficult to contain. He wanted to shout, swear, to break things, to inflict damage. The sense of grievance was overwhelming; what was happening to him was unjust and incomprehensible. He hadn't done anything to merit such punishment.

'It's not fair,' he mouthed silently but the noise inside his head was deafening, reverberating around his skull like a riotous crowd.

He needed to act, to take a stand, to demonstrate to his tormentors that he wouldn't submit to their tyranny. He needed them to know that he wouldn't be taken. He telephoned the offices of the Midlothian Advertiser and asked politely if he could speak with the so-called reporter who had misled him so perfidiously.

The receptionist said she would put him through to the newsroom.

'News,' said a gruff, disinterested female voice.

'Hello, may I speak with Bryan McGarvey?'

'He's not here, he's out on a job,' said the voice.

'Ah, off to stitch up his next unsuspecting victim, is he?'

The tone of the voice changed, appearing suddenly to take a greater interest in him.

'Sorry, who am I speaking to?'

'There's no need for you to apologise, you're not the person who has behaved unethically and immorally and who shall shortly be the subject of a lengthy complaint to the Press Council.'

'Can I tell him who called?'

George said nothing.

'Is there anything I can help you with?'

'Yes, you could pass on a message for me.'

'Of course.'

'You could tell him that he's the sperm of Satan and the most underhand, pusillanimous little shit I've ever met in my entire life.'

The gentleman seated at the table behind him rose to his feet and began to applaud which, in turn, attracted the attention of several members of staff. who stared at George in a manner disconcerting enough that he decided to leave the premises in case any of them recognised him from his photograph in the papers.

The morning was silvery grey and cold with a sunless, portentous sky. He'd spent the night first on a bench in the Botanic Gardens and then, when it became too cold to remain outdoors, in the passengers' waiting room at Waverley Station where he'd been able to remain until the station masters changed shifts at 05:00 and the new one told him he'd have to leave. He considered standing his ground and arguing that, as a member of the travelling public intent on catching the next available train (a necessary lie), he was entitled to remain on station property, but he caught the man looking at him in such a suspicious way, that he thought discretion the greater part of valour and bid a smart retreat.

His bones ached from the interminable cold – even in the station waiting room he'd been obliged to walk briskly around in random directions to prevent his limbs from seizing – and he could no longer feel his toes. The temptation to return home was, at times, almost irresistible but he knew that to do so was to surrender to the so-called authorities. He wasn't going to be beaten by them, he kept telling himself.

He decided he couldn't spend another night outdoors and that he'd have to find accommodation, irrespective of the dangers of being identified and reported to the authorities. His likeness had appeared in the media and so the more people with whom he came into contact, the greater was the risk of being spotted. Initially, he didn't recognise the photograph of himself published by the Midlothian Advertiser, and subsequently by other media outlets, nor could he understand where they'd obtained it from. It was a younger version of him in unfamiliar surroundings. Then it struck him: it was a close up of his face in Melvyn's graduation photograph that hung on the living room wall, which must have been snapped by the McGarvey fiend on his smartphone camera while George was out of the room.

He found a rather rundown guesthouse just off London Road, intentionally off the beaten track and where, he guessed, there would be a relatively small and unchanging clientele, minimising the chances of him being identified and reported. A corollary of such logic, however, was that the standard of accommodation was necessarily poorer. The first thing he noticed when he entered the foyer was how worn the carpet was; in places it was completely threadbare and in others it was held together by odd squares of grey gaffer tape. The air was suffocatingly heavy and there was a pervading smell of damp.

The reception comprised a square hatch cut into a plasterboard wall and behind it stood a portly, sub-continental male watching horse racing on a small portable television set sat on a grey plastic bucket seat. The tail of the man's crumpled shirt hovered around his navel and he wore jogging bottoms with an elasticated waist that sagged around the top of his buttocks, low enough to reveal the apex of his pubis. He was so hirsute that there appeared to be no determinate point at which his chest hair stopped and his pubic hair began, George observed. When he said he required a room, the man asked for his name, which he considered a reasonable request given his desire to check-in to his guest house, so he told him it was Django Reinhardt, an alias he'd prepared in advance. The man said nothing, staring searchingly into George's eyes like he was reading a complicated instruction manual. George felt deeply uncomfortable and so he pretended to be interested in something on the wall behind him. The man asked him to spell his name and George hesitated, momentarily forgetting the correct spelling, and it took him several goes before he got it right, which, he thought, made him look rather suspicious.

'You don't look like a jingo or whatever you call it,' the man said in what George assumed, after a moment's pause, to be a sarcastic tone.

'Well, I can assure you that I am,' he replied resolutely.

The man misspelled Django Reinhardt on a photocopied pro forma and then asked for George's address.

'No fixed abode,' he replied confidently, as per his plan.

'Surprise, surprise,' the man said with a sigh, then he picked up the form, screwed it into a ball and dropped it onto the floor. 'Look, I don't care who you are, as long as you pay.'

George produced a bundle of £20 notes he'd withdrawn from a cashpoint and handed two of them over. The man's eyes widened as he surveyed the notes for what seemed like an unnecessarily long time.

'If you're planning to bring any company back to your room - '

'Company?' George interrupted.

'I should warn you that the police raid this place a couple of times a month.'

The man handed over a Yale key attached to a wire coat hanger and pointed George in the direction of a narrow corridor whose walls had been defaced with obscene graffiti. Mention of the police had made George nervous and he felt a sudden urgent need to be away from the place.

'Actually, I've changed my mind. I don't need a room after all,' he said hurriedly.

The man laughed and returned his attention to the horse racing. George stood holding the key with his arm extended for several moments, but the man made no move to take it. George felt himself burning with indignation. He couldn't decide if he was being intentionally ignored or not.

'I'd like to cancel my reservation,' he said in a louder tone.

'Up to you,' the man replied, without taking his eyes off the TV.

There was another long period where, again, the man pretended to be unaware of George's presence although he knew, logically, that couldn't have been the case.

'Could I have my money back please?' he demanded firmly.

Without looking up, the man pointed to a piece of A4 paper – adhered to the wall by four pieces of yellowed Sellotape – on which had been written in green biro: NO

REFUNDS.

'But I'm not asking for a refund,' George protested. 'I've expressed a desire to withdraw my custom before consuming your services, so technically the transaction is void. I think you'll find, if you read relevant passages of the Consumer Rights Act, that I am entirely within my rights to do so, after a reasonable period of reflection. It's known as a cooling off period, which vendors are obliged, under the law, to respect.'

The man continued to ignore him.

'So, could I please have my money back?'

'Fuck off.'

George made a judgment then that he was unlikely to convince the hotelier of the merits of his argument and that, as he'd paid for the accommodation, he should use it. Clearly, the fat sub-continental gentleman hadn't recognised him, which was to his advantage, and he calculated that, if what he said was true and the police raided the premises twice a month then, it not being a leap year, there was only a one in 15.2 chance of them doing so on the single night when he was a guest. It was what was known in betting circles as a long shot, and so he resolved to remain and began to make his way down the corridor to his room.

'No luggage?' the man called after him.

George decided to ignore him. He already knew too much.

The bedroom was compact with only a single bed, covered with a faded orange candlewick cover, and a rickety chest of drawers fashioned from medium density fibre board, leaving little space to walk around or even to stretch. A communal bathroom served six bedrooms and it had clearly seen better days. A row of wall tiles along the edge of the bath were yellowing and several were missing, like a smoker's smile. The toilet bowl contained a soiled sanitary towel and the area around it was dominated by severe fungal staining. The shower, in George's opinion, was not fit for human use, and in any case, there were no towels.

The rest of the so-called facilities left much to be desired. Fire precautions, such as they were, would never have passed muster with even the laxest regulatory regime – the battery had been removed from a smoke alarm attached to the ceiling of his room and its wires were exposed – and multiple, small faecal deposits on the floor suggested a rodent infestation.

Despite the filth George slept soundly and he rose early the next morning and departed immediately, leaving his key on the reception desk. It was another bitter November day and a veneer of frost had gathered on the pavements and car windscreens and people brushed past him hurriedly on their way to work, expelling clouds of grey, smoky breath through their nostrils. Painful rush-hour noise gathered around his ears like a Black Friday crowd, pushing and jostling, competing for his thoughts. The day stretched before him like a vast, unknown landscape and he wondered what he would do to fill the hours. He hadn't planned for this and when there was no order or routine, he became anxious. Suggestions flooded into his mind unprompted; possibilities followed by warnings, threats, calculations of risk. His head felt dazed and disordered, leaving him unable to focus on a single idea. It was like he was searching for the end of a ball of string in a mess of irregular loops and knots, a starting point that might allow him to at least plan how to untangle it, but no matter how hard he tried, he couldn't find it.

He glanced at his smartphone. It was Wednesday, when his normal routine was to walk to the local newsagent mid-morning to buy a copy of *The Sentinel* and then to Romy's Café on Corstorphine Road, where he knew he could get a cup of tea with milk, and no interruptions to read Roz's column. Naturally, he couldn't go to any place where he might be recognised but he resolved that he'd try to approximate his routine as best he could. He found a branch of WH Smith where he bought a copy of the newspaper and went in search of a suitable venue.

The Stevedore Café on Leith Walk had been open since 4am, according to the notice of its opening hours posted in one of its frosted windows, and by the time George entered shortly before 10:20, most of its clientele was asleep. Contrary to its name, it didn't sell coffee, or tea. The tiled floor was wet and there was a strong smell of stale beer and the sort of strong disinfectant normally associated with public toilets. A barrel shaped woman with a harsh face the colour of boiled ham stood behind the bar, wiping its dull wooden surface with a damp beer towel. Before he reached her, he was approached by a thin, unshaven man with a long, earthworm-shaped scar that ran from his temple and over his cheekbone to the top of his upper lip, who asked if he wanted to buy some DVDs.

'What kind of DVDs?' George asked.

'The cheap kind,' the man replied.

George asked him if he had a list of titles. The man said that if he told him the titles that he wanted, he would visit an associate nearby who would provide him with the discs. He required money upfront, he added, assuring George that several of the pub regulars would vouch for him. George told him he regarded his business model as flawed and inefficient and that he'd garner more custom either by travelling in tandem with his associate or, preferably, by retailing his DVDs from a single point of sale – either a market stall, a shop or online.

'Who the fuck urr you, Alan fucking Sugar?' the scarred man demanded in a gruff, unfriendly manner.

'No, the name's Django Reinhardt,' George said, offering his hand.

The scarred man spat on the floor and departed the premises.

George bought a pint of India Pale Ale and sat down and, as he looked around, he noticed how much he appeared to stand out from his surroundings; he was still wearing the suit he'd chosen for his court appearance with a navy silk tie and pocket handkerchief, but those who were still awake seemed to pay him no attention. It occurred to him that he hadn't eaten for more than 24 hours. Apart from experiencing slight nausea and weakness in his legs, he appeared not to have suffered any ill effects. He knew that, sooner or later, he'd have to consume something, but until he could prepare his choice of specific foods cooked according to his requirements, there was no possibility of that happening.

He wouldn't allow his standards to be compromised by the malevolent forces ranged against him. To allow a morsel not prepared according to his strict routine to pass his lips would represent a surrender, which he would not countenance. At 10:57 he picked up *The Sentinel* and turned to the op-ed section, and at 11:00 he started on Roz's column.

After reading for three minutes, he stopped. He found he couldn't focus properly, and his breathing had become shallow and irregular. He tried to read some more but he didn't feel able to continue. Every treacherous word felt like cold steel pressed into his heart. He pulled the notebook and pen that he'd bought in the supermarket from his pocket to try to write something, but his fingers felt fat and numb. Fumbling ineptly, he dropped them both onto the hard, wet floor. He reached down to retrieve them, feeling helpless and conspicuous, aware of the barmaid's eyes trained on him. He picked up the notebook and spread it open on the tabletop and wiped it flat with his red fist and, with the other hand, clutched the pen in a claw-like grip and forced himself to create words, rows of comforting words, words of his own.

The claim that Lennon was killed by the CIA at the behest of powerful, neoliberal extremists at the heart of the American military-industrial complex, is supported by a significant body of evidence that lends it considerable credibility. The

CIA has an institutional predisposition to orchestrating assassination attempts on troublesome individuals, no matter how powerful, from Franklyn D Roosevelt to Ronald Reagan, suggesting there is, at the very least, strong circumstantial evidence pointing to its involvement in Lennon's execution. Many of the so-called 'facts' relating to the case are deeply flawed, including the suggestion that the man convicted of his murder, Mark David Chapman, acted alone. Chapman was portrayed in the mainstream, corporatist media as a nerd and an obsessive loner, in the tradition of a Lee Harvey Oswald or a John Warnock Hinckley. However, far from being the 'super fan' with a warped mind, the killer possessed not a single Lennon album, single or book and his actions, before and after the shooting, were remarkably calm – hardly the behaviour of a freakish flake. Nor did his actions, in the weeks and months leading up to the shooting, square with his supposed image as a penniless itinerant. His passport revealed that he'd visited several unlikely locations, including Georgia, Japan, the UK, India, Nepal, Korea, Vietnam and China. Most suspiciously, he felt the need to visit Beirut, the war–torn Lebanese capital, then a hotbed of CIA activity, and Hawaii, home to a CIA training camp. Nor has it been explained how these extensive travels were funded. It has also been suggested that Chapman spoke Russian! In prosecuting a state–sponsored conspiracy, the CIA would have drawn on its long experience of using mind-controlling drugs and techniques such as hypnosis to produce a 'sleeper assassin', similar to those fictionalised in the film The Manchurian Candidate. Typically, the 'sleeper assassin' is embedded in society for several years under the guise of a convincing legend, before being activated at the appointed moment. Such 'sleepers' doubled as convincing 'patsies', or fall guys, upon whom such killings can be solely blamed. As with the assassination of President John Fitzgerald Kennedy, nearly two decades earlier, the conspirators didn't bank on

troublesome forensic evidence that would challenge their
version of events. In the case of Lennon's shooting, the bullet
holes on his body formed in a tight pattern, more indicative
of a trained professional marksman than a firearms novice
like Chapman who, supposedly, had never fired a gun
before. Moreover, the autopsy report and death certificate
suggest all the gunshot wounds were on the left side of his
chest while eyewitness accounts have Chapman standing to
Lennon's right, suggesting there was more than one shooter.

George placed his pen on the table and, calmly, took a sip of beer. Although he felt something approaching hatred towards Roz for writing such baseless bile, he was composed enough to respond to her. He picked up his smartphone and typed a text message.

'I hope you're pleased with what you've done, my treacherous offspring. You have ruined my life.'

'Shit,' he thought, 'my phone ... the phone ... the fucking phone ... the signal ... they'll be tracking the signal ...' How could he have been so stupid? He grabbed hold of his possessions and left the bar with an almost full pint of beer sitting on the laminate table and he walked hurriedly south, along Leith Walk in the direction of Princes Street. He wasn't yet sure what he would do or where he would go, he just had an instinct to keep moving. At the Playhouse roundabout he spotted a tram stationed at York Place and he ran to board it. He bought a ticket all the way to the airport, but when the tram stopped at Haymarket, he waited until just before the doors were about to close and jumped off. A bus pulled up at a nearby stop, heading in the direction of Granton and he hurried to get on before it pulled away. He took an aisle seat on the bottom deck, immediately next to the exit. The bus was almost empty but for a couple of Chinese students on the backbench, chatting in what he took to be Mandarin or some dialectical variation. He rode the bus for a few stops and waited for it to stop at Dean Village. Another passenger boarded – an elderly lady carrying a wicker shopping basket – and just as the doors were about to close behind her, he leapt from his seat and alighted. The bus had already started to move, and he stumbled as his feet hit the pavement, but he managed to check his balance and avoided falling. As the bus moved past him, he caught the students staring at him.

He walked across Dean Bridge and, without stopping, he threw his phone over the side into the Water of Leith. Glancing backwards he watched it hit the foaming current and he breathed a sigh of relief. He started to think seriously about other silly mistakes he might have made – simple, avoidable errors that might land him in trouble. He was conscious of not leaving a trail of his movements on CCTV cameras across the city, so he found a nearby charity shop where he bought an overcoat, a scarf and a baseball cap to conceal his identity. He'd had the foresight to withdraw the maximum daily amount from a cashpoint immediately after leaving Mary at the court, to avoid revealing his location from subsequent withdrawals. Following the guesthouse fee, the purchase of clothing, the coffees and the notebook from the supermarket, he estimated he had enough cash to keep him in food and fuel for several days without having to break cover.

He knew he couldn't trust his family, who seemed only too willing to throw him to the wolves. Melvyn didn't have the courage to face him – he'd sent his wife along to drive him to the court to do his dirty work. His relationship with Melvyn had never recovered from the episode with the Malign Gillies. Not properly. Although he'd taken his son into his confidence, giving him a tremendous amount of responsibility at an early age, he felt he'd never repaid him with the level of loyalty he'd expected.

He'd given him total control of his defence at the industrial tribunal, an invaluable gift to a young Law student, and yet he never trusted Melvyn had full belief in his innocence. Throughout the case, he'd been only too willing to accept the word of George's employer at face value and to give the benefit of the doubt to the Malign Gillies, rather than to fight for his own father's basic rights. Melvyn talked in lofty terms of 'principle' and 'reputation' and of abstract notions like 'the bigger picture' and 'the wider issue'. George had been obliged, continuously, to bring him back to the specifics of the case, the facts as they stood, that, irrespective of how inappropriate, insulting or intimidating his behaviour might have appeared – and he challenged the other side to prove beyond reasonable doubt that it had been any of these things – they had failed to follow the due process of the Law. For all their expensive lawyers and their heavily resourced personnel department, they'd failed to issue him with an initial written warning or to document properly an initial verbal warning. Moreover, the verbal warning was not prefaced in terms that indicated it was an official verbal warning, nor was there an independent witness present; the final written warning (which was, in effect, an initial written warning) was improperly dated, allowing insufficient time for him to prepare a response. At no time was it communicated to him, either verbally or in writing, what the employer's disciplinary policy was, how it would be conducted and what his rights were under such a policy. There was more but he really didn't need to continue; Melvyn knew that the other side had conducted the entire disciplinary process in a slipshod and ultimately illegal manner and that, under the letter of the law, George was entirely in the right. Yet, constantly, his son counselled him to moderate the tone of the language George chose to use in official communications – to be more 'sensitive' and 'respectful' to the Malign Gillies and his employer, to the point where he began to wonder if, in fact, Melvyn was seeking to undermine his case from within.

George couldn't face another night exposed to the elements. He thought about hiring a car, which would double as transport and accommodation, but he would be obliged to use his real name and to produce his driver's licence, so he dismissed the idea. Instead, he decided to visit the only person he knew he could trust.

He arrived at Linda's house late in the afternoon and positioned himself on the opposite side of the street, at the gable end of a terraced row of houses, tucked in slightly so that he was out of sight. Her curtains were open and a ground floor window was raised slightly, suggesting she was in, but he knew he couldn't just walk across the road and ring the bell in case she had company who might recognise George and turn him in. He no longer had his smartphone, and he couldn't call her from a call box because he couldn't remember her number. The intense cold made his hands sting and his face felt numb and immobile like it did after an injection from the dentist.

Darkness stole in without warning, like a surprise cavalry attack, taking George by surprise. It was nearly December and the shortest day would soon arrive, when everything was dead, and night was at its most ruthless. He had been standing still for no more than 15 or 20 minutes but when he tried to move, he found that his lower limbs were frozen solid and that he had to walk a few paces before he felt them again. There was a crippling pain in his lower back and every breath generated sharp, excruciating spasms in his spine and shoulders like sparks from a welder's torch. He slowed his lung movement to a series of short, shallow gasps which made him feel faint and bloodless. His lack of food had started to bite, and he felt searing hunger pains stalking his stomach.

A light switched on in Linda's house, but he remained in place. The temptation to move from the cold into the warmth was strong but he held his ground. Patience and silence were more than principles for him now; they could be the difference between freedom and incarceration. They were underrated as virtues by today's younger generations who were dominated by the showy and ostentatious – lazy, superficial individuals who were light on self-discipline and heavy on instant gratification. In his experience, they were values that, more often than not, helped one to prevail. To wait, to hold one's counsel, to keep everything that one has in reserve, to place the burden on others, to force them to act first, to show their hand – these were the principles to which he subscribed. To do otherwise was to leave oneself exposed and to place oneself at the mercy of others. To act is to err – that was a lesson he had learned early, and it was one which he'd followed with commitment and dedication.

It was late when he came to, prostrate on the pavement with a cold slab of frozen stone pressed hard against his cheek. A dog walker had roused him from unconsciousness and, as he pulled him upright and propped him against a wall, he slapped his face and asked him repeatedly if he was alright. Was he on medication? Had he fainted? Did he want an ambulance? No, he didn't want an ambulance. The dog-walker thought he should see a doctor. He'd see a doctor when he was ready, he insisted. Leave me alone you nosy bastard, what concern is it of yours? Take your dog and piss off. In his confused and foggy state, he didn't know if he said any of those things or just thought them. The dog walker's expression didn't change. He lifted George onto his feet and propped him against a parked car.

'Are you sure you're alright?' he asked.

George's mouth wasn't working. He imagined himself telling the dog walker he was fine but no sound emerged from his lips. He fought the pain in his legs and back and struggled to stay upright. Across the road the light in Linda's living room had been switched off and her car was no longer there. He managed to lift an arm slightly and he pointed to his wrist with a finger. The dog walker looked at his watch.

'It's half past midnight,' he said.

Where had she gone at this time of night, George wondered. Was she with someone?

Would she be back before morning? Was he destined to spend another night rough? He gestured for the dog walker to continue on his way and tried to gesture with a benign blink of his eyes that he would be fine. He managed to struggle forward a few steps in the direction of Linda's house and, through incredible strength of will, to remain on his feet. From the corner of his eye, he could see the dog walker watching him. He willed the man to leave and eventually, after what seemed like an eternity, he heard him whistle to the dog followed by the sound of footsteps moving off. At least now he knew that there was no one in Linda's house although, by that stage, he couldn't have cared less. He opened her gate, let himself into her garden and waited for her to return.

Chapter 12

Roz was beginning to regret telling Ruaridh she was pregnant. She would have told him eventually – she'd seen how destructive holding something like that back could be with her own mother – but she wished she'd held off just a bit longer as he'd insisted on travelling with her to Scotland. He wouldn't hear of her going all that way on her own – not in 'her condition'. Everything she did now was judged against its appropriateness to 'her condition', as though it was contagious or terminal. She tried explaining that she wouldn't be walking all the way to Edinburgh, she'd be catching a plane and hailing a taxi, neither of which would require much in the way of strenuous effort, but he wouldn't hear of her going alone.

When he told her he didn't want her suffering from the stress and anxiety of her father's disappearance on her own, she tried to talk him down, pointing out that George hadn't actually 'gone missing', he simply hadn't returned home after leaving the court and that there was no reason to panic. Ruaridh recalled her telling him that he had returned home for lunch at precisely the same time every day since he was married, and probably long before, and that any deviation from such an established pattern certainly was a reason to panic. Surprised at his speed of thought and determined not to be outwitted, she said he couldn't just up-sticks and abandon his market stall.

'Fuck the market stall,' he declared with abandon. 'Some things are more important than money. And besides, Fruit and Veg Andy said he'd set up for me and put his boy on the stall for a couple of days until we get back.'

Of course, she couldn't tell him she didn't want him

along because she hadn't told any of her family about him. She'd managed to put him off accompanying her to Susan's funeral, despite his repeated offers to do so, by pointing out that he'd never met her mother and that it might be awkward being introduced to everyone for the first time while they were wailing with grief as her coffin was carried past. He had already told his mum about her – his dad died when he was 12 – and she was desperate to meet her, apparently, though Roz expressed bewilderment at why that should be the case and said he ought to suggest she moderate her expectations because, if they ever did meet, she would be in for a big disappointment.

By the time they had set off for the airport, however, she found herself glad of his company and of having the support of someone who wasn't her brother to help her deal with another of her father's misadventures. She called the police in Edinburgh from the Heathrow Express, unconvinced that Melvyn had had been forceful enough in trying to get them to treat George as a missing person, whose safety was in question, rather than just another 'no show' at the court. She was told by a duty officer it was too early in the morning and she was urged to call back later. When she challenged the officer by insisting that unlike her local branch of Marks and Spencer, she should be able to call the police at any hour, especially as it was an emergency, the officer changed his tack.

'Madam, we can't mobilise a search party for every person who doesn't return home in the evening,' he told her, with what she was quick to complain was a hint of arrogance.

He took slightly more interest when she informed him that her father was a suspected sex offender who had failed to turn up for a scheduled court appearance earlier in the day and was, therefore, a fugitive from the law, but he maintained his position that there were established procedures for such people and that, he was confident, all available resources would already have been deployed for his search.

The smell was the first thing Roz noticed about her parents' home as she entered using the set of keys she'd had since childhood, and which still fitted the locks. It was the same odour she'd detected in George's car when he collected her from the airport ahead of her mother's funeral. It reminded her of an acrid cocktail of sweat, airlessness and stale food from a care home in Croydon she'd visited for a feature she was writing at the time. It was the unmistakable scent of decay and helplessness that, she thought at the time, gathers around elderly people no longer able to care for themselves. It had never existed in the house when her mother was alive, and she felt the pull of tears in her eyes at the thought that, left to his own devices, George was adrift and neglected.

The house was freezing and eerily quiet and Ruaridh was surprised that for a man of such apparently fastidious habits, George's living quarters were so chaotic. Items of discarded clothing lay draped over chairs and on door handles; used cups and dinner plates collected in piles, and a sea of yellowing paperwork washed over surfaces. The floor was strewn with several copies of the same local newspaper that carried an article about George on the front page. The copies were spread haphazardly, spilling their contents as though they had all been read individually to ensure that the content in each was the same. Elsewhere, framed pictures and family photographs had been removed from walls and were propped against the skirting boards below. In their place had been pinned a hectic collage of dog-eared posters, pages torn from newspapers and magazines and post-it notes with scribbled messages in red and green ink, all of which seemed to be linked by a network of biroed arrows as though they were combined factors in a complicated mathematical formula.

Books lay spatchcocked on every surface, at stages of completion, all of which seemed to have some relevance to the Beatles or John Lennon. A giant jigsaw of the Sergeant Pepper's Lonely Hearts Club Band, described on the box as 'The Hardest Puzzle Ever', took up most of a coffee table and a life-sized cardboard cut-out of Lennon, dressed in early Beatles' trademark grey, collarless jacket and drainpipe trousers, stood in front of the mantelpiece surrounded by four battered electric guitars.

'This stuff was all kept in the attic when my mother was alive,' Roz offered in half- hearted mitigation.

'Does George play the guitar?' Ruaridh asked.

'No,' she replied.

He gathered a sheaf of printouts of various web pages to clear a space for himself on the settee.

'Don't mix these documents up, Dad will have them arranged in a particular order,' she scolded.

'They're not documents, and I haven't mixed them up. I've kept them in the same order as they were.'

She fussed around him, ensuring that everything remained in its place and that any item that had been moved, even by an inch, was reinstated. Ruaridh found a well-thumbed notepad that contained hundreds of pages of George's distinctively tiny and tightly formed handwriting. The title had been written on the cover with a black ink marker in a fanciful style that reminded Ruaridh of toilet block graffiti from his schooldays.

JOHN LENNON
THE LIFE AND TIMES OF A ROCK 'N' ROLL LEGEND

The telephone rang and even before Roz picked it up, they both knew it was Melvyn. She had been ignoring his calls on her mobile since they left Plumstead. Her column about George was due to run in that day's edition and she knew he'd have read it. Ruaridh could tell from her reaction, without hearing her brother's side of the conversation, that he was clearly angry.

'I'm entitled to write what I like, and it needs to be said by someone,' Roz said, somewhat high-handedly, he thought.

There was a long silence as, Ruaridh guessed, Melvyn was contributing his tuppence worth.

'Well, I'm afraid I don't accept that, Melvyn. If an alternative point of view is not discussed, then what hope is there of anything changing?'

Silence.

'I know you're a lawyer.'

Silence.

'I know that you have.'

Roz had told Ruaridh following Melvyn's phone call the night before that her brother appeared more concerned with something George's lawyer had told Melvyn's wife about a previous conviction than with the fact that he'd gone missing. Roz didn't know about the conviction – she thought it might relate to a dispute her father had had with a former work colleague several years before. She had recently moved to London for her first job in journalism at the time and so she didn't know the details. Melvyn would still have been at university, she said, and she thought he had been roped into the affair by her father because he was studying law, but she couldn't be sure. From what she remembered, her mother had dismissed it as a storm in a teacup – her father's 'latest obsession' – and it was never discussed again. There was certainly no mention to her that it ended with George having a criminal conviction on his record.

'No, Melvyn, I don't agree that it's an open and shut case.'

Silence.

'Even with a previous conviction.'

Silence.

'I know that I am not aware about the details.'

Silence.

'So, it was to do with that business at Carlton Stenhouse?'

Silence.

'Well, actually, I would like to be told, but you know better than me any mention of it was taboo as far as Mum and Dad were concerned.'

Silence.

'What I want to know is why you have never so much as mentioned it if you know so much about it.'

Ruaridh began to flick through the pages of the notebook. Roz had told him about her father's 'interest' in Lennon, but he was surprised by what appeared to be more like the obsessive devotion of a teenage fan than a pensioner pursuing a hobby, not least by the amount of effort and detail that appeared to have gone into writing it. He turned the cover to find a list of chapter headings and, on the next page:

A Short Note on the History and Career of the Author

I, *George Eric Lovelace, was born on November 6, 1944 at 28 Cloverbank Street, Edinburgh, the son of Eric Walter Lovelace, a Royal Navy Gunnery Instructor, and Agnes Catherine Brydon. I was educated at Corstorphine Primary School and Craigmount High School before attending the University of Edinburgh where I took a Bachelor of Accountancy degree (BAcc), specialising in tax management. My parents were decent, unpretentious, gentle and unsophisticated people who never used bad language and never had a bad word to say about anyone. At a time when people were more trusting and society more stratified along class lines than today, they were very deferential to those they perceived as their betters, particularly ministers, teachers and doctors. They were not particularly ambitious and rather fatalistic about their position in society. Getting*

*married, settling down and having an uneventful life seemed
to be the order of the day. They were not at all materialistic,
very public spirited and caring. They saw it as their duty to
help people in need and Agnes took it upon herself to care
for Mrs Shaylor, an elderly neighbour, while my father did
odd jobs for her and tended to her garden.*

Roz had told Ruaridh shortly after they met that her
father wasn't the easiest person to get on with and that he'd
never had a friend. What struck him more than anything was
how casually she dropped in this item of information, almost
as an aside.

'Not a single one, not even when he was a child?'

'Nope.'

'What about at school? He must have had friends at
school.'

'None means none.'

'Don't you find that a bit strange?'

'I guess he enjoys his own company. Is that so unusual?'

Ruaridh thought for a moment.

'Frankly, it is, yes.'

'Why are you making such a big deal about this? A lot of
men don't have friends. They don't socialise with each other
in the way women do.'

'Yes, they do. I've had loads of friends all through my
life.'

'Well, you're the one who's odd, not Dad. And where are
all these so-called friends of yours? I never see any of them.'

It irritated him that his conversations with Roz always
seemed to end on a put down. He wondered why she did it.
He knew he didn't have her sharp wit but even if he did, he
wouldn't use it in that way. He hadn't travelled as widely as
her, and he couldn't quote from books or talk intelligently
about the people he admired like she did. That's not to
say he didn't have opinions on politics and religion and

important affairs, but she never listened to him or engaged with him when he tried to make a point. Even when he knew she disagreed, she didn't try to argue with him, she just went silent. Like the time she got embarrassed when he had a conversation about Brexit with Elias, the waiter at the Rawalpindi at the end of her street. Elias agreed with him Brexit was a good thing for the country because it would mean fewer immigrants – but Roz stormed out of the restaurant before they'd even eaten their starter and he'd had to pay for an entire meal because they'd ordered it. She spent the rest of the evening and most of the next day in silent fury. She finally condescended to discuss the matter only after she'd sunk a few vodkas.

'Doesn't it occur to you that Elias and his family are immigrants?' she said.

'But he agreed with me. He said he thought controlling immigration is a good thing.'

'Well, if you can't see what's wrong with that argument, there's no point trying to explain,' she replied.

'And anyway, why are you so hostile to Brexit? Your paper was its biggest cheerleader.'

'Forget it, Ruaridh, just forget it,' she said.

As he surveyed the debris of George's life, he had a sudden revelation about the way Roz viewed the world. He saw in the confusion and disordered mess of a man, whose sense of order and fastidiousness defined him, the same contradictions that made his daughter so difficult to understand. Roz, the successful journalist and confident spokeswoman for the important issues of the day, who drank herself senseless in a drab, forgotten corner of a city and a nation whose greatness her written views claimed to represent. The powerful and elegant phrases she crafted gave little away about the fear and uncertainty in her own mind or of the disordered nature of her life - of projects being started and not finished, whims indulged and tangents pursued without any proper notion of her final destination or even direction of travel. He moved in with her because he thought that having a partner would bring some purpose and order to his life, and yet he now saw the daunting challenge it would be to bring any sense of permanence or stability to hers.

'Well, maybe it's not as simple as that, Melvyn.'

Silence.

'Why should he plead guilty, even to a lesser charge, if he hasn't done anything wrong?'

Silence.

'But you know what Dad's like. It's just how he is. Half the time he doesn't even know he's doing it and he doesn't mean any harm.'

Silence.

'And the lawyer thinks prison is a realistic possibility? Surely he can't be serious.'

As a family, we led unremarkable, but austere lives. Eric and Agnes were always very mindful of attending to my physical needs but, as was common at the time, they were rather distant and less attentive to my emotional wellbeing. I was brought up to respect my elders, to conform and be well behaved at all times, and not to push myself forward. 'Little boys should be seen and not heard' and 'manners maketh the man' were much quoted sayings. My perceived aloofness and lack of self–confidence in adult life were almost certainly a result of my upbringing. My mother died on July 22, 1947, when I was not yet three years old. I was given the news by Mrs Shaylor, rather than by my father, who never mentioned Agnes again. The day after her funeral he burned an album containing the only photographs of my mother in existence in a metal dustbin in the garden.

Primary schooling was a very regimented affair with rote learning the methodology of choice. Discipline was very strict and reinforced by use of the tawse (belt). Pupils were regularly belted for even the most minor misdemeanours or lapses. I learned to write on a slate, since paper was in short supply because it was wartime. Secondary education was little better. Overall, the standard of education was dismal, with only a few of the teachers at all inspirational.

As a teenager I became interested in numbers and I read voraciously about Arithmetic, Algebra, Geometry and Trigonometry. This was despite the fact that my Maths teacher was one of the poorest. All my free time was spent at the local library where I would read for hours on numbers and the relationships between them. On one occasion my parents were summoned to the school by the head teacher who told them that I had a precociously developed number sense. My parents didn't know what this meant and did nothing to encourage me in developing this talent.

At university I already knew I wanted to become a tax accountant and so I tailored my degree choices to that specialism. After graduating I held positions with several accountancy firms, attaining only low-to-middle ranking positions. I failed to achieve the level of success I craved and believed myself to be capable of, largely due to the shortsightedness and incompetence of the directors and senior managers with whom I worked.

'Well, what about the thing that the detective at the police station asked? No, about if he's ever had mental health issues.'

Silence.

'All I'm saying is that it's worth considering.'

Silence.

'No, I'm not a psychiatrist all of a sudden, but I can see what's in front of me. You don't need to be a cardiologist to know when someone's having a heart attack.'

I was forced to leave my penultimate job following

a personal misunderstanding with my immediate line manager, who took offence when I asked him if he would like to join me on a holiday in Spain. To my mind, this was a perfectly reasonable request and I pointed out that I knew of many people who spent leisure time with work colleagues, but he didn't see it that way and he rebuffed my offer with quite unnecessary rudeness. The matter could and should have rested there, but it subsequently got quite out of hand and resulted in me being summarily dismissed on a charge of gross professional misconduct. I fought it all the way as far as an industrial tribunal, at which point my employer surrendered and agreed to compensate me for unfair dismissal. While my position was vindicated entirely by their capitulation, they refused to reinstate me and so I resolved to appeal and to continue with my campaign to free my name, which resulted in the police becoming involved and me being charged on a trumped-up offence. I was determined to fight the case through the courts, to the House of Lords and the European Court of Human Rights if necessary, but was dissuaded at the eleventh hour when Melvyn, my son, made an impassioned plea for me to drop it and to plead guilty. Thankfully, the case received no publicity, and the facts were shielded from the wider public.

Ruaridh wondered why Roz had never revealed this information to him. The passage only mentioned Melvyn so perhaps, he thought, it hadn't been revealed to Roz. He questioned why and whether that would have been possible. Could such a secret be kept within a family? And if it could, should he now reveal it to Roz? Would there be any benefit to it, or would it just make her more anxious? He thought he should keep quiet for now.

When Roz hung up, he saw that she was shaking.

'He's outraged. He thinks I've made things worse for Dad by writing about the case.'

'Really?'

'Yes, really. He says all it's done is to make him look guilty and that it's made it more difficult for him to plead guilty to a lesser offence. I don't think he should plead guilty anything because what he did doesn't amount to criminality. That was my point.'

'I agree with you. If he hasn't done anything wrong, why should he plead guilty to anything?'

'Melvyn said that kind of hubristic claptrap might wash in the pompous musings of the broadsheet op-ed pages but that this is the real world. If he pleads guilty to a lesser charge, there's less chance that he'll go to jail.'

For the first time he could remember since meeting Roz, she sounded unassured.

'Fuck,' Ruaridh said.

'Don't say "fuck", don't say "fuck".'

She appeared to be at the point of crying.

'I need a drink,' she said, sounding desperate.

Ruaridh didn't respond. She hadn't had a drink since she told him she was expecting, or as she had put it: 'I'm pregnant, but I'll probably get rid of it.' She insisted she hadn't smoked either but he didn't believe her. He hadn't pressed her on her plans because, he reasoned, if he didn't give her the chance to be categorical, then there was still a chance that she would keep the baby. The situation was not dissimilar to his position at her flat. He was never officially asked to move in; he stayed overnight after a particularly long session in the boozer because he didn't have enough money for a taxi to the lock-up where he was dossing, and he'd never left. He made a point of not referring to them as 'living together' because he feared that if he ever did talk about their relationship in explicit terms, she might kick him out.

He reckoned his best course of action was to demonstrate his commitment to her and the baby through deeds rather than words because words didn't seem to have much impact on her, so he'd agreed that he would stay off booze and drugs for as long as she did and he promised to take responsibility for her health, and that of the baby, even if she seemed unconcerned with both.

He continued to thumb through the ... what was it exactly? He couldn't decide if it was supposed to be a diary or a notebook or just a collection of thoughts. Whatever it was, he was sure George couldn't possibly have any serious expectation of it being published. There didn't appear to be any proper sequence to the chapters, and it was difficult to follow what central point, if any, he was trying to make.

He knew a little about The Beatles – how could you not when there was a documentary about them on BBC4 or The Music Channel virtually every other week – but he didn't know about much of the detail George had written. It certainly looked like he'd done his homework; there were lots of little numbers attached to words that were explained in tiny, written notes at the bottom of pages.

'This book's very strange.'

'How is *that* book very strange?' Roz demanded derisively.

'I don't know, it just seems to jump randomly from one thing to another. Just when you think you're learning about a subject that's interesting, he goes off down a side road onto something different.'

'There speaks the Times of London's literary critic?'

Ruaridh thought Roz was upset after the phone call with Melvyn and so he decided not to push the matter any further.

She grabbed the notebook from his hands.

'You shouldn't be reading it anyway,' she said sharply.

Ruaridh was woken at 6 a.m. by Roz whose urgent movement suggested she was up. When he opened his eyes, she was already dressed.

'What are you doing?'

'Nothing. Go back to sleep.'

She left the room, closing the door behind her. There was a damp chill and Ruaridh could sense, even with the curtains closed, it had been raining overnight. He was still tired from the early start the previous day, but he couldn't have spent another moment on the spongy mattress of Roz's childhood bed, with its sharp spring coils digging into his ribs. He got up, dressed quickly, and followed her downstairs to find that she'd already put on her overcoat and was about to leave.

'Where are you going?'

'It's none of your business. Leave me alone.'

'OK, it might be none of my business but at least have some breakfast before you go.' He tried to put an arm around her, but she arched her shoulders and pulled away.

'I don't have time. I have to get to her before she leaves for college, or school, or wherever the fuck it is she goes.'

Her head dropped and she stared at her shoes, her face framed by a hanging cloak of hair. It was the first thing Ruaridh had noticed about her when they'd met, how unusually straight and smooth her hair was and how her cheekbones, when she smiled, drew his attention into to her sharp, green eyes. She didn't make a sound, but a couple of tears fell. Ruaridh put his arm around her shoulder again and this time she allowed herself to be led back into the house. They walked together to the kitchen, which was tidier than the lounge and without the smell, and he lowered her gently onto a chair at the dining table. Conscious she didn't like to be fussed over, he left her alone and filled the kettle and put some bread in the toaster.

'I can't let him go to jail, he'd never survive it,' she said quietly.

'He's not going to jail. It won't come to that.'

'If he pleads not guilty and it goes to trial, there's a good chance he will.'

'That's just Melvyn's view and he's a lawyer. Lawyers always want you to plead guilty because it makes their lives easier.'

She wiped the tears from her face with the back of her hand and sighed. Ruaridh handed her a mug of tea and insisted she take a couple of sips. After a few moments she appeared to have calmed down.

They arrived at the address at 7.15 a.m. in the hire car they had collected at the airport, and found the curtains drawn, with no apparent sign of life inside the house. It was an impressive looking modern villa with a large garden. Three expensive looking German cars sat at the at the top of the driveway with flagstones, despite the time of year, that had recently been whitewashed. Melvyn had told Roz the name of the girl's father and it hadn't taken her long to track down where the family lived. Ruaridh decided there was no way of stopping her from doing whatever it was she planned to do – and she refused to tell him – so he reasoned the best he could manage would be to be with her when she did it. They sat inside the car and waited for movement.

'I don't suppose it would make any difference if I pointed out that you could get arrested for this?'

'Nope.'

'As well as being harassment, it's also witness tampering.'

'So now you're a lawyer, are you?'

'Only saying.'

'Well, don't.'

He felt guilty about being there. Despite telling himself he had her best interests at heart, and that he wanted to protect her, really he knew he had to keep track of her movements because she was carrying his baby and he couldn't trust her to be out of his sight, not even for a couple of hours. He was exhausted after two sleepless nights and he had difficulty staying awake. As he fought sleep, he recalled a story she told him shortly after they met. She probably wouldn't remember telling him – she was pissed at the time – but it had stuck in his mind. How could it not have done? As with much of what she told him, it was the casual way in which the material was relayed as much as the content that was so shocking.

She was ten years old, it was a Saturday morning, that much she recalled clearly, when her mother summoned her from the garden where she was playing and told her they were going on a trip. She remembered the bus journey into town – the unsteady old back-ender winding its way through suburban roads with its characteristic, choking smell of diesel and cigarette smoke. The journey was memorable principally because of its rarity; George was still working in a well-paid job and they had a family car that sat in the driveway, but it couldn't be used that day, Mummy had said, because she wouldn't be able to drive afterwards.

Roz said George was away from home for the weekend – at a record fayre or a fan club convention, she couldn't remember precisely – but what was important was that he wasn't to know about their trip. It was a big secret that he shouldn't be told, her mum said. It seemed, initially, like an exciting game for Roz though Melvyn seemed less sure, and even as she thought about it on the bus, she began to feel a kind of sadness that her Dad wasn't included, especially as he'd been so happy when he left.

She remembered the short dash from the bus stop in the pouring rain to the white, terraced building with its thick, stone pillars. It looked from the outside like an office building but when they passed through the heavy, glass panelled doorway, she was surprised by its medicated smell and the women dressed in starched, white uniforms and peaked caps.

Even when her mother was wheeled away on a trolley, down a corridor and out of sight, she didn't feel anxious or threatened because there was orange juice and colouring books and soft words of reassurance from the ladies in white that Mummy was only going to see the doctor and that when she returned in a few moments she'd feel much better. Roz believed she was being braver than Melvyn, who sat still and tight-lipped, refusing any offers of comics and treats.

Susan didn't look better when she returned on the trolley. She was red-faced and hunched and she too looked like she'd been crying. Small movements seemed to hurt, and she said she wouldn't be able to manage the walk to the bus stop, so a taxi was ordered. They spent the journey home in silence; Roz wanted to play I-Spy like they sometimes did on Sunday afternoon drives in the countryside, but she sensed that her mother wasn't well enough, so she contented herself with spotting cars with registrations that ended with P.

For the next couple of days, Susan remained in her bedroom under a pile of bedsheets, with the curtains drawn and a bottle of pills on her bedside table. Melvyn kept repeating the same thing, that Mum was not to be disturbed. The house was silent, with the phone off the hook, and no one spoke above the level of a murmur. When their father returned from his trip he was smiling and in a mood of rare jollity, but soon it turned to anger and then he became morose and withdrawn. He shuffled in and out of Susan's bedroom carrying trays of soup and coffee, but he didn't stay for long and he barely spoke to her. He removed his clothes from their wardrobe and moved them ro the spare bedroom. When Roz asked why he was sleeping apart from Mum, he said it was to give her some peace until she was better. But he never returned, and they slept apart for the rest of their married life.

Roz looked over at Ruaridh, who had fallen asleep, and she wondered if she could risk lighting a cigarette. She decided she couldn't – even if he wasn't wakened by the smoke, he'd certainly smell it later. Neither of them had

had a drink since she told him she was pregnant and, as far as he was aware, she hadn't smoked either, although she'd sneaked a few cheeky puffs leaning out of the bathroom window. She wondered how long she could stay dry for. If it hadn't been for him, she'd have cracked halfway through the first day. Despite her enduring scepticism about him and their 'relationship', she couldn't ignore that he alone was responsible for her current alcohol sabbatical, which was the lengthiest she could remember. She could tell from the absence of heartburn and general hangover fug that her body was grateful even if her brain wasn't yet ready to start handing out plaudits.

The first time she saw Ruaridh had been on an early summer evening when he came into The Star Inn on Plumstead Common Road with three labourers from one of the local building sites, who appeared to have transported a good deal of its debris on their clothing. She liked the pub, which distinguished itself from most of the others in the area by not smelling like it had an undiscovered, long-dead Alsatian lying in the cellar. She would have spent more time there if it weren't the only pub in the area where there was the remotest chance that she might bump into someone she knew professionally. As well as catering to an element of the local, hard drinking hoi polio, it was also frequented by some pioneering middle-class settlers who looked like they baked their own sourdough bread and might occasionally read a book or watch something on BBC2. Unlike the local competition it had boardgames and ran quiz nights rather than fruit machines and pool tables, and while it screened football matches on a solitary television screen hung discretely in a corner, it didn't feel the need to advertise the fact on a large, branded tarpaulin above the door. Ruaridh stood out among the group as the only one who didn't laugh uproariously at every sexually explicit rejoinder voiced by the group. He was taller, and slimmer and, sweetly, Roz thought, he looked like he had dressed as a lumberjack for a provincial clothing catalogue photoshoot.

She was seated alone at a nearby table, reading the latest Madeleine Thien, and she was required to pass the group on her frequent visits to the bar to replenish her glass with large measures of vodka and tonic. They ignored her on her first couple of trips, but by her third the builders had clearly become convinced her repeated purchase of alcohol was a thinly disguised cover to satisfy her carnal craving for cement encrusted beer bellies. Her initial refusal to acknowledge their recurrent entreaties for her to improve her mood led one to conclude that, contrary to their earlier suppositions, she must, after all, be 'frigid'.

Having collected her glass from the bar, she halted momentarily and turned to address the spokesman for this opinion.

'Actually, I have quite a strong sexual appetite,' she declared loud enough for the other dozen or so customers and staff in the immediate vicinity to hear. 'Some of my many lovers might say it's voracious.'

To the gallery of widening eyes, she added: 'That said, if you three were the last men on the planet and the future of the species depended on our procreating, I'd be over there, at the other end of the bar, grinding my crotch on a door handle to satisfy myself.'

As she turned to return to her seat, there was a collective, appreciative roar from across the room as the builder struggled to retain a semblance of his dignity.

'Awright darling, keep yer hair on, just trying to make a bit of small talk,' he said.

Roz stopped again, turned and walked the two or three paces back towards the speaker until she was level with the circumference of his bulbous stomach. He was the smallest, and fattest of the three and, emboldened by several large vodkas, she stood to her full height. Dressed in what she modestly agreed were sensationally tight, black denims and four-inch stiletto boots, she suddenly felt the full weight of her sexual power, like a marble Renaissance statue holding up a lumpy bag of washing. Her chin hovered above his nose and, with her free hand, she reached down and patted his groin.

'Well, you know what they say about men who make small talk, don't you?' she said with a straight, humourless face.

The collective clientele of the room erupted in a round of whoops and hollers and this time everyone in the builder's group, joined in with the laughter.

'Fair play to you, darling. Fair play,' the emasculated labourer cried cheerfully.

A short time later, Ruaridh approached her table, carrying a large vodka and tonic. She had almost finished her drink and was quietly relieved she wouldn't have to return to the bar as she was still coming down from the exhilaration of the confrontation.

'I'd like to apologise for the behaviour of my, eh, acquaintances,' he said quietly and, she thought, shyly.

She was pleased to hear that he had a Scottish accent as it gave her a welcome sense of Celtic solidarity. She looked him up and down and tried not to smile at his pristine, Caterpillar boots.

'Where are you from?' she asked.

'Glasgow,' he replied.

'Well, I'll try not to hold that against you,' she said, pushing a chair out from under the table with her foot.

Ruaridh came to with a start and was immediately aware that Roz was no longer in the car. He looked out to see her striding across the garden towards a girl who had emerged from the front door of the house. The girl had short, dark hair that looked roughed and unwashed. She wore no make-up and was dressed in jeans, flat shoes and a baggy grey fleece that made her look plain and sexless. From a distance she could have passed for a boy, and while he knew she was seventeen, she could have passed for younger, he thought.

The girl approached Roz warily across the closely trimmed lawn and they met at the turn of the driveway. Her expression remained fixed on Roz as they talked. To him it seemed like the moment of dazed unreality, immediately after a bomb is detonated, when all the energy appears to have been sucked from an area prior to the noise of the explosion and the chaos of flying debris. But then nothing happened. The detonator appeared to have fizzled out and the expected explosion didn't come. Ruaridh wondered what Roz could possibly have to say by way of a preamble before stating who she was and why she was there. He anticipated a rapid change in the girl's expression and tried to guess what might be the point of revelation, but it didn't happen; instead, her faint smile moved slowly down her face like melting wax and her gaze stayed fixed as she nodded attentively. Roz's gestures became more animated and expansive – she had her back to Ruaridh but he could tell she was crying – while the girl remained composed and at one point moved forward and touched Roz's shoulder and then withdrew it quickly.

When it was clear that Roz had finished what she had to say, the girl began to talk, calmly, it seemed. Ruaridh wanted to wind down the car window so he might hear what she was saying but he didn't want to draw attention to himself and possibly alarm the girl, so he tried instead to gauge from her expression what she was saying. Her head was tilted slightly to the left, as though she was looking up into Roz's face and her posture was open and suppliant. There was an inquiring look in her eyes and her lips moved slowly and intermittently. Ruaridh was sure he could lip-read a few words.

'Are you ok? Are you sure you're ok?'

The girl moved closer and again she extended her hand and placed it on Roz's shoulder, only this time she allowed it to remain there, her fingers extending gently across the nape of Roz's black coat. They remained in the same position for what seemed to Ruaridh like an uncomfortably long time and he feared this might simply be a preamble to a sudden outburst of negative emotion. He wondered if they had reached an impasse, each unable or unwilling to contribute further, in a silent pact to remain there until the other moved or spoke. The morning was beginning to break through the darkness and in the blue, hazy dawn, a shroud of drizzle gathered around them, its miniscule droplets resting on their hair and clothes like motes of dust.

The front door of the house opened, and a tall man emerged. Upon seeing Roz and the girl together he assumed an exaggeratedly disapproving expression, like a villain in a silent movie. Despite his swift, strident steps toward the pair, Ruaridh was able to command every detail of his appearance. His distressed drainpipe jeans and casual, light tan slip-on shoes; his candy-striped shirt with open collar, fanned across the lapels of a mustard, American sportscaster's blazer. His predominantly perfectly bald head and belly, despite his lofty frame, seemed comically out of proportion to the rest of him; a thick leather briefcase swinging from his right hand, in a rising parabola, gaining momentum like a weapon being primed to launch. Behind him emerged a squat woman dressed in a lime green twin set and a pair of scarlet, patent kitten heels, like the dwarfish foil in a Benny Hill sketch, causing Ruaridh to choke on his laughter.

Upon seeing her father, the girl removed her hand from Roz's shoulder and, in doing so, it appeared the spell between them was broken. The scene appeared suddenly animated as the girl shifted hastily, turning to place herself in the space between Roz and her father. His expression changed from anger to entreaty, his lips moving hurriedly. The woman dropped her handbag and moved across the grass, her diminutive legs scuttling like a cartoon insect.

Although Ruaridh still couldn't make out what they were saying, he could see the urgency in their mouths. Their look was intolerant and disproportionate. It was one familiar to him; the first look he remembered from the earliest time in his life. It spoke to him of domineering control and helpless, powerless fear; of unrelenting volume and the remorseless threat of pain; of his mother, cornered and tearful and his father standing brutish and bullying. It reminded him of minicab meters ticking over while suitcases were stuffed with bedsheets and towels; of sleeping on the floors of people he barely knew in towns he'd never heard of; of smelly bed-and-breakfast lodgings and refuges with no space to be alone. Constantly changing schools and teachers and never getting to say goodbye to friends he knew he'd never see again; of freezing water, eating out of tins and no television; of watching his mother's resolve slowly weaken until her spirit was broken. Long, tearful calls in dank, urine soaked phone boxes; of sickening, grovelling apologies and painfully stilted reunions; of the gradual build-up of tension and the transparent inevitability of the cycle of pain being repeated.

He forced himself to leave the car and he ran across the garden towards the group. When he arrived, he grabbed Roz to move her out of harm's way. She was stunned and immobile and he had to manoeuvre her across the grass, her heels catching on the lawn. He bundled her into the hire car, strapped her in and then he moved swiftly around to the driver's side. As he closed the door, he heard frantic threats of police and arrests. As he pulled away, he watched through the wing mirrors the final gestures of threatened recrimination playing out behind them.

Chapter 13

Straiton, South of Edinburgh, earlier on the same day

Linda liked to go supermarket shopping in the early hours. There was something illicitly pleasurable about venturing into the darkness, scoping the deserted aisles at a satisfyingly lingering pace without a thought for another soul. It felt as though she was flouting a social convention, like working on Christmas Day (she used to enjoy that too) or missing a royal wedding on television.

It appealed to her sense of individuality, reminding her of a recurring childhood fantasy where she had the power to freeze the world in its tracks with a click of her fingers, suspending people in frozen animation while she walked among them in the streets and entered their homes, studied their faces, rifled through their belongings and read their diaries to discover what they really thought. Shopping at this hour also had the benefit of allowing her to take her time and weigh up her options, to read labels on packets and jars, and feel the fruit and veg without attracting looks or having to queue behind harassed parents or dithering pensioners.

On this occasion, there was a purpose to her visit. Barbara Boddy had texted her earlier in the evening to ask if she'd seen the piece by Rosalind Boucher in that day's Sentinel. Wasn't she the daughter of Susan Lovelace, she asked, implausibly, as if she didn't know? Did Linda know the identity of the mystery man mentioned in the article? There was a rumour it might be George. Such a scandal, if true. She didn't mention what the article was about or where the supposed rumour had originated, though Linda could guess it probably wasn't far from Barbara Boddy's pot-stirring imagination. She replied curtly that she hadn't read the article, which was true, and left it at that.

For the rest of the evening she tried to forget about the message, but it had panicked her, and she knew she wouldn't be able to sleep if she didn't read the article. Mention of George in the context of a 'scandal' was something she'd been expecting to hear for years, although she couldn't pinpoint why she felt that, or what sort of scandal it might be. He was one of the most straightlaced people she knew, hardly gossip fodder or tabloid exposé material, and yet there was something about him that she felt made him a target for trouble. But what kind of trouble? She was never quite able to say. He was not the sort of personality to get mixed up in anything criminal – he was far too unadventurous for that – and he was as far from a rabble rouser as it was possible to be. He wasn't reckless, seditious or violent. If she were to assess him in her role as an actuary, she'd be hard pushed to identify any risky behaviours at all, other than his single infidelity with her – she felt if he'd had other affairs, she'd have known. He wasn't a heavy drinker or a gambler and the notion of him taking drugs was preposterous. So, what was it about his personality that made this most predictably conformist man, at the same time, so bewilderingly unfathomable?

He could be insensitive, sometimes incredibly so, and she had often become frustrated at how deaf and blind he could be to her feelings. But was that really the stuff of scandal? She'd never have described him as misanthropic, not when she saw him around his children, and yet some of his behaviours, she felt, were often wilfully cruel – the long silences, the lack of interest in her concerns, his failure to comfort her if she was angry or upset, his constant changing of the subject when she wanted to discuss something that she felt was important. Yet, when she complained to close friends – the pair she'd confided in about her relationship with George – they dismissed such things as classic male traits. He was 'just a typical bloke', they said, and counselled her not to expect any deep or sensitive reactions from a man.

But he wasn't a typical bloke – that's what had attracted her to him in the first place. He preferred the company of women – Linda never knew him to have any male friends, other than the husbands of Susan's girlfriends – and he had no interest in team sports, cars or drinking in pubs. He could be incredibly kind and thoughtful, but in practical ways like doing odd jobs around her house and driving her places. Often, she arrived home from work to find he had restocked her kitchen with groceries. But he never expressed his feelings in words, nor did she pressure him to do so. Despite their affair lasting several years, there was always a temporariness to it that she didn't seek to correct. Perhaps she felt, intuitively, that he wasn't capable of anything more and so she was comfortable with the seat-of-the-pants informality of their relationship. Neither of them had professed love, which was one of the few aspects of their relationship that she looked back on with any sense of gratitude.

Linda didn't believe anyone should have regrets – mistakes were simply experiences to be learned from – but her affair with George had come the closest. Reading Barbara Boddy's message delivered a familiar, dull ache she felt on the rare occasions that she thought about their time together. She'd never managed to locate precisely where in her body the pain lived; it seemed to exist everywhere and nowhere, and it took her some time to realise that it wasn't an illness or injury, but the physical manifestation of her deep and profound regret. The feeling of shame.

She tried, unsuccessfully, to locate *The Sentinel* on her smartphone. She made marginally more progress on her home computer, even locating the right page on the paper's website, but she'd barely caught sight of the article when a box flashed up asking her to pay a subscription, using her debit card, which was a technological trial too far.

217

Driving to the supermarket, she rehearsed in her mind what the article might be about, poring over every word of the text message for any clues it might contain. She knew it couldn't have mentioned her by name, otherwise Barbara Boddy would never have had the nerve to contact her. She wondered too about its timing; surely it was no coincidence it had surfaced so soon after Susan's death? Was this perhaps Roz's crude idea of payback – avenging her mother's memory in the most public way possible? George had always insisted that none of the children knew about their relationship, but then he was hopelessly naïve about such things and she never trusted his judgment.

It was almost one o'clock by the time she reached the news stand in the near-deserted store. It hadn't occurred to her that all the previous day's papers would now be bundled and tied at the checkouts and that some of the next morning's editions would already be laid out on the shelves. She approached a skinny, porridge-faced boy in a green branded uniform, who didn't look like he was old enough to drink coffee far less be out of bed and working at such an hour, and she asked him to untie one of the bundles. His face flushed with alarm, like she'd just ordered him to empty the till and race off with her to her cougar's love nest in the Wester Hailes high flats.

'Eh, we're not supposed to...' he began scratchily, but instantly relented after Linda confected an expression of such post-menopausal menace, he plainly realised that breaching a sacred company directive was preferable to battling the gathering shitstorm now threatening to engulf him.

Surprised and a little embarrassed that her hands were trembling, Linda rifled through the newspaper until she came to the opinion-editorial section and quickly scanned the pages for the article. The raw text looked benign enough, just a few columns of print beneath Roz's flatteringly youthful picture by-line. No screaming headline about betrayal or infidelity

218

or ruined lives; no grainy, snatched photographs of figures sloping furtively in and out of cars and backstreet hotels.

She always made a point of looking for Roz's column when she bought the paper, which wasn't often, and what she read she didn't particularly like. She found her style thorny and judgmental.

Her most vivid memory was of a truculent teenager with contemptuous eyes. Susan had complained about her smoking pot when she was fifteen and she made oblique reference to underage sex. Linda was surprised when Roz landed a job on a national newspaper because she hadn't excelled at school and had only just managed to scrape a place at university.

She started to skim read the column, desperate to get to the end so that she'd know the worst, but, as her brain fought to keep up with her eyes, she realised she wasn't taking any of it in. She returned to the start, consciously slowing her thoughts, scanning the text, line-by-line, trying to absorb its meaning. She heard a couple of young girls at the checkout muttering giddily to the malnourished shelf-stacker. Something had amused them, and she wondered if it was the sight of a flushed, elderly woman, dressed in a leopard print onesie and running shoes, rifling through yesterday's paper. If only they knew why she was there – searching for mention of a humiliating sexual perfidy from her past – their laughter would surely be louder and more damning.

As she read, she felt the stabbing pain of shame and regret grow deeper. Susan's funeral had been enough of a trial, but she had forced herself to attend the service at least, as she knew her absence would be noticed and then questioned. She had long ago hoped that, in time, she could forget about her time with George, her greatest regret that was so out of character. When she considered now what did then, she didn't recognise herself. At the time she'd barely considered Susan's feelings beyond labouring under the delusion that she was somehow doing her friend a favour. Everyone knew Susan and George had a barely serviceable marriage, and he was clear with her that they hadn't slept together since Melvyn was born. She somehow convinced herself their relationship wasn't adulterous because, for both, it was all about the sex and in that sense she wasn't taking anything away from Susan. She saw no contradiction in giving George what he wasn't getting at home.

The furtiveness of it had made her feel young again and the threat of being caught only added to the excitement. She was flattered that George appeared to find her so desirable, that she inflamed such passion in him. She realised he was probably frustrated by the enforced celibacy of his marriage, but she delighted in imagining she was more attractive to him than Susan and that her sexuality alone was responsible for his rampant libido.

Of course, now she knew better. Having sex with George was far from the erotic Shangri La she'd imagined at the time, when she was lost in a mirage of idealism and vanity. The sex may have been frequent and frenetic, but he did little to reciprocate the attentions she paid to satisfying him. There was no tenderness and, for someone married with children and, she imagined, experienced, his technique was clumsy and unpractised. She thought perhaps it was a symptom of their circumstances – snatched opportunities on car seats and borrowed hours in hotel rooms meant everything was hurried and functional. As George explained in mitigation, following another rushed and unsatisfying encounter, that limited-over cricket was, by its nature, quicker and more physical and it required more speed of delivery, than the traditional five-day test format. Linda told him that, just once, she'd have settled for five minutes.

She never considered herself a risk taker, particularly not with sex, and she should have foreseen that going to bed with a married man was out of character for a reason.

The experience of sex as subterfuge left only the memory of its deceit. Just as she had betrayed her friend, she felt cuckolded by the act itself because, she realised, sex is only ever meaningful in the present, in the urge, and when the urge leaves you, the whole enterprise seems like a ridiculous waste of time.

After her husband died, she missed the intimacy of being with someone with whom she had shared experiences and she made the mistake of believing she could replicate that feeling with George, if only they spent enough time together. But it never happened. That's not to say they didn't have good times – she wouldn't have stayed with him for so long if they hadn't – but too often their enjoyment seemed coincidental. They took pleasure in different things and so their experiences never seemed to be shared. There was no emotional connection.

Following Frank's death she threw herself into her job because she knew from previous traumas and tragedies how comforting the company of numbers could be. They were perfect and true, immutable and enduring, and independent of context or judgement. They didn't wither or disappear on a whim. She was an atheist because she thought numbers were more dependable than any supposed god. Belief in them didn't require blind, irrational faith because they were incontestable, infinite and eternal, and their beauty was absolute. She was initially attracted to George because they both saw meaning and purity in numbers, but it wasn't enough to keep them together. Perhaps, if circumstances had been different, things might have worked out between them, but she doubted it. There was a problem with George, and she still hadn't worked out what it was.

She ended it with him eventually and the guilt was immediate. It ate at her from within and, in time, it began to show on the outside; she was convinced of that. She did everything she could to delay the onset of ageing with cosmetics, potions, diet and exercise and for a while it worked, but then it caught up with her like a revenue inspector nailing a tax dodger. Every morning glance in the bathroom mirror felt like finding another brown envelope on the doormat – another line, another unflattering angle; her hair was thinner and more brittle, her skin looser and paler.

Frank died 30 years ago to the month and it occurred to her that their nineteen years spent together now accounted for less than a quarter of her life. For most of the rest of it she'd been alone. Had she not spent those wasted years of furtive shadow-dancing with George, would she be happier? Could she have met someone who was kinder and more worthy? Might she even have remarried? Perhaps, she thought, but probably not. There was to be no life after George, not in that sense. No relationships. Certainly no more affairs. Was that because of George? Was it because of who or what he was? Her only comfort was she hadn't planned it that way, it's just how things had worked out. The one thing she was able to conclude for certain was how lucky she'd been with Frank.

She closed the newspaper and dropped it in the trolley which she pushed along the next available aisle, feigning interest in a shelf of sauces and pickles. After a few moments, confident she wasn't being overlooked, she retrieved it and tried again to read the article.

By Rosalind Boucher

Let me preface this column by declaring an interest. The subject I have chosen to write about was inspired by a man who's very close to me. Some may accuse me of abusing my position, rightly pointing out that most people aren't in the privileged situation of being able to use a platform in a national newspaper, with access to hundreds of thousands of readers, to grind personal axes. But I believe the case of this man, whose name I can't reveal for legal reasons, highlights an issue that affects many more people and, for that reason, is worthy of public discussion.

The man in question has been charged and, if convicted, he faces possible imprisonment, for an alleged action that some people might regard as a natural expression of human sexuality – it is claimed he had an erection. He didn't expose his erection or do anything with it. He simply experienced it while dancing with a girl who, while several years younger than him, is an adult. Her complaint, that this man became aroused while in her company, was enough for Crown prosecutors to decide there was justification for him to be charged with sexual assault.

She couldn't read anymore because her heart was beating fast and she felt the stabbing pain to the point where she thought she might faint. She dropped the newspaper into the trolley and tried to walk but her legs felt too weak to move. She recalled the first proper conversation she ever had with George, at one of the painfully stilted, formal gatherings thrown by Susan when she still made the pretence of having a working marriage. She and Susan had met at a therapy group shortly after Frank died after her GP convinced her, erroneously it transpired, that she was suffering from depression. At that first drinks party she'd known Susan for only a few weeks, and it was the first time she'd been to her home. She was the only member of the group who was invited, and she'd felt flattered.

She saw another side to the demure woman who convinced the group she was in thrall to a domineering and emotionally absent husband. Susan drank too much, and she spent most of the evening on a sofa, flirting volubly with a wiry obstetrician who clearly had a convincing line in hilarious anecdotes. George, meanwhile, stood apart from the crowd, mute and preoccupied. Occasionally he replenished guests' glasses and offered them crisps and nuts from cut glass bowls, but that was as far as his interaction with them went. If someone talked to him directly, he responded curtly and functionally but didn't seek to prolong the exchange.

After she got to know him properly, Linda was amused watching those who had never met him try to engage with him in conversation – 'the uninitiated', as she called them – as they slowly realised that a simple, informal chat wasn't going to be as simple as they'd imagined. After a few moments, their posture became stiff and restless and their eyes roamed in search of reassurance that the world beyond remained the same. Wary of being rude, they refocused their attention, and tried to adapt to George's peculiar, stop-start way of communicating, before they finally gave up the ghost and extricated themselves from his company.

She was attracted to him from the outset. He was tall, slim and slightly greying and, while no means film-star handsome, well maintained for his age. He dressed like the captain of a golf club in a pristine navy blue, double breasted suit with a matching blue and red striped tie and handkerchief. In one hand he held a tumbler of whisky, and with his other hand he reached down periodically to collect salted peanuts from a bowl that he dispatched purposefully into his mouth. Only after he'd stopped eating did Linda notice that his lips were still moving. The room was divided into small gatherings of people, each of which he regarded in turn, his eyes dashing from one to the other. Every minute or so, he glanced at his watch.

Linda was nominally involved in a conversation with a couple about whom she could no longer recall a single detail, but her attention was focused on George. After a while she excused herself and walked over to him but, as she stood beside him, he failed to acknowledge her and continued to talk quietly to himself.

'Hi, you must be George,' she said brightly.

He didn't reply.

'Are you counting?'

He glanced at his watch and mapped the digits on its face with an index finger. Then he turned to look at Linda.

'Monitoring,' he said, unsmiling.

'Monitoring what?' she asked.

'In the previous 25 minutes, around 40 per cent of the conversation in the room has been broadly work-related – that is to say, people discussing various aspects of their jobs and job-related activities.'

'Really?' she asked.

'Really.'

She noticed a couple of bloodied nicks on his face where he'd cut himself shaving and, on the shoulders of his suit jacket enough flakes of dandruff for it to be classed as a minor problem. Even if Susan hadn't already rehearsed her marital problems at their counselling sessions, Linda would have known from these signs alone that she and George didn't get on.

They were the sort of thing that, with Frank, she'd have taken care of, tidying up and smoothing over before he was presented to the world.

'33 per cent might be classed as involving the mundane fundamentals of domestic affairs – childcare, schooling, the cost of living, neighbourhood disputes and so on – and 15 per cent have involved the purchase and operation of various items of mechanical and electrical hardware.'

Linda put on her most convincing confused look, but he failed to elaborate.

'Such as?'

'Cars, mainly but also video cassette recorders and hi-fi systems.'

'Ah,' she said.

'And these conversations were conducted almost exclusively by men.'

'Of course.'

'With the exception of the lady in the scarlet frock whose sole contribution to the conversation was to ask who Bang and Olufsen were.'

'Typical.'

'And the remaining ten per cent of conversations might be referred to as an unclassifiable mélange of directionless trivia with frequent references to the sexual act.'

'Mélange?' she asked, smiling.

He glanced at her questioningly, as though unsure about whether she expected a response.

'Not a collection or a mix?'

'No, a mélange.'

His face remained deadpan, his voice flat and monotone. She considered teasing him further but thought better of it.

'Sounds intriguing.'

'All of it has emanated from that party there,' he said, pointing at Susan and the wiry obstetrician.

Linda couldn't help laughing.

'Naturally, I'm rounding up,' he added, soberly.

'Naturally.'

'That's Simon Poynter with my wife.'

'Yes, I was introduced to him when I arrived.'

'He's an obstetrician.'

'Yes, I know.'

'He and Susan are having an affair.'

What shocked Linda more than the information was the dispassionate tone in which it was delivered, as though it was just another detail of his time and motion study of the group's conversation.

'I'm not supposed to know. But I do,' he added.

At that first meeting Linda found George to be vulnerable and even a little sweet; he was unconsciously funny, and she wondered if his reticence in company was perhaps a result of his being sidelined by Susan who was clearly the more sociable of the two. Her therapy group was full of husbands who complained their personalities had become subsumed within the entity of their marriage because they had domineering wives. As she was leaving the party and, perhaps feeling the glow of too much wine, she pecked him on the cheek and told him how handsome he looked in his suit as, gently, she brushed some of the dandruff from his collar.

I don't wish to dwell on the merits of the case – not least because, at this stage in proceedings, the law forbids it. That it has come this far, I believe, says much about the recent shift in power relations between men and women. Women of my mother's generation could expect to have their bottoms pinched and even their breasts fondled as part of everyday office badinage. Anonymous reporting websites recount often shocking historic cases of women being sexually assaulted in the workplace and, when they complained, were disciplined or even sacked without any proper investigation for maligning older or more senior male colleagues. These cases were horrific; they offend our sensibilities, and no right-thinking person wants to see a return to such behaviour by men and to a system that allowed them to get away with it. But I question if, in seeking to rebalance relations between the sexes, we've overshot the mark. Last week I read a report of an employment tribunal case brought by a female teacher offended by male colleagues making derogatory comments about women drivers. In another case, reported earlier this year, a nine-year-old boy in America was suspended from school for sexual harassment after he described his teacher as 'cute'.

In the past three years there have been 47,300 cases of sex discrimination accepted by employment tribunals, according to figures published by the Ministry of Justice. This compares with 22,400 cases of disability discrimination and 15,500 for race discrimination. Sex discrimination accounts for the fourth highest number of cases heard by tribunals; only allegations of unfair dismissal, unauthorized deductions and Breach of Contract account for more cases.

The problem with George was that having been shown a modicum of attention, he was hooked. Offers of practical assistance – running Linda to work when her car was off the road, lifting heavy items, performing DIY tasks – became suggestions of meetings for coffee and lunch dates. She drew the line at dinner, recognising where he appeared not to, that it represented the graduation of their acquaintance onto a different level, that couldn't easily be interpreted as casual or innocent. Nevertheless, he became a fixture in her life without her really planning or wishing for it. All the while she tried to gently apply the brakes to his attentions.

At the start it was flattering to be the subject of such interest but soon it became too much. He was like a dog wearing a plastic neck funnel – incapable of focusing on anything other than what was immediately in front of him, which, most of the time, seemed to be her. When she expressed an interest in a particular singer or band, he bought her a cassette of their latest album; when she praised a writer, he read their books obsessively; when she broke her wrist playing tennis, he registered for first aid classes so he could be of assistance should she suffer a similar injury in the future.

The more she got to know him, the more she saw how he interpreted simple gestures of kindness and understanding as more meaningful than they were intended to be. A hand on the arm, or even standing close to him, was imbued with romantic significance while the mildest rebuke caused him to be grossly offended. Her recounting a conversation she'd had with a male colleague at work was enough to send him into a jealous rage and then, with equal haste, the matter was forgotten. He seemed unaware of these idiosyncrasies until they were pointed out to him and then he would deny them or insist they were normal behaviour.

No one wants to see a return to the bad old days of the sleazy Seventies, and nor should we forget how far we have come. But equally, we should not confuse casual sexism with sexual harassment or sexual harassment with sexual abuse. If I asked my mother and her friends about their experiences at work in the 1970s, most would complain about the office creep or the dirty old man in the store-room, but they'd object in the strongest terms if it was suggested that they were more tolerant than women today. There's a double standard in a society where sexual imagery is ubiquitous and yet, when anyone who shows a modest human reaction to that imagery, they are denounced as depraved. It's like feeding free booze to an alcoholic and then complaining when he gets drunk.

Though George was different in many ways from any man she'd ever met, Linda recognised in him an honest desire to be like everyone else. He often failed comically, but his relentless determination was commendable and sometimes heroic. Though he could often be cold and precipitate to the point of rudeness, he had an endearing formality, like an old school gentleman who never swears and opens doors for ladies.

She couldn't fathom what, considering this, had prompted him to drop his trousers in the middle of her kitchen while she was making him a cup of tea and to present her with a fully alert erection. Other than a goodnight kiss at the end of a party six weeks before, she'd given him no reason to suppose she was interested in a sexual relationship of any kind, far less one with the husband of her friend. Her first instinct was to giggle at the absurdness of this half-naked, middle-aged accountant grinning like an expectant schoolboy as his penis swayed like a shop sign in a breeze. She stifled a laugh, as she continued to proffer a mug of tea, for fear of prompting

229

one of the intemperate outbursts.

'I don't quite know what you think is going to happen, George, but I'm afraid you're going to be disappointed,' she said calmly.

His grin remained fixed.

'What I mean is that I'm not going to have sex with you.'

'Oh, that's unfortunate. Why ever not?' he inquired, like he was asking his bank manager why he didn't qualify for a favourable mortgage rate.

'Well, for a start, because you're married.'

'Susan doesn't love me. And I don't love her,' he protested.

'Well, that may be so, but Susan is my friend.'

'What's that got to do with it?'

Susan's abortion changed everything. It wasn't so much the timing that surprised Linda – Roz was 12 at the time – nor George's claim that they hadn't had sex for years. What shocked her most was that Susan chose to recount every detail of her unsatisfactory affair with the father of her unborn child (a family friend who had 'taken advantage' of her) at a group meeting with such negative disinterest, like she was discussing a washing powder that didn't get her clothes properly clean.

It wasn't just that she appeared to have such a low regard for her husband, in whose ignorance she seemed to revel, but if anything, she was even more contemptuous of her lover. She had no feelings for him, she announced dryly; she didn't even like him particularly, although he could make her laugh when she was drunk. The only time she laughed in George's company was when he humiliated himself with one of his gaffes, but that wasn't the same thing, was it? Sex with Simon was just something to make her feel like she was human, that involved touching and sensing another person without always expecting some catastrophic breakdown along the way that would leave her imagining she'd lost her mind. George thought he looked like a Nazi bus conductor, she added matter-of-factly.

Even if George found out about their affair, he wouldn't object, she insisted, which was worse than if it were to destroy him because it confirmed what she already knew, that he felt nothing for her at all. She couldn't be sure if his lack of emotion was a way of punishing her, or if he was genuinely so insensitive that her betrayal hadn't affected him in any way at all. She couldn't possibly love someone who was capable of such detachment, but then she added that clearly, she must have some feelings toward him, even if it was just the anger she kept buried deep within her, that she couldn't express or rid herself of. That, she said, came from somewhere she couldn't identify. Was it normal? Was she normal? She asked the group.

'Of course, you're normal, Susan,' the others chorused, although Linda wasn't so sure.

Susan would rather not have had to explain any of it – her affair with Simon Poynter, her pregnancy, her absence of feeling toward her husband – she told the group. She was seeking an abortion but, in the meantime, she would initiate sex with George, for the first time in years, to cover her tracks, in case he ever found out about the pregnancy. The ensuing silence in the echoing hall, where every cough and shuffle on the hard, plastic seats was magnified, felt long and oppressive. The group leader, a frail, soft-spoken Irish woman, told Linda on her first visit that after a few visits she'd stop noticing the overpowering smell of adolescent gym hall sweat, but she hadn't believed her. Not until then.

When we judge such cases, we should be mindful that often what we feel most strongly about is the abuse of power rather than the seriousness of the crime. A television presenter who gropes a 16-year-old girl in his dressing room may be a sleazy, slobbering creep who betrays the trust

231

placed in him by the girl's parents and the general public, but betrayal of trust is not a crime. The same girl may well have been groped by a 15, or even an 18 or 19 year-old boy round the back of the chip shop the night before but we don't regard that as being remotely in the same context, far less as an offence that the police should be troubled with. The girl may even have had sexual intercourse with her boyfriend when they were both 15, both breaking the law, but a law that is routinely ignored in the name of common sense and police staff rotas.

The first time Linda had sex with George, he brought along a pornographic video he acquired by mail order from a post office box number in Hamburg, which he described as 'research'. Linda had never seen a sex film before and, from the luridly blurred cover shot of what appeared to be a fully operational gangbang in progress, she had no intention of starting now. George appeared disconsolate when she told him to put it away, like a child being told he wasn't getting any pudding. She asked him if Susan had ever consented to viewing such material, and he conceded she hadn't. He blushed and dropped his navy Y-fronts with white piping.

'Susan must never know about this,' Linda said solemnly.

'I don't see why, she wouldn't bat an eyelid,' George replied dispassionately.

'Because she mustn't. It would create all sorts of difficulties.'

'Difficulties for whom?'

'For her, for us, for your children.'

'Why should it affect my children?'

'She mustn't know, George.'

'Fine.'

'Promise me she won't find out.'

'She won't find out.'

'Promise me, George.'

'I promise. She won't find out.'

No one should excuse bad behaviour by older men, and it goes without saying that that includes the all too frequent examples of abuse that rightly end up in the courts. But we should also be wary of seeking to legislate maleness out of existence. No should always mean no, but if we allow the politically correct, zero tolerance agenda to override common sense, then we lose the ability to discriminate between what is shocking and dangerous, rather than what may be inappropriate but ultimately harmless.

The next soiree thrown by Susan was noticeably different from the first one Linda attended. The crowd was thinner and it had a bottom-of-the-barrel feel – bored neighbours vying for a place at the head of the buffet queue, comparing notes on their experience of local schools; local society worthies with wine halitosis and friends of Susan who looked like they'd become lost on their way to a pottery night class. Susan was winking drunk by the time Linda arrived and Simon Poynter was nowhere to be seen.

'He's NFI'd,' she replied when Linda inquired about him.

'NFI'd?'

'Nae fuckin' invited,' she said, trying to wrap her lingering Canadian drawl around her idea of the Edinburgh vernacular, before falling away, laughing.

George hovered around Linda with the same self-satisfied expression he'd worn since she had consented to them sleeping together. He had changed in that time, appearing more outgoing and voluble, and his dress sense appeared to have changed from gentlemen's outfitter to supermarket casual. He was energised by a sexual charge that Linda found flattering, but his unceasing attention was sometimes exhausting. He seemed to have two modes – sexually aroused and asleep – and she felt like he was taking out a lifetime of enforced celibacy and frustration on her.

Anyone else would have rightly regarded his behaviour as a flagrant insult to his wife. Linda could see that, while he might be able to understand, technically, the meaning of terms such as empathy and loyalty, he didn't necessarily feel them, at least not in the way other people did.

She was chatting idly to a balding drone from Intermediate Life Drawing – several large glasses of wine had slipped over in quick succession, making her more tolerant that she might otherwise have felt – when George approached and placed his hand on her backside. Without acknowledging him, she eased it free and handed him her half-empty wine glass.

'Be a sweetie, George, and top me up, would you?' she asked, glancing around the room to see who might have caught sight of such a gesture of intimacy.

Fortunately, Susan was standing with her back to them and everyone else seemed otherwise engaged. George took hold of the wine glass but remained standing, eyes glazed over from the booze and wearing an idiotic grin. The man, who had monopolised most of the conversation, continued unabashed though she had little memory of what he said.

'Come with me now, there's something I need you to see,' George said with the forced precision of someone aware they have had too much to drink.

He didn't drink as much or as often as Susan, but when he did, it was like he was quenching a thirst. Linda was glad to be rescued from the dull life drawer, but she didn't want to offend him by cutting him off in the middle of his story.

'I'll be with you shortly,' she told George, gently but insistently. 'I'm talking to this delightful gentleman.'

Linda smiled and did her best to follow the thread of his conversation which included, she vaguely recalled, the embarrassing fate that had befallen a hapless nude model at one of his recent classes.

'Nude, you say?' George interjected.

The man halted his speech briefly and gave an unconvincing smile.

'As I was saying, the model in question was perhaps carrying a larger undercarriage than was healthy for a lady of her age, particularly around the -'

'What, totally nude?'

The man stopped talking and the veneer of tolerance washed from his face.

'Yes, totally nude. It's a life drawing class.'

George stood motionless with a fathomless expression, his eyes flickering like they were lit by a loose connection. The man stepped backwards and tendered his open palm as an invitation for him and Linda to move on. George took her by the arm and led her in the direction of the doorway, laughing leerily, as though sharing a joke with himself.

'I demand that you come with me now,' he announced haughtily, leading her from the room.

She was aware that some guests were looking at them and she smiled, doing her best to project light-hearted normality. Conscious that George seemed unaware of the signal his behaviour was sending, she followed.

In the hallway he manoeuvred her against a wall and began to kiss her hungrily.

'George, not here, what if someone sees us,' she protested, feeling her heart racing.

He pulled up her skirt and placed his hand roughly down the front of her knickers.

'George,' she said, removing his hand and smoothing down her dress with some urgency. There were traces of her lipstick around his mouth and she reached over to thumb them off. He grabbed her hand and began kissing her again. The effects of the wine and the nervousness she felt at being caught gave her a feeling of sexual excitement and she kissed him back. As his hands reached again for her skirt, she pushed him away.

'We can't do anything here. Is there somewhere we can go?' she asked breathlessly.

He led her to the top of the stair and, when they reached the landing, he began to kiss her again, vigorously. He moved his body closer and held it tightly against hers and she felt the prominence of his erection pressed against her stomach.

'Not here, George, what if someone needs to go to the bathroom?'

He released the pressure of his body on hers and, as she stood upright, she felt nervous and lightheaded. He took hold of her hand and pulled her and she allowed herself to be led down the hallway. Linda had never been upstairs in his house before and she was surprised at how unlived in it seemed. The carpets and curtains looked like post-war hangovers from previous owners and there was no occasional furniture or paintings on the walls. It struck her that the rest of the house was the same – sterile and untouched by the personalities of either George or Susan. Both, it appeared, were reluctant to leave any imprint of themselves on it.

They arrived at one of four identical oakwood doors and George's grin widened as he turned the tarnished brass handle before leading her into what she assumed was a spare bedroom. Fearing that other guests might find their way upstairs, she closed the door behind them. The room was in darkness with only a strip of light at the foot of the door from the hallway offering any sense of orientation. She felt dizzy at her sudden lack of vision and her legs buckled as she became aware of a small build-up of cold moisture that had gathered at the back of her neck.

She felt the warm, reassuring grip of George's hand on hers as he led her hurriedly a few paces forward until her shin hit something hard and she sank to her knees, feeling sick with pain. Realising it was the base of a bed she laughed, and only then did she become aware she'd been holding her breath. She gasped and began sucking in air, hungry for oxygen.

George lifted her to her feet and put his hand over her mouth to silence her as he eased her onto a mattress and the soft springiness gave way beneath her weight. She heard him unbuckle his belt and unzip his trousers and he lowered himself on top of her. His weight was difficult for her to bear and she struggled to pull her pants down over her thighs. The smell of his aftershave hit her, and the danger and illicitness of the circumstances made her feel a tingling of excitement between her legs. She felt the firm tip of his erection against her midriff and she squirmed with anticipation. His actions were rough and frantic and she whispered for him to slow down and to relax. She was transported back to her early teenage sexual encounters with boys who, lacking a basic geography of the female form, assumed that if they continued to push hard enough and for long enough, sooner or later they'd find themselves buried in something warm and wet. She wanted more than that.

She took hold of his hips tried to hold him still above her, to regulate his movement, to enjoy the anticipation and sensations of their bodies coming together. She was aware of George's open mouth hovering above hers and the feeling of his hot, anxious breath on her face as he ground his pelvis against her harder, groaning with delight. He stopped and she became aware of a warmth spreading across her stomach. He flopped on top of her, his body limp, and breathed heavily with relief and exhaustion.

In the stillness of the room, she suddenly became aware of an event. She couldn't tell where it had happened or even what it was – a sound or a movement – all she was able to deduce was that it had occurred independently of her and George.

'Shush,' she whispered sharply.

'What?' George said.

'Shush,' she repeated.

She held her breath and forced herself to be perfectly still and she willed George to do the same to prevent any noise that inhibited her ability to focus. She screwed her eyes shut tightly and mind conjured kaleidoscopic illusions of white light. Her ears pulsed with the deafening sound of silence. There it was again.

George said nothing. She refocused, emptying her mind of everything. She heard breathing. It wasn't her and it wasn't George. It was coming from somewhere else in the room. Then she heard movement, a swishing sound that appeared to confirm her worst fears.

'Is there someone else in the room?' she whispered so quietly George didn't hear.

She repeated the question, but he remained silent.

In the moment of shocking realisation, she summoned the strength to push his body from under her and to free herself.

'My God, this isn't one of the kids' rooms, George? Tell me this isn't one of the kids' rooms.'

She stood up, straightened her clothing and made for the doorway.

Human nature hasn't changed so fundamentally in a generation. What has changed is our tolerance of bad behaviour. We no longer accept that there should be any circumstance in which a woman is degraded by the words or actions of a man, particularly one who has power over her through age or position and rightly so. Men guilty of historic abuses are not judged by the mores of the time that the abuse took place which, at best, turned a blind eye to it or, at worst, tolerated it or even condoned it. They are condemned retrospectively by more enlightened attitudes which hold that, even if everyone around them was behaving similarly, they should have known better. A corollary of such an outcome is that those women who lived through such times and were on the receiving end of the abuse may feel complicit because, by implication, they too should have known better than to let it happen without shouting about it from the rooftops.

Linda wondered if Roz was right and if things really were so different today. She often read in magazines and heard on television that it was so, but she didn't believe it. For times to change, it required people to change and she wasn't sure that had happened.

She couldn't read any more. She dropped the newspaper in the basket and left it stranded in the aisle. She walked across the car park in tears, shrouded by the orange, fluorescent glow of the streetlights, wishing she hadn't made the trip in the first place. She felt ashamed, not only for what she'd done all those years ago, but doubly so for having spent the intervening time fearful about what Roz knew and might reveal. Of course, she'd given some thought to the impact the episode might have had on her and how much it may have damaged her, but not enough. She drove home slowly, feeling sick and lonely. Her hands trembled on the steering wheel and cold tears stung her eyes like they were punishing her. As she approached her house, she saw the silhouette of a figure standing hunched in the driveway. She opened her car door.

'Hello, George,' she said.

Chapter 15

The New Town, Edinburgh, later that morning

Melvyn could recall precisely the discussion that led him to re-evaluate everything that had happened in his life up to that point. He was still young enough that every adult experience was novel and many were challenging, but this was more so than any before, leading him to question if the world was as it appeared to him and whether he should accept it at face value. Studying law, he was taught to question everything, to take nothing for granted and to be sure of all the facts before prosecuting an argument. If that should be the case in his professional life, then why should he not apply the same standard of inquiry in his personal life? As he learned about different things, met new people, faced fresh challenges, he began to doubt his faith in his own judgement.

Graduating from adolescence to adulthood, from school to university, listening to new and diverse voices, hearing other people's stories and opinions and watching how they communicated and engaged with each other, he wondered if his understanding and expectations were the same as everyone else's – whether he was normal.

The discussion that made such an impact on him took place during a tutorial on moot – the language and practice of legal debate – when his tutor Dr Dan, a likeable hippy but given to infuriating tautology, described the atmosphere in a courtroom during a criminal trial. He explained how a group dynamic is often formed between the various parties – prosecution, defence, trial judge, defendant, witnesses – when the first ripples of emotion start to wash over the room like waves on a shoreline. From there, tension can build, giving way to stronger currents that generate their own momentum. According to Dr Dan, in those circumstances it was incumbent on the criminal lawyer to recognise those flows and to use them to his or her advantage. Identifying a point in proceedings when the mood of the court starts to change in your favour, and to seize those opportunities, was a test for every counsel, he said. The legal system is based on a zero-sum game principle, where winning is the desired outcome and, as such, you must convince the jury or sheriff of the merits of your argument, and that how something is said is often as important as what is actually said. To meet that challenge, you must be able to identify when there is a lack of conviction in your adversary's argument and to capitalise on those weaknesses.

Melvyn watched as his classmates nodded appreciatively, scribbling in their notepads, while he sat motionless, without the faintest clue what Dr Dan was talking about. He felt sick. The same sickness he experienced after waking from a recurring dream he'd been having since childhood, in which he was alone on a bus as it pulled away from a stop, with his parents standing on the pavement, waving him away. He didn't know why he was on the bus, where it was headed or why his parents had abandoned him. He tried to scream at the driver to stop, but he'd lost his voice. He tried to cry, but no tears came. He tried to show how scared he was, but none of the passengers paid him any attention. He continued to experience different versions of the dream, particularly at times of stress, like when Anthony died, but there were some constant elements – he was always a schoolboy with the same helpless fear of being driven into the unknown.

Dr Dan's discussion cemented in Melvyn's mind what, until then, had been a vague but compelling suspicion that, somewhere along the line, he had missed something important that everyone else knew about and, from that moment, he felt deracinated from his own reality, barred from a secret no one would let him in on.

The feeling recurred when he listened to people recount

stories of small talk and casual friendships struck up whilst they bought something from a shop, or stepped into a lift, or waited in a queue, or visited their doctor – anything that involved personal interaction, that contained within it, terms and ideas familiar to others but not to him. Giving someone space, gauging their mood, watching their expression, valuing their feelings, letting them express themselves – all were abstract phrases he heard that, like convoluted idioms in a foreign language, gave a hint of their underlying meaning, but which he could never use convincingly for fear of misapplying them or using them inappropriately. They were, to him, intangible notions like antimatter or black holes used by other people whose understanding of them was informed and whose word he was obliged to accept because he didn't know any different.

When he and Mary went to the cinema together during the early years of their marriage, they often discussed afterwards what they'd taken from the film they had seen and he wondered if they'd been sitting in the same theatre. To him, the pleasure of watching a movie was like ticking off a checklist; the satisfaction of charting its progress methodically, waiting and spotting the first inciting incident, the timing of the first main reversal, pulling together the symmetry of the main plot and subplots and, if the film was any good, of drawing together all the critical elements as it reached a satisfactory conclusion. Mary talked about the strength of the characters and of their motives and desires, of themes and mood; elements which, if they were intentional by the writer or director – and Melvyn wasn't convinced they were – had passed him by entirely.

Perhaps if he had been able to address this absence in his understanding when he was younger it would no longer have such a hold on him now, but he hadn't, and even contemplating it was like clinging to a rising balloon. The older he got the more fearful he was of letting go because of the embarrassment he knew he would face for having allowed it to persist. It would redefine him at work – how could a man who wasn't right in the head be responsible for running a multi-million-pound business? And it would affect his relationships – how would Mary feel if he were to admit that all the foundations on which their marriage was based – love, affection, devotion and loyalty – were empty terms he used but didn't understand, their meaning and efficacy he took for granted, like shampoo or engine oil, because all the work had been done by other people?

Now, as he sat around the boardroom table with his wife and father-in-law and Robert's nieces lined up against him like a firing squad, he felt the same fear he experienced in the lecture theatre with Dr Dan all those years ago. For all the words being spoken and the arguments developed, which he gave every impression of following and appreciating, there was an important part to all of them that he knew, instinctively, everyone but him understood. Connections were made and conclusions drawn following a logic that he simply couldn't follow. Nebulous, elusive terms like perception, reputation, value and allegiance were thrown around like balls for him to chase and, just when he'd given up on one, another was cast in the same direction from which he'd just returned empty handed.

'We can't allow things to slide indefinitely; every hour we stay silent is another hour of falling share prices and devalued stock,' said Elspeth for whom Melvyn had created a sinecure position with an ambiguous enough title to keep her convinced of her continued value to the company while simultaneously preventing her from being able to do any real damage.

'I don't see how we can do anything other than remain silent,' Rhona asserted. 'If we make any statement about George, then we simply invite further questions about his whereabouts and, if it were revealed that we don't know,

243

we will look even less in control of the situation than we do already.'

'What I don't understand is how he could just have disappeared from the face of the earth,' Robert complained rattily.

Melvyn had yet to contribute to the meeting and he felt his silence had become conspicuous.

'He hasn't disappeared from the face of the earth. Clearly he still exists, somewhere,' he said, making what he thought to be a necessary point.

'Oh, for Christ's sake, Melvyn, don't split hairs, not now, not at a time like this,' Mary chided.

He felt betrayed by his wife who was aware of the efforts to which he'd gone to track down his father and yet still she sided with her father. He had left numerous messages on George's mobile, urging him to get in touch, until there was no space left on his voicemail; he'd forced his way into George's house and turned the place upside down, ransacking every drawer and cupboard for clues to his whereabouts; he'd contacted all of his father's acquaintances which, in truth, wasn't a long list, without success and, of course he phoned the police who needed no reminding of his absence.

Since his disappearance from the court two days ago now, the only contact George had made was an abusive text to Roz. Melvyn had done everything in his power to find his father and yet Mary appeared to give him no credit for his efforts. Far less did she seem to appreciate what a difficult character his father could be and the strain it put on Melvyn, having had to assume the main responsibility for looking after him since his mother's passing.

'Elspeth is right. We must do something. We can't sit around waiting for George to turn up while the reputation of the firm goes down the toilet,' Robert said. 'I didn't devote most of my life to building up a reputation in this community only to see it destroyed by a -'

'Yes, I think we know that we have to reach a decision today on the way forward,' Mary interjected. 'That's not in question.'

If there was an absence in Melvyn's understanding of the world, then he was sure it existed for his father's too. What appeared normal to Melvyn as a child and a young adult, after all, had been shaped by the attitudes and behaviours of his parents. Only when he was old enough to compare his own life story with those of his peers, did he start to question his perception of what, if anything, was commonplace. If this absence existed, why had it never been identified or even noticed by his parents? More presciently, why had it taken 18 years and a chance discussion prompted by a university lecturer for him to identify it? Why, in the multitude of his childhood experiences and in all the conversations he'd had with his parents as he was growing up, didn't they do or say anything to indicate that his view of normality was anything other than, well, normal? Why were they seemingly unable to explain to him how the world worked – not in a physical or philosophical sense, but in practical ways such as how to make and keep friends, to start and hold a conversation, to avoid upsetting people and getting on their nerves, to behave generously, or to show someone you love them and keep showing them you love them without having to think about it.

While he had reflected on those questions periodically throughout his life, he had long ago concluded that it was neither possible nor desirable to chase any conclusive answers. He would have to consider apportioning blame and he was either unwilling or perhaps unable to do that. He couldn't blame his father who had given everything he could to teach his children everything he knew – the value of numbers and equations, symbols and proofs, formulae and reactions and every other fact in his possession that might provide them with a helping hand, stand them in good stead,

245

show them the way. He gave them all of his time – all the time he had. He gave them the security of routine and repetition: meals at the same time every day, always on time for school, bedtime before the watershed. He gave them love in the only way he knew how, not an emotional, effusive love but a pragmatic demonstration of unconditional devotion, which Melvyn believed, when viewed in its entirety, amounted to something more valuable than embraces and mawkish words of comfort. If his father had the same absence in his understanding, that made him ill-equipped to deal with the multitude of everyday situations that other people took as read, then he had taken steps to adapt, to forced himself to learn new skills and coping mechanisms, to convince others, and perhaps himself, that nothing was amiss.

Nor could Melvyn lay blame for this absence on his mother, whom he understood had been incapable of coping with the demands of life. He learned from a memorable discussion with his mother when he was a teenager that she felt she was misled into believing George was something he wasn't and that, by the time she discovered the truth, it was too late for either of them to do anything about it. Coming from a French speaking province of Canada, she was separated from him by language and culture which, she recalled, encouraged her in the mistaken belief that his reticence and solitariness were signs of his British reserve. Far from interpreting them as constituting an 'absence', she believed they were rare qualities and virtues that highlighted his innate modesty and courteousness. Despite the obvious chasm of understanding that existed between them, he never heard his mother complain. It was the only time he remembered his mother discuss her relationship with George in such terms and because of that, it had lodged deeply and colourfully in his mind.

It was a glorious, warm and sunlit day during the long

school summer holiday, the morning after one of his parents' Saturday soirees. Linda Walker had left her headscarf behind the night before and George volunteered to drive to her home to return it. While he was away, Susan was secreted with Roz in her bedroom, discussing something in hushed tones, which Melvyn assumed was an issue of female only concern. He thought it a bit soon for his sister to have her period, but he was by no means an expert on menstruation which he recalled only in sketchy detail from a sex education class at school. They emerged a short time later and it appeared that both had been crying. Melvyn always felt uncomfortable around tearful people and he sought to avoid them, but his mother was insistent that he join her and Roz in the lounge, because there was something she wanted to discuss with them.

In the aftermath of the previous night's revelries, the room had a musky, penitent smell of stale tobacco and smeared lipstick. Half-drunk glasses and overflowing ashtrays littered surfaces like forgotten clues at a crime scene, while wine-spattered cushions were strewn on the floor still bearing the retained impressions of overfed backsides.

Susan collected the cushions and reconstructed the sofa, with the offending marks turned downward, and she insisted on the three of them sitting tightly together while her fist clutched a crumpled ball of toilet paper that she had used to mop her eyes. Roz was still crying and was clearly determined to continue the conversation they'd been having in the bedroom. His sister rarely cried, and he recalled this occasion for the volume and ferocity of her tears. Though Melvyn had no evidence to support a notion that had long been lodged stubbornly at the back of his mind that, for reasons he couldn't even begin to explain, their state of upset, and the conversation that followed, somehow involved Linda Walker.

'You would never leave us, would you, Mum?' Roz

asked, haltingly.

Melvyn thought this an odd question for his sister to ask as it had never occurred to him that their mother would go anywhere.

'Where would I go, without my children?' she asked.

'You might go to Canada,' Roz said through her tears.

'Why would I go to Canada?'

'Because that's where you're from. It's where your family lives.'

Susan cupped Roz's face in her hands and kissed her forehead.

'You are my family, and my place is here. With you.'

'But how do we know you won't go? How can we be sure?'

'Because I'm telling you now that I never will.'

'But you might,' his sister insisted. 'This isn't your home; Toronto is your home and you're miserable here. You said so yourself. I want you to stay here with us, with Daddy and Melvyn, but I don't want you to be miserable. It makes me scared that one day you won't be able to stand it any longer and that you'll go without telling anybody.'

Roz was skinny and shilpit, with the androgynous look of a child on the cusp of puberty. Tears ran down her pale, freckled face, between the tiny pimples on her pink cheeks. Recalling it now, Melvyn found it difficult to reconcile the tough, redoubtable adult with the crumpled little girl, drowning in his oversized jumper, with strands of flyaway hair matted to her cheeks as she clung to her mother and broke her heart. Whenever he thought about that day, and he often did, he believed the feeling of undulating nervous energy that coursed through his chest and stomach was one of the closest times he ever came to experiencing proper sadness.

'When he does show up eventually, that's only the start

of our problems,' Robert prognosticated. 'We're not out of the woods at that stage, not by any means. Then he must go to trial, and we can only hope he does the decent thing and pleads guilty. I mean, can you even give us that guarantee, Melvyn?'

The old man sat hunched over the boardroom table that Melvyn imagined had seen hundreds of clients smooth-talked over the years – all of them small potatoes compared with the many high ticket, complex cases the modern company handled, concurrently and across multiple jurisdictions, under his leadership.

'No, I can't, Robert, because he's told me he's innocent. So why, in those circumstances, should he plead guilty?'

'Oh, for Christ's sake, Melvyn, of course he's guilty,' his father-in-law bellowed, his jowls shaking like an excited bloodhound. 'Everyone knows he's guilty, even your own sister knows it, though according to her too-clever-by-half reckoning, it's the fault of the child he molested.'

'She's not a child,' Melvyn corrected dryly.

'It's a mystery to me that she gets paid for writing that drivel, but then my views are probably not progressive enough for today's generation. In my day *The Sentinel* was a reputable newspaper.'

'Come on now, Dad, we agreed we wouldn't make this personal,' Mary said.

The problem for Melvyn was that he knew his father might well be guilty under the letter of the law, but still believe himself to be innocent. He'd been here before, after all, as a 19-year-old second year law student, who was suddenly and unwillingly appointed by his father as Lead Counsel for the Defence in the matter of George Eric Lovelace versus Carlton Stenhouse LLP and latterly, in the case of The Crown versus George Eric Lovelace. To be assigned such a level of responsibility at that age should have been a matter of pride to the young Melvyn, but then he discovered the material facts of the case and that no other paid, qualified lawyer could be found who was willing to take on the work.

The case was presented by his father as perfectly straightforward. George Eric Lovelace, an employee of Carlton Stenhouse LLP, had approached a colleague, his immediate superior, and suggested they spend a holiday together in Andalusia, Spain. Said superior, one Martin Mungo Gillies, had declined the invitation. Conscious that the motive behind his invitation may have been misunderstood, Mr Lovelace sought to clarify his position and repeated the invitation, which was again declined. This second refusal led to a cooling in the relationship between the two named and resulted in Mr Lovelace being charged with gross professional misconduct and summarily dismissed.

Judging this action to be both unfair and disproportionate, Mr Lovelace subsequently appealed against the dismissal. The original decision being upheld, Mr Lovelace sought to bring the matter before an industrial tribunal, accusing his erstwhile employer of unfair dismissal. Conceding that it had acted unfairly and disproportionately, the firm of Carlton Stenhouse LLP withdrew and agreed to settle the matter privately. While substantial and generous compensation was subsequently paid to the claimant, the firm, acting perversely and contrary to the rules of natural justice, refused to reinstate Mr Lovelace to his former position.

Those were the facts, according to George, but in testimony disclosed to Melvyn there was another, quite different interpretation applied to them. Mr Gillies claimed to have been quite taken aback by Mr Lovelace's initial invitation to go on holiday. The pair had been colleagues for several years and yet, to Mr Gillies' recollection, they had never engaged in a conversation that was not work related. Mr Gillies did not recall ever discussing anything remotely relevant to his personal life with Mr Lovelace, far less a liking for the south of Spain, and he did not consider them to be anything other than colleagues. When Mr Gillies refused the invitation, his junior colleague reacted in an unnecessarily aggressive way. In the course of subsequent days, Mr Lovelace took issue with a number of routine work-related requests made by Mr Gillies that in the past he had fulfilled without question and, on several occasions, raised his voice, including at a departmental meeting which caused some embarrassment to Mr Gillies.

Mr Lovelace subsequently approached his senior colleague a second time and reiterated his invitation for the pair to holiday together. On this occasion Mr Lovelace stated that he had an 'intellectual desire to holiday with a homosexual' and that 'everyone in the office knew [Mr Gillies] was queer'. Mr Lovelace added that he had 'no desire to bugger or be buggered' but that he would like to have the opportunity to 'act a bit faggy' in an environment where such behaviour would not be considered abnormal. In his evidence, Mr Gillies said he had been left bewildered and alarmed by Mr Lovelace's comments, which he considered crass and believed constituted an unwelcome invasion into his personal affairs.

He had always sought to keep the issue of his sexuality private and he resented such an intrusion by Mr Lovelace. He told his junior colleague that if he didn't drop the matter, then he would have no option but to lodge an official complaint through the company's personnel department. According to Mr Gillies, Mr Lovelace appeared to take this as a challenge and went out of his way to make it clear to Mr Gillies that he did not believe he had acted inappropriately. When Mr Lovelace approached him a third time, reiterating the invitation, Mr Gillies feared the matter would not be resolved unless he made an official complaint.

In written testimony by one Charles Forsyth, Personnel Director for Carlton Stenhouse LLP, Mr Lovelace was summoned to an initial meeting to discuss the complaint against him. While he agreed with 'almost every word' of Mr Gillies' account, he refused to accept that he had done anything wrong. Despite being given the opportunity to apologise to Mr Gillies and to agree to desist from any further such approaches, Mr Lovelace continued to insist that he had done nothing for which it was necessary to apologise. When informed that his failure to do so would result in further disciplinary action, Mr Lovelace appeared instead to become obsessed with procedural detail, in particular to the company's apparent failure to follow industrial relations law to the letter. The company concluded that, under the circumstances and given Mr Lovelace's continued uncompromising and confrontational attitude, it had no option but to proceed with disciplinary action.

'I know we agreed we wouldn't make it personal, Mary, but I simply can't understand the man's attitude,' Robert said, his face scorched with righteous anger.

Turning his attention to Melvyn, he continued: 'It doesn't seem to me that you are in any way embarrassed by what has happened.'

A static silence hung in the air as Melvyn faced the collective frowns of the four faces on the other side of the table.

'I ... I don't see why I should feel embarrassed. I've done nothing wrong,' he pleaded. Robert erupted.

'Oh Jesus Christ man, your father has dropped us all in the shit and you sit there insisting you've got nothing to be embarrassed about!'

Melvyn felt his head fill with blood as fear took hold, not of being outwitted – he knew he could more than hold his own with his supposed adversaries – but rather of being exposed emotionally, that he would not understand the human expectations made of him.

'It's not like this is a one off, is it?'

The volume of Robert's voice plummeted to almost whisper, and his tone altered, leaving Melvyn confused and unnerved. He preferred the safer ground of the old man's high decibel anger because the sight of gobbets of white spit flaying from his snooker ball face was easier to read than his current expression of coiled neutrality.

'In the jargon of our law enforcement colleagues, it seems Mr Lovelace Senior has "previous" with this sort of behaviour.'

He scanned his father-in-law's features and listened intently to the register of his voice, monitoring its timbre for any giveaways. Robert's jaw continued to tremble – aftershocks from his previous outburst – and, while he thought he detected a slight upward movement of his lips, redolent of a thin smile, he couldn't be sure.

'Oh yes, we know all about that, don't we?' he said, leering across the table at him. 'He's done this before, hasn't he? Don't think we don't all know about your family's dirty little secret.'

Melvyn glanced at Mary in the hope that she might offer a clue or some sign of support, but her eyes remained fixed on the printed agenda sheet on the desk in front of her.

'And despite that, you continue to protect him and to insist that he's innocent. For the love of God, what kind of man are you?'

'Dad...' Mary said, finally believing that her father had crossed a line.

'He hasn't done this before. The facts of the previous case you refer to were quite different from this one,' Melvyn protested quietly.

Robert scoffed.

'He has a previous conviction for sexual harassment, we know. His lawyer told Mary all about it.'

'Dad.'

'Something which, in more than 20 years of marriage, you failed to tell her.'

'Dad.'

'Don't you think that's something you ought to have told your wife about at some point?'

'Dad, please.'

Melvyn remained impassive.

'The facts of that case were quite different from this one,' he repeated.

Having ignored a written warning, urging him to apologise to Mr Gillies and to agree to desist from further abusive behaviour, Mr Lovelace was suspended from duty pending further disciplinary action, according to testimony disclosed to Melvyn. Despite this, Mr Lovelace continued to turn up for work, insisting his suspension was illegal and unenforceable as Carlton Stenhouse LLP had failed to follow proper procedures. Considering this, the company moved to immediate dismissal on the grounds of gross professional misconduct.

Mr Lovelace then lodged a claim for unfair dismissal which Carlton Stenhouse LLP moved to defend, and a date was set for an industrial tribunal hearing. Feeling somewhat out of his depth, Melvyn described the details of the case to Dr Dan and handed him all the relevant documents. After studying them overnight, Dr Dan told him that while the company may have failed to follow proper procedure to the letter his opinion was that, on the balance of the evidence, George had behaved in an abusive and unprofessional manner and had been inflexible when the company had sought to resolve the issue between the two parties. For those reasons, he felt the tribunal judges would almost certainly side with the employer and that his father should be advised to withdraw, rather than potentially losing and having to pay his own legal costs and those of the company.

George chose to ignore the advice, insisting that 'if Dr Dan was an Advocate worth listening to, he'd be practising the Law rather than teaching it'.

Under instruction from his father, Melvyn signalled his intention to proceed with the case but on the afternoon before the initial tribunal hearing was due to take place, he received a letter delivered by courier from Carlton Stenhouse LLP in which it announced its intention to withdraw and to settle the matter privately. Melvyn was summoned to a meeting of the company's chief executive, personnel director and senior solicitor the following morning where an attempt would be made to 'conclude the matter amicably and to the satisfaction of both parties'. It was suggested that neither Mr Lovelace nor Mr Gillies should be present at the meeting 'to help facilitate an environment where the case can be discussed dispassionately'.

At the meeting, held in the Carlton Stenhouse LLP offices in Charlotte Square, Melvyn was taken aback at how friendly and accommodating the two men were. Mr Forsyth, who insisted on being addressed as Charlie, explained it had been Mr Gillies' strong desire not to proceed with the tribunal case because he did not wish to be subjected to the publicity that would certainly accompany it. He was a very private man, Charlie explained, who had experienced a great deal of stress; he had lost weight, been placed on medication by his doctor and his relationship with his partner had broken down as a result of the case.

Mr Gillies wished the matter to be resolved without any further delay. Carlton Stenhouse LLP was prepared to offer Mr Lovelace the most generous terms to end the dispute. Clearly, he stated, it was no longer possible for Mr Lovelace and Mr Gillies to work together and so, to bring the matter to a full and final settlement, if Mr Lovelace withdrew his claim for unfair dismissal, the company would allow him to resign, with no stain on his professional character and with a lump sum worth two years of his existing salary, tax free, to be paid to him with all his pension rights intact. In addition, the company would give him a favourable reference that he could present to potential future employers. Mr Gillies was prepared, in those circumstances, to withdraw his complaint and so there would be no mention of 'the recent unpleasantness' in Mr Lovelace's employment record.

Melvyn returned home like a conquering hero, flushed with what he regarded as a first notable success in his fledgling legal career. He had held his own with a major financial institution and emerged with a deal that he regarded as outstanding, given the circumstances. George didn't see it like that. He regarded it as an 'unprincipled stitch-up' and an 'invitation to collude in a shabby and worthless compromise'. The company had erred in its treatment of him, he insisted, and nothing less than his reinstatement to his former position and a full and unconditional apology would suffice.

The single agenda sheet fluttered gently in the hands of Mary whom, Melvyn noted, couldn't look him in the eye. He found direct eye contact deeply unsettling, but he had practised it assiduously throughout his professional life as he'd been told on good authority that it set apart the strong-willed and trustworthy from the impressionable and shifty.

'We need to make a decision today,' she said purposefully. 'And what we feel, Melvyn, is that - '

'What you feel?' he asked pointedly.

'- What we feel is that we need to ... what we feel is that you have to take a stand on this. Are you going to stand-by your father, irrespective of what he may or may not have done, or are you going to support the firm?'

'I don't see why I should have to make a choice between one and -'

'Oh, for God's sake man...' Robert interrupted.

'Dad, please, let me deal with this. You need to give

us a sign that you're prepared to get a grip of this. It has happened and none of us can change that, but we can take steps to lessen the impact it has on the business. And frankly, it would be better all-round if your father was to plead guilty and for you to lie low for a while until all the publicity dies down.'

She stared at the sheet of paper as though she was reading from a script.

'The alternative is for a trial date to be set, probably several months down the line, creating an ongoing mood of uncertainty, followed by several days of damaging media coverage during the trial, all potentially affecting the share price in a negative way. In those circumstances, we can't afford to have the son of the defendant remain as chief executive of the business.'

The next set of official papers relating to the case received by Melvyn included a sheriff court citation and evidence documents disclosed by the regional procurator fiscal. They revealed that on a stated date George Eric Lovelace had visited Martin Mungo Gillies at his home where he used threatening and aggressive language, causing the witness fear and alarm. The purpose of the visit was, according to Mr Lovelace, to set the record straight about a prior invitation for the pair to holiday together. It is alleged Mr Lovelace became agitated and increasingly preoccupied about Mr Gillies' personal circumstances, leading the witness to fear that some sort of physical attack with a sexual motive was imminent.

'So, what are you saying, Mary? That if my father doesn't plead guilty, then I should resign?' Melvyn asked with the same, quiet and controlled tone he had maintained throughout the board meeting.

No one spoke and, for the first time, he felt genuinely

angry rather than nervous or bewildered. The ground had shifted in his favour and he no longer felt like he had any cause to be on the defensive. It was no longer a personal matter about what his father may or may not have done and the damage his behaviour might or might not do to the company. Now it was about him and his continued stewardship of the company; it was professional and they were on his territory.

'And if I'm not chief executive of this company, who are you suggesting should be?' he asked, slowly and deliberately.

Still, they remained silent. Melvyn knew that none of them had the balls to speak up because they were afraid of him. Namely, they were afraid of his ability to make money for them, which, he noted, they were happy enough to bank and spend, but not to acknowledge his unique and central role in generating or to thank him for. They were sponges to his stone – rabbits and he was a lion. They knew that the whereabouts of his father and his innocence or guilt were of little consequence compared with the enormous, massive, tangible improvements he had made to the firm over the years for its scale, profit and turnover. These were matters that he knew and appreciated better than them. They were the bottom line and at the end of the day that was all that mattered.

He had a clarity and focus that everyone else in the organisation lacked and that was how he had been able to transform a small, provincial legal practice into a successful multi-national firm. He had brought vision, resilience and credibility to the business not because he had a First from an ancient Russell Group university or because he knew the right people or greased the right palms. He had built a business empire because he had been relentlessly single minded about chasing the numbers – nothing more, nothing less. So why, he wondered, should he ever again feel at the mercy of youngers and lessers who weren't fit to change the batteries in his calculator? Of course he'd turn his father in. Faced with the choice, he'd talk his father into pleading guilty – he'd done it once before and he'd do it again. No question.

Chapter 16

Straiton, South of Edinburgh, the same morning

In his later years, Lennon struggled with the notion of being a rock 'n' roll star. After decades of performing, drug taking and hell raising, he was beginning to discover what it was like to lead a 'normal' life, keeping house while his wife assumed responsibility for the business side, his music and her artistic interests and their growing property portfolio. This reversal in power relations between the pair was, in part, down to their Avant Garde ideas about the changing roles of the sexes in society – that the man should not be regarded automatically as the breadwinner and the woman the homemaker; that traditional boundaries were breaking down and more couples were now 'doing their own thing'. Lennon was entering a stage when the realisation was perhaps dawning that his life no longer stretched ahead infinitely, that his best days may be behind him already and he might possibly have been asking himself what he had to show for his existence – not in terms of money or material possessions, but in the quality of the relationships he had with his children and those around him. He barely saw his eldest son, Julian, with whom he had always had a distant and fractured relationship. He felt bleak about the future and sometimes, Yoko recalled later, she would wake in the night to find him crying, fearful that she would die before him and that he'd be left alone, bereft, without direction or purpose. Perhaps he had begun to ask how one copes when one outlives one's spouse, irrespective of how happy or otherwise a marriage had been, and found that one has nothing of value or purpose to live for.

George heard Linda pottering around in the bathroom and

he put down his notebook and started to dress. He looked at the silver carriage clock on the mantelpiece – it was just gone ten o'clock, which meant he had slept for the greater part of seven hours. He made his way to the window and pulled the curtain back a fraction and shivered at the frozen scene outside and the thought of being out there again alone; exposed, caught in its chilling embrace. Nothing moved on the road and he knew that, for the moment at least, he was safe. But for how long?

Despite the long sleep, he remained exhausted, his fingers and toes still numb. Linda had dragged him into the house after finding him collapsed on her doorstep. She had then manhandled him onto the sofa and provided him with a duvet and a hot water bottle. He fell into a deep sleep almost the moment his head hit the cushion but, in his semi-conscious state, he was lucid enough to make her swear she would not turn him over to the authorities. While she assured him that she was not in touch with any of his children, she did admit she had received a call from Roz, who asked if her father had been in touch. She had told the truth – that he hadn't. She asked Linda to call her immediately if George showed up or got in touch, but she assured him she wouldn't – not yet at least, until they'd had a chance to talk. In fact, she appeared as angry as he was with Roz for the travesty of a column she had written, which made him feel a little more assured.

Linda entered the room dressed in a light pink towelling bathrobe and a pair of pink slippers, and she moved briskly to the window to open the curtains. Daylight swarmed into the room, stinging his eyes and forcing him to shy away from its concentrated rays, and he sought refuge on a chair at the back of the room that was mostly in shadow. It was the first time he'd seen Linda in a bathrobe since their relationship ended more than 20 years before and, while there was nothing remotely erotic about her appearance, it rekindled in him a sense of familiarity and fondness.

He was conflicted, because he no longer found her physically attractive and yet, in his mind, there was an enduring sense of closeness to her. Her hair was grey and the skin on her face, once smooth and shiny, was now flaccid and matt and her figure bulged, repellently in places. He felt it unlikely, if not inconceivable, that he could now muster an erection at the sight of her nakedness the way he used to do. His thoughts had become conflicted because, while sex in general was an issue of diminishing importance in his life, it continued to define how he felt about women and the idea of it still defined how he thought about them. He had always liked attractive ladies and the more attractive they were, the more he liked them. He felt easier in their company than in that of men because, even if there was little or nothing else that they had in common, there was always the prospect of sex, no matter how remote, that helped him to retain an interest.

It never mattered to him that, in the most cases, the physical act of having sex never happened, not least because he was married and there were considerations of fidelity, but that, in a sense, was not an issue of overriding priority. The prospect, possibility, even the notion of of sex was something that helped him to communicate with women, in whose company he might otherwise have felt inept or uncomfortable.

Linda asked him if he'd had a comfortable night and if he felt better for his rest. When he offered a positive response to both questions, she went to the kitchen to prepare breakfast, which he looked forward to with some relish. Quite apart from the fact that he hadn't eaten for 48 hours, Linda was one of the few people who understood his dietary requirements and didn't quibble about them, and he felt confident she would provide him with a menu that was both acceptable and nutritious.

She appeared a short time later carrying a tray that

262

contained a pot of coffee along, with two mugs and a small jug of milk, a plate with four slices of toasted plain white bread, a dish of butter or margarine, two shelled boiled eggs in a small ramekin, a plate containing slices of orange, cheddar cheese and a separate plate of sliced ham. After enquiring about the provenance of the bread, the butter or margarine, the cheese and the ham, he requested a single slice of bread with cheese but no margarine or ham. He declined the offer of coffee because, he told her, he didn't have his tube of sweeteners with him. He never ate boiled eggs, he reminded Linda, adding that he was prepared to forgive the oversight as it had been more than two decades since she had last cooked for him. She retired to the kitchen and returned with a glass of water.

They ate and drank without talking – one of the reasons George felt comfortable in Linda's company was that she shared his dislike of conversation during mealtimes – and afterwards he returned his plate and glass to the tray.

'I've been thinking about Roz's column and we shouldn't be too critical of her because, whatever she did, it was for the right reasons,' Linda said after a few minutes.

'What makes you think so?' he asked.

'She may have gone about it the wrong way, but her argument was in your favour.'

'She said I was guilty,' George protested.

Linda thought for a moment before responding. That was another thing he liked about her; she didn't state anything without giving proper consideration to the matter at hand.

'Well, that's not true exactly because, if I understood her correctly, she doesn't believe you should be charged with a behaviour that she doesn't consider to be a criminal offence.'

'That may be the case, but she accepts the girl's version of events over mine. Whatever she believes that version amounts to, is immaterial. Clearly, she doesn't believe me when I say I didn't do what the girl says I did. Not only that

263

but she chose to share with the readership of her newspaper that she doesn't believe me.'

Linda turned her head and fixed her gaze in the direction of the window.

'I'm not sure I believe you either, George,' she said calmly.

Had it been anyone else uttering such a contemptible slur, he knew he would be furious but because it was Linda, he couldn't summon the same level of anger. Instead, he felt perplexed and a little disappointed.

'Why should you say such a thing?'

'Because I know you.'

She faced him with a smile that suggested ... actually, he didn't know what it suggested because it wasn't an explanation. It was simply a statement that, while factually accurate, entirely failed to convey why she didn't believe what he said.

'Oh, I'm not saying you meant to do it or even that you were aware you were doing it, but I think you can't help yourself,' she continued. 'You often act in ways that don't make any sense at all, that's your problem, George. You behave like you set the rules and anyone who doesn't follow them is ignorant or stupid, or simply doesn't have your level of understanding. You do what you do and that's all that matters, and it's not that you don't care about the consequences – you're not even aware that there are consequences. You live your life in your own way, according to your own standards, but you take no account of the feelings or needs or desires of others, particularly women.'

'That's not true, I was brought up to be a gentleman. I have the utmost respect for women,' he protested.

'Oh, I'm sure you believe that entirely, and I've seen you in action – standing up for any lady who enters a room, holding doors open for them. You're always first to let them go first, top up their drink or light their cigarette, but that's not really the same thing as having respect for them, is it?'

'Isn't it?'

'You behave like you respect them but you're just going through the motions. These are things you do by rote because they have been drilled into you. You're like Pavlov's dog: the moment you see a woman lift her coat you rush to help her on with it because you've been taught to believe that's the appropriate thing to do. But what if it's not? What if the woman wants to put on her own coat or get her own drink? What if she thinks you're being patronising and that by rushing to help you're implying she needs help, that she'd not capable of doing those menial tasks themselves?'

'Well, I'm not,' he insisted.

'But how do these women know that?'

'It's obvious that I'm being gentlemanly. That my intentions are honourable.'

'Why do you suppose that it is obvious? They can't read your mind. Most actions can have different, often conflicting motivations and can be interpreted in different ways. Just because you think you know that your motives are pure doesn't make them so. They might think you're doing it for purely selfish reasons, because you want to have sex with them.'

George blushed and stared beyond Linda.

She continued: 'What happens in situations where you haven't been taught to behave or react in a certain way, when things don't go according to your expectations, when it's just you and another person, a community of two, and your conflicting worldview is pitted against the other person's, when it's a battle of perceptions, your word against theirs? What happens then, George? Perhaps that's when we see the real you.'

He continued to stare straight ahead, speechless, without the remotest idea of what she was talking about. All he knew was that she believed he was guilty and he didn't know why.

'I've been in situations when you have behaved very badly, in ways that are so wrong they're quite unconscionable, but you don't see it. You can't see it because it's new and unfamiliar and you don't have the handbook that tells you how you're supposed to be. Even when you're told you're wrong, you refuse to accept it. You need convincing, corroboration, and you'll try to make out that it didn't really happen that way, that you've been misjudged, misrepresented, that the world is against you; that it's not you who's in the wrong, it's other people; they're being oversensitive or prudish or judgmental; they're persecuting you and impugning your motives.'

He couldn't judge properly from the tone of her voice where this conversation was heading. Was it leading to some purgative conclusion where his ignorance and lack of understanding would be exposed, where his deepest thoughts and reasoning would be held up to scrutiny, where his actions would be found wanting and where necessary consequences would follow? Was it a prelude to her dismissing him from her home, never to return? He waited tentatively for the denouement, frozen with uncertainty. He knew with some conviction that he wouldn't like what was coming because it was clear she was criticising him, in his view in quite defamatory terms, but at least he'd be able to understand it, to comprehend what it meant and to act accordingly. Her unreadable smile waned. Should he stay silent, he wondered. If he did, it might suggest he agreed with what she'd said, but if he spoke he knew for sure that he'd betray his ignorance and his lack of comprehension.

'And at the centre of everything is sex.'

That statement at least he could agree with but not, he suspected, for the same reasons as her.

'It's not your insensitivity around sex that sets you apart, George – Christ knows I've known lots of men who are crass and ham-fisted in the bedroom – it's how you behave afterwards. The real abuse happens later when you deny the right to complain. You act as if nothing remotely out of the ordinary has happened and to suggest it has is just the latest episode in some puritanical conspiracy against you. You're the real victim because all you're trying to do is to live your life according to a strict set of principles against which no one quite measures up.'

'Are you finished?'

'Not even close, George, not even close' she said in a quiet, moderate tone and with her eyes narrowed.

He had asked out of a genuine sense of curiosity, but he could tell from her reaction she thought that, somehow, he was doing her down.

'It's just that I need to go to the bathroom,' he pleaded.

'And the worst of it is that you are most abusive to the people who care about you; those who have gone out of their way to care about you, despite the many obvious challenges. You allow us to get so close and then no further. There is a quaint formality about you that is superficially attractive because it makes you seem so ... I don't know, vulnerable. But after a while, we start to realise that is all there is to you. It is seductive to imagine that your cool detachment is a moat to keep us at bay for long enough until you lower the drawbridge and we'll be ushered into the courtyard of the inner you, where we'll meet the real George, the sensitive, caring, understanding and giving George. But that never happens – in fact, it goes the other way. You summon us close enough until we drop our defences and then you commit an act of such unspeakable cruelty that we find it difficult to imagine you as the same person we knew. You make us question our principles and character, to wonder if really, we are the ones at fault because we're too demanding or complaining or narrow-minded or inconsistent, too accountable to human impulse. You make us apologetic and wary of our own judgment, afraid of our next move, convinced that you are right and we're wrong, in every respect. You force us to lose faith in our expectations that the world is essentially a compassionate and predictable place, and to believe instead that it's frightening and hurtful and flawed. You make us doubt our own sanity.'

She stopped talking and the room fell silent. He waited for a few moments, paralysed by indecision. Was this the end?

'I really need to go to the toilet, Linda,' he said.

The car journey to his house was spent mostly in silence. Linda's face remained expressionless as she drove and after their conversation, neither felt that there was anything left to say. The last of the afternoon sun emerged suddenly from behind a mountain of blue clouds, like a stage act reappearing for its final encore. George closed his eyes and let the sun's rays, magnified through the windscreen, settle on his face like a balm; for a few blissful moments he felt quietly contented. He tried to imagine how it would be to feel like this all the time, without having to think about anything other than what surrounded him – the tranquilising hum of the car's engine, the certainty of its slow but constant forward movement and the calming tincture of nature's heat on his skin. During this all too brief interlude, when he was not required to do anything; when there were no questions or accusations or expectations; when time and space and ideas were other people's concern, he thought that this was perhaps the happiest he'd ever been.

'You will go, won't you, George?'

He'd promised Linda that if she drove him home and collected some essentials from his house that he would call Melvyn and ask him to drive him to the police station, to allow him to hand himself in.

'I said I would, and I will.'

'Will you plead guilty?'

They hadn't discussed that issue and he felt aggrieved she should raise it when they were already on their way.

'I didn't do it, Linda.'

The car was stopped at a set of traffic lights and she turned to face him.

'It's probably best for all concerned if you do. Why put the girl through the agony and embarrassment of a trial?'

'But I didn't do it.'

'Everyone thinks you should plead guilty.'

'By everyone, you mean you and Roz.'

'And Melvyn.'

'Melvyn?'

The lights turned to green and she began to drive again.

'Melvyn does not believe I'm guilty.'

'I didn't say he believes you are guilty. I said he thinks that you should plead guilty.'

George couldn't believe Melvyn would ever suggest such a thing.

'How do you know?'

'He told me so.'

'When?'

'Yesterday.'

'You didn't tell me you spoke to him yesterday. You said you only spoke to Roz.'

'I spoke to both of them.'

'You're lying.'

The car pulled up at another set of traffic lights.

'I'm not lying, George.'

He asked her to park a couple of streets away from his house and to walk from there in case the police had it under surveillance. He would remain in the car and wait for her, he said. If she were approached by anyone, she was to tell them that she was his hired cleaner. Linda asked him why it mattered, when he had already agreed to hand himself over to the authorities, but he said he would rather do it his own way. He handed her his house keys and told her where to find everything, including his notebook and his tube of sweeteners. She took the keys, got out of the car and walked away, without looking back.

He didn't know now if he could trust her, not after what she'd said in her house and her lying about not speaking with Melvyn, and he wondered if he should follow her. He noticed she had left the key in the ignition and he thought, perhaps, that he could drive her car away instead. But to what end? Where would he go and what would he do? Could he really save himself? He felt sickened by what she told him about Melvyn and part of him still hoped it wasn't true. He expected his son, of all people, to believe in and support him because he alone had witnessed the pain and suffering that he'd been through at the hands of that vindictive little shit Gillies.

Melvyn had been at George's side throughout the entire episode and he knew, better than anyone, how the legal process could be manipulated to ruin the life of an entirely innocent man. Melvyn knew George had already been the blameless victim of a debased legal system and a motivated, vexatious litigant who had set out to destroy his career and his reputation. And his son was instrumental in ensuring that Gillies achieved both goals.

It was Melvyn who counselled him to enter into a shabby Mephisthophelean pact with his employer, who promised a mature and sensible compromise but delivered an unqualified condemnation of guilt. It was Melvyn who advised him to plead guilty to the egregious charge of sexually harassing the malevolent homosexual Gillies, to spare him the indignity of a public trial when it was George who was deserving of compassion and redemption. But, at the end of the day, he knew he could have no quarrel with Melvyn then. He may have put his head in the noose, but George released the trap door on himself.

He had forgiven his son's misguided actions because he was a teenage student, barely into long trousers, but now he was older and George was wiser; Melvyn no longer had youthful naivety as an excuse. George may have been responsible for his own destruction once, but he would not make the same mistake again. If what Linda had said was true, that Melvyn wanted him to sacrifice his name and reputation on the altar of another malicious accuser and a corrupt criminal justice system – his son the traitor, the colluder, the self-interested quisling – then perhaps there was nothing left to save.

Linda appeared from around the corner at the wheel of his car and she parked it on the other side of the road. He got out to meet her and a gust of cold air ripped through his lungs, causing a stabbing pain. She said the house was empty of people and that no one was staking it out. She handed him his notebook and his tube of sweeteners, as planned, and immediately he felt calmer.

'The key's in the ignition,' she said.

He nodded.

'You'll go straight to Melvyn, won't you?'

He said nothing.

'George, you promised.'

'That was before you told me about the phone call.'

'Listen, you have to hand yourself in. What do you think will happen if you don't? That they'll forget all about it and you can go back to living your life? That's not going to happen. It must be dealt with. You can't avoid this any longer.'

He hoped she'd stop talking and just let him go. He couldn't bear to be with her any longer and he inched closer to his car.

'George,' she said loudly.

'Alright, I'll do it. I'll go to see Melvyn.'

She smiled, moved forward and wrapped her arms

around his shoulders, pulling him closer to her. Instinctively he backed away, as he always did when people tried to make close physical contact with him, but his legs were too weak to resist even her strength and he surrendered.

'You're your own worst enemy, you do know that, George?' she said staring directly into his eyes.

He felt his face redden and he looked away, longing for her to let him go. She pulled him closer to the point where he could feel her hips pressed tightly against his and she kissed him on the cheek.

'For goodness sake, George, what is that?' she demanded suddenly.

He looked at her blankly.

'I'm flattered at my age ... but really, you are incorrigible.'

'What are you talking about?' he asked.

She pulled his jacket tail up and touched the top of his right thigh.

'What the hell is that?' she asked, handling the bulge in his trouser pocket.

'It's my tube of sweeteners,' he replied.

'Do you always carry them there?'

'Yes, of course.'

'Did you have them in your pocket on the night of the company dance?'

'I would have done, yes.'

'Don't you think that might be important? I mean, to your case.'

'I don't know,' he replied. 'I hadn't thought about it.'

Chapter 17

Central London, later the same day

The call that Martin had been expecting came at the worst possible time. It was just after 4.30 p.m. and he was in the middle of an email exchange helping his political editor to draft the script for a live interview with the Prime Minister, who was on a state visit to the United States, and had agreed to an outside broadcast on location at Camp David in time for the Six O'clock News.

His head was filled with a multitude of detail about the special relationship, the latest growth figures and every other issue he could think of to press the PM on while they had him captive, and the last thing he needed was a distraction. The call came through the switchboard, so he had to wait for a few seconds until the girl at reception transferred it. He was tempted to hang up and screen all calls until the programme was over, but his indecision caused a split-second delay and before he had time to act, he heard the caller on the end of the line.

'Hello, is that Martin?'

The voice had an Eastern European harshness that was unfamiliar, but he knew this was the call he dreaded.

'Speaking.'

'Hello, Martin, it's Tony Grozdana.'

He thought silently for a moment.

'Tony, from the Taverna, you remember?'

He didn't.

'The Athena Taverna.'

Still nothing.

'In Holloway.'

'Ah, Tony.'

Tony, or Greek Tony as everyone called him, though from

memory Martin was sure he was Kosovan or Macedonian or something like that. His relief was followed quickly by bewilderment about why Greek Tony should be calling him out of the blue, at his workplace, after all this time. It must have been 20 years since he last stepped foot in the Athena Taverna, he reckoned.

'How did you get my number?'

'One a my customer, he tell me he think you work at BBC,' Greek Tony replied in the same heavily accented pidgin English that Martin remembered from two decades before.

'Listen, it's great to hear from you, Tony, but could you possibly call back another time? It's just that I'm really up against it at the -'

'Is your wife, Martin, she here,' he interrupted.

'My wife?'

'Yeah, your wife, she here.'

Martin thought of his wife, on the floor beneath him, putting together a piece for the *Today Programme*.

'If you're talking about Roz, she's no longer my wife.'

'She very drunk. She lie on the floor.'

Yes, this was the call he'd been expecting, ever since Isla had come home from school in tears because a boy in her class claimed her grandfather was a nonce and that her mother had written about it in the paper.

'You come, you come take her home.'

'Roz is not my wife. We're not married anymore,' he tried to explain, but Greek Tony was having none of it.

'You come. You come take her home now.'

'Tony, I can't come now, I'm busy dealing with something that's very important.'

'Your wife, she no important?'

'Of course, she's important but she's not my wife.'

'You come take her now. I no wan' her here no longer because she very drunk and she bad for business. My

274

customer, they complain.'

Martin recalled Greek Tony's often hysterical reactions to the slightest setback and he found it difficult to believe his customers had become so discerning in the intervening years. From what he remembered of the Athena it was, even by 1990s standards, a depressingly substandard hovel of last resort for the low maintenance imbiber.

'Look, Tony, I'm sorry but I can't leave what I'm doing to traipse halfway across the city -'

'What a kind a man are you?'

The question hung as Martin struggled to think of a suitable answer. He considered putting the phone down, but he knew Tony would call back and he didn't want his domestic intrigues being played out for the entertainment of his colleagues – not again.

'You tell me what kin' a man he leave his wife -'

'SHE'S NOT MY WIFE. HOW MANY TIMES DO I HAVE TO TELL YOU?'

His raised voice attracted furtive glances from colleagues. The atmosphere around him at work had been tense since Roz's column was published earlier in the week. He still hadn't read it – he couldn't bring himself to – but Deborah had, and she'd given him a flavour of its content. He knew which of his team had read it from their awkwardness around him and by the sudden silences that descended when he walked into a room. One had left a copy of the paper lying on his desk, helpfully opened at the appropriate page. He had an idea who the culprit was, or at least he was confident he could narrow it down to a handful of the crew who had been shortlisted for redundancy earlier in the year, only for their jobs to be reprieved when the union threatened to strike. He could have found out for sure by reviewing CCTV footage but he wasn't about to do that. Whoever the perpetrator was, he or she knew they held the upper hand and so, he supposed, did Greek Tony.

'You come now, or I call the police. You hear. I call police.'

The rush hour traffic crept slowly along Portland Place as Martin emerged from the

BBC building into the early evening chill. He had asked his deputy to take the reins – he'd worked with Chris for most of his career and he didn't have to explain why he needed to get away. If any of the senior management questioned his whereabouts, he was to say Isla had taken ill at school. He wondered where Ruaridh was and why he wasn't the one dropping everything to rush to Roz's aid. He still had Melvyn's mobile number and he'd called it to see if he had a contact number for Ruaridh but it went straight to voicemail, so he left a message, urging him to call back urgently. He even called Isla on the off chance that she had a number for Ruaridh – she didn't – and he had to make up a story to convince her that there was nothing the matter with Mummy. He'd also dropped by Deborah's desk and told her he had to leave to take care of a troublesome spot, as in 'ex marks the...' which was their code for 'Roz trouble'. She smiled and wished him luck.

It took a while to find a free cab and, while he was waiting, he Googled the Athena Taverna because he couldn't remember the address. The only times Martin had been there were to meet Roz when she was working as a junior reporter on the local paper in Holloway. After she changed jobs she continued to drink there, inexplicably, even when the last of her ex-colleagues had moved on. Unsurprisingly it had no website, nor did it appear to feature on any online business directories. The cab driver had never heard of it and so he chose to drive aimlessly around the area for 30 minutes before finally admitting defeat. He also stopped at the office of a local minicab firm on Holloway Road to ask for directions and they were equally useless, though the driver said they were being deliberately unhelpful because he was competition. In the meantime, Martin tried Melvyn's number again but there was still no answer. Eventually, just as the meter hit £53, Martin spotted the bar tucked away in a side street near Archway Underground station. He asked the cab driver to wait.

He remembered the Athena as a sad, stultifying hovel and despite these low expectations, he was still taken aback by the grimness of its atmosphere as he entered. Its purpose appeared not to have changed – to peddle low quality alcohol to the unfortunate and the incorrigible. It had the same dirty junk shop yellowness with a lick of emulsion as a half-hearted nod to modernity. Even the punters were the same, only greyer skinned and more beaten-up by life. The bar was small and functional with a couple of beer taps and a gantry that consisted of a few aged bottles of obscure liqueurs. The bar's real business was in strong peasant wine stored in vats in the cellar and decanted into bottles cradled in wicker baskets to hide its industrial origins.

Roz was seated at a table in a corner, awake but only just, her hands cupping her chin to hold her head upright. Her eyes looked like darkened hollows in the dry, bloated landscape of her face. As he approached, it was clear from the smell that she had wet herself.

A fatter, balder version of the Tony he half-remembered from another life approached him.

'You have car?' he asked aggressively.

'I have a taxi waiting outside,' Martin replied.

'I help.'

They took an arm each and spirited her limp body across the bar, her feet gliding serenely above the floor. The taxi driver glowered as they manhandled her onto the back seat, and he warned Martin that he'd have to pay for the cleaning bill if she was sick. Martin agreed and he handed Greek Tony a £20 note for his trouble.

He sat on the back seat with Roz's hunched and

unconscious frame leaning into him. He called Deborah.

'She's in a bad way, I can't leave her alone like this.'

'No, of course you can't,' she said. 'Keep her safe and give me a call later.'

He never failed to be impressed by Deborah's compassion, especially given how Roz had treated her, blaming her for their break-up, but she had got it all wrong. It's true they were friends while he and Roz were married but nothing more than that. She was sympathetic and supportive and, if anything, she encouraged him to do all he could to hold their marriage together.

'Are you remembering Isla's got a friend coming for a sleepover?' she asked.

'We could always cancel.'

'Don't be silly.'

'No, I feel bad about landing all of this on you again. When will my responsibility for this woman ever end?'

He caught the eyes of the taxi driver staring at him through the rear-view mirror.

Deborah didn't respond. He had asked her the same question so many times it had become rhetorical.

'We can put her friend off until next weekend. She'll understand.'

'No, she's been looking forward to it all week and, besides, it's no trouble at all. They're good girls. They will shut themselves away in her bedroom and watch something on Netflix. I won't even know they're there.'

'Are you sure?'

'I'm sure.'

By the time they reached Roz's flat, the smell had drawn the attention of the driver who demanded an extra £20 on top of the charge to fumigate the cab. He remained seated resolutely at the wheel, brooking no request for assistance, as Martin struggled to lift Roz's limp frame into the street. Once outside, he bundled her over his shoulder and carried her, fireman style, to the front door. Only then did it occur to him that he would need her door keys.

He bent forward and laid her down on the step and felt through the pockets of the thin gingham jacket she wore over a mini dress but found nothing other than an empty cigarette box and a lipstick.

'Roz, where are your keys?' he asked, without response.

He reached down and shook her by the shoulders. Her head rocked back and forward, and she groaned in discomfort.

'ROZ, YOUR KEYS. WHERE ARE YOUR KEYS?'

Her eyes opened slightly, revealing narrow strips of red glaze and then they closed again.

'Come on, Roz, we need your keys to get you inside. Help me out here.'

Her eyes opened again, wider and she stared into his face with a look of studied incomprehension.

'Martin ... Martin, why are you here?'

'I'm here to get you home and into bed, now tell me where your keys are.'

'Handbag,' she slurred.

Shit, her handbag, her handbag, where the fuck is her handbag? He didn't remember seeing it at the bar; it was possible it might have been there, under the table perhaps, and that he had missed it, but then again it was equally likely she arrived without it, having left it somewhere else entirely. Fleetingly, he wondered if he should return. He imagined his deranged figure standing in the street with his piss-soaked ex-wife hoisted over his shoulder, trying to find a taxi driver sympathetic or desperate enough to pick them up. And for what? To arrive at the Taverna possibly to find that the handbag wasn't there, because in truth, it could be anywhere in London. Suddenly, he remembered he had a spare set of her keys at home. They had agreed he should have a set, in case of an emergency. Though neither had been explicit at the time, it was just such an emergency he had in mind. He rang Deborah again.

'You're not going to believe it,' he said.

Roz lay shivering on the frozen step, so he removed his overcoat and wrapped it around her, leaving him to brave the zero temperature in his shirt sleeves. By the time Deborah came running toward him almost two hours later, he was pacing up and down the path, slapping his arms around his body like a prisoner in a Siberian gulag. She reached down and stroked Roz's hair.

'Poor lamb. Will she be OK?'

Martin shrugged.

'I don't know what she's on. It's taken more than drink to do that to her.'

She handed over the keys.

'The girls are in the car, parked further up the street. I didn't want Isla to see her mum like this.'

'Thanks. What did you tell her?'

'I said Mum had a bad cold and we didn't want her to catch it so she couldn't see her.'

He smiled and kissed her.

'You're an angel.'

He carried Roz into the flat, found her bedroom and dropped her on the bed. Even by London standards, the room was small. The flat was surprisingly tidy for someone who lived so chaotically, and he wondered if that was Ruaridh's influence. Issues of cleanliness and personal responsibility had been covered at length during their discussions about access to Isla, and Martin had made it clear to her that he would not allow her to visit Roz if she lived like a drunk. And he had to commend her that she never had. Outwardly she was normally pristine, which he suspected was part of a pact that she'd made with herself that, so long as she offered a façade to the world that was ordered and respectable, then it mattered less if everything within was dysfunctional and chaotic.

The room was featureless and sterile. Aside from essential items of furniture – a bed and a wardrobe – it had nothing. The walls were dirty white and bare and there were no decorations or ornaments, no designs or artefacts, nothing of her personality to distinguish the space in any way as hers. The few possessions she had, mainly books and records, he guessed, remained packed in cardboard boxes on top of the wardrobe. It was a vignette of loneliness and controlled despair that said to him Roz was clinging on by her fingertips.

Isla had mentioned there was 'something wrong with Mummy's new flat' after her first couple of visits, but she was too young to articulate what it was. Generally, she had come away from time spent alone with Roz quiet and withdrawn which was why they decided that their access visits should take place at Martin and Deborah's place. Then, one day she stepped into the car with unusual purpose.

'I know what it is about that Mummy's flat,' she announced triumphantly.

'Oh, yes...' Martin replied.

'She doesn't want to live there.'

He knew Roz found it hard to make friends; during their marriage, the only people they ever socialised with were his friends and work colleagues. He wanted her to be outgoing and popular, for the rest of the world to see in her what he did, and he did his best to support her and encourage her in company, but he failed, and he was left to wonder if it was even possible to make other people like someone. How can you be there for them all the time, to make sure they say the right things at the right time? How can you make them what they're not?

He felt guilty undressing her while she was unconscious, even if he had done it regularly when she was his wife. He held her under her arms and knees and lifted her through to the bathroom and lowered her gently into a warm bath. In the cramped space, she was forced to sit upright and, as he sponged her shoulders, her head rocked back and forward slightly. Her breasts had all but disappeared and the outline of her ribcage was visible. Years of smoking were starting to take its toll on her skin which wasn't as fresh as he remembered. If she stopped now, she might get away without any further damage, but he knew there was no chance of that happening. He found it difficult to believe she was the same person with whom he'd fallen in love all those years ago.

He dried her down with a bath towel and put her to bed, making sure she was lying on her side in case she was sick, then he switched off the overhead light and sat on the floor in a corner of the room, against the wall. It had been an exhausting day and his limbs ached. He hadn't eaten since breakfast, but he didn't feel hungry, which was just as well because he knew there would be no food. Roz rarely cooked; the preparation of meals to her was an afterthought. She regarded it as an annoyance forced onto her by others – yet another means of highlighting her inadequacies.

When Isla was a toddler, mealtimes were occasional, haphazard events that produced whatever was at hand or could be bought at the last minute in fast food outlets and at late-night service stations. Martin bristled at the memory of returning home after work to learn that his baby daughter had been fed bits of cheese or a few slices of salami.

He sat in the darkness of the room with only the orange glow from the streetlights piercing gaps in the drawn curtains. He listened to the wash of traffic in the distance and the occasional snap of firecrackers. He'd forgotten it was Guy Fawkes night and he felt guilty he hadn't arranged to take Isla to a display. Not that it mattered now; if he had, it would just be another burden to be foisted on Deborah at the last minute. He gazed at Roz's head lying on the pillow and the thought came to him, quite coldly, that he was sure she would die soon.

He had known her for 20 years, lived with her for a little less than half of those, and still he had no idea who she was. There were things she could do, even now, that surprised him, not the drinking and drug taking – he'd long since accepted there was no bottom to the pit of abuse into which she could plunge herself. But in other ways she remained composed and self-assured and he had even wondered if she behaved obtusely just to punish him; to show him that no matter how low he thought she could sink, she could still outsmart him. He might be the one with the fancy job, the nice home, the loving family, but they were just trappings. She might be a drunk, but what she had was permanent and more valuable. She could be languishing desperately in a rehabilitation clinic, unable to eat, and yet she could still produce a brilliantly lucid and persuasive piece of writing that took his breath away. For all her years of excess and self- destruction, she never missed a deadline.

A corollary was that when she wasn't abusing her organs with alcohol, which wasn't often, she abused her talent, writing about issues she didn't care about and taking disingenuous positions because she felt bored and she had the intelligence to carry it off. When they were younger, he feared and admired her smartness in equal measure, when everything she wrote was weaponised and relentless on issues that mattered to them both. When he felt brave enough to challenge her, her arguments invariably left him bruised and undermined and, when he thought he couldn't feel any more emasculated, she could write a searing piece for whatever paper she was working on, arguing the case from his side, only more effectively.

Her writing was grown-up and persuasive, and she never took the easy option. She didn't support the Iraq war, but she offered a detailed and well researched rebuttal to the charge that, in failing to do so, she was effectively emboldening a murderous tyrant. One of her greatest achievements, she maintained, was dissuading her then editor to support a judicial review of the Parliamentary vote that enabled the invasion. Even after the truth about the war came out, she stood by her stance that it wasn't the job of journalists to try to overturn democratic decisions.

But, over time, her writing had changed. When it came to Brexit, she was shrill in support of a second referendum even when many of those on her side of the debate had long since moved on. She maintained that Crossman had appointed her to be the sole Remainer voice on the paper and, as such, she was obliged to take the stance she did. She insisted that it was also a position she agreed with, but Martin saw the lack of conviction in her voice. The Roz he knew would never have allowed herself to be seduced like that, to sacrifice intellectual rigour for political convenience and embrace an argument she knew in her heart was on the wrong side of history.

He had avoided reading her most recent column, but watching her now as she slept off yet another staging post in her campaign of self-destruction, he thought he should do so now. She was deteriorating beyond his control and one day he would have to explain to Isla who her mother was, what she did and why she did it, to account for her actions and, possibly, to excuse them. He knew their daughter would want to know why her relationship with her mother was different to that of her friends, why she couldn't see her every day and why they couldn't be alone together. Martin knew all he could do was to explain the facts, but the facts wouldn't be enough. She'd want to know the reasons and he had a duty to try to find out.

He would be able to tell Isla that she had a loving but not a fit mother; that once, for a short time, they had lived together after he had convinced himself, despite every impulse warning him against it, that the proper place for a child was with her mother. He could tell her how he'd called Roz at her flat countless times of the day and night to make sure that their daughter was safe but got no response; how he had tried to reach her so many times without reply that his ear burned on his old Nokia brick mobile; how he convinced himself that Roz must have had told him they were going away, to Scotland or to visit friends, and that it had slipped his mind; how he'd rung every friend and relative he could think of and every hospital within a 50 mile radius, frantic for news; how finally he drove over and forced the door open with a fire extinguisher and found his toddler daughter terrified, tearful, untrusting; how she'd stripped herself naked to rid herself of the stench of her pyjamas; how she was so hungry she'd emptied the bin looking for food. He could tell her how he'd tracked down Roz to the squalid flat of a drug addict; how she was so drunk and high on amphetamines that it was 36 hours before she was capable of coherent speech; how she'd cried herself hoarse for days, begging him not to report her to social services or the police and vowing it would never happen again; how he was so angry he felt he might kill her; how, finally, he convinced himself that reporting her, seeing her jailed, her career ended, his daughter deprived of a mother was not the right thing to do. He could tell Isla how all those things had happened, but not why. Only Roz could do that.

He Googled *The Sentinel* and scrolled down to her column. He found it hard to read her words – to reconcile the authority in her voice with the merits of the argument she sought to put forward. Roz's great talent had been to combine conviction with persuasiveness but this felt like a familiar pattern of her taking a position she didn't believe in for the sake of expediency. The more he read, the clearer he could see the cracks in the edifice, where she forced the circumstances to fit her thesis, conflated fact with opinion, bent credibility. It was understandable that she would want to support and protect her father but at the expense of what and whom? Her argument, he believed, would make reasonable people doubt their own reality.

If George was responsible for doing what the girl claimed – and she was a girl – was it right to insist that she should just have to accept that that's what men do and put up with it? Part of Roz's conceit was to monitor the pendulum swing and alert her readers when it passed the level of acceptability. She tolerated the merits of a case for so long until she could claim that its proponents had gone a step too far – that red tape, political correctness, health and safety had, in the parlance of the popular prints, 'gone mad'. To do so now, over the issue of men abusing their power over women in whatever guise – age, position, wealth, physical strength – was the sort of feeble, carpet-lifting thinking she hated. It was outrageous to suggest that a man of George's seniority and experience could ever be a victim in a power relationship with a 17-year-old girl. Rather than see her father for what he was, it was easier for her to blame society, liberal politicians, the media, an entire generation – everyone, that is, except the person accused. Of course, it was still an allegation and he had yet to be convicted, but there was no smoke without fire. Why would a girl make up such a story? Martin had long suspected his former father-in-law might be capable of such a thing. He'd always felt there was a problem with George.

His phone rang and he dropped it. He scrambled to pick it up and answered – it was Melvyn. He didn't have a number for Ruaridh. He said he and Roz left Edinburgh for London the day before because Ruaridh was due to travel to Chichester to attend a weekend craft fayre.

'Is it urgent?' he asked.

Martin told him about Tony's phone call and the state in which he had found his sister.

'Is it urgent?' he repeated.

Martin sighed.

'No, I don't suppose it is,' he said resignedly and hung up.

He Googled craft fayres in Chichester and found a listing for a contemporary craft show at Midhurst Rother College. He called the main college number, which was answered by a caretaker who said everyone had left for the day but that the exhibitors would be in at nine o'clock the following morning.

'Sorry I can't be of more help.' The man said.

'No problem, I'll call back then.'

Martin bowed his head and felt the pain of regret for Roz. He didn't blame her for what she had written. He couldn't blame for her how she felt or for who her father was. When Isla asked him why her mother was the way she was, he could tell her about the night she could never forget. It was one of the first things she had told Martin after they'd met, when she was drunk – it wasn't a story she would have wanted to tell when she was sober. He would be able to tell Isla that it was the single most significant moment in her mother's life because it had forced her, suddenly and brutally, to confront the worst realities of the world. 'It made me an adult', was the expression she used.

He could tell Isla how her mother was 14 at the time and studying for her pre-Christmas exams. Melvyn was at a friend's and, the only other person in the house was Susan who was in bed, doped to oblivion after George had uncharacteristically encouraged her to take more of her sleeping pills. He had never done so before; he was sceptical of the power of medicines, as she remembered clearly from her childhood.

'They will do you good, put you to sleep,' he assured her. 'You need the rest after what we've been through.'

She told him how unlikely and insincere his words sounded. It was as if he had planned things to be the way they were because he wanted the house to be quiet and empty of people. His mood was low and fragile, she remembered. He had recently lost his job over an argument with a colleague, the details of which had never been explained to Roz. In fact, her parents had gone out of their way to obfuscate and to make sure that she knew as little as possible about the situation. She wasn't particularly interested; she had friends whose parents had lost jobs and they'd always got another one and she was sure her father would do the same. She had other more important things on her mind.

She could not recall precisely what had alerted her to the reality that something was wrong. It might have been a noise, a smell, perhaps just a feeling that made her leave the pile of books on her bed and venture downstairs. All was quiet, but it occurred to her that it was too quiet; there was no sound from the television or the rustle of newspaper. She wondered if her father was reading one of his Beatles books or perhaps listening to a record with headphones on, but when she checked in the rooms, all were empty. She decided he must have gone out, but that didn't make sense. If that were the case, it would have been planned, arranged in advance and discussed. He never did things on a whim.

She opened the front door and gingerly made her way into the front garden. She was not wearing slippers and the cold path was painful on the bare soles of her feet. The luminous glow of a perfectly full moon and a pageant of brightly lit stars made it feel more like a late autumn dusk than a midwinter night. The air was clogged with acrid chimney smoke. She breathed more deeply and detected another scent, not quite as strong – unnatural, industrial, a car engine.

She looked around the gable end of the house toward the garage to see if her dad had started the car, intending to go somewhere, but it was closed. At the foot of the door, she noticed movement – a white, creamy, billowing movement like the formation of clouds. She was confused. Her mind seemed to slow down, and it took several seconds for her to realise that the substance was coming from inside the garage.

She rushed toward it and tried to open the upward-lifting slide door, but it wouldn't budge. She knew it didn't lock from the inside, so she thought perhaps it had been jammed shut by frost. She rushed around to the side door and tried the handle, but it was also locked. She tried to force the door with her shoulder, an effort she knew was futile, but it seemed to take some time for that realisation to be communicated to her limbs. She tried to shout for help, but her voice was weak and useless.

She picked a boulder from the driveway and smashed it through the garage window. In doing so the tips of two fingers were slashed and blood began to seep from the ends. The sight made her nauseous but she didn't feel any pain. She chipped away at the remaining shards with the stone until the frame was free of glass and she threw herself through it, landing painfully, her head smacking on the concrete floor. The room was clogged with thick, bitter smoke that caught in her throat and stung her eyes, making her convulse.

She tore off her pyjama top and held it close to her face, allowing her to take a few, shallow breaths. She manoeuvred around the car, her progress interrupted by items littered in her path – tools, bits of garden furniture, offcuts of wood – until she reached the driver's side. She pulled open the car door and George's leaden body fell away onto the floor. She switched off the car engine and checked his condition. He was unconscious but he appeared still to be breathing. His eyes had rolled upward and his mouth was filled with saliva. She put her hands under his arms and dragged him towards the exit. He was a dead weight, and she could manage only a few inches at a time. She was crying frantically.

'Don't die, Daddy, don't die. I love you very much, Daddy. Please don't die,' she said.

She knew the slide door at the front entrance was her only

chance. If she couldn't open it, he was done for, perhaps they both were. She pushed at the door, shoved it, kicked it, slapped it with her open hands but still, it would not budge.

'Stay with me, Daddy, don't leave me, Daddy.'

Finally, she noticed the locking mechanism had been pulled shut from the inside and so she slid it in the opposite direction and the door glided open, releasing a rush of air into the garage.

Inside the ambulance, his face clamped with an oxygen mask, George regained consciousness and Roz could see how disappointed he was to still be alive. He clasped her hand tightly in his and pulled her toward him and warned her not to tell anyone about what had happened. It was their secret, no one else's business, not even her mother's.

'It made me an adult' she told Martin, her eyes red with tears. She never referred to it again.

Chapter 19

Saughton, in the west of Edinburgh, the following day

George had left Linda with a feeling of relief. After sitting awake for most of the night in his car in a lane near Musselburgh and reflecting on it a greater length, he realised it could never have worked between them. He couldn't imagine why he ever thought it could. She had never been committed to him, or to the things he was interested in, any more than Susan was. He could see that clearly now. Her suggestion that he should go to Melvyn and that, together, they should turn him over to the authorities was so far removed from his thinking that they could hardly have been further apart. How could she believe such an action was honourable? And that little piece of theatre at the end, concerning the tube of sweeteners, as if that had convinced her of his innocence where his word had failed; how could he have taken that as anything other than an egregious slight against his character? Either she trusted him, or she didn't.

He thought that perhaps he should have felt some sadness at the realisation, in the way people do in love stories when it becomes clear they cannot be together, but the feeling simply was not there and for that he wasn't ready to reproach himself; instead, he decided that he could never have loved her, even when he'd convinced himself otherwise. He thought he had known what love was; he imagined it to be the sensation he had experienced with Linda all those years ago – the desire to be near her, to involve her in his thoughts, his plans, his interests, his hopes and ambitions, to share with her his joys and his disappointments, to give her the benefit of his experiences and his learning. But perhaps that was not love after all.

He felt certain that she, like Susan, was concerned only with herself and her opinions. Looking back, it occurred to him that neither had accepted in whole what he thought or held to be true; in fact, both challenged him in almost every respect. If he suggested a course of action, invariably, it was not the right one. If he offered an opinion, both returned it, amended as though nothing he said or believed in had any validity without their input. Both became bored quickly when he tried to involve them in his passions and did little to hide their feelings of disinterest. In fact, both justified them as quite normal, insisting there was no reason why they should feel the same way as he did about John Lennon or The Beatles or anything else that he held dear – that such interests were hobbies, pastimes, ephemeral in nature and removed from what really mattered. They were wrong.

After they parted, he drove to the hardware store on Dalry Road that he'd identified the week before as being fit for the purpose he had in mind. He had not returned after that initial visit, in case the proprietor recognised him from the papers and put two and two together. It was a small shop; no bigger than a few metres square and stacked from floor to ceiling with every kind of merchandise possible for building and home improvement purposes, from the smallest nail to the most powerful power drill, the kind of store that was commonplace in his youth, but which had given way to the preponderance of large DIY multiples. What it offered, that was lacking in the high-volume chain stores, was the element of personal service.

George admired the proprietor from the outset. He had bought a packet of nails as a means of testing his suitability and attention to the task in hand, without any frivolous diversion into small talk, and he had passed with flying colours, convincing George of his suitability and that this should be the outlet where he would source the materials needed for his mission. The man was bald and stocky, dressed in a traditional brown canvas apron, and he had a proper, groomed moustache that didn't look like it had been grown for charity purpose or as a homosexual affectation.

George found the owner in his rightful spot behind the counter and asked him if he could cut him a length of hosepipe, of around six feet. The owner asked him what gauge of hosepipe he wanted, and George told him the wider the better. He fulfilled the request without further ado and asked him if he wanted anything else. George told him he also wanted a small roll of duct-tape. The man offered him a choice of three sizes, and he opted for the smallest and cheapest. He only required a small amount, he said. The man calculated the total amount of cash due, took the money, handed over some change, and within a few moments George was on his way.

'Looks like it's clouding over,' the man said as he exited.

He decided to ignore him. Perhaps he had misjudged him after all, he thought.

It was a short drive to the lock-up just off Calder Road. It was in a row of ten units, stone built and with a corrugated tin roof. He obtained it from the council, for a peppercorn rent of £60 a year in 1996 and the price had never increased. Over the years it cost him a tidy sum, given that he had little reason to use it, but knowing it was there, available when needed, gave him peace of mind and he always felt it was worth the cost.

Occasionally, once every couple of years, he paid a visit to check the lock hadn't seized or that the roof hadn't sprung a leak, and amazingly nothing had ever gone wrong. He found the occasional dead rat inside and the door had been defaced with some quite vulgar graffiti that had never been removed, but none of that had really bothered him. It was a facility with a single, straightforward use, as far as he was concerned.

He nosed the car forward into the tight space until it was

closed entirely within the lock up. There was no overhead light, so he had to complete his preparations with the door open which carried a risk of him being overlooked, but it was mid-morning and there was no one around so he decided to take a chance. He inserted the end of the hosepipe into the exhaust and closed it off with several turns of the duct-tape – enough to ensure there was a proper seal – then he fed the other end through an inch-wide gap in the rear window on the driver's side. He pulled the garage door down until it was closed, and then he locked it. He had the only key to the only door and there were no windows; he wasn't going to make the same mistake as he did the last time. He sat in the driver's seat of the car, switched on the overhead light and began to write his final chapter.

Lennon was pronounced dead on arrival at St. Luke's-Roosevelt Hospital Center, in Upper Manhattan, at 23:15 EST on December 8, 1980.

George hadn't learned about Lennon's death until later in the morning, 07:13 GMT to be precise, when he was wakened by Susan who had heard the tragedy reported on the Today programme. His reaction was one of disbelief and initially he was convinced that Susan had confected the story as some despicable scam to unsettle him. He told her she was a liar. She told him he was an idiot and handed him the radio, which was broadcasting an interview with William Pobjoy, Lennon's former headmaster at Quarrybank High School. The moment George discovered the truth, he cried uncontrollably.

Lennon was shot four times, at point-blank range with hollow-point bullets which expanded upon entering his chest, severely disrupting his tissue and virtually destroying vital organs as they travelled through his body. His cause of death was given as 'hypovolemic shock, caused by the loss of more than 80% of blood volume'. One of the most comforting and yet unsettling, observations made by any of those present during Lennon's final moments was that of Dr Stephan Lynn, the emergency room doctor who received Lennon. He said: 'If [Lennon] had been shot in the middle of the operating room with a team of surgeons ready to work on him, he wouldn't have survived his injuries'. These words are a source of great comfort to me as they indicate Lennon's injuries were so severe, he would have had virtually no chance of surviving no matter how good the quality of care or the speed with which he was treated. And yet they also struck me as peculiarly flippant and insensitive coming from such a highly qualified professional gentleman as Dr Lynn, given that the odds of anyone being shot in an operating theatre with a team of medical professionals in attendance are so remote as to be statistically insignificant. Having conducted extensive research of gun-related crime in the years since Lennon's death, I have never come across such an incident ever being reported. December 8, 1980 was an unusually warm winter's day in New York, and, for Lennon, it was packed with frenetic activity as he fulfilled various professional duties. Portentously, it began with a frustrating disruption to his usual routine of visiting the Café La Fortuna, near his home on New York's Upper West Side, for morning coffee. On this particular day the cafe was closed, so he departed from the family apartment in the Dakota Building, bordering Central Park at around 10:00 EST, and made his way to a local barbershop where he had his hair cut in a 1950s 'Teddy Boy' style.

Though the events were several years apart, George came to associate Lennon's death with the first day of his criminal trial when, finally, he came face-to-face with his own assassin, the Malevolent Gillies. Both days began in a similar vein. In normal circumstances, George would have breakfasted early before departing for work at around 08:00 GMT but, having been dismissed from his job, unfairly, and having since been victimised by the police, the Procurator Fiscal's Office and the Crown Office in what was shaping up to be one of the great miscarriages of justice perpetrated in a UK court, he was preparing for trial. With his appearance scheduled to begin at 11:00 GMT, quite remarkably he too visited his local barber to have his hair cut, though not in a Teddy Boy style.

Later in the morning Lennon was visited at his home by a photographer from Rolling Stone magazine, whose brief was to shoot the cover for the January issue. The camerawoman wanted to photograph Lennon alone, but he insisted on Yoko also being included in the shot. The resultant image, of a naked Lennon entwined around Yoko dressed in black, has become iconic, winning several global awards for creativity. To me, the picture is an aberration. Art is all very well, but surely there must be a point to it. Why a 40-year-old man, no matter how much of a creative genius, should feel it necessary to commit himself to such a humiliation in the name of art, is beyond me. I read that the picture was intended to symbolise a child clinging to its mother, which left me even more bemused and angry. Lennon was no child and Yoko was not his mother. They were husband and wife, for pity's sake, and it would have befitted them to act as such. After the photoshoot, Lennon gave what would be his last interview, to a DJ from the RKO Radio Network. At 05:40 EST, he and Yoko left their apartment to fulfil an appointment at the Record Plant Studio to mix a song 'Walking on Thin Ice', intended for their follow up album to the recently released Double Fantasy. As they departed the building, they were approached by several people seeking autographs. Among them was Mark David Chapman, a 25-year-old security

*guard from Honolulu, Hawaii, who had travelled to New York
with the intention of murdering Lennon. Silently, Chapman
proffered a copy of the Double Fantasy album to Lennon
who obliged with an autograph. After signing the album,
Lennon asked, 'Is this all you want?' and Chapman smiled
and nodded in agreement. The moment was immortalized in
a photograph taken by the DJ from RKO.*

Melvyn and George had arrived at the court building
shortly before 09:00 GMT and they were ushered into a
holding room to await the official start of proceedings. George
insisted on Melvyn, as his legal representative, dressing
appropriately in a business suit. As his son didn't possess a
suit, he'd had to lend him one of his, which was several sizes
too big and which draped around his thin teenage frame in a
most ungainly manner. Susan had expressed her disapproval
of Melvyn representing George in quite strident terms. Not
only was it a distraction from his forthcoming university
exams, she argued, it was also 'horrendous' that he should
'force' his son to be party to such a 'crazy, self-glorifying
venture' that was bound to fail.

While they waited, they rehearsed his opening statement,
line by line. George was not confident that Melvyn was fully
conversant with all the key points. He had spent the previous
weeks carefully drafting the statement, expressing in precise,
emphatic detail how a simple extension of friendship had
been, at first misrepresented, and then transformed into a
hateful vendetta that determined to destroy him. Melvyn
appeared distracted and he did not engage with the process
on a level that George felt would do justice to his case.
Several times he had to ask him to pay more attention.

The swearing in of the jury took longer than expected and
it was close to 12:30 GMT before George was led into the
courtroom, to the dock. Melvyn was already seated at the
solicitors' benches in front of the trial judge. The prosecution

counsel were dressed in robes and they wore wigs; they looked professional, confident and competent compared with the hunched figure of Melvyn who laid bundles of papers George had prepared for him on the table in front of him and began to leaf through them hurriedly as though he were reading them for the first time.

George looked across to the public gallery where he saw the Malevolent Gillies enter. He had not seen him since being forced from his job several months before and he was shocked by the change in his appearance. He had lost a considerable amount of weight and his face was yellow and gaunt and almost unrecognisable. His appearance at work was always immaculate; it was one of the things that, initially, George admired about him, that he took care to dress smartly, always wearing cufflinks, polishing his shoes to a high shine, never wearing the same shirt on consecutive days. Now he was dressed lazily, in a cheap looking, casual jacket and jeans and a floral-patterned shirt that appeared not to have been pressed. He was unshaven, which made his narrow jaw appear dirty, and his dry, thinning hair was not combed properly.

George kept his eyes trained on Gillies whose gaze remained fixed firmly ahead in the direction of the Sheriff as though he were paying close attention to the proceedings. From his peripheral view George could see his quarry's eyes flitting erratically, and occasionally he swallowed as if his mouth was dry. It looked to him like he was making a determined effort to remain perfectly still, but he was aware of a slight trembling motion in his shoulders. Suddenly, Gillies turned his head to face George. The movement was so quick and unexpected that it gave him a fright but then, just as quickly, he returned it to its original position. The meeting of their eyes was so fleeting as to be almost imperceptible, but it stayed with George long afterwards.

After mixing their song at the recording studio, Lennon and Yoko began their return journey home at around 22:30 EST. She suggested they go to a nearby delicatessen to buy something to eat but Lennon was keen to return home to see their five-year-old son, Sean, before he was put to bed by his nanny. The December night was exceptionally mild and instead of driving through the Dakota's archway into the safety of the inner courtyard, they ordered their limousine driver to draw up at the kerb in the public street outside. As Lennon exited the car, Chapman emerged from the shadow and moved toward him, still clutching his autographed copy of Double Fantasy.

He called out Lennon's name and, before the musician had time to respond, Chapman produced a .38 handgun. Here, accounts differ: some claim the assassin immediately opened fire, others say he dropped down into a combat position before unloading five shots. The first bullet flew over Lennon's head and the remaining four entered his chest. By now fatally injured, he staggered the few steps into the porter's vestibule, blood gushing from his body, and he scattered a handful of cassettes of the music he had just recorded across the ground. With Yoko screaming, the porter immediately rang the alarm that went straight to the police, then he knelt down and attempted to administer a tourniquet around the chest of the dying Lennon but, realising such action was futile, he removed the musician's blood-spattered glasses and covered him with his jacket. By 22:51 EST, the first police officers were on the scene and they were greeted by Chapman, his hands raised in supplication, who immediately confessed to the shooting. Within two minutes, Lennon's body was bundled into the back of a patrol car and rushed to the nearby Roosevelt Hospital at 59th Street, near Central Park. Ono followed close behind in another patrol car. Lennon was admitted to the emergency room, into the care of Lynn who, due to the massive loss of blood,

immediately administered a transfusion and, holding
Lennon's exposed heart in his hands, began to massage the
organ vigorously in an attempt to restart circulation – but to
no effect. At 23:15 EST. Lennon was pronounced dead. At
around the same time, the hospital public address system,
tuned to a local radio station, began to play The Beatles'
song All My Loving.

The start of the trial did not go well for George. Melvyn's performance was stilted and stuttering, and he failed to cover most of the points his father believed were crucial to his case. He focused mainly on providing a chronological description of events which, to his ear, did not give the jury an accurate picture of the deviousness of which the Malevolent Gillies was capable, nor the remotest intimation of the suffering George had endured at his hands. Nor did Melvyn follow his explicit instruction regarding the issue of Gillies' sexually promiscuous character. To say that he was angry would be to grossly understate his frame of mind but, as they returned to the holding room for the lunchtime recess, he resolved to take a more diplomatic tack with his son.

Susan had always advised him that to display anger openly, no matter how justified, was counterproductive, and that positive encouragement was more likely to achieve a desired result.

He never fully understood why this should be the case; if you are angry because of a failing by another person, then surely pointing out that failing in the strongest terms possible is most likely to achieve optimum results, he thought. But what he discovered, through experience, was that expressing one's anger over a particular issue most often led to that anger becoming the subject of the ensuing discussion rather than the matter at hand and, for that reason, he committed himself to a 'softly softly' approach with his son.

'Well, that was a wholesale disaster, so we really need to

up our game this afternoon,' he began.

Melvyn said nothing.

'I'm not blaming you entirely, Melvyn. Perhaps I was not clear about what I wanted. Did I not say that first impressions count?'

The room was small and featureless, with only a small desk and two chairs. Melvyn sat on one of the chairs and leaned forward, holding his head in his hands and sighing loudly as though exhausted. George thought perhaps Melvyn had not heard him.

'Did I not say that first impressions count?'

Still his son said nothing.

'When we resume this afternoon, you must drive home at every opportunity that what we are dealing with is evil, pure and simple, that this man has set out to ruin my life and that he will stop at nothing - '

'I'm not going back in,' Melvyn said calmly.

At first George wasn't sure he'd heard his son properly and so he carried on.

'- that he will stop at nothing to destroy me. Not content with robbing me of my job and blackening my name, he then set out systematically to...'

'I'm not going back in,' Melvyn repeated.

George felt his anger, which he had been trying to suppress, suddenly rise to the surface and he had to breathe deeply and control his thoughts to prevent a full-blown explosion.

'Of course you are going back in, Melvyn. You just had a bad morning, that's all. I take on board that you are a student with no experience of a real-life courtroom and I'm not expecting miracles. All you need to do is to follow my instructions properly. That's all.'

Melvyn's head began to shake and it took George a few moments to realise that his son was crying. He didn't know where to put himself. He hadn't seen Melvyn cry since he was ten years old and he thought he was past all of that.

'Come on now, son, don't be a baby. We have had a row, that's all, there's no need to cry. Pull yourself together and dry your eyes – we have a lot of preparatory work to go through before we return to the courtroom this afternoon.'

Melvyn raised his head and fixed George with a look that was so intense it left him quite startled. His eyes were bloodshot and fiery, and his mouth was open with a cloud of saliva visible. His fists were clenched and shaking.

'I SAID I'M NOT GOING BACK IN THERE YOU FUCKING FREAK ... WHY CAN'T YOU UNDERSTAND THAT?'

'Melvyn, mind your language and keep your voice down or someone will - '

'SHUT UP, SHUT UP, JUST SHUT THE FUCK UP.'

'Melvyn, this isn't helping - '

Melvyn stood up to his full six feet and ranged over his father with his hands balled, raised as if he was going to strike him.

'SHUT UP, YOU FUCKING MADMAN. SHUT UP.'

George backed away and presented his open palms as a way of trying to calm his son.

'Ok, ok, I'll be quiet, I'll be quiet.'

Melvyn dropped to the squat position of a pugilist, his weight resting on his front foot, and he seethed with white saliva leaking through the corners of his closed mouth. He continued to sob, breathing heavily through his nose like a riled bull, readying itself to charge. George backed away and bowed his head in submission to indicate that he did not present a threat and he resolved to wait until his son's tantrum subsided. He couldn't recall precisely how long they stood like that because, as he trained his focus on the worn grey marble flooring, he appeared to lose track of time. Fearful of being physically assaulted, he dared not shift an inch, not even to look at his watch. Eventually, he became aware of movement but even then, he refrained from lifting his head. He heard Melvyn sniff several times followed by the sound of papers being shuffled, then footsteps coming toward him and he saw all the case documents dropped on the floor, dozens of papers spilling out of their folders onto his feet and across the room.

'There's something wrong with you, Dad. You've got a problem and you need help,' Melvyn said quietly, before exiting the room.

George was determined to fight on, and, in fact, his son's resignation even bolstered his resolve. He had come this far without the support of Susan, and one more Judas in the family was not going to divert him from his intended course. He had to inform the court that he had parted company with his legal counsel and that he intended to represent himself. Proceedings were suspended for the rest of the afternoon to give him time to prepare, and that night he maintained his vigil outside the home of the malevolent Gillies, in the hope of divining some additional 'smoking gun' evidence that might further elucidate his malign character. Lennon's killing changed all that. The shock destroyed him and robbed him of the will to continue and, later that day, he changed his plea to guilty.

He closed his notebook and laid it on the passenger seat along with his pen. Then he switched on the engine. He looked at his watch – it was a little after 13:30 GMT. He thought, not for the first time, that perhaps Melvyn had been right, perhaps there was something wrong with him. He certainly felt different. His life had been a struggle and it was consoling to know it might have been easier if he were normal – that is to say, more like other people. Perhaps then something could have been done to fix him. But it was too late to have such thoughts now, at his age. This was his choice, and he would honour it. He read, a long time ago, that before shooting Lennon, Chapman tried to kill himself and failed. It angered him that, for a large part of his life, he had more in common with his hero's assassin than with his hero. Now that would change. He took a deep breath and sucked in the hot, bitter air.

Chapter 20

Straiton, South of Edinburgh, a month later

'I hope you're not rushing back to work.'

Roz forced a smile and shook her head. For the life of her, she couldn't recall the man's name. He was a friend of her parents; she remembered him vaguely, turning up at dinner parties when she was younger. Simon, that was it, Simon something. But then he disappeared off the scene, which was not unusual with friends of her parents. He was at her mother's funeral, she remembered that. There was an image in her mind of the look of discomfort on her father's face when he was forced to make small talk with him. God, George hated that. She smiled at the thought.

'Especially not in your condition.'

What condition was that, she wondered. A condition of abject boredom, of trying desperately to engineer a none too offensive means of extricating herself from Simon whatshisname before she parted company with her sanity? Oh, you mean because I'm pregnant, she thought, well, why not fucking say that instead of hiding behind your pathetic, male inhibitions? Did she say that or just think it? She couldn't be sure. She wished she'd taken Linda's advice and dispensed with the funeral idea altogether. Losing both parents in a matter of months was exceptional, after all – people would understand. She knew that, but she insisted it should go ahead. She wasn't doing it for other people, she was doing it for her father. Susan had had a funeral and so George would have a funeral – it was only fair. And God knows he'd suffered from lack of fairness all his life.

It wasn't fair that he didn't have friends, that he couldn't look you in the eye, that he couldn't sustain a conversation that extended beyond clichés and pleasantries. It wasn't fair that he couldn't hold down a job or get on with work colleagues in the way other people did or succeed in his career because the stupid personal stuff got in the way. It wasn't fair that he'd never met anyone with enough expertise to help him; that he chose the wrong woman to marry and ruined her life but that both were good people and good parents, too good to end their marriage at a time when they were told that marriages were for life. It wasn't fair that his children endured and suffered, for years, the consequences of his actions and behaviour, but that he couldn't see how much they were suffering, far less do what was needed to end it. It wasn't fair that his life was ruined by other people's ignorance and inertia. The very least he deserved was a funeral.

At first, Roz felt sympathy and now, after weeks of being buffeted by a tornado of shock, horror and grief, she felt only sadness. Her grief was more than the sum of its parts. Losing a parent at her age was within the range of reasonable odds; losing two felt like the house had stacked the pack. Both parents dying in quick succession and leaving her an orphan at 44 felt like vindictiveness. She never believed she could feel so totally, helplessly bereft and alone and for what? A father who could have been saved if perhaps more people had taken the time and trouble to try to understand him or if she and Melvyn and Susan had had the courage to confront him.

Because of her pregnancy, she couldn't even take something to help her through the pain, but she didn't want to. Her GP had prescribed beta blockers and antidepressants – Valium was out of the question in her 'condition' – but she flushed them down the toilet, not because she felt that she deserved to suffer but because she didn't like the idea that her unborn child should be punished for her need to medicate. The pain would stop with her; she wouldn't pass it on to the next generation.

'The last thing your dad would want is for you to become ill because you've pushed yourself too hard.'

Oh, fuck off! Just fuck off you hateful, closed-minded, pusillanimous cocksucker, she thought. How the fuck would you know what George would want? How the fuck would anyone know what he wanted, or didn't want or thought or felt? He didn't even know himself. All he really knew was how to keep going, press on, move forward without a backward glance at the devastation he was leaving in his wake. Roz knew he must have known he was different, though he never admitted as much. Roz sensed it when he said the wrong thing, smiled when he shouldn't, was unfazed by bad news. He showed how different he was every time he didn't get a joke, was over familiar or obsessed about something trivial; when he launched into a semi- psychotic rage for no apparent reason, broke down over something inconsequential, or when he betrayed himself in a million other tiny, nuanced ways that only those who knew him could even begin to understand.

'Roz, sorry to tear you away. Can you come through to the kitchen and give me a hand with the sandwiches?'

Linda draped a proprietorial arm around her shoulder and led her away. Good old Linda – there was a woman with a perfect sense of intuition.

'Thank you,' Roz said quietly, as they left behind a slightly crestfallen looking Simon whatshisname.

'I could see you were struggling.'

Linda ... kind, understanding, forgiving Linda, who she should have hated for carrying on with her father while her mother was slowly doing herself in on prescription drugs;

307

who thought she was being oh so very discrete and that no one would ever know about her dirty little secret with her best friend's husband, but who hadn't figured on having an affair with the world's most artless and indiscreet man, who thought keeping his condoms in the glove compartment of his car constituted covering his tracks. She knew all along and she suspected her mother did as well, although such was the code of silence surrounding George that no one ever mentioned it.

She was young at the time, 12 or 13, and heartbroken that someone else should come between her parents, especially someone so close and unthreatening, a devil in disguise. She felt endangered and undermined, that the safety of her family and her home were being threatened, and that everything that she knew and valued might be swept away. But she never tried to stop it because, even at such a tender age, she understood that the only way to keep things the same was to say nothing. The truth was she couldn't hate Linda because she was the one person who had held their family together, who understood George perhaps better than anyone and who didn't make any judgements.

Linda had offered to host the wake at her home. They both knew they could expect only a handful of guests, which had ruled out booking a hotel and her parents' house was out of the question, because of the ruinous state George had left it in. Roz was upset at how she felt it reflected his deteriorating state of mind. She had stood in the middle of the lounge, surrounded by the detritus of his obsessiveness, and felt numbed to her core.

Melvyn had offered to pay a professional firm to clear all the 'rubbish' their father had accumulated over the years, in readiness for the house to be put on the market. It was the least he could do, he said, because he couldn't make it to the funeral. The civil service sexual harassment tribunal was due to start on the same day and he had to be there to ensure it began without a hitch. He hadn't taken a day off work since George had gone missing, not even when his body was discovered in a lock up on the other side of the city, whose existence had only come to light when police queried a regular payment to the council on his bank statement.

But Roz put her foot down and told Melvyn, in no uncertain terms, that she wasn't having strangers come into her father's house and tramping on his memory. All that 'rubbish', as Melvyn called it, was George's life – those dog-eared scrapbooks of decades-old cuttings from newspapers that no longer existed; fraying ticket stubs for concerts and cinema showings with George's enjoyment rating out of ten biroed on the back; the countless boxes of seven-inch singles of early recordings on obscure record labels. All that 'rubbish' was his legacy in lieu of a life less ordinary, his version of other people's family photographs and hand-written letters from friends and loved ones, cherished personal gifts, sporting accolades, curriculum vitae charting solid career progression and all the other memorabilia that a normal person can reasonably expect to gather. All that 'rubbish' was the essence of who he was, and it required handling with as much love and care as he'd put into collecting it.

She couldn't face doing it now; she could not even imagine a time when she might have the strength to cross the threshold, but that time would come. She had to get stronger and fitter so that she could fight to clear her father's name. Of course, the case had died with him and proceedings were no longer active, but that was not the same as his name being cleared. There was a stain on his character that she would work to remove with Linda's new evidence about the sweeteners and his medical records which, she imagined, must surely must count for something.

She felt the tears coming again and she had an overwhelming desire to be alone. She went to the bathroom, locked the door and sat on the floor. In her handbag was the diary that had been found in the car with George, which she took out and began to read again. None of it seemed new; it contained all the pet intrigues and arguments she had heard him recount as far back as she could remember. She smiled at his meticulous detailing, his touchingly formal delivery and the plausible exaltation in the way he reported anything he considered shocking or salacious.

She remembered Ruaridh reading the notebook at her parents' home and commenting on what he thought was a lack of reverence for a person her father had professed to admire or even to love. But Ruaridh had missed the point. George didn't feel love in the same way other people did, or sympathy or regret or compassion or sadness, all he could do was to learn, as best he could, how to be spontaneous and, to those who knew him, he sounded like an actor delivering his lines. Because she suspected he didn't experience emotion in the same way most others did, or expected him to, he never properly understood people. He could see how they looked and dressed, what they did for a living, how clever or successful they were because these were tangibles that he could add to a chart. But he didn't know why they behaved the way they did, what they felt, what made them laugh or cry or what moved them to anger or pity.

Because he could not express his feelings in words, he did so through actions. The act of writing his book was a gesture of love itself. Just to read it was to misrepresent it because its value was not in the words and their meaning but in its endeavour, in the hundreds of yellowing, thumbed pages, its tiny letters and coded notations, its voluminous research and its exemplary commitment to accuracy. George didn't understand people, how they functioned, communicated or interacted. He was more comfortable with things because they were animate, predictable and dependable and in the pages of this faded, fraying exercise jotter, was his most meaningful attempt to connect with the world.

There was a gentle knock on the door.

'Roz, are you in there?'

It was Ruaridh. She smothered her nose and mouth with a tissue to mask the sound of her tears.

'Come on, we'd better get going if we want to beat the traffic.'

Lovely, gentle, devoted Ruaridh. She decided she would stay with him and have his baby because all she had to do was to let him take care of her. There was nothing more to think about or question or interpret. He loved her and that was all that mattered. She had been suspicious of him when they met because she couldn't understand his motives: Why her? Why them together? Even the tone of his voice sounded alien, but it occurred to her it was because he was genuine. What he felt for her and expressed was real and she wasn't used to hearing that. It was what an authentic expression of love sounded like. Suddenly, she felt warm. She closed her eyes and put her face in the path of the sun's rays streaming through the bathroom window and she smiled. The feeling was soothing and radiant and, for a few moments, she imagined it was summer.

About the Author

Carlos Alba is an award-winning journalist and author. His debut novel *Kane's Ladder* was published by Polygon in 2008 followed, in 2011, by *The Songs of Manolo Escobar*. His third novel, *There's a Problem with Dad*, was inspired by his experience of observing, over several years, a family member with undiagnosed, high functioning autism. Carlos now works as a freelance journalist, as well as running a public relations consultancy, Carlos Alba Media, in Glasgow where he lives with his wife Hilary and three children, Molly, Michael and Carmen.

Acknowledgements

There's a Problem with Dad was several years in the making and realised only after a lot of internal debate about whether it should be written at all.

The idea came from another book, Shoot the Damn Dog: A Memoir of Depression, by a former journalistic colleague Sally Brampton, and specifically from a passage where she recounted her experience of growing up around a father with undiagnosed Asperger's syndrome (AS). Her description of his symptoms, and the effects they had on her and other family members, immediately struck a chord with me as they were almost identical to behaviours exhibited by a family member of my own.

That initial spark posed two immediate questions. Was I qualified to write about AS and, even if I felt I was, should I do so?

There followed a long process of reading about and meeting people with AS, also known as high functioning autism; considering and interrogating the condition (some people would even question its description as a 'condition'); asking who is affected by it; who should make decisions about it and its 'treatment'; and critically, who has the right to define it? Who owns it?

Is it solely the 'property' only of those with AS – some people would argue yes – but, if so, why should loved-ones and friends who are nevertheless affected by its impact be denied a say? That didn't seem fair to me.

I also faced the question of whether it was proper and desirable write about the neurology, as I perceived it, of a family member – even one who had since passed away? What about the effect it might have on people who knew and loved that person? If they objected to me writing about their parent, sibling, cousin, spouse, or friend, was that sufficient reason not to address the issue?

A lot has been written about autism but comparatively little about undiagnosed, high functioning autism. Yet millions of people live with it into middle and old age either ignoring it and its consequences or unaware they have it. Part of the explanation for that is perhaps because it is a comparatively recent focus of study – AS was first given a medical classification in 1994 – and also perhaps because diagnosis is a lengthy and laborious process.

The compromise I reached was to write a novel – to use the 'research' I'd accumulated over years of observing someone with undiagnosed AS, but to elaborate on that and the issues it raised through a character who is entirely fictional. While my family member was undoubtedly the starting point for George Lovelace, the character evolved during a lengthier journey.

In helping to realise George, Susan, Roz and Melvyn I'd like to thank my two dedicated and tireless editors at Ringwood – Rowan Groat and Olivia Simpson – who left no stone unturned in ensuring that all the characters were as alive as they possibly could be and that they had the best chance of doing justice to the big issues raised in the novel.

I'd also like to thank Sandy Jamieson and all of the team at Ringwood for recognising something in the work that they judged was worthy of an audience.

Thanks to the authors of the many books and papers I read about autism and Asperger's syndrome, particularly Professor Tony Attwood, arguably the world's foremost authority on the subject, who was also a patient and generous sounding board.

To all of the neurodivergent people who gave me their time and assistance over the years, patiently explaining what it's like to think differently in the hope that I might somehow 'get it', there's not enough space to express my thanks, but special mentions to David and Curtis, Andy, Ding, Eloise, Tay, Helen and Tony.

While I wouldn't presume to know what it's like to live with high functioning autism I hope that at least some of those who do might recognising something familiar in my story.

More from Ringwood

Some titles from the Ringwood, available from the website in both print and ebook format, as well as usual outlets.
www.ringwoodpublishing.com
mail@ringwoodpublishing.com

What You Call Free

Flora Johnston

Scotland, 1687. An unforgiving place for women who won't conform.
Pregnant and betrayed, eighteen-year-old Jonet believes nothing could be worse than her weekly public humiliation in sackcloth. But soon she discovers that a far darker fate awaits her. Desperate to escape, she takes refuge among an outlawed group of religious dissidents. Here, Widow Helen offers friendship and understanding, but Helen's own beliefs have already seen her imprisoned once. Can she escape the authorities a second time?

ISBN: 978-1-901514-96-4
£9.99

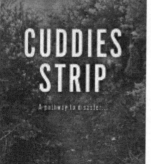

Cuddies Strip

Rob McInroy

Cuddies Strip is based on a true crime and faithfully follows the investigation and subsequent trial but it also examines the mores of the times and the insensitive treatment of women in a male-dominated society.
It is a highly absorbing period piece from 1930s Scotland, with strong contemporary resonances: both about the nature and responsiveness of police services and the ingrained misogyny of the whole criminal justice system.

ISBN: 978-1-901514-88-9
£9.99

Inference

Stephanie McDonald

Natalie Byron had a happy life in Glasgow. She had a steady job, supportive friends and a loving family – or at least, she thought she did. The morning after a date, Natalie wakes up inside a strange house, in a strange bed, sleeping next to a man named Jamie who claims he is her boyfriend. Outside the window are rugged cliffs surrounded by endless sea. All her things are here. But this isn't her life and Jamie certainly isn't her boyfriend. Fearing she's been kidnapped, Natalie flees, but not one person on the island will help her. When everyone around her insists that her life in Glasgow is nothing but a delusion, Natalie begins to doubt her own sanity. But there is one thing Natalie is sure of. She needs to get off this island.

ISBN: 978-1-901514-68-1
£9.99

Murder at the Mela

Leela Soma

Newly appointed as Glasgow's first Asian DI, Alok Patel's first assignment is the investigation of the brutal murder of Nadia, an Asian woman. Her body was discovered in the aftermath of the Mela festival in Kelvingrove Park. During the Mela, a small fight erupted between a BNP group and an Asian gang, but was quickly quelled by police.

This novel peels away the layers of Glasgow's Asian communities, while exploring the complicated relationships between Asian people and the city.

ISBN: 978-1-901514-90-2
£9.99

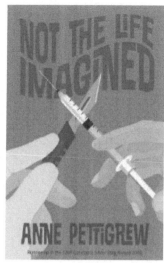

ISBN: 978-1-901514-70-4
£9.99

Not the Life Imagined

Anne Pettigrew

A darkly humorous, thought-provoking story of Scottish medical students in the sixties, a time of changing social and sexual mores.

Beth Slater is shocked at how few female medical students there are and that some people, think they shouldn't be there at all. Devastated by a close friend's suicide, Beth uncovers a revealing diary and vows to find the person responsible for her death.

Beth charts the students' changing, often stormy, relationships over two decades. In time, indiscretions surface with dire consequences for some.

Where the Bridge Lies

1941 The Clydebank Blitz robs Nessa Glover of her husband and five children. Struggling with her new reality she becomes a shipyard welder, and finds herself drawn into trade union activism. One day she visits Harmony, a commune built on notions of equality and unity, led by the charismatic Fergus Abercrombie. 1980. Keir Connor is a traumatised war correspondent. When his father dies, he is left with a letter. His journey leads him on to Harmony, now Laggandarroch, a residential school for disadvantaged children, as he tries to unlock the past. One thing is sure: Harmony is key.

ISBN: 978-1-901514-66-7
£9.99